While the Lights Are On
Life Goes On 3

Surviving the Evacuation

Frank Tayell

Life is never quite as simple as fiction. The good are never quite as kind. The bad are rarely as evil. But sometimes they are.

Surviving the Evacuation: While the Lights Are On
Life Goes On, Book 3
Published by Frank Tayell
Copyright 2020
All rights reserved
All people, places, and (most) events are fictional.

The author has asserted their moral right under the Copyright, Designs and Patents Act, 1988, to be identified as the author of this work. All rights reserved. No part of this publication may be reproduced, copied, stored in a retrieval system, or transmitted, in any form or by any means, without the prior written consent of the copyright holder, nor be otherwise circulated in any form of binding or cover other than that in which it is published and without a similar condition being imposed on the subsequent purchaser.

ISBN: 9798676443689

Other titles:
Post-Apocalyptic Detective Novels
Strike a Match 1. Serious Crimes 2. Counterfeit Conspiracy
3: Endangered Nation & Work. Rest. Repeat.

Surviving The Evacuation/Here We Stand
Book 1: London, Book 2: Wasteland
Zombies vs The Living Dead
Book 3: Family, Book 4: Unsafe Haven
Book 5: Reunion, Book 6: Harvest
Book 7: Home
Here We Stand 1: Infected & 2: Divided
Book 8: Anglesey, Book 9: Ireland
Book 10: The Last Candidate, Book 11: Search and Rescue
Book 12: Britain's End, Book 13: Future's Beginning
Book 14: Mort Vivant, Book 15: Where There's Hope
Book 16: Unwanted Visitors, Unwelcome Guests
Life Goes On 1: Outback Outbreak
Life Goes On 2: No More News
Life Goes On 3: While the Lights Are On
Book 17: There We Stood

For more information, visit: www.FrankTayell.com
www.facebook.com/TheEvacuation & twitter.com/FrankTayell

Part 1
Zombies Can't Run

Canberra & Queensland

11th & 12th March

11th March

Chapter 1 - The Conspiracy So Far
Bonner, Canberra, Australian Capital Territory

As the sun rose over Canberra, so did the flies, forming a buzzing replica of the clouds of breakfast-barbecue smoke billowing above the recently barricaded rear gardens. But no smoke rose from the abandoned suburbs to the north of the defensive wall.

"They're not interested in the bodies. D'you notice that?" Mick Dodson asked. "The flies hover above the zombies, but they don't land."

The streetlight flickered on, off, on, off; an unnecessary signal to those standing watch that dawn had arrived. One by one, the searchlights and spot lamps went out, leaving the roundabout on Shoalhaven Avenue in artificial darkness. Slowly, day's first light smoothed the shadows into distantly spaced, mostly one-storey, single-garage homes. Neatly fenced, occasionally hedged, dotted with trees, and ringed by parched, and often charred, moats of lawn. Once home to clerical staff and administrators, teachers and nurses, and the other essential workers who kept the lifeblood of Australia's capital pumping. Now they were lifeless. Evacuated.

Many bore the smoke-black scars of the conflagration two weeks ago. Those fires, begun a week after the outbreak, had led to the evacuation of the northern and eastern suburbs of Canberra. With most of the city's firefighters already deployed to the bush, swathes of the city had burned before the blazes were brought under control.

On most houses, charred or not, wooden boards covered windows and doors. Those weren't repairs, but reinforcement, defences added during the panicked first hours of the outbreak three weeks ago, when misleading rumours made it unclear whether the nightmare was global or confined to Manhattan. Before the location of the first outbreak was confirmed, the virus had spread at subsonic speed as the infected escaped aboard passenger jets. Nowhere was safe from the undead. Not even Australia.

Some aircraft had been shot down. A few had landed at airports where they'd been quarantined. Many had crashed. One of those downed planes had slammed into the outback only a few hundred kilometres from Broken Hill, where Mick Dodson worked as a Royal Flying Doctor medic and pilot who refused to retire, and where Tess Qwong had been a police inspector ever-grateful she no longer patrolled a city's beat. Three weeks later, Mick Dodson was still a pilot and medic. His daughter, Anna, had risen from an independent backbench rural representative to a senior member of the cabinet. Tess had been appointed deputy commissioner with the Australian Federal Police. It was a grand title considering that under a dozen, mostly elderly or injured, coppers remained in Canberra.

"I'll tell Dr Smilovitz about the flies," Mick Dodson continued. "He's a fella who'd be interested."

Daylight now more formally arrived, Tess Qwong took a closer look at the four corpses they had killed during their night's unexpected sentry duty. "I'm more interested in their clothing," she said, brushing away the pestering insects; they might not be interested in the zombies, but they were very interested in her living flesh. "The coats are too warm for the weather, so they were originally worn for protection."

"They were city folk," Mick said. "Bet they fled to the bush when news of the outbreak struck. Didn't know the rules for surviving out there, so came back. But not quickly enough."

Tess turned around, looking across the roundabout which created a junction with Mirrabei Drive. A few of the sentries further down the rampart were pacing back and forth. A few of the newer conscripts had taken the all-clear signal as the okay to relieve themselves. Crucially, no sirens were sounding and no one was screaming. "Reckon the wall works," she said.

"They've been building these types of walls in Singapore, have they?" Mick asked.

"So the report goes," Tess said. "Create a line of cars along the middle of the road, with a skirt of corrugated metal to stop crawlers. Bolt fencing to the bodywork to provide protection to the sentries standing guard. Lay planks and ladders across the vehicles' roofs to create a walkway. Not a bad system, quick and easy, utilising whatever is close to hand."

"And the Singaporeans call them crawlers?" Mick asked.

"No, but that's the *polite* translation," Tess said. "You should read some of the briefing notes Anna brings home."

"That hotel suite isn't home," Mick said. "Home is the outback. Sixty thousand years of ancestral history is calling to me. It's where I was born. It's where I'll be buried. But a hotel isn't a bad place to spend a few nights, even if I've got to share the suite with you and my daughter."

"And here I was, about to offer to cook you breakfast when we got back."

After the Rosewood Cartel had dropped mortar bombs on Broken Hill's runway, Mick had flown Tess to Canberra to report the cartel's activities directly to the cabinet. And to report the departure of Liu Higson and the Guinn siblings for Vancouver aboard Lisa Kempton's private jet.

As much as life had changed for Mick, it had changed even more for his daughter. Anna was the youngest member of the Australian parliament and independent representative for the Division of Parkes, a rural constituency containing four hundred thousand square kilometres, one hundred thousand people, and her childhood home of Broken Hill. After the outbreak, Anna had jumped from the backbench to a backseat in the cabinet. As the number of suicides and disappearances among her colleagues had increased, and after the mirror-cabinet had been dispatched to Tasmania, Anna had been promoted again, to the front-bench position of Minister for Housing and Agriculture.

"You should still read the reports," Tess said. "If you can find the time to watch every bad action movie ever made, you can find time to read some of the briefing notes."

"A bloke's allowed to enjoy his retirement," Mick said. "And you'll tell me anything important."

A distant gunshot crinkled across the low roofs to the north. Tess turned around, peering across the roundabout northwards, up Mirrabei

Drive, but the young trees were still taller than her perch atop the barricade.

"Only one shot," Mick said. "Probably just a shadow. How many of the conscripts d'you reckon have ever used a gun before?"

"Can't be many," Tess said, "or you and I wouldn't be on guard duty. But I think we're turning a corner. One of Anna's reports was from the Minister of Defence, Ian Lignatiev. He estimates only ten thousand zombies remain in the outback and bush."

"And that's why I don't bother with those reports," Mick said. "I got a different number from that Canadian scientist."

"You mean Dr Avalon?" Tess asked.

"No, from the normal one, Leo Smilovitz," Mick said. "He reckoned there are about a hundred thousand zombies out there now. He extrapolated the figure from the reports on rural fuel shortages to come up with an estimate on how many people had fled into the outback. Smart fella," he added, offering a rarely given measure of approval. "But as long as everyone remains locked down in the camps and cities, in the farms, mines, and cattle stations, the troops currently deployed will have it down to a thousand by the end of March. If we can re-establish proper communications so teams can be rushed to local outbreaks, we can return to nearly normal by the end of April."

"Only if you've a weirdly twisted definition of normal," Tess said. "April is too ambitious. If we had soldiers in the outback, it would be different. Or even police. But we've hardly any to deploy here in Canberra."

"I trust Dr Smilovitz more than *Mr* Lignatiev," Mick said. "Leo Smilovitz worked on this kind of thing before the outbreak. What did Lignatiev do but complain not enough money was being spent on the military?"

"Maybe the bloke had a point," Tess said. "And I know why you don't like Lignatiev, it's because of all those publicity photos of him flying a helicopter."

"Just because he was in the cockpit doesn't mean he was flying," Mick said. "It certainly doesn't make him a pilot. Rule six."

"That's your third rule-six since nightfall," Tess said. "You didn't tell me what Avalon and Smilovitz thought of the Guinn siblings. You *did* remember to ask, right?"

"No worries, I'm not so old I forget so easily," Mick said. "Leo's professional opinion is that the Guinns were weird. The brother more so than the sister. Out of their depth, and possibly obsessional. And this is from a bloke who works with Dr Avalon. He *knows* weird."

"Fair dinkum, but what did the siblings tell Dr Smilovitz they were doing in Canada?" Tess asked.

"Looking for the girl Pete left behind," Mick said. "And Leo believed them. Good man, that scientist. And a good judge of people. And so am I, and I don't think Pete Guinn was lying."

"Someone lied," Tess said. "Look at the evidence. Before the outbreak, a private jet belonging to the billionaire, Lisa Kempton, landed in Broken Hill. Aboard were two pilots, apparently two of Kempton's most trusted employees. And also aboard was Pete Guinn. If he was telling the truth, he's a bloke who sold carpets, and whose sister used to write computer code for Kempton a long time ago."

"I like Corrie," Mick said. "Nice woman. Bit reserved. Spent too much time talking to kangaroos, but that's more common than you'd think."

"And she was maintaining the dingo-fence near where the infected plane crashed," Tess continued, citing the evidence.

"You can't suspect she had anything to do with that," Mick said. "Who'd want a plane-load of zombies crashing on their head? If Captain Hawker and his SAS team hadn't rescued them, both the Guinns would be dead. And, later, it was Liu who *volunteered* to billet them in her house. With her past, if you suspect Liu Higson of some connection to a drug cartel, I'll prescribe you a week of sleep and I don't care how short-handed we are."

"I'd take that prescription," Tess said. The dawn chorus, conducting an early reveille from atop a tree at the centre of the roundabout, was cut short by the chronic coughing from a trio of chain-smoking conscripts, emerging to light up what had to be the last of their supply. "But no, of course I don't suspect Liu of anything other than wanting to rescue her daughter from Vancouver."

"And you've seen the footage the Guinns sent back?" Mick asked. "They're doing what they said, finding out what's happened in North America."

"Anna still has the footage of Michigan," Tess said. "But I've seen the interviews the Guinns recorded in Pine Dock and Nanaimo. Liu's account of what she saw is just as useful. And with millions of refugees arriving by plane and ship, we're hearing plenty of stories of how the world fell apart. No, it's not that I distrust the Guinns. Not as such. With rioting in the cities, with chaos in the skies, regaining order here in Australia took us too long."

"Only because the satellites are down," Mick said.

"Partly, and partly due to shock and panic which still hasn't subsided," Tess said. "Too many infected arrived by air. Too many planes crashed in the bush. And too many people fled into the outback, faster than we could evacuate the non-essential civilians to the coast."

"Which is exactly what Dr Smilovitz told me," Mick said.

"I'll agree he has a point," Tess said. "But *my* point is that, in Broken Hill, we were coping with the undead until the cartel arrived, and those criminals were in Broken Hill before the outbreak. Maybe even before Lisa Kempton's plane landed. Last year, we received a warning about how the Rosewood Cartel was looking to expand their operations in Australia. We were told to watch for criminals with the three-leafed tattoo, and carrying three gold coins."

"Like that bloke who attacked Liu and Pete in Joey Thurlow's cafe," Mick said. "But when a bloke is carrying a silenced pistol, you don't need to be a police inspector to know he's a professional assassin."

"Deputy commissioner, if you please," she said, her fingers brushing the Australian Federal Police shield-badge around her neck and the only indication of her rank, office, and authority. "Deputy commissioner, even if I'm still getting a police inspector's pay."

"Don't expect sympathy," Mick said. "Because I should be enjoying my retirement."

"You refused to retire two years ago," Tess said. "So who's to blame if you're here?"

"If I'd known being helpful would have led to me standing on the roof of a car, holding an assault rifle, protecting Canberra from zombies, I'd have… actually, I don't know what I'd have done."

"Moved to Tasmania?" Tess asked. "Or New Zealand, or Samoa. Except they're no better than here. And everywhere else is far worse."

"Not much worse," Mick said. "In Timor, we're holding the airport in Dili, and the port of Kupang. We'll retake Timor before the fleet reaches Malaysia."

"Now you're sounding as optimistic as Dr Smilovitz," Tess said. "Anyway, what puzzles me is why that assassin went after Pete Guinn."

"For the plane," Mick said. "That's what you told me. And they tortured the pilots for the code which would unlock the only plane in Broken Hill capable of taking them back to South America."

"Those killers were Aussies," she said. "There's more to it. More than the Guinns said, and maybe more than they knew. You don't send a professional hitman after a bloke who sells carpets. You certainly don't send a serial killer, a butcher who flayed people alive over days. Did the serial killer work exclusively for the cartel? And does that mean that every victim, here and across the world, wasn't a random murder but actually a cartel assassination? And why did the killer go to Broken Hill?"

"What you're really saying is, rather than playing soldier, you want to be hunting the serial killer," Mick said. "You're annoyed that you can't. I never thought I'd agree with Erin Vaughn on anything, but our attorney general is right; a serial killer who goes years between victims isn't a priority when we're digging mass graves. The outbreak changes everything." He pointed down at the corpses. "The first week after Manhattan, the soldiers were deployed to the outback, to the airports. Now they're overseas helping with the evacuation. The police are clearing the outback and restoring order to places like Melbourne." He pointed at the roundabout where new conscripts were being shown how to fall-in. "And for soldiers, we're using civil servants and civilians who don't know how lucky they are not to be in one of the coastal cities."

"How lucky we are, too," Tess said. "In three weeks we've put together an invasion fleet."

"Two invasion fleets," Mick said. "But you know how I hate using military terminology. A million people aboard a fleet of cruise ships heading to Hawaii. Another million gone to Malaysia. Some might be retired soldiers or reservists, but most are refugees, and they've got a short voyage to learn to be soldiers. All because we're not ready for so many refugees so soon. That's the real problem here. Politicians like Ian Lignatiev and Oswald Owen treat this like a war, when it should be a relief effort."

Another gunshot sounded, this one more distant, and not nearly as loud as the reaction from the conscripts behind them. In turn, that was drowned by the yell from the handful of NCOs as they shouted the new troops into their teams.

"Maybe that's the root of my anxiety," Tess said. "My gut says this is the wrong way of doing absolutely everything, but despite the hallway outside our hotel suite being one of the corridors of power, I can't change what's happening. I didn't ask last night, was there any word from Liu on the pilot's grapevine?"

"She's still ferrying people out of Vancouver. VIPs to Guam, not children now they've got those 787s playing air-ambulance."

"VIPs like President Trowbridge?" Tess asked.

"Him?" Mick asked. "I don't think anyone's heard from Trowbridge since General Yoon sent the message he'd been sworn in as the U.S. president. Bloke's dead if you ask me. Good riddance. Never liked the idea of a president. Having that ambassador and the Governors of Guam and Hawaii run things as a triumvirate is far more sensible." He sniffed. "Smells like breakfast."

"It smells like beef," Tess said. "They're slaughtering the cattle."

"You knew they would," Mick said. "And I'd say that's our cue to call it a night. We'll grab some steak, take it back to the hotel, and we can watch a movie. I've a good one I've been saving, about a ghost who rides a motorbike. And don't tell me you've anything better to do."

"Give me a pen, I'll write you a list," she said. "Hang on. Do you hear that? Engine. Approaching. Fast."

Day had now completely banished night, leaving a clear view of the street: the burned wreck on the parched front lawn of the smoke-blackened house; the undead bodies shot at sunset whose arrival, coinciding with Tess's inspection, had led her to spend her night standing watch on the wall. The broken windows, the trampled lawns, the scattered junk dropped by fleeing householders, greedy looters, and frantic refugees. But beyond those, in the distance, and approaching at speed down Shoalhaven Avenue, was a black four-door with dust on the windscreen, dents on the fender, and suitcases strapped to the roof.

"Hold your fire!" Tess called. "Hold your fire!"

"Rule three," Mick called loudly to calm the nerves of the conscripted civilians. "Zombies can't run. They certainly can't drive."

"But will they brake?" Tess whispered. "Get ready to jump and run back."

The car was heading straight up the road, towards their section of the wall. A wall built strong enough to deter an un-human fist but nowhere near strong enough to withstand two tons of speeding metal. The car didn't slow, but it should have. At fifty metres away, the driver swerved around a charred trailer, abandoned in the middle of the road. But the driver hadn't seen the pile of timbers dumped behind. Thirty metres away and speeding too fast to slow, as it slammed into the debris, both wheels on the left-hand side rose, spinning in the air while the foremost right-side wheel slammed into an abandoned tyre. Pivoting on one rear wheel, the car spun and flipped, landing on the passenger-side doors. Metal screamed as the car spun, scattering suitcases as it rolled onto its roof, grinding to an upside-down halt among the undead corpses.

Tess had already jumped down from the wall in an instinctive leap. An eye-blinding bolt of pain shivered up her left side, a jarring reminder of Sydney and the stab wound that had curtailed her dreams of promotion and returned her to the town in which she'd grown up.

"Stretchers!" she yelled, limping towards the wreck until the pain subsided sufficiently that she could run. Keeping her eyes on the corpses around which she picked a path, she gave the car barely a glance until she heard the moan. Her gun was drawn and raised before she heard the words.

"Help."

"No worries, help's here," she said, though she didn't holster her weapon. Something was wrong. Very wrong. More so than was usual even for these supremely strange days.

Three women were in the car, all in their early twenties. Two conscious in the front. One unconscious in the back. All three were dressed in nondescript T-shirts and cotton trousers. Suitable for the long southern summer that only at night was beginning to show signs of turning to autumn. But most of the car's interior, like the roof before the car flipped, contained bags. Soft holdalls in the back, unlike the hard cases which had scattered across the road. But if those cases' spilled contents were anything to go by, these people had been transporting food. Enough cans and packets to open a store. But that wasn't what had raised Tess's internal alarm.

"Help us," the driver whispered.

"Shh!" Tess said, turning from the car, stepping back along the road, looking among the corpses for the crawler. She could hear it, that dead gasping wheeze, near but not deadly close, not yet. She stepped off the road, onto the parched strip of lawn belonging to a partially burned house, circling the car, scanning for movement.

Just as wood snapped, Tess realised the danger wasn't from road or car. She spun around as a four-metre-wide section of the smoke-blackened, two-metre-tall, faux-picket-fence collapsed. Three zombies fell with it, but Tess aimed at the fourth, a grotesque figure with an oozing stump instead of a hand, a seeping hole for an eye, and two knives embedded in its chest. Previously, the monster had stood behind the now fallen trio. As it lurched over them, red-brown pus sprayed from its missing hand.

Again, instinct took over, and Tess aimed for the centre mass, firing two shots before three weeks' nightmare experience reasserted control, and she shifted aim to its head. The zombie fell and she stepped back. Firing at the zombies on the ground, two shots and then three. The crawling creatures moved and rolled, thrashed, and bucked, trying to stand while also trying to claw at her, but they failed to do either before hot lead took them to an eternal peace.

Tess stepped back another pace, aiming into the rear garden of the smoke-blackened, one-and-half-storey Scandi-barn where the undead traipsed through a gap in the far fence. Dozens of them. Trampling across sun-scalded grass, heading straight for the crash.

"Walking like that," Mick said calmly as he came to stand by her side. He raised his rifle, a fully automatic HK416 with a suppressor he'd been given by the SASR in Broken Hill and rarely went anywhere without. "Walking one zombie after the other, reminds me of processionary caterpillars."

Tess held her fire while he began his. The bullets left the gun as a soft whisper, which gained a barking echo when Major Belinda Kelly reached their side. On the old soldier, nose, lips, and mouth added topography to a face that was mostly scars. Kelly's walking-story of experience was mirrored by the conflicting ranks she wore on her jet-black utility uniform. Her shoulder-board insignia marked her as a major, while the crown sewn to both sleeves reminded the world of the warrant officer she'd recently been. Now she was in command of the capital's northern defences.

"Reckon we've found the source of the incursion," Kelly said, putting down the last of the approaching undead. "I make that seventeen hostiles."

"Over here," Mick called to the approaching conscripts who'd been brave enough to follow Major Kelly, but wise enough to take their time. "Who's got the stretchers? Let's get these people out of here."

"They'll have to go to quarantine," Kelly said.

"The airport facility is empty," Mick said. "I'll drive them, if you give me a couple of people to watch them during the journey."

"I'll secure the house," Tess said, stepping over the corpses.

"I'll get you a backup team," Kelly said.

"No need," Tess said. Most of the recruits were greener than lettuce, and as familiar with combat; she didn't want to fret about friendly fire as well as feral teeth.

Beneath her feet, the singed fence creaked. The charred grass crackled. The glass from the broken window crunched. Tess kept her gun raised, sweeping left to right across the empty garden, then more slowly from right to left, taking in the broken windows and burned back doors.

The fires had begun during the early days of the outbreak, while she was still in Broken Hill. Hasty back-garden cookouts during the early power cuts had sparked and spread. With fire crews already deployed to the bush, the blazes had grown. With water supplies restricted, bringing the inferno under control had taken too long. Homes had burned, and the most northern and eastern suburbs had been evacuated. The wall had been built. But each day, each night, the undead traipsed in from the north, following the road convoys of refugees. But unlike the car-bound humans who kept to the blacktop, the undead wandered aimlessly, arriving in ones and twos, tens and twenties, with no pattern or consistency. In turn, this placed a shifting pressure on the wall, testing the untried conscripts, exhausting the handful of experienced soldiers. Subsequently, it had been decreed the suburbs would be reclaimed. More conscripts had been brought in, and today they would go house-to-house, street-to-street, and create a new, taller, stronger, and more permanent, wall on the very outskirts.

Tess crossed into the next garden, and then the one beyond where tumbled concrete besser-blocks created a narrow channel down which the undead had been forced. An artificial passageway ending at an alley running parallel to the road, and which was, currently, empty. She didn't lower her gun, but listened, waited, counting to thirty before heading back to the scene of the crash. Mick and the injured car passengers had gone, though Major Kelly remained with three obviously nervous conscripts.

"We're clear," Tess said. "They made their way into that back garden during the night. The noise of that car galvanised them to push down that fire-weakened fence."

"Thank you, Commissioner," Kelly said. "The car's occupants were looters, by the look of that gear."

"And they drove all the way from Mildura," Tess said, pointing to the upside-down sticker on the bumper of the upturned car. "So maybe not looters if they drove from that far away. Maybe shop owners, coming with the last of their stock."

"Which is ours now," Kelly said in what was not quite a question, not quite a statement.

"Ours, yes," Tess said. "Detail some people to take it to the emergency reserve at the museum. We'll distribute it after the beef is gone."

"We'll take all that can be salvaged to the emergency food reserve, yes, ma'am," Kelly said.

Tess caught the caveat, but didn't argue. Kelly would claim and distribute most of the supplies among the conscripts. Some might make it to the food reserve, though during the last three weeks, very little had.

"You heard the commissioner!" Kelly added, addressing the trio of conscripts in a parade-ground bark. "Pack everything up. But be careful where you put your hands."

"Did Dr Dodson take the patients to the airport?" Tess asked.

"Aboard a van we're calling an ambulance," Kelly said.

"Then he's left my car," Tess said. "So I'm driving home for a few hours sleep. G'day, Major."

"Before you go, ma'am," Major Kelly said in a tone Tess had last heard just before she'd ended up spending an entire night standing guard.

"You want to ask another favour?" Tess said.

"We're five non-coms short," Kelly said. "Three are crook. Two disappeared. I can run a double team, promote a couple of promising recruits and put them on guard duty here, but we'll still be short."

"I've a cabinet meeting at four," Tess said. "I really need to get some sleep before then."

"This will only take an hour," Kelly said. "Two at most."

Tess doubted it, but she could hardly say no. "What do you want me to do?"

Chapter 2 - Team Stonefish
Bonner, Canberra

Ten minutes later, with her water bottle refilled, but her heart singing for coffee, Tess stood in front of the leaderless six-person squad. Three women, three men. The oldest had at least a decade on Tess, while the youngest should still have been in school. All wore green coats, the same cut, style, and, unfortunately for the large man with the pancake physique, the same size. Despite the designer swoosh on the breast, they were as close to uniforms as these recruits would see for a long time.

"G'day," she said. "My name's Tess Qwong. I'm a deputy commissioner with the Australian Federal Police, but a couple of weeks ago, I was an inspector in Broken Hill. Any of you served in the military? Police? No worries. Despite what some people might say, this isn't war, and it certainly isn't policing. Do you see the singed rooftops on the other side of the wall? A string of end-of-the-world barbies got out of hand, and we evacuated those suburbs. Now we're reclaiming them. Bet you all heard the shooting a few minutes ago? You know what it means?"

"Zombies," the young man said, removing his cap so he could scratch his very recently shaved, and already sunburned, scalp.

"How old are you, mate?" Tess asked.

"You going to ask anyone else that?" he asked. "Or just me."

"Fair point. Good on ya for volunteering."

"You mean we had a choice?" the young man asked.

"I guess not," Tess said. "What's your name?"

"Hay-Zach," he said.

"Zach? G'day," Tess said. If the teenager wanted to rename himself, she wouldn't judge. The one silver lining in the apocalypse was being able to escape a little of your past. "This isn't war, but that doesn't mean there's no danger," Tess added. "We're going house-to-house searching all the properties in the empty suburbs between here and the Mulligans Flat Nature Reserve."

"Just us?" Zach asked.

"Everyone," Tess said. "Each team has been allocated a couple of streets. By lunchtime, we'll be done. This afternoon, you'll be building a new and more permanent wall, taller than that one."

"And then we'll guard it?" a woman with silver-grey hair asked. She couldn't be more than a year older than Tess, so it was probably dyed, but instead of opting for the colour of her youth, she'd fully embraced the shades of her future. Her trio of nose rings appeared to be gold, while her suit jacket looked designer, and her boots were the kind of op-shop rejects an optimist would call vintage.

"A couple of weeks ago," Tess said, "if you told me I'd be here, doing this, I'd have said you'd spent too long fishing for flies in the noonday sun. So I'll be honest and say I don't know what you'll be doing tomorrow. Do you know one another? No. You should. From here on in, you'll serve together. You're a team. A unit. Mates. In the worst of times and the best of times, both of which are ahead of us all. So, who are you?"

"Elaina Slater," the woman with the trio of nose rings said. "I was a primary school teacher in Wagga Wagga. The entire school was evacuated to Tasmania, but I thought I'd do more to keep them safe by volunteering here."

"Clyde Brook," said the man with the sparse goatee, carrying one of the squad's two shotguns. "My husband and son were sent to Tasmania. Only one of us was allowed to go with him."

"My wife took my son," said the forty-year-old man with the pancake chest, carrying the other shotgun. "My ex-wife," he added with a sad sigh.

"And what's your name, mate?" Tess asked.

"Shane Morgan. I was a... I was in finance."

"I'm Sophia Peresta, and I had a yoga studio," the tall woman with the braided hair said. "Just opened. Took me five years to save up enough to qualify for the loan. Are all the kids being evacuated to Tassy? Because my daughter's at the crèche at the university."

"Not all, and I don't think any more will be sent away from here," Tess said. "From now on, the planes and ships are being used to evacuate people from the harbours in Indonesia, the Philippines, Malaysia and across the Pacific. We need to get the civilians out so we can send the soldiers in, secure the towns and cities there, like we're doing here. Retake the farmland, the industrial buildings, the countries, the islands, the continents. I won't say it'll be quick, but the offensive has begun."

"Why are there only two shotguns?" the last of the group asked. Not so much pushing fifty as holding it at bay, she had a bad scissor-cut to match her badly fitting dungarees, which certainly didn't match the sapphire necklace and earrings.

"What's your name?" Tess asked.

"Bianca Clague. I'm a pastry chef from Adelaide."

Tess doubted it. The jewellery spoke of money, and the cut gems matched her cut-glass accent. Old money, but that was worth no more than her jewels, and she knew it, so was claiming a more useful prior profession.

"This morning," Tess said, "two fleets of cruise ships, tankers, and freighters departed. Aboard each fleet were a million people. Some are conscripts like you. Some are soldiers. Some are refugees. One fleet left Perth, heading up to Malaysia where they'll secure the peninsula. The other set sail from Brisbane. They're making for Hawaii and then to the Baja California Peninsula in Mexico. But first, they're stopping in Samoa to refuel and to collect rifles and ammo the Americans have flown in. That's why you've only got a couple of shotguns. As terrifying as the zombies seem, the dangers *we* face pale in comparison to elsewhere in the world. You blokes know how to use those?"

Clyde gave a precise nod. Shane looked a little uncertain.

"I can give it to someone else," Tess said.

"No. No, I know what I'm doing," Shane said, a tremor to his voice.

"Okay, we'll call that rule four," Tess said. "Guns are always pointed at the ground. We'll climb over that wall, and split into two teams. Team A, that's Zach, Bianca, and Shane, you'll take the right. Team One, Elaina, Clyde, Sophia, you're on the left. We'll walk up to our section, eyes open, guns pointing down. When we get to our set of streets, we'll go door-to-door. Any that are open or unlocked, give a yell, and I'll go in. You're watching my back, understand? Good. What's rule four, Shane?"

"Guns at the— Oh, sorry."

"Use the shovels to knock the zombies down," Tess continued. "If there are more than two zombies, you retreat. Rule three, zombies can't run. But humans can. So retreat carefully. Don't flee. Remember to yell a warning to the rest of us. Two zombies or less, you knock them down. Shotguns, you move in and shoot them on the ground. Never shoot if they're moving, upright, or inside. You leave them to me. Okay?"

"Welcome to the ever-evolving abnormal," Bianca said.

"Everyone got their gear? Shane, mate, what's in your bag?"

"Everything I own in the world," he said.

"As long as you can carry it," Tess said, eyeing the pack that was nearly half the man's height. "Everyone got water, because I don't know when you'll get more."

"Is that rule one?" Zach asked.

"Sort of. Rule one is check your boots," Tess said.

"And rule two?" Elaina asked.

"Remember rule one."

They were the last team to climb over the wall. Ahead of them, Major Kelly's double-strength squad had already reached the next roundabout and were heading north up Burdekin Avenue.

"Why shovels?" Bianca asked as their squad walked north. "We don't have shotguns because there aren't enough. But why shovels?"

"Same reason as you've got those jackets," Tess said. "It's what was available in a warehouse here in the city."

"Logistics wins wars," Elaina murmured.

"Exactly," Tess said, giving a wide berth to a charred car outside an equally burned house. "And we've got a logistical nightmare on our hands. General Yoon wants us to resupply her army. You've heard of General Yoon?"

"The prime minister mentioned her," Shane said, already out of breath. "On her radio broadcast three nights ago. She's the American general, yes?"

"The Canadian general running the relief effort in most of North America," Tess said. "But Canada isn't the only front. Indonesia, Japan, Singapore, and Korea all need assistance, and that's before we even begin talking about India. As for China and Russia, they're not even talking to us. We've got to ramp up production of everything. By the coast, we're building giant desalination plants, and the electricity generating stations to power them. A by-product of those water plants is salt, from which we'll get chlorine another coastal factory can turn into bleach we can use to disinfect our clothes. Washing detergent comes next, but until we've got the bleach, we're exhausting our wardrobes faster than a jackaroo at a weekend-long wedding."

A gunshot echoed, out of sight, but loud.

"Barrels down, guys," Tess said as both Clyde and Shane raised their shotguns. "A single gunshot is someone eliminating one of the infected. Two shots mean the same thing, just fired by someone with bad aim. More than two is when you pay attention." She patted her holstered sidearm. "And when you see me draw my weapon, that's when you get ready. Remember rule three?"

"Zombies can't run," Zach said.

"Right. Best foot forward, because we've a couple more streets before we get to our section."

After twenty minutes, Tess was lost. Her badly photocopied map only had half the street names, and none of the side roads. She'd assumed she'd be able to ask other teams the way, but they seemed to be out ahead on their own.

"This is us," she declared, reading the street sign. "Jackamos Street. Are any of you locals?"

"I am," Bianca said. "But I've never been here."

Tess pointed at the map, then along the street. "We'll check the houses on this street and Eugene Vincent Street, which should be that road up the top of the hill." A gunshot carried on the wind, but distant. Faint. "We shouldn't have too much trouble," Tess added. "We're on a hill and there's a fair number of streets between us and the Mulligans Flat Nature

Reserve to the east. That's where that shot came from, and the direction the undead will come. There are some patrols out there, hunting them, but that doesn't mean we'll let our guard down."

"What's that smell?" Bianca asked.

"Burst sewage pipe," Clyde said. "Blocked first, then burst. Water's evaporated. That smell comes from what remains."

"An incentive to get the job finished," Tess said. "Team A—"

"Team Stonefish," Zach said. "We're Team Stonefish."

"You are? No worries. Stonefish, you're on the right. Team One—"

"Funnel-web," Elaina said. "They're way scarier than a stonefish."

"Team Funnel-web, take the left," Tess said. "Shotguns, you watch the rear, but keep those barrels down. Don't go shooting anyone in the back. One person walks up to the front door. If the windows are smashed, if the door is broken, call me. We don't care if the door is unlocked, just that it's closed. And if it *is* closed, check the back. If the backdoor is shut, too, then you chalk the footpath outside with a tick. You've got chalk? Off you go."

Tess stayed in the middle of the narrow, sloping road, watching the two teams nervously approach the obviously shut front doors. Both houses had the clean lines and unmarred brickwork of the recently built, and both in a cubist-interpretation where they'd clearly recycled the same architectural plans. Other houses on the street were brick one-storeys, or taller Scandi-barns. Some had new solar tiles, others had red terracotta, but she'd find similar mix-and-match components across the entire continent-country. Of far more immediate interest was the complete absence of cars along kerbs and in driveways. These houses had been recently lived in, and just as recently fled.

This was the heart of the problem. Before the nature of the outbreak was truly known, before she had arrived in Canberra, before the last prime minister's suicide, and even before the fires, a warning had been given that outlying suburbs might have to be evacuated. *Might*. But the warning had been taken as doctrine. Residents had weighed their future as a choice between walking to the centre of the capital with what little they could carry, or driving away with everything they could cram into their car. Some had taken a few hours to cook all the food they couldn't take with them. Some of those hasty cookouts had got out of control, only hastening the owners', and their neighbours', departure. With the suburbs emptying, and most of the fire-crews fighting bushfires, or having joined the rescue-or-destroy mission in the outback, homes had burned before the blazes were under control. Clearly, the people on this street had taken one look at the rising pillars of smoke and fled. No doubt many were now among the undead unwittingly returning to the place they'd once called home.

Team Funnel-web moved to the next house. Seeing that, Zach called for his team to hurry.

"It's not a race, mate," Tess called. Zach waved acknowledgment, but didn't stop hurrying on to the next building while Shane, awkwardly due to the heavy weight of his pack, bent to mark the footpath.

Zach would learn. Hopefully, he wouldn't learn the hard way. She turned around, looking down the slope, beyond the handful of streets and to the distant trees of… She took out her map to find the name. Mulligans Flat and the Goorooyaroo Nature Reserve. And beyond those, the gloriously sharp mountain peaks. Canberra was an alien city to her, a name from the news, barely more relevant to her daily life than Seoul, Washington, or Pyongyang.

"Commish!" Bianca called.

Tess turned to see Bianca waving to her a good deal further up the street. She'd stopped outside a single-storey peach-brick with a stormy-grey ceramic tiled roof. To the right of the door was a closed garage, while to the left were a trio of wall-height windows that must originally have been designed for an office, then repurposed for a home. The windows were curtained, but the front door was broken open.

"Step back," Tess said as she advanced, drawing her sidearm. "Do you see the splinters on the doorframe? Those marks were made by a crowbar."

"Was it looters?" Shane asked.

"Defo," Tess said. "Long term, it doesn't matter. Once this street is secured, these houses will be re-allocated among the refugees."

"Oh," Shane said, adjusting his pack. "I thought that might happen."

Zach, meanwhile, had crossed to the trio of wall-height windows and was trying to peer in. "You hear that?" he asked.

"Yeah, there's something in there," Bianca said.

"Broken door means we go in and check," Tess said. "Shane, go back to the footpath, keep your eyes on the side of the house. Shotgun pointing down, remember? Zach, you go with him, and keep your eyes on the road. Bianca, you stay here, by the door. Come in if I call, otherwise, stay outside."

"Yeah, no worries," she said.

Gun raised, Tess stepped inside, quickly sweeping through the living room and kitchen. The photos mostly showed a young baby. Sometimes with parents, sometimes with grandparents. The floor was littered with soft toys, but she doubted the mess had been created by looters. The thieves probably *were* responsible for dropping the trio of canvas tote bags in the corridor leading to the bedrooms. An odd mix of crockery and utensils had spilled out of one, while small glass jars of baby food had fallen from the other.

Tess stepped over those, through the open child-gate, and into the hallway, moving with determined certainty towards the source of the noise.

The zombie was in the master bedroom. Male. About thirty. He'd been tied to the bed, swaddled in a sheet, around which long chains had been wrapped under the frame. The snapping sound came from his teeth gnashing up and down. The rattle was from the chains moving and shaking. The sound of cloth ripping was dulled by the blood and fluid seeping through the pale sheets.

Tess took aim, and fired. One shot. But it was followed by a second, this one from outside. Tess dashed out of the room, down the corridor, over the scattered toys, registering the broken glass in the front window as she sprinted to the front door. Outside, Zach was crouched, while Bianca gripped the barrel of Shane's shotgun, keeping it pointed downward.

"Trouble?" Tess asked.

"Not really," Bianca said.

"Sorry," Shane said. "I… it just went off."

"No worries," Tess said. She waved the all-clear to the other team. "Give the shotgun to Bianca, and take the shovel." She turned around, breathed out, and went back inside, completing her sweep before returning outside. "Only one zombie. Zach, you've got the chalk?"

"No worries," he said, and scrawled a large Z on the footpath. "They'll come and collect the body?"

"Yep," Tess said. "And disinfect the house."

"You mean someone has to live there?" Zach asked.

"Defo," Tess said. "Could be refugees passing through, or recruits being trained, or workers for the new factories. There are millions of refugees at sea, and millions more desperate to catch a boat or plane. Next house. Eyes open."

"There won't be enough beds for everyone," Bianca said.

"But there *will* be enough roofs," Tess said.

"And steak for brekkie," Zach said. "That's what the major said, we'll get steak every day."

Tess shook her head, and glanced over to the other team, already moving from the front door towards the rear garden. Clyde seemed to have taken charge, and seemed to know what to do. The man was probably ex-military. Retired when he'd become a dad, but hadn't come forward when the call-up was issued, not until his son had been sent to relative safety.

"Sorry, Zach," she said. "The steak is a one-off. There's a station to the north. Big place, big herd, but it needs too much water to keep running. We told them to send the herd here for slaughter and canning, but not until after we'd built the canning factories. They sent the cows too early. Since we've no food to keep the herd alive, and no factories to make the cans, let alone process the meat, we're slaughtering them instead. We'll freeze as much as possible, but the rest is being cooked. And when it's gone, it'll be gone for a decade. We'll keep enough breeding stock to reintroduce them, one day, but it's a veggie diet until then."

"No more snags or burgers? Are you serious?" Zach asked, wistfully forlorn.

"Sorry, mate," Tess said.

A shout came from ahead. The other team had reached the junction, and had already begun searching the houses to the right. Elaina stood on the kerb, while Clyde and Sophia stood much closer to the front door.

"Finish checking these houses," Tess said, and went to check on the other team.

"The door's open, Commish," Elaina said. "We'd have gone in, but we didn't want to spoil your fun."

"House keys are in the lock," Clyde said, pointing to the dangling boomerang-shaped fob.

"And no car in the drive," Tess said. "The owners, before leaving, left the keys so a looter wouldn't break the door down."

Inside, it was quickly apparent the homeowners had accurately foreseen the future. Looters *had* emptied the kitchen and bathroom cupboards, and removed most of the tools from the rack in the garage. But, perhaps because they'd *not* had to exert themselves forcing an entry, they'd refrained from excessively wanton destruction.

"No zombies," Tess said, returning outside. "Lock the door. Mark the footpath with a tick. And— Oh, strewth, they're going the wrong way."

Team Stonefish had reached the junction, and were now heading north up Ben Blakeney Street, and toward a brown-brick one-storey half covered in scaffolding. The tall and tidy fence ringing the property had been partially removed to allow access to the garden while it was being landscaped. From the scaffolding running up and across the roof, solar panels were being installed.

"Stonefish!" she called. "Shane, Zach, Bianca!"

All three slowed and turned. Before Tess could call out again, a figure lurched out through the gap in the fence. Grey trousers stained with blood, faux-leather jacket ripped to shreds, face contorted by savage burns and twisted with infected, undead rage.

"Move!" Tess called, raising her gun, but she didn't have a clear shot. She ran forward as the team turned towards danger. Zach stepped back, while Bianca half-raised the shotgun, but Shane charged forward, swinging the shovel up over his head.

"No, Shane! Get back!" Bianca called.

But the man was trying to make up for his earlier mistake. He swung the tool in a vicious, curving downward hack that completely misjudged the distance. The edge of the shovel smashed through the zombie's arm, ripping flesh from bone. Momentum spun Shane ninety degrees while the heavy weight of his still-slung pack carried him forward another half metre, and straight into the monster. Its left arm was a dripping stump, but the right was a clawing hand which curled around the bag's shoulder strap, tugging Shane forward and down. As its teeth bit into the man's shoulder, a simultaneous yell came from both Shane and Zach. A scream from Shane, fury from Zach as the young man charged, swinging his shovel low at the zombie's legs.

Even from ten metres away, Tess heard bone snap. The zombie fell, and so did Shane. Shane's heels and elbows dug into the grass, as he tried to get clear. The zombie thrashed more violently, pivoting and rolling onto its broken leg, and far enough from Shane and Zach that Tess dared risk the shot. She fired. One shot, straight into its forehead. The zombie collapsed.

"Back to the road!" Tess called as she crossed to Shane, now lying on his side, hand curled around his bleeding shoulder. "Shane, mate, let me have a look. Some people are immune, remember?"

But even as she spoke, Shane coughed and spasmed. His arms jerked. His legs kicked. Rolling onto his back, arms and legs kicking like a beached turtle, his dead eyes filled with insatiable bloodlust. His mouth snapped, and Tess stepped back.

"Sorry, mate," she said. She fired, and her gun had an echo.

Tess stepped back, turning to look for the new danger, but the second zombie was dead. Shot by Bianca, the slug having smashed through its skull. A metre to the left, and it would have slammed through Tess's back.

"Good shot," Tess said. "Zach, you okay?"

"He's... He's..." Zach stammered.

"Bianca, take Zach back to the middle of the street," Tess said. "Wait for me there." She walked around Shane's corpse and that of the zombie who'd infected him, over the zombie Bianca had shot, and into the garden. The two dead zombies wore non-descript clothes which could have come from the back of any wardrobe, but the soles of their boots were so clean they'd been found very recently in a shoe shop's stock room. In the rear garden, a set of shattered plate-glass sliding doors led into a sunroom. Beyond was the looters' stash: dozens of bulging bags and twice the number of stuffed suitcases.

"Zach, mark the footpath with an L and a Z," Tess said when she returned outside. "Those zombies were looters, and they've been living here for at least a week. That's their stash house, filled with supplies scavenged from a dozen properties. At least a dozen."

"They must have thought other looters wouldn't search a building site," Bianca said.

"Probably," Tess said.

"What do we do about Shane?" Zach asked.

"His body will get a burial," Tess said. "That's why we mark the kerb."

"He'll be buried with the other zombies?" Zach asked.

"They were all people a month ago," Tess said. "But I'll have a word with the coroner. Make sure Shane gets a plot of his own."

She wouldn't. All the bodies would be cremated in a recently expanded industrial furnace, Shane's with them. Hers, too, if that was her fate. But Zach didn't need to know that.

With Shane's sudden death, she merged the two squads into one. Calling it Team Stonefish didn't cheer up Zach. Nothing would, except time. The next six houses were locked. At the seventh, Tess let Bianca enter first, but she came back outside almost immediately.

"Suicide," Bianca said, swiping away the flies following her.

Tess pulled her scarf around her mouth and went in.

The house was nothing unusual: a three-bedroom one-storey shared by a couple, their five-year-old daughter, and their dog, judging by the photographs dotting the wall. The body was in the en-suite bathroom, off the master bedroom. The tub was full, but he lay on the floor. Polished shoes. Dress shirt. Tie, but no jacket because he'd wanted to have easy access to his left wrist on which a fifteen-centimetre-long incision ran along the artery. In the sink was a bloody scalpel. On the sink-counter, a dusty octagonal bottle of Cognac kept company with an open bottle of sedatives.

Yes, it was suicide. Just another suicide. Tess didn't breathe out in relief only because she'd then have to breathe in just as deeply, and the flies were already buzzing around the blood on the floor. She'd lost count of the number of suicides she'd attended since arriving in Canberra. With each report of a newly discovered corpse, she still expected to find a mutilated body, tortured by the serial killer from Broken Hill. But no, this was just another sad tale of someone who couldn't accept the new reality.

But then, in the floor-to-ceiling mirror next to the bath, she saw the reflection of his partially hidden face.

Carefully, she opened the cupboard beneath the sink. A few bottles of shampoo kept company with a lone bottle of shower gel, but there was no sign of the toothbrushes missing from next to the sink. The owners of this house must have taken them when they left because this dead man didn't match the picture in the photographs. In fact, Tess was certain this man owned a mansion over in Redhill.

As she walked back to the front door, she took out a notebook and pen, and quickly jotted a note. "Clyde, Zach," she said, handing the note to Clyde. "Go back to the wall. My police car is parked on the other side, next to the major's ute. The keys are beneath the seat. Drive to Parliament House. Tell the sentries there, and anyone who stops you, that you've got a message for Anna Dodson from Commissioner Tess Qwong. Then drive back here with the minister. Run."

"It's bad news?" Bianca asked as Zach and Clyde jogged down the street.

"It's a friend," Tess said. "So the minister will want to see for herself. Keep watch here, while I take a proper look around the house."

Chapter 3 - And Then There Were Five
Bonner, Canberra

"Yes, that's him," Anna Dodson said. Once a teacher, very recently an unexpectedly elected protest candidate, she'd been appointed Minister for Wellbeing in the first post-outbreak cabinet. Now she was Minister for Housing and Agriculture. "That's Aaron. Senator Aaron Bryce. Will that do for a formal identification?"

"More than enough for these times," Tess said. "I thought I recognised him, but with someone so high profile, I needed to be positive."

"Was it suicide?" Anna asked. "It looks like suicide, Tess, but was it?"

"I have a few questions before I answer that," Tess said. "Let's talk in a different room." She pointed at the doorway, and then followed Anna back into the main bedroom, the hall, and into the living room.

Being a decade older than Anna, while they'd crossed paths in Broken Hill while children, it was Mick Dodson whom Tess had grown to know first. As a new constable, while he was already an experienced flying doctor, they'd attended many a remote emergency together. But since Tess had returned to Broken Hill, she'd grown to know Anna, then a teacher.

"Whose house is this?" Anna asked.

"That's one of my questions," Tess said. "The senator had a house in Redhill, right?"

"Not just a house," Anna said. "It's a mansion. His father-in-law paid for it."

"Sir Malcolm Baker, who got rich from coal and pokies, yes?"

"By owning the company that made the gambling machines," Anna said. "I don't think he's ever put a coin into a slot himself."

"And Aaron's wife, she's not here in Canberra?"

"She's at their place near Brisbane," Anna said. "Has been since before the outbreak. The marriage was in trouble."

"Genuinely in trouble?" Tess asked.

"You mean was it a come-on?" Anna asked. "No, he is truly miserable. But he's seemed— I mean he *was* getting happier. I thought it was because of the distance between him and his marriage, and his father-in-law."

"And since the outbreak, he's been your assistant?" Tess asked.

"He was offered my job," Anna said. "I got it because he turned it down."

"He didn't want it?" Tess asked.

"He didn't even want to be Minister for Water," Anna said. "But I made him accept it, and kept him close. He was good with figures. Good at seeing the whole picture, thinking ahead. But he didn't want responsibility for people's lives."

"I thought he wanted to be prime minister one day," Tess said. "It was in all of the papers."

"Because his father-in-law paid them to print it," Anna said. "His wife had ambition, but he didn't. Not really. Certainly not since the outbreak."

"Beyond a good night's sleep, a good meal, and a long shower, who does?" Tess said. "He was thirty-nine years old, in an unhappy marriage, and in a stressful job. Add in the apocalypse, and suicide isn't a surprise. Except this isn't his house. Do you recognise the people in those photographs?"

Anna looked at the pictures. "They're strangers to me," she said.

"Are you sure?" Tess asked. "When did you last see the senator?"

"Yesterday morning," Anna said. "We were working on the Murray-Darling problem. Even reducing cotton production to ten percent, and felling all of the almond groves that aren't mature enough to produce nuts this season, we'll still be two thousand giga-litres short. But we can't reduce cotton any further because we need it for so much more than just clothing, so production will have to be scaled up next year. No matter what Oswald Owen says, Australia won't be a one-month rest-and-reequip stopover for the refugees. We have to assume a population increase of one hundred million by the year's end, with the increased water consumption that goes with it."

"That sounds like a tough problem to crack," Tess said.

"Yes, but we were close to a solution," Anna said. "We'd developed an agricultural strategy to see us through the winter, and which would provide enough water for Oswald Owen's industrial expansion. I thought that was enough of a victory for one week so I sent Aaron to bed."

"At what time?"

"Early. After dawn, but not too long after."

"And you thought he went to his mansion in Redhill?" Tess asked.

"No, he's been sleeping in the hotel, just like us."

"In the same hotel?" Tess asked.

"He's two floors down," Anna said. "In a single without a view. He gave up his suite to a couple of families. The ones whose kids race their bikes up and down the halls. Now, I'm playing my cabinet-minister-card and ask why are there so many questions?"

"Because he came here to kill himself," Tess said. "He didn't go to his hotel room where he'd be found by you when he failed to show up to work. He didn't go to his mansion where you'd have sent me to look for him. He came here. An unassuming house in an unassuming street in an abandoned suburb. Take another look at those photographs."

"Why do— Oh," Anna said. "You mean the girl." Anna stood and walked to the shelf and picked up the family portrait. "I suppose she looks a *little* like Aaron. Or as much like Aaron as she looks like the man in this picture. That's what you're saying?"

"Asking," Tess said. "I heard the rumours."

"They were just stories," Anna said. "I suppose it's possible she's his daughter, but I'm sure he would have said something. Does it matter?"

"I don't think so," Tess said. "Not now. There's no car outside, so Senator Bryce walked here in smart shoes and a suit and tie, with a scalpel, sedatives, and a bottle of Cognac almost as old as Sydney. He ran the bath, took a drink and a fistful of pills, and then he slit his wrist. Lengthwise, so he knew how to do it properly. But he didn't get into the bath. I think he might have changed his mind, might have stood, grabbed for a towel to stem the bleeding, but the sedatives kicked in, and he collapsed. It would have been painless."

"And he came here because of the girl in this picture?"

"Perhaps. Or perhaps not. But I'll write this one up as suicide." Tess checked her watch. "Strewth, it's not even ten o'clock."

"Did you think it was later?"

"I've lived a lifetime this morning already," Tess said. "And last night wasn't much better. Mick and I did a turn on the walls."

"You brought Dad here?" Anna asked.

"He brought himself," Tess said. "But I kept an eye on him, and he on me. And he went back to the airport at dawn. They were still short-handed so I stayed to help. Trouble found us just before we found Aaron. Lost one bloke to zombies down the street. There's enough time to write this up to include it in today's prime ministerial broadcast."

"No, I don't think so," Anna said. "Unless you do."

"People will have to know at some point," Tess said. "This is the seventh parliamentary suicide since the outbreak, and the first since the old prime minister died last week. Not counting Maggie Lee."

"No, I'm sure she went to find her family," Anna said. "She was talking about it for a week. Maybe she'll return. But that's why we sent so many to Hobart. It's hard to go walkabout when you're stuck on Tasmania. We'll have to recall some. I always thought it was a mistake sending so many away like that."

"You mean, you'll have to recommend to the prime minister that some be recalled," Tess said with a thin smile. "How are things on Tassy?"

"Better than here," Anna said. "And they'll hate to be back, but it has to be done. Can this be kept quiet for a few weeks?"

"Two at most, but don't hope for more than one," Tess said. "The coroner will be discreet. My team will stay quiet if we buy their silence with some lighter duty. I was thinking we could send them to the airport where your dad can keep an ear pricked for whispers."

"A week is more than long enough," Anna said. "By then, General Yoon will have crossed into the U.S., the fleet will have reached Hawaii, and we'll have reinforced Singapore."

"A week," Tess nodded. "And how are you doing?"

"Me?"

"We haven't had much time to talk," Tess said. "We share a hotel suite, but the rare times we're all there, your dad insists on watching movies."

"Bad movies."

"I know, right?" Tess said. Both women smiled.

"I'm tired, Tess," Anna said. "Fraying at the edges, but I can see the light at the end of the tunnel. There's still unrest in some cities, zombies in the outback, and bandits in the bush. But the problems are getting smaller, more manageable. With the quarantine zones at the airports, we're controlling the infection. Thanks to the draft, everyone is working, even if they're guarding a wall rather than fixing our communications problems. It's possible that not having satellites has actually helped. No one's waiting for orders from us, but getting on with running things locally. Medically, our biggest challenge is disease in the refugee camps. Instead of worrying about starvation, we're dealing with logistical problems, so things could be a lot worse."

"Like twenty thousand head of cattle being driven to Canberra a month before their time?" Tess asked.

"Exactly," Anna said. "General Yoon now has more recruits than she can equip. All refugees are being sent to farms, new and old, across the American Plains. But until harvest, they'll require food. I don't know how much food is in storage across America, or how much is accessible, and I doubt General Yoon does, either. Soon, the ships and planes arriving with refugees will return with food aboard, not soldiers. Which is why the slaughter of those cattle is so deeply frustrating."

"Because of how much is being wasted, you mean?" Tess asked.

"Because of how small things have these huge knock-on effects," Anna said. "We just pushed two million refugees onto ships, and sent them away because we don't have the resources to keep them here. Some are soldiers, yes. But most are civilians. I won't even call them conscripts. Most of the million who sailed from Brisbane won't even have firearms unless they collect them from Samoa. Which is assuming the Americans have flown them in like they promised. We're also assuming they'll be able to get more ammunition from Hawaii once the island has been secured, otherwise I don't know what they'll be fighting with when they get to the Baja California Peninsula. We're moving fast because we'll starve if we move slow. But I wanted to speak to you about the cattle." She reached into her bag and took out a large envelope. "The attorney general has three warrants for you to serve. Dad will fly you."

"Arrest warrants?" Tess asked, opening the envelope. "And they're printed. This must be serious. I don't recognise the names."

"You've got a summary of the evidence, and the witness statements. Eight in total."

"But for three separate suspects and three separate crimes," Tess said, glancing through them. "This isn't sufficient to press charges, let alone take to trial. It's why we shouldn't have an attorney general running the police."

"Let's not have that argument again, Tess," Anna said. "The packet includes some background information culled from the databases we could access. It's enough to arrest them and bring them back to Canberra. What happens at trial doesn't matter. The key goal is to *arrest* them, publicly. We want to announce their detention on the broadcast later this week."

"As an example to everyone else?" Tess said, quickly scanning the sheets. "Five of the statements are connected to the cattle. This one, Bradley Metzger... Where's Camp 23?"

"Ballina," Anna said. "Two hundred kilometres south of Brisbane. It's a refugee camp with three desalination plants, a coal power station, and the usual coastal factories to make the parts. I think there's canning and a pipe manufactory. Or there should be by now. There's been an outbreak of dysentery."

"It says. And we're to pick up some meds at the airport on our first stop." Tess tapped the page. "What's the crime in Ballina?"

"The first shipment of coal has arrived at the coast. The turbines have already been there for two days. Without the new power station, the desalination plants can't run. Without them, there's not enough water for the other eight camps nearby and inland. That's nearly seven hundred thousand refugees. In a month, it'll be three million. It's why we dispatched the fleet from Brisbane four days early. We can move people to the city to inhabit the rooms those conscripts were billeted in. We'll buy ourselves two more weeks, but it'll be a month before those ships return. We're trying to house hundreds of thousands in towns of tens of hundreds. The infrastructure can't cope. Without water, we'll get more riots, and we've barely got a lid on the trouble in Melbourne."

"Got it. Metzger's being removed for incompetence, and charged with criminal negligence. Who do you want running the place? Mick?"

"No, we've put together some management teams from the refugees who came from Jakarta, and they'll arrive at the coast in two days."

"So you're sending me and Mick on ahead. Without backup, I assume?"

"It's not me," Anna said. "This is Erin Vaughn's mission. But she has a point. A deputy commissioner and the father of a cabinet minister probably won't end up hostages. Or worse. We shouldn't need an army. I don't know whether those three will go quietly, but it's really about whether the rest of their people will still follow the law."

"No, we shouldn't need an army to serve a warrant," Tess said. "But I'm assuming you have one in reserve in case it goes wrong?"

"The SASR," Anna said. "They're waiting at Ballina. In a couple of days, they'll parachute into Honolulu to retake the airport. I don't want to use them because it might delay that operation. And since the fleet is already at sea, nothing but bad weather will delay when they reach Hawaii. Losses will be fewer if the SASR are already there."

Outside came the sound of an engine.

"The coroner is here," Tess said.

"I can speak to them," Anna said. "And to your team. I'll send them to the airport afterwards. You better get going."

"You know, it's days like this I wish I'd taken over my mum's restaurant," Tess said.

Chapter 4 - Frankenstein's Mistake
Canberra and Beyond

With civilian road traffic banned, it was an easy drive to the airport, delayed more by barricades than traffic. Most of the new barriers were as empty as the roads, their guards deployed to the outer walls and suburban security. Her badge got Tess through the rest, and through the gates at the airport where she drove straight to the hangar Mick had claimed as his own personal garage. Outside, the runway was empty, though every other spare metre of tarmac was occupied with 747s, A380s, and 787s, with civilian props and military fighters parked beneath the shade of the jumbos' wings. Inside the hangar, she found Mick elbows-deep in the partially disassembled engine of a Pilatus PC-12.

"Ah, there you are," he said. "Do you want to speak to those refugees?"

"Who?" Tess asked

"The ladies who were in the car that crashed up by the wall," Mick said. "You've come to question them, right? I put them in quarantine over there." He pointed beyond the hangar's wide doors, out across the crowded airfield and to another hangar, recently painted with a giant red cross.

"D'you know, I'd forgotten about them," Tess said.

"They say they were bringing supplies here, didn't want them to go to waste," Mick said. "They're lying. Reckon they were planning on setting up a black market."

"Since all their supplies were confiscated, let's believe the best," Tess said. "But that's not why I'm here. I need to give the ground-crew chief a heads-up to expect a few more recruits later."

"More aircrew? Good on ya," Mick said. "They kidnapped nearly everyone last night. And half the pilots," he added pointing at the stationary planes. "Probably would have taken me, too, if I'd been here."

"Who's they?" she asked.

"The air force. They want to launch a satellite, so they've taken everyone they can grab, and flown them to somewhere in the Marshall Islands. Presumably because that's where the rocket is."

"A communications satellite? That can't come soon enough."

"And won't," Mick said. "Not if they think spaceships and planes are similar enough that aircrew can double as astronauts. So who are these recruits?"

"After you left the wall," Tess said, "I was drummed into leading a team to clear some of the suburbs. We found a body. A suicide. Aaron Bryce."

"No? Truly?" Mick asked, finally abandoning the engine to which he'd been giving three-quarters of his attention.

"I sent for Anna to identify the body," Tess said. "I knew it was him, but with a cabinet minister, I needed to make it official. She wants to keep this news quiet for a few days. The conscripts I was with need work here as a bribe, and so you can keep an eye on them. But that's not why I'm here, either. We've got a job. You and me. From the attorney general."

"Erin Vaughn? Since when does she think she can give me a job?"

"Anna asked," Tess said.

"Of course, that's different," Mick said. "And what does Anna want us to do?"

"For you to fly me up to Queensland to serve three warrants."

"Three arrests?"

"Yep. All senior people administering important facilities," Tess said, holding up the envelope Anna had given her. "One police officer should be enough. If it's not, the military is ready, but hopefully they won't be needed."

"And you want me to fly you?" Mick asked. "Where in Queensland?"

Tess glanced at the notes. "Camps 17 and 23, Ocean Shores and Ballina."

"That's not Queensland," Mick said. "Ballina's in New South Wales. Ocean Shores? Is that near Mullumbimby? Didn't think they had an airport."

"Queensland is our first stop," Tess said. "Then we're flying to the airport at Ballina. They should have three desalination plants operational by now. Because they haven't, and because of what sounds like incompetence, they had to bring forward the departure of the fleet from Brisbane so they could use the space in the city to house the refugees who can't be housed further along the coast."

"And why are we investigating?"

"Because the incompetence has also led to an outbreak of dysentery. Our first stop is the airfield at the Durham Gas Refinery. We'll pick up some meds aboard a broken freighter that was forced to make a landing. Then on to Ballina and Ocean Shores."

"If Ocean Shores is where I think it is, we'll have to drive from Ballina," Mick said. "Or pick up a helicopter. Durham's the place sixty kilometres north of the Jackson Oil Refinery?"

Tess shrugged. "You tell me. It's not my beat."

"If we can't refuel at Durham, we'll top up in Jackson. And we need a plane that can carry prisoners as well as cargo? There's nothing for it, we'll have to take *Frankenstein's Mistake*." He walked out of the hangar and over to a Beechcraft Super King Air sporting RAAF colours.

"A pilot really named this plane *Frankenstein's Mistake*?" Tess asked.

"No, I did," Mick said. "Even before our new aerospace corps pressganged my ground-crew, we were short-staffed. The majority of the experienced mechanics and pilots were sent to the coastal airports to ensure a quick turnaround of the refugee flights." He stopped by the plane. "We'll have a range of three thousand three hundred kilometres, a speed of five hundred and seventy kilometres per hour. And we should have capacity for eleven passengers. But open a dictionary, look for demarcation, and a picture of this plane will be illustrating the definition." He opened the door. A ramp quietly, and quickly, unfolded.

"That's neat," Tess said.

"Try walking up it," Mick said. "It's an engineer's solution to a problem that wasn't there. Do you see those rails on the ramp, and then inside? The cargo sits on those so they can be rolled up the ramp and to the tail where they're locked in place for the flight."

"So a pilot can load the plane without help?" Tess asked. "Where's the problem?"

"They didn't consider weight distribution. They took out the seats, replacing them with those two fold-down benches, you see? Flush with the cabin walls."

"Those are benches?" Tess asked.

"Good enough for aircrew being flown a short hop, but that leaves the cargo at the back, making her tail-heavy. Worse, the engineer's design only considers there ever being a full load. The cargo has to be stacked from the back, otherwise the locking mechanisms won't work. We don't want cargo sliding around as we fly."

"Then let's take a different plane," Tess said. "Looks like you've got plenty."

"The jumbos are too big for Durham. The Hercules arrived flying on one engine, so she's out of action. Trying to get anything else out of that jumble of planes will take us all day. Yesterday we had a trio of C-17s here, but they went east. No, we'll have to take this freak of science. Are you happy carrying prisoners in there?"

Tess clambered inside, unfolded a bench, and tested the webbing-harness straps. "They're civil servants. Administrators. They won't be trouble."

"Rule nine," Mick said. "Better to be prepared than dead. There's some spare handcuffs in the office."

"Any chance there's some coffee there, too?" Tess asked.

The take-off was surprisingly smooth, and the ascent even smoother. That didn't stop Mick grumbling about engineers, but Tess began to relax as the plane soared north over the suburbs she'd been guarding during the night and the outer-burb she'd cleared that morning.

"What's our ETA?" she asked.

"It's an eleven hundred kilometre flight. We should manage five hundred kilometres an hour. Maybe a bit more," Mick said. "So we'll get in around one-thirty if the wind's in our favour. Two-thirty if it's not. How long will you need in Durham?"

"An hour. Probably less," Tess said. "How long will it take to load the meds?"

"That depends on what they are," Mick said.

From the envelope Anna had given her, Tess extracted the printed summary. "The broken plane is one of twelve aircraft which flew out of the airport in Dili."

"In Timor Leste? That's the Presidente Nicalau Loboto International," Mick said. "I've been there."

"You have? When?" she asked.

"After Operation Astute was over," he said. "I flew in medical supplies. Short runway, if I recall. What type of planes were these?"

"Assuming they're the same as the plane stranded in Durham, they're 737-NGs," Tess said, glancing at the notes. "Korean charter, but flying the UN flag. They were carrying medical supplies from an airport warehouse, loading them even as the airport was overrun. One plane was lost over the Timor Sea. According to the Timorese pilots who made it to Darwin, the captain and co-pilot were infected and the one soldier they had aboard crashed the plane into the sea."

"But eleven aircraft made it to Darwin?" Mick asked.

"Where local pilots took over, and flew the planes to the refugee camps at Cairns, except for one plane which, suffering engine failure, had to land at Durham."

"That's good flying to find the airfield," Mick said, with professional respect.

"The pilot's name was Elaine Lassiter," Tess said, reading from the notes.

"Ah, there you go," Mick said. "She's one of mine."

"A flying doctor?"

"And former Border Force," Mick said grudgingly. "But I fixed all the mistakes she learned from them. What's on the plane?"

"Among other things, twelve crates of metronidazole."

"The antibiotic? I've a box of that back at the runway," Mick said. "How big is a crate?"

"Doesn't say. There's a lot of other gear aboard. There's a handwritten note here, saying they've sent another twenty thousand workers to the Jackson Oil Refinery to increase the strategic oil stockpile. They need the medical supplies. If the plane can be repaired, they want it to hop the sixty clicks south."

"Don't they need those supplies in Durham?" Mick asked.

"Not yet," Tess said. "The gas refinery is part of phase-three of the expansion plans. The oil fields are the priority. We need diesel to power the temporary generators until new, more permanent, power stations are built. Not to mention the fuel for the road convoys. Ramp up production now on everything, everywhere. I think Anna said phase-three of the plans won't be implemented until after winter."

"It's Oswald Owen's plan, not hers," Mick said. "That bloke wants to dig out our country's bones, leave her an empty crater in the ocean. You know his problem? His and Ian Lignatiev's, and even our new prime minister? They're treating this like a war. Calling it a liberation of Hawaii, an invasion of Mexico, an advance to the Panama Canal. Each time I tune in to the PM's daily news update, I expect to hear a promise it'll be over by Christmas. But this isn't a war, it's a relief effort."

"I know, Mick," Tess said. "You've mentioned that once or a million times. You reckon we'll be at Durham by two?"

"Give or take, and out of there by three. If we can't refuel, we'll have to go to Jackson. It's another fourteen hundred kilometres to Ballina. But we should make it before dark."

"If not, we'll wait at Jackson," Tess said.

"Not in Durham?" he asked.

"Nope," Tess said. She held up the sheaf of papers. "Because I've not got to the good part yet."

Chapter 5 - Judge, Jury, and Executioner
Durham Gas Refinery, Queensland

"Wake up," Mick said.

"Do I have to?" Tess asked, but she began stretching herself awake as best she could in the close confines of the co-pilot's seat. "Talk about a long morning after the longest night. Are we there?"

"Pretty close," Mick said. "Picked them up on the radio a minute ago. Do you see the smoke ahead?"

Beyond the cockpit lay a wide arid expanse of shadowy reds, stark pinks, and so very rare dots of green. Ahead, though, a thin column of smoke rose to the nearly cloudless sky.

"Talk about the never-never," she said.

"Ah, it's not that remote," Mick said. "Not if they have a runway."

The wavering grey column of smoke was nearly mirrored by the ruler-crisp black line of the runway, startlingly vivid amid the crushed ochre dust. Between the runway and a low tower and squat hangar was an empty helipad and busy stand crammed with three small planes, none bigger than their Beechcraft. A kilometre beyond, a black dagger of road cut through the umber soil to a jungle of shining steel pipes belonging to the refinery itself.

"There's the 737-NG," Mick said. "Overshot the runway, by the look of her. Doubt we'll get her in the air. Brace yourself."

"Smooth landing," Tess said as Mick taxied the plane to the far end of the runway. "Your engineer mate did a nice job on the engine."

"The RAAF tuned her up," Mick said. "And he's no mate of mine. Bloke's a professor."

"Ah," Tess said. "Am I sensing some personal rivalry at the root of your dislike for the bloke? There are the cattle trucks, to the west of the runway. Only twelve of them. No sign of the cattle. No sign of people, either." She unbuckled her harness, stood, and crossed to the locker.

Inside, beneath Mick's assault rifle and one of her own, and above the strapped-in-place storage locker with the outback-emergency packs she'd have insisted on even if Mick hadn't, was her holster. Smoothing down the red and black flying doctor's jacket and trousers that had been the only uniform available at Canberra's airport, she adjusted her badge and buckled on the gun belt. To the two spare magazines in the holster-clip, she added another two to her pocket, though if she had to fire even one bullet, they were in deeper trouble than a gun could save them from.

Outside, a brushed-clean red and yellow pick-up ambled towards their plane.

"The welcome wagon is in no hurry," Tess said. "You radioed them to say we're picking up the meds?"

"And inspecting the cargo freighter," Mick said.

"Did they ask any questions?"

"Nothing unusual," Mick said.

"How long will you need?" Tess asked.

"Call it an hour," Mick said. "But I'll keep this monster ready for take-off. We can be back in the air faster than you can strap in."

Adjusting her badge one last time, she opened the cabin door. The ramp automatically extended, clattering to the baked tarmac. Awkwardly, she clambered down to the runway, thinking Mick might have a point about the professor turned engineer who'd tinkered with the plane.

"G'day," she called to the truck before waving away the squadron of flies who'd also come to inspect the new arrivals. But where the insects buzzed close, the truck had stopped ten metres from the wing. Driver and passenger had climbed out. Both wore corporate blue jumpsuits with wide-brimmed hats that bore the same company logo.

"You're the pilot?" the driver asked. Mid-thirties, five-nine, she was well tanned and well built from a hard and remote life. The driver was about a decade younger, with the too-muscled arms of a young man who was beating bush-boredom by pushing weights.

"Deputy Commissioner Tess Qwong," she said, holding up the badge she'd hung around her neck. "Australian Federal Police. And you are?"

"Talya Bundeson," the driver said. "This is Rob-O Hansen. Over the radio, you said you were the flying doctor."

"That's me," Mick said, making an awkward show of climbing down the ramp. "Mick Dodson, surgeon emeritus with the Royal Flying Doctor Service. The father of a cabinet minister gets a police escort these days. Prime Minister's orders. And it's her orders that brought us here. We're on a mercy dash to grab the meds from the back of that cargo plane."

"There's none there," Talya said. "Because of the heat. We moved everything into the hangar."

"Good on ya," Mick said. "I'd buy you a drink, but I've a long way to fly before nightfall. I could do with one for the plane, though."

"Your daughter is the prime minister?" Hansen asked.

"Strewth, Rob-O," Talya said. "Bronwyn Wilson's in her sixties. He means he's the father of Anna Dodson. The… the… um…"

"The Minister for Housing and Agriculture," Mick said. "That's her. And I want to see if that Boeing will fly again."

"Not easily," Talya said. "You'll need a new compressor, a new combustor, and probably a whole new engine, but you'll need to bring in a new undercarriage first. A prop is all that's preventing her from belly-flopping into the dust."

"Ah, pity," Mick said. "How are you for fuel? Can you top us up?"

"Sure," Talya said. She frowned. "Are we supposed to charge you? I guess not."

"Mick, if you can get her loaded," Tess said, "I'll go and have a word with the person running this place."

"You want Judge Munsch," Talya said. "Up at the refinery."

"Great," Tess said. "Can you give me a ride?"

"Leaving you to help me, Rob-O," Mick said. "Do you know rule seven?"

"There are rules?" Hansen asked, suddenly flushing with anxiety at a test for which he'd not studied.

"Rule seven," Mick said, "never let an old bloke do the heavy lifting."

Leaving Mick and Hansen to walk to the hangar, Tess climbed into the passenger seat of the airfield's service vehicle as Talya Bundeson took the wheel.

"I'm guessing few planes have arrived recently?" Tess asked.

"Not yet," Talya said. "Not compared to Jackson. We heard they've got a million new workers at the oil refinery."

"They spun you a yarn," Tess said. "They've been told to make provision for up to a million by the year's end. We'll provide the resources for housing, however many *are* sent. *When* they're sent. *If* they're sent."

"Because we can't take that many here," Talya said. "We couldn't manage a tenth. There's not enough shelter and nowhere near enough water."

"Same problem as everywhere," Tess said. "Most likely, it'll be workers from Jackson who are transferred here once they've finished expanding the oil refinery. But we're still talking months away. Natural gas is in phase-three of our plans, and we're still figuring out phase-one."

"That's the scheme the prime minister was talking about on the radio?" Talya asked.

"That's it," Tess said. "You've been listening to the broadcasts?"

"Sometimes. Some days," Talya said.

The airfield's main gate hadn't been reinforced, and nor had the fence ringing the runway. Designed to stop wildlife, it might slow the undead. The sentry, armed with a hunting rifle, might stop a handful of zombies, but not a swarm.

"Have you had many zombies out here?" Tess asked.

"A couple," Talya said as they drove through the gate. "None for a week. But I thought they'd all been killed."

"Not yet," Tess said. "How did a judge come to run a gas refinery? My notes say a woman called Sandra Toyne was managing the facility."

"The judge's brother worked here," Talya said, gritting her teeth loud enough for Tess to hear the molars grind. "After the outbreak, he went to get the judge. Ms Toyne disappeared."

"Why isn't the judge's brother running the place?"

"He died. A week ago," Talya said.

"But you've been running the airport for a while?"

"Only for a week," she said. "But I've worked here for five years."

Tess didn't ask her next question because the answer was in front of her.

A hundred metres from the entrance to the refinery, and ten metres back from the road, stood a three-metre-high, four-metre-wide wooden box. Steps led up from both sides. At the top was a lever to operate the trapdoor situated beneath the noose.

As with the airport, a low fence ringed the refinery. By the entrance to the car park, the gate had been recently reinforced. It stood open, but was guarded by a miserably dehydrated man standing in the shade of a blanket. Two corners were tied to the gate, the other two held up by poles dug into the mineral-rich soil. With obvious reluctance, the sentry trudged from under the blanket's shadow and into the still-hot sun, making space for the car to drive through.

The car park was far from crowded. Talya pulled the truck into a spot next to a corporate-blue minibus. From how Talya tensed, Tess could tell she wanted to say something, so, before she could, Tess got out.

Of the twelve vehicles in the lot, nine were adorned in corporate blue, one in sporty red, but it was the two battered utility trucks that were of interest to Tess. Both had a grassland logo very out of place among the refinery's steel-forest of metallic pipework. She walked over to the nearest truck, brushing the dust from the logo before turning back to Talya, who'd exited her vehicle, and now stood by the still-open driver's door.

"I smell beef," Tess said. "There's nothing to feed cattle here, is there? We had the same problem in Canberra. The cattle arrived before we were ready for them. Had to slaughter the lot. Wasted a good deal. The Davenport Downs Cattle Station is about five hundred kilometres north of here, right?"

Talya glanced back at the guard, who'd reclaimed his spot of shadow by the gate, then returned her gaze to Tess's badge. "Yes," Talya said. "Yes it is."

"Thank you," Tess said. "I'll make my own way from here, but you should wait. I won't be long."

The main entrance was unguarded, and the doors were unlocked. Inside, behind a rounded blue-plastic reception desk, a woman had been watching a tablet until Tess entered. She was dressed in black rather than blue. A shotgun leaned against the wall behind the desk. When she jumped to her feet, Tess saw a holstered gun at her belt, the flap unbuttoned. The uniform was brushed clean, not washed, nor ironed. The hat didn't fit, and the hair beneath was too long for a roughneck.

"I'm Commissioner Tess Qwong. I'm here on a mission from the prime minister. I need to speak to the judge, but my plane leaves in twenty minutes."

"I... yes, ma'am," the receptionist said, and hurried to the doors before turning around. "Please wait here. I'll be... I won't be long."

As she went through, Tess walked over to the row of clean but cheap armchairs. The building's fans burred, circulating the air, but not chilling it. Of all the places likely to have enough electricity to create an iceberg in this scorched desert, it was surely a natural gas refinery that had its own power station.

Her eyes fell on the gallows outside, but she turned away, scanning the rest of the room. There were no magazines on the low coffee table, only a spray of prospectuses for prospective investors. But who else would fly out this way? At the airport, she'd seen an RV with an awning, a few tables and chairs. There'd be a better-equipped social club wherever the refinery workers slept, but they'd work their shifts and fly home or to the coast for their R&R. That was before the outbreak, of course.

With a clunk, the doors swung open, and the receptionist stepped through. "Ma'am, commissioner," she said. "Please come this way. Please?"

"Thank you. You're understaffed?" Tess asked, noting the fear in the receptionist's eyes, the tremble in her voice. "If you're doubling-up as a security guard and receptionist, I mean."

"We're... we're... I..." the woman stammered, a reaction far more illuminating than any words would have been. "It's in here, ma'am," she finished instead, pointing at a door labelled *Meeting Room A*. She opened the door, and followed Tess inside.

The floor-to-ceiling windows offered a vista only of interest to investors. The curtains had been drawn back, offering a view of giant pipes and a cloudless sky, and providing almost all of the room's light. With the furniture's current configuration, the room could seat about thirty, split between six low benches, three on either side of a narrow aisle. At the front of the room, furthest from the door, were two tables covered in black cloth. Behind the large table dominating the centre and rear of the room were the flags of Australia and Queensland. To the left was a smaller table on which was a laptop. To the right, a solitary chair was placed behind a scaffolding and wire enclosure.

The stale air dripped with terror, but oddly not from the middle-aged woman sitting on the chair behind the scaffolding and wire enclosure. It was a dock. She was a prisoner. The man sitting at the laptop was a clerk. The other man, standing behind the prisoner, was a guard, meaning the woman sitting in front of the flags was the judge. Over her white shirt and black suit jacket, she wore a black cloak that was closer to an academic gown than judicial robes.

"G'day," Tess said. "Commissioner Tess Qwong, Australian Federal Police. You must be Judge Munsch." Tess turned to the prisoner. "I know you. You're Teegan Toppley."

"My reputation's spread far and wide," the prisoner said.

"You have interrupted proceedings," Munsch said.

"Apologies for that," Tess said calmly. "But we're in a rush. Been an outbreak of dysentery at a couple of the refugee camps by the coast. Got to grab some meds from that downed 737 before the bug sweeps along the coast. Apologies again that I won't be able to stop long enough to enjoy this show."

"The administration of justice is not entertainment," Munsch said.

Behind Tess, the receptionist shifted from foot to foot. The guard behind the prisoner looked equally nervous. Behind the judge was a second door. A single rather than the double through which Tess had entered, and it was propped open. Possibly to let in some air. Possibly to conceal another guard or two.

"You knew our plane had landed," Tess said. "You knew I would come here. You had this ready. A judge. A clerk. A convict. Space for observers, but not for a jury. You're the judge and jury. Are you the executioner as well? I saw the gallows. It's hard to miss."

"If death is the sentence, I do not shy away from its administration," Munsch said.

"My pilot's name is Mick Dodson," Tess said. "Don't know if you've heard of him. You'll have heard of his daughter, Anna Dodson."

"The aboriginal politician?" Munsch asked.

"The Minister for Housing and Agriculture," Tess said. "I just want to make sure we all know which direction the future's leaning. You keeping a record of this, mate?" she added, turning to the clerk. "Good. Canberra will want a copy."

"So you have come to stop me?" Munsch asked.

"Ironically, no," Tess said. She turned to the convict. Teegan Toppley looked utterly different to the photographs taken before her trial in December. Her hair was now mostly grey and ragged, shaved short in prison. Though she had the physique of a runner, not a fighter, behind her narrowed eyes a calculating brain measured angles and distance, waiting to strike.

"Teegan Toppley," Tess said. "According to the interview you gave that gullible journalist, you're forty-six. According to the honest court reporter at your trial in December, you're fifty-nine. Claimed not to have committed a crime here in Australia since you were twenty, but you'd also not set foot here for two decades until you needed treatment. Cancer, right? And it was a success. After which you donated a hundred and fifty million dollars to charity. That's what they got you for. Tax evasion."

"Just like Capone," Toppley said, offering a most charming smile which had entranced a nation during the nightly-news updates of her trial.

"How'd you come to be here?" Tess asked. Toppley wore corporate blue, like the ground-crew at the airport, but with a large PZ199 stencilled on leg and chest.

"I was aboard a prison transport and here it stopped," Toppley said. "The how and why is as much a mystery as my original arrest."

Tess nodded, and turned to the windows showing a view of dirt and steel. "If I'd been running this place, I'd have put some palm trees out there. I guess the cost of watering them would have been considered profligate by the owners. Or maybe they only prefer plants after they've been stuck underground for a million years." She turned back to the judge. "The mine owners and refinery managers are working with us now. Helping us expand production, creating a stockpile with which we can clothe, feed, and arm the world."

"We must all do our part," Munsch said.

"Glad you agree," Tess said. Slowly, she reached into her pocket and took out the envelope. "Communication is difficult. Accessing databases is nearly as tough. Everything stored on the cloud is inaccessible. But we've got some local databases. We've got some local knowledge thanks to the operation down in Jackson. And we've got some witnesses who offered evidence. The pilot of the Timorese freighter and a worker who escaped from here." She held up one of the sheets of paper. "Your name is Lisa Munsch. You're a court clerk from Brisbane. Your brother was a roughneck and former union rep. After the outbreak, he flew to Brisbane, collected you and some of your mates, brought you back here. In the intervening weeks, the facility's manager disappeared."

"We searched for her," Munsch said.

"I'm not here about that. I'm here about the cattle."

"You would have us starve?" Munsch asked. "You send us workers. You don't send us supplies."

"Your brother launched a raid on Davenport Downs. He attacked a convoy of cattle destined for Perth. He died. As did two others of your people, and seventeen workers from the cattle station. But three survived, and we've got their statements."

"As you say, my brother died," the judge said. "The surviving members of that raid returned here. They were punished for their deeds."

"But you didn't return the cattle," Tess said. "You didn't report the crime. As a result, Davenport Downs sent word by air to the other cattle stations, warning them of murderous rustlers. And as a result of that, five thousand head of cattle were delivered to Canberra a month too early. The canning and processing plants aren't finished. There's no feed for the livestock. The cows had to be slaughtered. Some will be eaten. Some frozen. Most will be wasted. In a few months' time, people will starve because of that waste."

"That's why you are here?" Munsch asked. "The guilty have paid for their crimes. We have the records."

"Which you can cite during your own trial," Tess said. "This is a warrant for your arrest." She placed the printed sheet on the table in front of the clerk. "In addition to the statement from the survivors of the raid, we've evidence from the pilot, and from one of your workers who escaped."

"You're arresting me?" Munsch asked.

"I'm not arresting you, no," Tess said. She took the handcuffs from her belt and put them on the desk, next to the arrest warrant, and addressed the clerk. "Tomorrow, a new management team will arrive and take charge of this facility. *She* can come with me. *You* can dismantle the gallows. Or it can go the other way." She turned to face the receptionist. "Whoever you are, whoever you *were*, you're no match for the regiment of Special Forces who're ready and waiting for the order to clear this place out." She turned to face the guard behind Toppley. "Civilisation might be in disarray, but we'll not abandon it so easily. It's your choice."

"Judge, jury, and executioner," Munsch said slowly. "It is so easy for you, isn't it, Commissioner. You arrest, charge, and walk away with no consideration of what comes next. Yes, I *am* the judge. Yes, I *am* the jury as well, because it would be criminally unjust to ask others to take that responsibility. And yes, *I* am the executioner because it would be unconscionable to ask others to do what I dared not. I take upon me the hard choices so that others do not have to. So that *you* do not have to."

She stood, and walked around the table. The crude robes covered most of her body, but from the way the suit jacket and shirt hung, Tess doubted the woman wore a holster. The sentry behind the convict, holding his shotgun, had taken a step back. But that could have been to make space between him and Toppley as much as to create distance between him and the judge.

"You're right," Tess said. "Sometimes, yes, it falls upon an individual to make that choice, to take that decision. It has nothing to do with a badge, with a law, but with a far deeper division between what is obviously right and what is manifestly wrong. And once that decision is made, right or wrong, the consequences must be faced." Tess tapped the clerk's desk, and stepped back. "So make your choice, or face the consequences tomorrow."

"Arrest this woman," the judge said.

The receptionist looked at the clerk. The clerk looked at the sentry. The sentry looked at the convict, who shook her head and smiled. All the while, the judge stared at Tess and Tess stared at her, arms folded.

The clerk stood up, and took a step back, away from the desk, indicating he wanted no part in the proceedings. But the receptionist stepped forward, picking up the piece of paper Tess had laid down. She glanced at it, then replaced it, picking up the handcuffs instead.

"Now arrest her, Nicole," the judge said.

"No," the receptionist said. "She has a warrant from Canberra. If you have any authority, it's superseded by the government. And if they don't have any authority, neither do you."

"You can't be serious?" the judge said. "This is the time you develop qualms? I mean, this, *now*, is the time?"

"Yes," the receptionist said. "Hold out your hands, please."

The judge looked to the guard, to the clerk, and then back to the receptionist. "You will regret this, Nicole. Without order, people like that woman, Toppley, will come to rule places like this. The weak will be murdered. The strong will kill. There will be no turning back."

"Maybe not," the receptionist said. "But if they send the soldiers in, everyone will die tomorrow."

"Very well, Nicole." The judge held out her hands.

The receptionist stepped forward, then looked down, turning the handcuffs this way and that, seeking how to operate them.

"Not like that," the judge said, stepping forward. "Like—" She grabbed the receptionist's collar, reaching for her holstered gun, but the judge was clearly as unfamiliar with hand-to-hand combat as Nicole was with handcuffs.

Even as Tess drew her weapon, the judge hauled the sidearm from Nicole's belt. Nicole grabbed the judge's wrist, and both women stepped towards one another, wrestling with the gun. Tess stepped forward even as the sentry levelled his shotgun, but it wasn't that weapon which discharged.

As the sound of the gunshot faded, the judge collapsed, blood spreading across her white triangle of shirt. The receptionist stepped back, dropping the gun. Tess holstered her own.

"Put that down, mate," she said, waving her hand at the sentry. "It's over." She stepped forward and knelt by the dying woman's side.

"We all pay in the—" the judge whispered, but choked on blood before she could finish her final words.

Tess breathed out. "That wasn't how I wanted this to end, but it *is* an end. Canberra doesn't know about the gallows, so get rid of it. Over the next few months, thousands of workers will come here. Production's got to come first if we're to save the planet. What happened here will be another sad story of the nightmare-times which no one will want to remember."

"Commissioner," Toppley said, holding up her own wrists, tied rather than cuffed. "I originally arrived with two hundred and twenty others. When I was led from the... let's call it a cell, there were four others still alive."

"There's only five of you left?" Tess turned to the sentry with the shotgun. "Go fetch the other four. Take them out to the car park. Move!" She turned to the clerk. "Untie Toppley." She turned to the receptionist. "That was self-defence. No charges will be filed. I'd suggest you pick up that sidearm. You might need it."

The sunlight seemed far brighter, but the air not as hot, as she stepped outside, followed by the receptionist, the clerk, and Teegan Toppley. Talya Bundeson waited by her truck, while the gate-guard sheltered beneath his awning.

"The judge shot herself," Tess said, loudly. "She was under arrest for her involvement in the theft of cattle and for the murder of their drovers. A new management team will arrive tomorrow."

Talya nodded. "Renee Jenson," she said.

"You know her?" Tess asked.

"I gave her the truck," Talya said.

"Yes, she made it to Jackson," Tess said. "And she is one of the witnesses, one of the reasons I'm here. This woman has the arrest warrant. You should give it a read."

The gate-guard turned on his heel, walking away in a direction opposite to the airport.

"And you're giving anyone who wants to run time to do so?" Talya asked.

"There will be no further reprisals," Tess said. "No more repercussions. We don't want people running off into the outback where they might become infected." That last part was true. The other was not. She turned to Toppley. "You were given those clothes here, right? PZ199."

"I assume the Z stands for zombie, the P for prisoner," Toppley said. "It's a touch gauche, don't you think?"

Before Tess could reply, the sentry appeared from a side door with four tied and chained convicts following behind. One of whom Tess knew. Personally.

The first convict to step outside was a woman. In her early twenties, her frazzled hair matched her confused expression as the eyes behind the taped-together glasses darted left and right, calculating whether this change of events implied safety, or more danger. Thin, five-five, but she'd be taller if she stood straight. Her corporate uniform, on which was stamped PZ197, hung loose on her frame. Behind her came PZ209, a tall man, late forties or early fifties, with short grey hair and three weeks of white stubble on his chin. His head was bowed, his shoulders squared, his muscles tensed. Behind him, PZ194, a wiry twenty-something, had rolled up his sleeves revealing arms with as much sunburn as tattoos. A beak nose jutted out between strands of his long, lank hair which partially hid his rabbit teeth and matching eyes that darted this way and that.

But slouching along at the rear came the familiar frame of PZ201, a man with a barrel chest and a crate gut. As a boy, and with the girl he'd gone on to marry, he'd tormented Tess, the foreign girl with the mistake for a name. As a man, he'd delighted in pestering the copper he'd envied and feared. She'd locked up him more times than she could remember, often after a fight to put on the cuffs. The last time she'd seen him was in Broken Hill, after the outbreak, when he and his wife had been scamming foreign students billeted in some chalets the self-serving couple owned. He was a petty crook with petty desires, consumed by equally petty jealousy. It was no surprise to see Stevie Morsten in chains, but it was odd to see him out here. And as he saw her, his smile widened.

"Hello, Princess," he said loudly. "It's Princess Wrong. Ha."

"What did you do to end up here, Stevie?"

"Done nothing," he said. "Got lost."

"My name's Commissioner Tess Qwong," she said, addressing the prisoners. "You're all coming with me to a refugee camp on the coast."

"What if we don't want to, Princess?" Stevie Morsten asked.

Tess pointed to the noose, swinging in the barely perceptible wind. "Do you really want to stay?"

Chapter 6 - Con-Air
Above Queensland

In the car park, she had the convicts' hands untied, and their heavy chains removed. During the procedure, in sight of the gibbet, no one spoke, not even Stevie Morsten, though his lips moved in silent calculation. Toppley kept her eyes on Tess, while PZ209 kept his on Talya's truck. But though the convict looked, he didn't bolt. Tess trusted her instinct, and that warned her the grey-haired man was far more dangerous than Stevie Morsten, but like Toppley, PZ209 had realised the plane was the fastest way away from the gallows.

"We're flying in that?" Stevie asked, as he climbed down from the back of the fire-service truck when it stopped thirty metres from the Beechcraft Super King Air.

"Like I said, Stevie, you can always stay here," Tess said.

"My mates call me Steve-O, Princess," he said. "But you can call me *Mister* Morsten."

"Stevie Morsten?" Mick Dodson asked as he climbed out of the Beechcraft. "Is that you?"

Stevie looked down, suddenly cowed. Clearly remembering a night twenty years ago when he'd had his first, and only, confrontation with Mick, whose pledge to do no harm hadn't extended to the alley behind a pub.

Tess nodded to Mick, and they walked around the plane, out of earshot of the prisoners and Talya who was now conferring with the other ground-crew worker, Rob-O Hansen.

"What's going on, Tess?" Mick asked. "How'd Stevie Morsten end up here? Is that young woman the judge?"

"The judge is dead, Mick. It was worse than the evidence led us to believe. The judge was hanging the convicts. About two hundred were here, and these are the survivors. Don't ask me what crimes they committed, but we've got to get them out of here, and get word to send in the army. Maybe the air force as well."

"That's Teegan Toppley, isn't it?" Mick asked. "Well, I know what *she* did. You want to bring them all with us?"

"If we leave the convicts behind, they might be killed by those who want to eliminate the evidence, and it won't stop with these five. It'll be a bloodbath. But if we take these people away, maybe the guilty will stay their hand."

"I've got her balanced and loaded for one passenger," Mick said. "Blame the engineer's storage system. She'd be heavy, but manageable. With five passengers, I'll have to unload all the crates by the wings."

"Will weight be a problem?" Tess asked.

"Only for the bits of the flight that involve defeating gravity," Mick said. "But look at it this way, I guarantee we'll be able to land."

Again confounding Mick's criticism of the engineer, it barely took three minutes to slide out the crates he'd loaded in the front half of the plane. Within ten, the convicts were all aboard. As Mick gave the plane one final inspection, Tess walked over to the airport service-truck where Talya and Rob-O stood, nervous and expectant.

"The new management team will arrive tomorrow," Tess said. "What happened here is over. It's done. What matters is how we face the dark days ahead. Pass the word."

She headed back to the plane, knowing her words wouldn't be enough. There might be reprisals by those who considered themselves victims. There might be desertions into the outback, and so more zombies unless the unforgiving landscape killed them first. The hands at the cattle station, and perhaps even the roughnecks down at the Jackson Oil Refinery, would demand a reckoning for their dead mates. But those weren't her problems today. They almost certainly would be in the days ahead, but first she still had two more warrants to serve.

She climbed aboard the plane, closing the door even as Mick powered up the engines.

The fold-down benches ran along the cabin, opposite each other. Rather than seatbelts, webbing harnesses were bolted to a sprung rack on the fuselage. Though all the convicts were now buckled in, none were cuffed or otherwise secured. Toppley, PZ209, and the young woman sat on the starboard side. The younger man sat next to Stevie, who sprawled with his legs splayed across the aisle.

"Princess! Princess!" Stevie called with the enthusiasm and wit of a toddler. "When are you serving drinks, Princess?"

"We're flying to the coast," Tess said, addressing them all. "To a small town where we're building canning factories for fish, other factories to make the cans, foundries and metal recycling centres, power stations, and desalination plants. In short, there's work. There's a bed. Clothes. Meals. There's life. There'll even be pay."

"And our crimes will be forgiven?" Teegan Toppley asked.

"Forgotten," Tess said.

"In my case, I find that hard to believe," Toppley said.

"I spent last night shooting zombies attacking the wall around Canberra," Tess said. "So believe it or not, but I'm looking forward to seeing the sea."

"What about some nuts?" Stevie asked, laughing uproariously.

"Quiet, Mr Morsten," Toppley said. "Never kick a gift horse, because it has twice the legs to kick back."

"Eh?" Stevie asked.

"Buckle up, Tess," Mick called as the plane began to roll down the runway.

She pulled herself to the cockpit, strapped herself in, and put on the headset.

Five minutes later, they were in the air, heading west, and she relaxed, but only a fraction. "How long until we land?" she asked.

"Around dusk," Mick said. "Three hours. Maybe four. Maybe less."

"Did I ever tell you how reassuring I find your rigid devotion to precision?" she said.

"What happened back there?" Mick asked.

"You should ask what went wrong," Tess said. "The survivors of that cattle raid correctly identified the logo on their ambushers' vehicles. That pilot from the 737 correctly identified the cattle trucks. The escapee who made it to Jackson identified the judge, and our attorney general was able to find the name among the records of court staff. All well and good, and which gave us just cause to charge them with the cattle raid and those murders. But that's only a third of the story."

"You mentioned hanging," Mick said.

"She was executing convicts," Tess said. "According to Toppley, there were two hundred plus, and those five are the only survivors. But that's only a third of the story, too. At the refinery, the wrong vehicles were in the car park. Only one didn't sport the company colours, not counting the two stolen during the cattle raid. Inside, the air-conditioning wasn't on. I could hear the fans turning, but no cold air blew out. There simply aren't enough experienced crew to run that place. So what happened to the old hands?"

"Do you think they got the colonial neck-tie?" Mick asked.

"Or a bullet," Tess said. "We'll have to interrogate the survivors. Maybe dig up the graves."

"Do we?" Mick asked. "And does it have to be us?"

"It has to be done. Erin Vaughn's covering letter says she wants to make a public announcement of the arrest of the ringleader behind the theft of the cattle and those who are so poorly administering the refugee camps. She wants to demonstrate the federal government is still in charge, still administering the old laws. So there has to be an investigation. Quick rather than thorough. But it'll have to be done, and I reckon it has to be done by me. I just wish we'd had more information going in."

"Speaking of that, maybe you should find some backup for the next two warrants."

"Defo," Tess said. "I *needed* backup back there, but there were no coppers in Canberra. Not enough soldiers to secure the suburbs. There's no one but you to fly the plane, and no one but me to serve the warrants. Blame the lack of satellite communication, blame the confusion, but it's a bloody mess, Mick. That woman wouldn't have come quietly. If the gun hadn't accidentally discharged during the fight, I'd have shot her. It would have been a summary execution of someone guilty of carrying out summary executions. That's not how we should run a country."

"Sounds like the right level of hypocrisy to me," Mick said. "Each of us, and all of us together, we've got to hold on one more day, and then one more, until the days become weeks, the weeks become months, and we look back and realise we're through the worst of it."

Tess said nothing, but watched the landscape cycle from pink to crimson, with an occasional splash of green from a stubborn tree. An even rarer plume of smoke marked a small settlement. Miners? Soldiers clearing the outback? Refugees fleeing the city? The plane flew on before she could tell.

"Those convicts, do you think they know how to fly a plane?" Mick asked.

"Toppley might. Maybe PZ209. The others? Doubt it. You're worried they'll hijack the plane?"

"I wouldn't say *worried*," Mick said. "But do you remember that movie we watched on Saturday?"

"Which movie?" Tess asked. "And which Saturday?"

"Had that fella who's in everything. The movie about the plane full of convicts," he said. "I thought we could change our call-sign."

"You're not renaming this flight *Con-Air*," she said. "And that was Tuesday, not Saturday."

"Was it? I'm losing track of the days."

"I'm losing track of the hours," Tess said. "There's far more of them in a day than there used to be."

"You're getting old, that's all," Mick said.

"Says the bloke whose footsteps I'm following," she said. "What was the airfield like?"

"In Durham? Efficient. Under-crewed. Low on supplies."

"Did you refuel?"

"I only managed to get us a top-up," Mick said.

"Should we detour south to Jackson?" Tess asked.

"No, we'll reach the coast," Mick said. "And I'd rather spend the night by the sea. Been a while since I last saw it."

"Can't you fly higher?"

"With the weight in the tail, if I try to ascend, every degree I rise, the tail will add another, and we're liable to switch from a plane to a sail boat. Not very aerodynamic, your average boat."

"You're enjoying this, aren't you?" Tess said.

"Better to enjoy it than the other thing," Mick said. "Up here, I can appreciate the full depth of time, the breadth of the future. I can see the weight of the past and how lightly we ever brushed the soil."

"I can see a mountain ahead of us," Tess said.

"Nah, can't be," Mick said, even as they raced their shadow towards the dusty promontory. "That's just a hill."

As they flew over it, she saw it wasn't as high as she'd first thought, but she also saw the plane's shadow far, far too close. But the landscape below was morphing from the emptily expansive outback into the deceptively barren bush. Trees were more numerous, with an occasional ring marking a house, or line marking a road, though those all appeared to be running north-south, and disappeared behind as quickly as she spotted them.

"I tell you what we'll do when we get back to Canberra," Tess said. "We'll watch that movie about Capone."

"Capone, why?" Mick said.

"Tax fraud. That's what they caught Toppley for, wasn't it?"

"This is the Flying Doctor, I've received your Mayday. Can you receive me, over?" The urgency in Mick's voice woke Tess up.

"Mayday?" she asked. "Where are we?"

"Five hundred kilometres east of Durham, by the clock," Mick said, before returning to his radio. "This is the Flying Doctor. Are you receiving me, over?"

Below, the rolling bush was every shade of red from ochre to umber, but full of long shadows cast by shallow hills, dotted with more frequent clumps of pale scrub, desiccated during the long summer, now waiting for the ever elusive rains.

"They're transmitting, but not receiving," Mick said. "And now they've stopped sending. Look for smoke." He brought the plane into a slow turn.

"A wildfire?" Tess asked, still waking. "Not out here?"

"Nope. Car fire," Mick said. "It's a bus of kids, surrounded by zombies. Car ahead of them is on fire. Car behind is dead. They're trapped with some of their infected mates outside. It was a bloke on the radio, so they've got some adults with them, but you could hear the kids in the background."

"Can we find them?" Tess asked.

"He didn't know where he was," Mick said, "but he could see a helipad, so there might be a runway."

"Out here, must be a mine," Tess said. "There. Smoke. Two-o'clock."

"Got it," Mick said, straightening the plane. "If we can land, we'll have to," he added.

"Yes," Tess said. And she knew what would have to be done then.

Below, a curving dust track cut through the gently rolling shadows, turning and twisting around dry creek-beds, but leading to a rising pillar of sharp grey cloud. Nearer still, the track abruptly became a ruler-straight, quadruple-width, recently tarred, five kilometre stretch of highway running a few degrees off north-to-south. At the southern end, a helicopter squatted on a perfect square of tarmac, and near it billowed smoke from the lead vehicle in a car-bus-car convoy.

"Zombies surrounding the bus," Tess said. "Twenty to thirty. Probably at the lower end."

"No telegraph poles. No lights," Mick said. "They've turned the road into a temporary runway for a new mine. Must be that place up ahead. What do you think of the bus?"

"A twenty-five-seater Isuzu," she said. "Lime green, matches the Subaru behind it. Might even match the lead car, though that's too charred to tell. Hire-company vehicles, I think, though they're a long way from home."

"But is it damaged?" Mick asked. "We can't fit twenty-five aboard."

"Looks fine," Tess said. "But if it was working, why'd they stop?"

Though flying slow and low, the plane was already overtaking the smoke.

"Yep, it's a mine," Mick said. "Looks empty."

To the south of the temporary runway, beyond a fence, a dozen bright yellow construction vehicles were parked amid a cluster of huts and cabins.

"No lights. No smoke. No people down there," Tess said. "But no zombies, either. Just around the bus."

Mick turned back to his radio. "This is the Flying Doctor, can you hear me, over?" He paused, listening. "Nothing. Ground's sloping towards the mine. I'll bring her in over the bus, lure the zombies away. We'll stop about a kilometre from them."

"I'll warn our passengers," Tess said.

Chapter 7 - Trapped in the Never-Ever-Again
Humeburn, Queensland

The cockpit shook. The wings shuddered. The wheels squealed as the plane hit the ground heavy and hard. From above, the ribbon of road had appeared as smooth as silk, but the landing gear found every bump during the sharp deceleration. Even as the plane rocked and swerved, Tess unbuckled her belt for the second time in five minutes. This time, before going back into the cabin, she opened the locker at the rear of the cockpit.

During the flight, and with the convicts in the back, she'd worn her holstered sidearm. For what lay ahead, she'd need one of the two HK416 assault rifles. Before leaving Broken Hill, Captain Hawker of the SASR had given them to Tess and Mick. In part, it was an apology from the soldier for not having stopped the cartel gangsters. But the rifles, having belonged to two deceased soldiers, were also a reminder to the police officer, and ultimately to Mick's daughter, of those who'd been sacrificed during the outback skirmish.

On reaching Canberra, Mick had taken to ostentatiously carrying his rifle with him as a prompt to others that he possessed a seniority not entirely based on age. When she learned how few police officers remained in the capital, Tess, just as ostentatiously, wore her badge instead, leaving the rifle at the airfield. When she'd been dragooned onto Canberra's walls, she'd come to regret it. Now, after the gas refinery, the policy required revision.

Loading the rifle, she picked up two spare magazines, but pocketed the suppressor rather than attaching it. They knew zombies followed sound, and right now, that's what she wanted.

"You letting us out or what?" Stevie asked as she made her way through the cabin.

"Stay put, stay quiet," Tess said, unclipping the fire extinguisher from the bracket by the door. "We'll be back in the air in thirty minutes."

"You didn't answer my question," Stevie said. "*And* I never got my free drink."

"Dr Dodson will give you some water once he's turned the plane," Tess said. "But let me be as clear as I was up at the Durham refinery. That's Mick Dodson, the father of a cabinet minister. This rifle was a gift from the SAS." She tapped the stock. "And they're waiting for us at the coast because, if things had worked out differently in Durham, they would have gone in to clean it up. If you do anything stupid, you'll have the SAS hunting you through the outback."

"We understand," Toppley said. "And we shall sit quietly, meekly awaiting your return."

Doubt rising, Tess opened the door. Quietly cursing the engineer who'd replaced the steps with a ramp, she clambered down. The engines still burred, swirling a dust storm across the runway-road. Head bowed, she jogged away from the plane, to the clearer air behind and beyond.

After fifty metres, and a protest from her hip, she slowed the run to a walk. She was nearly a kilometre from the bus and the undead, though some of the figures were already moving towards her. Rule three, zombies couldn't run, so as she quick-stepped forward, she assessed the battleground.

The road sloped downward towards the mine for which this runway-road had been built. Designed to last a year or two and a few dozen flights, it was already in need of resurfacing. Even so, it would have required considerable effort and expense. In total, five kilometres had been paved. Divide that by two on the assumption that a plane wouldn't turn around once it had landed, and it was still more than all but the heaviest freight planes would need. And much wider. Wider than most highways, with room for eight lanes of car-width traffic, though without any lane markings. From the air, the runway-road didn't extend to the mine, nor did it continue far out into the bush.

To the east and west, hillocks and humps, and a few lonely mulgas, offered some cover, but zombies didn't hide. The engines would lure them to the plane, as was the case with the two walking-corpses to the east. A third staggered up from a dried creek. A hundred metres apart, but with the closest well over a kilometre away, they were a problem for later.

Turning her walk into a jog, she covered half a kilometre three times as quickly as the zombies approaching from the bus. Putting down the extinguisher, she raised the rifle and took the measure of her foe. Three women, one man, and they weren't miners. With their faces distorted by feral rage, covered in gore and wind-borne dust, it was impossible to guess their age. But they weren't young. They weren't children from aboard the bus. City-dwellers? Possibly. The passengers from the cars? Maybe. Behind those four, another two had detached themselves from the bus. That still left over a dozen beating at the thin metal and thinner windows. Had that been a scream from inside?

Tess raised the rifle, braced her feet, and fired. A single shot, another, another. Six shots to kill the four nearest. She shifted aim to the two behind, but they weren't close enough. Not yet.

Zombies couldn't run. Mick had declared it a rule, while Dr Avalon had decreed it impossible. Tess wasn't sure how much trust to place in the recently arrived Canadian scientist, but she'd not seen any running zombies. Not in Broken Hill, not around Canberra. They didn't think. They couldn't use tools or weapons. They existed only to spread and infect. A walking test tube to contain the virus was how Avalon had described them, the words relayed to Tess second-hand via Anna after the Canadian's surprise appearance.

And *now* they were close enough. Tess opened fire. Five measured shots, and the zombies fell. Tess picked up the extinguisher and walked on. Another seven had detached themselves from the bus. After thirty metres she stopped, taking aim. Her target: another civilian. The next wore the reinforced work clothes of a miner. She focused on the clothing, not on the faces. Not on how, one after another, they walked into gunfire, oblivious to death. Another seven down, thirteen bullets expended; since Broken Hill, there'd been plenty of practice. She ejected the magazine, inserted a fresh, picked up the extinguisher, and walked on.

Rifles and patience and wide-open spaces, that was how they would rid the world of the undead. How General Yoon was neutralising them in Canada. And it was why there might be battles, but this wasn't a war. No enemy came willingly to the slaughter. Only unthinking creatures. She just wished they didn't look like people. She followed the gently sloping road down the shallow hill, towards the bus, stopping twice more to shoot one, then another.

Two were by the bus's door, beating and kicking, smashing their arms against the glass. Only two?

Raising the rifle one-handed, she gave the car behind the bus a wide berth. The passenger in the rear seat was dead, a screwdriver through her undead eye. The other seats were empty, and she supposed their previous occupants were now among those she'd just shot.

By the time she was close enough to see the desperate fear on the small faces of the passengers inside the bus, three zombies were close to the door. Two wore mining clothes, one in active-wear more suited to a spin-class than the eternal grind of survival. All three were beating and clawing against the thin metal, leaving bloody smears as they smashed their hands to pulp.

Tess fired. Shifting position, to stand flush against the chassis to avoid a miss or ricochet travelling straight through the bus's thin walls, she fired again. Again. She raised a warning hand to deter the man who'd come to the door from opening it. As she did, she saw what little remained of the shredded front tyre, and what remained of the monster it had driven over. The torn tyre was planted firmly on the zombie's chest, the organs surely crushed, but its gravel-scraped head, abraded of almost all skin and hair, knocked against the road as it craned and twisted its neck. She raised the rifle and fired one last bullet before returning to the extinguisher. Rifle raised one-handed, she walked down to the still smouldering car, some thirty metres ahead. Not as close to the bus as she'd thought, and not the imminent threat she'd assumed.

The fire had begun in a gym bag thrown through the broken rear window. Around it were the smoke-stained remains of plastic jars and glass bottles. Roadside salvage, she supposed. She slung the rifle, and sprayed the extinguisher over the bag, then the back of the car, before turning her attention to the interior.

The car doors were closed. Only one charred skeleton was inside, in the driver's seat, a knife in its neck, another in its eye. She sprayed the engine and set the extinguisher down before backing up a pace, turning a slow circle, then crouching to check beneath the vehicles. After motioning again that the bus's passengers should wait where they were, she looked down the slope, towards the fenced mining compound a further four hundred metres away.

The gate sparkled while the fence, covered in rust, didn't even gleam. Inside were a handful of very old cabins, a score of smaller prefab huts, and the row of cartoon-yellow construction vehicles. But no undead. No living people either.

A distant crack came from closer to the plane. Another. A third. She walked a looping circle off the road and onto the dirt. In the distance, Mick stood by the Beechcraft's wing, his rifle raised. Other than him, and inside the bus, she saw no movement. Mick had shot the three approaching undead, meaning the immediate threat was vanquished. But the solution to one problem brought the next into clearer focus.

The bus's front tyres were ruined. The two cars were worse than junk. Even from here, she could make out the bullet holes in the helicopter, not that it was large enough for everyone, and not that she knew how to fly it.

The bus door slid open. The man on the steps held a cricket bat in his hands, and a mountain of responsibility on his shoulders. Long shirt, jeans, an old belt, worn sneakers, cheap wedding band, broken watch: not a miner, nor a soldier, and not at all dressed for the outback.

"G'day," Tess said. "I'm Police Commissioner Tess Qwong, out of Canberra. My pilot's a flying doctor. What happened here?"

"Your pilot's a doctor?" the man said, relief adding a tremor to his words. "Please, you've got to help. It's my son."

"He's sick?" she asked.

"He's dying."

She stepped up into the bus, and into a swarm of children, all wearing matching red and white tracksuits.

"Everyone move back," Tess said. "In your seats, kids. Is it just your son that's crook? Everyone else okay?"

She scanned the faces looking at her. Nine of them belonged to children around ten years old, a roughly even mix of boys and girls. A tenth child, about the same age, unconscious, was cradled in the lap of a fear-worn woman, the only other adult on the bus.

"Everyone's okay except for Brendon," the eleventh child said. A girl, in her early teens, her hair was cut too short for the emerald and silver clip above her ear. But that clip matched the engagement ring on the older woman's finger. Which, no doubt, made the woman her mother, though clearly not of every child aboard the bus.

"Brendon?" Tess asked. "Do you know what's wrong with him?"

"Diabetic shock," the father said.

"We don't know," the mother said. "He's not diabetic. But he wasn't bitten so it isn't *that*. He just collapsed this morning."

When Tess had seen the small faces at the window, and the ruined tyre, she knew a hard choice was ahead of her. Looking at the pale boy with the already blue lips, it was no choice at all.

"We're walking up to the plane," she said, straightening. "All of us, together. Leave everything here. No bags. Ma'am, what's your name?"

"Molly Birdwood," she said.

"Can you carry your son? Sir, what's your name?"

"Clarke."

"Clarke, you're last off the bus. I'm going first." She turned to the teenage girl who'd spoken. "You're going second. What's your name?"

"Shannon," the girl said.

"Hi, Shannon, I'm Tess. I'll walk to the edge of the road. When I call, you follow, bring this girl with you." She pointed to the girl sitting on the next seat. "Everyone else, from the front, come outside in pairs, holding hands. When we're outside, we'll walk to the plane. No one runs unless I say. Got it?" If anything, they looked even more terrified, but it was a new world for everyone. "Molly, you come last. Clarke, you follow. Everyone ready!"

Not waiting for an answer, or for more fear to set in, Tess jumped back outside. The road was still clear, as was the bush. Nothing had appeared inside the gated mining compound, nor between them and the plane.

"Shannon!" Tess called. "Come on!"

In under a minute, she'd hustled the children and parents outside and onto the red-dirt verge. She could see Mick, rifle in hand, his head turning from them back to the open cabin door. If Toppley wanted to steal the plane, now was the time, and if the notorious crook knew what was about to happen, she very well might.

"Let's pick up our pace," Tess said. She turned to the father. "What happened here, Clarke?"

"We were trying to get to the coast," he said. "We came from a cattle station about… I don't know how far away. About a day's drive."

"You're a stockman?"

"No. We lived in Townsville, but Molly's sister runs the hotel in Tambo. We went there after the news of the outbreak. We were going there anyway," he added, defensively. "We'd planned the trip for months. We were there a day when the police evacuated us to the cattle station. A couple of days ago, they said they were moving the children. Molly and I, because we've got Brendon and Shannon, we were given responsibility for these kids, too."

"Did they say where they were moving you?" she asked. "Tasmania?"

"Brissy," he said.

"Good news for you then," Tess said. "Brisbane's close to where we're heading. But if you were trying to reach the coast, how d'you end up here?"

"We got lost," he said. "It was one breakdown after another. Last night, they came at midnight. Hundreds of them. Zombies," he added. "We held them off until dawn. Mostly. That's when we fled. We split up. Driving in different directions. The rendezvous was a diesel-stop about fifty kilometres that way." He waved vaguely at the open expanse beyond the runway-road. "It was full of the undead. We kept driving. The road became a track, and then we saw the sign warning about planes. I thought we'd find an airport, but we found this."

"And what about the people in the car?" Tess asked. "How'd they get infected?"

"At the diesel-stop," Clarke said. "Tony went looting."

"He was in one of the cars?"

"In front," Clarke said. "The car stopped. I guess the fire started by accident. We were waiting for the smoke to clear, but the zombies came. We tried to drive out, and tore up the wheels. The others, they died one by one."

"I think someone in the car behind was infected, too," Tess said, glancing over at Clarke to get his reaction.

"Really?" he asked, and sounded genuinely shocked. "I didn't know. I mean, I guessed. I… it all happened so quickly."

"How long since your mate Tony turned?" she asked.

"I don't know. Two hours. Maybe three."

"And you came along that dirt track," she asked, pointing beyond the plane.

"Yes."

Rule three, zombies couldn't run. But they didn't tire, either. They didn't stop. Three hours worked out at fifteen kilometres, but she'd call it ten. Any zombies within ten kilometres, and close enough to the road to have heard this convoy pass, would have reached them by now. Similarly, any undead inside the mining compound would have made their way to the gate. It wasn't proof they were safe, the three zombies Mick had shot told her that, but it was close enough.

She had another few questions for the man, more details about the cattle station, and why they were travelling by road not air, but they were approaching the plane, and Mick was approaching them.

"The kid's crook," Tess said, pointing to Molly and Brendon.

"Did he report any pain?" Mick asked. "Let's put him down in the shadow of the wing."

"He said he was dizzy," Molly said, as Mick took the boy from her arms.

"When was that?" Mick asked.

"A couple of hours ago," Molly said.

"Four hours twenty minutes," the teenager, Shannon, said, holding up her wristwatch. "He's been unconscious for three hours and ten minutes."

"We thought…" Molly began. "For a while we thought he might have been infected. By *them*. But he wasn't bitten. It's not that, right?"

"No." Mick smiled as he lifted one closed eyelid, then another. "He'll be fine. Before dark, we'll be at a hospital. A couple of pills, a good meal, and a better sleep, and he'll snap around faster than a croc in a treadmill. The rest of you okay?" he added, turning to the other, terrified, children. "Tess, a word?"

They walked back towards the plane's open door.

"What's wrong with him?" Tess asked, in a whisper.

"Might be septic shock, might be something a lot worse. His heart's fluttering and weak. And there's still a chance it's the other thing."

"How long does he have?"

"It's the wrong question, Tess, and you know it. Sunset's not far off. Finding the runway after dark will be difficult. There's not enough fuel to stay up in the air while they find a way to reel me in."

"How much fuel is there?"

"Enough to reach a proper airport and proper hospital if we empty those crates from the back," he said. "And if the convicts stay here. And maybe you keep one of the parents. Maybe one of the kids."

"That's worse than I feared," Tess said. "The bus has lost its front tyres. It's not driving anywhere. There might be a few vehicles up at the mining compound, but the miners probably drove off in anything with enough range."

"I can be back here at dawn," Mick said. "Not before. And you know what rule three is?"

"Zombies can't run."

"The other rule three," Mick said. "Don't go walkabout in the middle of the night. I'll leave you the emergency packs. Not much water there, but enough if you sit tight, and stay inside. I promise to be back at dawn."

Chapter 8 - Old Mine, New Tricks
Humeburn, Queensland

"No, Clarke, you go," Molly said, pushing her husband onto the plane. "A son should be with his father if... if it comes to that."

And that should have been the most difficult part, but Tess had overlooked Stevie Morsten's reaction to being stranded in the zombie-rich outback.

"You're leaving us out *here?*" Stevie asked, looking to the other convicts for support.

"No, Stevie, I'm staying here, too," Tess said.

"Hear that, Kyle?" Stevie said, ostentatiously addressing the wiry man with the tattoos. "Maybe we should take a walk."

"Go ahead," Tess said. "Go for a walk, and keep on going, and in a week, you'll be back at the natural gas refinery, but I'm sure they've removed the noose."

"It's a trick," Stevie said, too slow to catch her meaning. "You'll shoot me in the back."

A dozen sharp retorts flashed across her mind, but professionalism kept them from her tongue. "It's not long until dark," she said. "And Dr Dodson will be back before dawn. There're some cabins behind the fence down there at the mine. That's where I'll wait for the plane. If you want to trek out of here on your own, go ahead."

With a last brief, but grim, word with Mick, she ushered the convicts off the tarmac. Molly and Shannon waved away the plane as it rolled along the road, picking up speed before darting upwards and skywards.

As the sound of its engines faded, Tess picked up one of the two bags of emergency supplies. Molly carried the other. Both packed by Mick, they contained the bare essentials to keep pilot and copper alive for two days if the plane crashed in the outback. Among eight, the water would be long gone by dawn.

"I'm not kidding," Tess said loudly. "Anyone who wants to walk out of here can. Mick will be back at first light. Their bus broke a couple of hours ago, and since we set down, only three more zombies have appeared. I'm not saying more won't appear during the night, but it won't be as many as in Canberra. It's about an hour until sunset, and another hour until proper dark. I'm going to wait in one of the mine buildings. Come with me or don't."

As she headed down the sloping road, Molly and Shannon at her side, she didn't need to look behind to know they were all following.

"You said they're convicts," Molly whispered. "How much danger are we in?"

"Not as much as you'd think," Tess said. "The big bloke, he's a yobbo I've locked up more times than I can remember. The older woman, that's Teegan Toppley."

"No, really?" Molly asked, half turning to steal a glance at the infamous crook.

"Who's that, Mum?" Shannon asked.

"She's a jewel thief," Molly said. "It was all over the news in December. They got her for cheating on her taxes, right?"

"Something like that," Tess said. "I don't know the other three but I freed them from illegal incarceration by a deranged court-clerk impersonating a judge. Technically, they're witnesses rather than criminals. I don't think they'll be trouble."

"What kind of jewels did she steal?" Shannon asked.

"It's not nearly as glamorous as it sounds," Tess said. "Molly, did you have any supplies on your bus? Water, particularly."

"Not much. We left most of it behind this morning."

"I had a few bottles in my bag," Shannon said.

"We'll grab it now," Tess said. "Any guns aboard?"

"No. Alicia had a couple of shotguns in her car. That's the one that caught fire."

That was both good and bad. Tess had her rifle and handgun, but had left Mick's rifle on the plane. While the extra firepower would be useful, the only person who certainly knew how to use a gun was Toppley. Out of all of them, she certainly *was* a criminal, and not just a tax cheat and jewel thief.

Tess stopped near the bus. Toppley wasn't far behind. The young woman with the taped-together spectacles followed the old crook as close as a shadow. PZ209 was a few metres behind her, his attention split between the outback and the mine ahead. And far, far behind him slouched Stevie Morsten and PZ194, the tattooed man whom Stevie had called Kyle.

"We're grabbing some water from the coach," Tess called, aiming her words at Toppley. "Keep watch." She climbed aboard. "Clear," she said a quick minute later. "Grab what you can, Molly. Anything that'll help us get through the night." She stepped down so Molly and Shannon could enter.

"Shame about the tyres," Toppley said, walking over to Tess. "How certain is your pilot to return?"

"I've known him since I was a kid," Tess said. "And worked with him since I first became a cop. He's a mate, as is his daughter."

"The cabinet minister?" Toppley said. "So a rescue would be guaranteed under the old regime. In these rather strange times, nothing is certain. Not even taxes."

Without another word, Toppley walked towards the helicopter. The woman with the glasses had stopped, head bowed, near the edge of the road and far from the pile of corpses. As Toppley hurried on, she began to follow, though hesitantly, clearly unsure whether being the notorious crook's shadow was safer than lingering close to the police officer.

PZ209 had left the road and now stood like a lighthouse, turning his gaze across the scrub-filled desert, though his gaze, too, lingered on Toppley as she strolled towards the obvious means of escape.

"It's only a few litres of water, and not much else," Molly said, pausing in the doorway, waiting for her daughter.

"And some flashlights and some books," Shannon said. "Which we'll want because it'll be a long night."

Stevie had seen Toppley angling towards the helicopter. Kyle in tow, both men had picked up their pace, overtaking PZ209, marching towards the helicopter in what was nearly a run.

"Can you fly it?" Stevie called out, overly eager.

"Bullet holes are contra-indicative of mechanical operability," Toppley said, finishing her tour of the machine, and heading back towards the road.

"What's that mean?" Stevie asked.

"It's been shot to scrap," Toppley said. "Blood on the hardtop, Commissioner. Blood on the seat. Bullets in the engine mount. A mix of 9mm and 7.62, judging by the holes."

"7.62?" Tess asked. "You mean from an AK-47?"

"I do," Toppley said.

"How d'you know all that?" Stevie asked.

"Everyone should have a hobby, Mr Morsten," Toppley said. "That machine won't fly anywhere."

"Any bullet cases on the helipad?" Tess asked.

"None," Toppley said. "Though my efforts at seeking clues no doubt fall far below your own standards. The chopper arrived here damaged. I would imagine it took fire during, or shortly after, take-off. In which case, it is unlikely to have flown from very far away."

Tess mulled that over as they walked the last few hundred metres to the gate, reaching the conclusion that it probably didn't matter, and certainly couldn't help.

The gate leading into the mining compound was very new, made of double-strength steel, a three-dimensional lattice frame, and steel posts embedded in asphalt as fresh as the runway-road. The renovations hadn't extended to the fence on either side. Decades-old, made of rusting wire, where each of the heat-warped support posts leaned in a different direction. A strong wind would push it down, while a gentle pull was all it took to tug the gate open.

"Wait here," Tess said. "I'll be five minutes. If there's trouble, head for the bus." That last was addressed to Molly.

"Trouble?" Stevie said, reigniting his faux-grievance. "You mean you didn't check this place first? I think I could sue you for that."

Tess didn't reply, but stepped inside the compound.

What she'd guessed from the air was confirmed up close. Half the buildings were as old as the fence, while the other half were as new as the gate and runway-road. To her left sprawled a tumbledown, L-shaped, high-set cabin. Wood-log foundations held the floor a half metre above the ground, while recent scaffolding held up most of the walls. Three metres of scaffolding and six fresh-sawn planks covered an age-warped wooden veranda, while wooden boards covered the window behind. But from how other windows weren't covered, this wasn't a post-outbreak reinforcement, but simply an outback repair.

Behind the cabin were another two partially collapsed shacks and the ruins of a dozen more, built at least fifty years ago and abandoned soon after. To her right were parked five excavators, five dumper trucks, a small crane and winch, and a bulldozer. All carried the logo of Harris Global, the sprawling multinational with scandals in Mongolia, accidents in South Africa, corruption charges in South America, and mining interests in a dozen more countries besides. But of far more interest than the monstrous yellow beasts, and the company which owned them, were the pair of grey utility trucks sheltering in their shadow. She'd not noticed those from the air. They appeared roadworthy, though the keys were missing. She guessed those would be inside one of the twenty-or-so new trailer-cabins arrayed behind the excavators. Each was the size of a shipping container, though made of wood and plastic.

On each hut, a long wooden pole jutted five metres into the sky, taller than a digger's front-loading bucket could accidentally catch. On those were strung wires, presumably bringing power to the huts from a generator. Since the wire arced over her head, it carried electricity to the decrepit L-shaped cabin, too.

While the ground was unpaved dirt, the heavy wheel ruts suggested she'd find the main excavation further north, lost to sight among the sloping ground. From the air, she'd thought she'd seen a few more huts and shacks to the north. She couldn't recall more than that, and nothing about the vague memory was particularly inviting. No matter. What was key was that no one had come to greet her. No one living or undead.

The sleeping hinges of the L-shaped cabin squeaked awake as she put her shoulder to the large, lock-less door. It opened an inch and stalled. Something heavy lay behind the door. Another shove, and she had the door open wide enough to see the arm, unmoving. Another push shoved the corpse far enough that she could ease inside. Rifle raised, she swept the room before giving the corpse a second, then third, look to triple-check it was dead.

"G'day!" she called, moving the rifle in a one-handed arc while extracting her flashlight. No reply came and the light found nothing in the shadows. She turned her attention to the corpse. But it was an obvious suicide-by-shotgun. A belt-tourniquet was wrapped around the dead woman's forearm above a stained bandage encircling her wrist. In her mid-forties, she wore boots, jeans, and a plaid shirt, but all of a designer, bought-in-the-city style, over which was a corporate windbreaker. A passenger from the helicopter? Or had she been here a lot longer? It was too soon to draw a conclusion.

Tess slung the assault rifle, and drew her handgun. With flashlight in one hand, wrists crossed, bracing her gun hand in a more familiar pose, she quickly searched the room. Scattered with easy chairs and salvaged tables repaired with scaffolding brackets, a TV squatted in one corner of the room, a dartboard in the other. A bar dominated the third, made of planking as old as the cabin, but with a half-empty whisky bottle and a trio of glasses on the countertop. Three glasses. So far, one corpse. But there were more bodies by the bus. She reframed her interpretation: *only* three glasses.

In the room's last corner, battered bookshelves stood sentry on either side of an equally battered door, repaired with plyboard from where one too many heavy boots had kicked it closed. The books, as well used as the door, looked just as old.

Beyond lay a corridor with doors either side, all of which were being used as storage. In some were old tools, in others broken furniture. Eight rooms in total, at the end of which was another door, leading outside.

Tess returned to the corpse and checked the shotgun. It was empty, as were the corpse's pockets. The woman had been down to one shell. Or she'd been left with one by the others who'd fled. One thing *was* certain, it would be safer waiting inside the cabin than outside.

She reached down, crossed the woman's ankles, and pulled the body through the door and onto the veranda. By the gate, she saw Molly turn Shannon away. Tess went back inside, grabbed the blanket from the couch, laid it over the body, and walked back to the gate.

"Trouble, Commissioner?" Toppley asked as Tess approached.

"One corpse, one shotgun, one shell," Tess said tersely. "Looks like she was infected. Killed herself. No sign of anyone else here. Hopefully the zombie who infected her was one of those I shot by the bus, but we'll assume the worst and that more are lurking in the outback. We'll be safer on the other side of the gate."

Stevie knocked into PZ209 as he sauntered inside. The grey-haired man's eyes narrowed, though his glare was entirely aimed at Stevie. In turn, Tess's childhood tormentor peered around in what, for him, was an attempt at nonchalance, but his fists, clenching in thought, betrayed his intent.

"This is a mine?" Shannon asked, looking in every direction except that in which the body lay.

"An old mine," Tess said. "Abandoned fifty years ago and recently re-opened before the outbreak. I reckon whatever they originally found here, decades ago, was too expensive, too difficult, to extract. With modern technology and techniques, they decided to have another go."

"It's quite an expensive stretch of road for simple exploration," Toppley said.

"Do you think it's a jewel mine?" Shannon asked.

"Shush," her mother said.

"Perhaps," Toppley said. "This is the right geography, but jewels are nothing more than coloured stones. Their true value is in the story associated with them."

Shannon's hand went to the sapphire hair clip which matched her mother's ring.

"Jewels or gold," Tess said. "Maybe silver, though this doesn't look like the right equipment. Maybe there are other machines further down that slope. But we're expanding the operation of all the useful mines. Coal and iron are our immediate priority. Oil, too. Zinc and lithium will come in phase-two. Ramp up production now, create a stockpile to supply the global relief effort. Since this place was abandoned rather than expanded, it can't have been producing anything we immediately need."

Stevie picked up the shotgun from where Tess had leaned it next to the veranda. He checked the chamber, then sauntered back towards them.

"Got to protect the sheilas, right, Princess?" he said. "You should give me some shells for this."

Saying nothing, Tess stepped forward, grabbed Stevie's wrist, turning it, and his arm, upward, spinning him off balance, before a quick sweep of her leg against his ankle knocked him down to the dirt. She stepped back. "The plane comes back tomorrow, Stevie, and Mick's flying it. You know Mick, and he knows you. And he won't hesitate to leave you behind if I, or Molly, or Shannon, aren't alive and well. Do you understand?" She turned away even as Stevie picked himself up. "We've an hour before dark. Everyone go into the cabin. Rest for a bit, because there'll be work soon. There are some mugs in the kitchen, so share out the water. One cup each. I'll check the rest of the site."

The new cabins were clearly labelled with laminated metal plates. The smaller units were one-person dwellings. The first she came to was locked, but the key was in the door and *Matt Sanderford* was on the nameplate. The interior had been divided in two. One half contained an unmade bed, a wall lamp, a closet. The other half had a chair, a TV affixed to the wall, and a small desk with a laptop. The power was out, but the laptop's battery hadn't run down, though it required a password to log in. She shut the lid.

No bathroom, no plumbing, and only a small air-conditioning unit. It wasn't bad, and better than standard, but it was still just a place to sleep and video-chat home. The closet was nearly empty, at least of clean clothes. From the pile of dirty linen, laundry had not been a priority immediately prior to the departure, or death, of the mining crew.

They would have heard about the outbreak, over the radio or satellite-internet. Soon after that some would have left. She turned back to the desk, checking the drawers, then the bunk. No photographs, no phone, nor any other obvious personal items. Matt Sanderford had time to pack before he'd fled.

The toilet block was adjacent to the showers, two separate units, both with three stalls. The water tank was empty. Behind the wash-block, a cabin, the maximum length a standard flatbed could carry, had been split in two. The door led into an office with desk, maps, a filing cabinet, a computer, radio, and a pegboard with vehicle-keys. According to the prominently displayed work order and licences, they were exploring a coal deposit for fifty square kilometres from the site of the Humeburn Valley Mine.

Behind the desk, the room was divided in two with a heavy and locked door leading to a medical room. But that door had an equally thick plastic window, and through it, she saw the corpse. Buzzing with flies, lying on the solitary cot-bed, one leg and both wrists secured with cord, a chisel through his eye. Meat-ants streamed to the body in a there-and-back double-column from a gap in the wall. In a week, only bones would remain. But it begged the question of what the ants had been eating before.

Back in the office, the radio sat on a table of its own behind the desk, and was partially disassembled. It was a minor frustration, but offset by the map on which it stood. A larger-scale map of Queensland showed her where the exploration was centred, and that was forty kilometres north of the nearest decent road. This wasn't just the never-never; it was the never-ever-again.

The generator was in a small cabin adjacent to the shower block. The reservoir was dry. The main fuel tank was empty, too, with only a trio of small fuel cans scattered beneath a large and otherwise empty rack.

Outside, she followed the rutted track beyond the temporary huts, through the ruins of more, older, shacks, on and downward. The dirt verge grew into an embankment, then into the slope of a hill, while the track became a snaking canyon covered in rock and scree fallen from both of the increasingly vertical sides. She was about to turn back when, low to the ground, she caught movement. Raising the rifle as she spun, she quickly took her finger off the trigger as a furry, large-eared, long-nosed, half-metre-long marsupial paused, tense, eyes fixed on Tess.

"Didn't mean to startle you," Tess said, but even as she spoke, the animal darted along the path, disappearing among the ruined buildings behind her.

Tess found herself smiling. That was something to tell Mick, that she'd seen a nearly extinct bilby. Her smile froze as, from the direction the animal had run, came a metallic click and clatter. Rifled raised, she walked on, slowly following the canyon-road until, with no warning, beyond a bend, it opened into an even deeper gorge running across her path. Ten metres wide and forty metres deep, it was crossed by a steel-plate suspension bridge. Made in sections and assembled on-site, it had replaced the older, iron-framed, wooden bridge, which lay at the bottom of the gorge.

Slowly, she reached for the pouch on her belt, and extracted the suppressor.

The bridge had a gate on either end, one metre high, secured with a simple latch.

She screwed the suppressor onto the barrel.

With no barrier running along the lip of the gorge, the gate must have come as an insurance-required standard fitting for the bridge. It hadn't stopped the zombies falling down to the gorge below where, now, they writhed, limbs broken, skin punctured, oozing dark gore onto jagged boulders. But on the far side of the bridge was the reason the rabbit-eared bandicoot had been running for its life. Three zombies pushed on the gate at the far end of the bridge. A man and a woman in heavy-duty denim, and another woman in pink culottes and a thin-strapped tank top. The gate rattled as they pushed onward, arms reaching across the distance, beckoning for Tess to join them. Instead, she sent a bullet.

Three shots whispered from the suppressed barrel, then a fourth as the third missed, only ripping away the ear of the undead man. She shifted aim to the crippled zombies in the gorge below, but held her fire. They weren't a threat and ammunition was limited. She checked the gate was secure, then headed back through the canyon, and to the cabin, with a better idea of what had occurred here.

Teegan Toppley sat on the hood of one of the grey utility vehicles, an axe handle across her knees.

"Are you thinking of driving out of here?" Tess asked while slinging the rifle.

"Drive where, Commissioner?" Toppley asked. "In none of my future plans did I see myself as a modern-day Ned Kelly. Or, considering the events of the last three weeks, a real-life Road Warrior. Of course, you're the one with the badge. And the keys, I assume?"

"If you don't want to drive out of here, why are you asking?"

"Because it's always wise to have a plan-B, Commissioner," Toppley said. "A woman told me that once, just after I robbed her."

"*After* you robbed her?"

"She caught me in the act. Otherwise, how would she have given me such wise words of wisdom?" Toppley smiled, and jumped down. "I can fly a plane, though not well, and I haven't tried for years. But I understand how debris on a runway can turn a landing into a crash. I saw your pilot drag that zombie off the road. How many corpses would make a landing impossible? How will your pilot know, if he arrives before the sun has properly risen?"

Tess pulled out the keys she'd taken from the office. "How will he know? He picked up the distress call from the bus's radio. We can use that to warn him off, though it can only transmit, not receive. I'd hoped to use the miners' radio, but it's been dismantled. Looks as if it broke weeks ago. To clear the runway, we've got that bulldozer."

"And a plan-B?" Toppley asked.

"These utes," Tess said, throwing a set of keys to Toppley. "Check the tank on that one." She took the other set herself, opened the door, and turned the ignition. "This one could make fifty kilometres, give or take."

"This will splutter to a stand-still after twenty," Toppley said. "Split the difference, and from what Mrs Birdwood said, we'll reach the diesel-stop where so many of her friends were infected."

"The track beyond the runway-road is the only way out of here," Tess said. "In the other direction, there's a gorge, a bridge, and the undead, mostly at the bottom of a creek. The sides are too steep for them to be a threat. Beyond the bridge are the mine-works. According to a map I found in the office, they were exploring for coal."

"Coal?" Toppley asked. "Where's the dust, the slag, the smell? Those are the wrong type of machines."

Tess shrugged. "Does it matter? We've enough fuel to reach the diesel-stop where Molly was attacked this morning, but that's about as far as we'd get before dark. If we syphon the fuel from those excavators and dumper-trucks, we'll have enough to get much further. Maybe not to the coast, but enough to follow the track to a road and that to a larger one, and to a working mine or cattle station. That's our plan-B for tomorrow, if the plane can't land."

"Agreed," Toppley said as if it had only been a suggestion. "I'll gather the fuel."

"We'll need to keep some diesel for the site's generator," Tess said. "But there are empty fuel cans in the generator room. Tubing and rags there, too."

"Indeed, and some are to be found much closer than that," Toppley said, pointing at the ground.

Tess took a cautious, and wide, step away from the truck. In the dirt, near the mobile crane-and-winch, lay a long length of rubber hose. "Someone's beaten us to it," Tess said. "We might have to make do with what fuel's in the utes."

Toppley shrugged. "I've been in worse situations," she said. "This morning, for example. Thank you for saving my life, Commissioner. I won't forget it."

Tess nodded. "I was there because of a raid on a cattle station. We didn't know about the executions."

"Nevertheless, I am grateful."

"How did you find yourself at the judge's less than tender mercy?" Tess asked.

"Unintentionally," Toppley said. "Along with my fellow guests at the correctional facility south of Darwin, I was taken to the airport and put to work. We dug, though I couldn't tell you why, though my theory is we were constructing an escape tunnel to Papua or something as equally unachievable. Civilians, convicts, it made no difference who we'd been as long as we dug."

"At the airport?" Tess asked, adding that to her mental list of things to investigate after she'd served the other two warrants. "So how did you get from Darwin to Durham?"

"Five days ago, we were gathered onto coaches and driven south to the refinery. With no warning, no explanation, we were issued with the clothing, regardless of who we'd been before, what our crimes were. Whether there had even *been* any crime. The following day, the judge began her trials. You'll want to know why she was executing us. There is no good reason, though from an overheard word or three, someone aboard the first coach witnessed something as we arrived. Or was *assumed* to have witnessed something."

"You were witnesses, being eliminated?" Tess asked.

"Essentially," Toppley said. "Perhaps I'm wrong, but that is what I choose to believe since it is more rational than the alternative. Michaela Bellamy was in prison for vandalism during a political protest in which she refused to identify her co-revolutionaries."

"The woman with glasses? She doesn't look the type."

"The protest was over the closure of a library," Toppley said. "I believe she took the fall for a group of teenage bibliophiles."

"Ah. What about the grey-haired bloke, PZ209?"

"I don't remember him being at the airport, and certainly not in the detention centre, but I've seen him before somewhere."

"In your past life?" Tess asked. "He's a mercenary?"

"Perhaps," Toppley said. "It's Stevie Morsten and Kyle Stokes who concern me. But you know them?"

"I know Stevie," Tess said.

"He says you're infatuated with him."

"That's a yarn lying so heavy it'll smother the truth," Tess said. "We grew up in the same town, and I've been knocking him down ever since we were kids and locking him up ever since I was a cop."

"Watch him," Toppley said. "And I shall find fuel for our plan-B."

"Keep an eye out for the undead," Tess said.

"Oh, indeed, Commissioner," Toppley said, knocking the axe-handle against her leg. "But what is life without a little risk?"

Chapter 9 - Million Dollar Rocks
Humeburn, Queensland

As Tess approached the large cabin, the door opened, and PZ209 stepped out, a hammer in his hand, four long shelves under his arm.

"Are you building a deck, mate?" Tess asked.

The convict stared at her, not glaring, not even angry, but calculating. "I'm barricading the windows."

"Your accent, you're American?" she asked, realising she'd not heard him speak before.

"Canadian," he said.

"You're a tourist?" she asked.

He tapped the hammer against the number stencilled on his leg. "I'm a convict," he said.

"Historically, that's a fast-track to citizenship," she said with a smile he didn't reciprocate. "Don't bother with the windows. We won't be spending our night here. Come inside, and I'll tell everyone the plan."

With half the windows by the dartboard broken and covered months ago, and with the generator still off, very little light found its way inside. But enough forced its way through the cracked timbers and dirt-veined windows for her to see the shotgun was missing from where she'd left it by the door. The bottle of whisky was gone from the counter doing duty as a bar. Behind the bar, inside the artificially walled-off kitchen area, Shannon and Michaela were sorting through the cupboards and crates for crockery and food, while Molly had folded up the chairs and was now moving the tables in front of the windows.

Stevie and Kyle had found a crate of beer, which, along with their feet, they'd planted on the table near the dark TV. The men sat in two of the lawn chairs, to which the miners had glued foam padding on arms and the back.

"It's the princess," Stevie said, waving his half-drunk bottle at her. "Fancy a stubby? We can spare one for royalty. If you ask nice."

Tess ignored him and walked over to the kitchen, while Molly walked over to her.

"I poured away the whisky," Molly whispered. "But they found the beer. As soon as they did…" She waved at the pair of men. "And if they keep drinking like that…" Again she trailed off as her daughter, and Michaela, came to stand on the other side of the high shelves doing double duty as a counter.

"You said there's a plan," PZ209 said.

"Has anyone heard of General Yoon?" Tess asked.

"Who's he?" Shannon asked.

"*She*'s leading the American army in Canada," Tess said. "Last I heard, they'd reached the Saint Lawrence River, and were about to march south, cross the border, and begin securing the United States. Since we lost contact with their most recent president, she's running all of North America. Those parts over which we humans have control."

"A sheila as a general? No wonder the world's spinning backwards," Stevie muttered.

"She's been so successful, that she's no longer taking new recruits," Tess said, ignoring Stevie. "She sent us a message asking for guns, for ammo, and for planes to move the refugees back behind her front line, but it's advancing faster than we can organise an airlift. She's using construction machines as tanks. Diggers, tractors, giant crane platforms. We'll copy a page from her playbook and spend the night on top of that bulldozer."

"Outside? In the open?" Stevie asked, pushing on the arms of the chair as he engaged in the monstrous effort to stand.

"Are you sure that's safe?" Molly asked.

"Far safer than staying in here with only an inch of rotten wood as our walls," Tess said. "A last stand in a rickety cabin is for the movies, and life isn't like a film."

"No one gets a post-credit scene, eh?" PZ209 said, his lips curling in what was almost a smile.

"I was going to say you can't go online to find out how it ends," Tess said. "An undead hand could easily smash through those walls. Or the floor." Everyone looked down, and took an involuntary step back. "But the dozer is too big to be knocked over," Tess continued. "It's too bulky to be damaged, too high for the zombies to reach us. Shannon can sleep inside the cab. The rest of us will need blankets or coats, but we can get those from the huts, and it won't be a cold night. We'll want shovels, too. Anything with a long handle, to push away the undead."

"Why not shoot them?" Michaela asked.

"We'll keep the bullets in case we've got to clear the runway tomorrow morning," Tess said. "Though I'd prefer using the bulldozer. Dr Dodson will return at dawn, but that road must be clear of debris to be used as a runway. Again, the bulldozer is perfect for that. But there is a chance Mick's delayed. Bad weather on the coast might leave us stranded here longer than we have water for."

"Didn't you bring any?" Stevie asked, finding a new issue in which to shove his wedge.

"Quiet," PZ209 growled. "Let her finish."

"How much water do we have?" Tess asked, turning to Molly.

"Three cups each," Molly said. "But there's none coming out of the taps."

"The water reservoir is empty," Tess said. "I found the tank near the shower block. It's the same with the fuel. Whoever was here before us drained both. Any joy finding tucker?"

"D'you like Vegemite?" Shannon asked.

"That slop?" Stevie growled. "That ain't food."

"Love it," Tess said.

"Yeah, it's ace, isn't it?" Shannon said.

"There's goulash too," Molly added. "A crate of twenty tins, each half a kilo. But that's it."

"We'll heat up a batch after Toppley turns the generator on," Tess said. "After we've eaten, we'll board the bulldozer, but leave the generator running tonight. Zombies follow sound. That's rule four. So if they get through the fence, they'll head to the generator, not to us, but we'll have enough lights we can keep an eye on them."

"And if the plane doesn't land tomorrow, we'll drive to the coast?" Michaela asked.

"In the two utes," Tess said. "I'll park them next to the bus. We'll use the dozer to clear a path, and to buy us a bit of distance, then jump in those, and drive to safety. We'll need some paint, too. At each junction, we'll paint an arrow to show which road we've taken, large enough to be visible from the air. But we'll probably reach civilisation before Mick finds us. Molly and Shannon, you're on dinner-duty. Michaela, right?"

"Michaela Bellamy, yes," the quiet woman said, then jumped as the lights flickered on, the empty fridge's motor sputtered, and the corner-fan began to whir.

"Looks like Toppley got the generator working," Tess said. "You're from Darwin, Michaela?"

"And glad not to be there anymore," she said.

"We need tools. Anything with a long handle," Tess said. "Can you take a look in those storerooms at the back, grab as many as you can find."

"I'll help you," PZ209 said.

Tess turned to Stevie and Kyle. "Jackets and blankets," she said. "You'll find them in the cabins behind the construction equipment."

"I bet *you*'d find them there, too," Stevie said.

The door opened, and Toppley walked in, but dressed in jeans and boots, a shirt, and a reinforced thigh-length beige coat with exterior padding on shoulders and forearms. "There's a zombie on the road," she said. "About two kilometres out, but heading this way. Ah, but isn't electricity a wonderful thing." She smiled, and reached into the coat's pocket. "And speaking of wonderful, I learned half the truth of what they were digging for."

"The maps said coal," Tess said.

"In the office, yes," Toppley said. "But digging for coal usually produces coal dust. There's a lack of it here. No, it was opal." She held up a stone the length of her finger, and nearly as wide. As dark as the expanse between the stars, the stone had iridescent veins, which shimmered as they caught the light. "Black opal."

"Is it valuable?" PZ209 asked.

"It's beautiful," Shannon said.

"Here," Toppley said, and tossed the uncut gem to the girl. "When cut, that one is probably worth a million dollars."

Shannon nearly dropped the rock in surprise. "A million bucks? No way!"

"Oh, yes," Toppley said. "And there are plenty more, and plenty which are far larger. Possibly larger than any black opal previously discovered."

"That's what they were mining here, not coal?" Tess asked. "Meaning most of those machines out there are simply camouflage for any aerial survey."

"You're asking my professional opinion?" Toppley asked. "I suspect they intended to explore for coal, but then found a seam of opal. They are working it by hand, sending it back by plane. Everything else here, yes, is camouflage to avoid declaring the find and so paying the tax. There is an ordered professionalism to the operation which speaks of experience. They have conducted this kind of illicit dig before. The runway was the giveaway. It's far larger than needed to take a crew away for a weekend's escape to the coast unless that plane was unusually heavy."

"Wow," Shannon said, then held out the stone to Toppley. "Here."

"No, keep it," Toppley said. "Assuming the commissioner doesn't want it as evidence? However, I should remind you that the federal government takes tax fraud rather seriously."

"Not anymore," Tess said.

"Let's see that?" Kyle asked, walking over to Shannon. The girl turned away, while Molly stepped forward. So did PZ209 and Toppley.

"Back up, mate," PZ209 said.

"Everyone has work to do," Tess said. "And there's a zombie approaching."

"So maybe you should share out those guns, Princess," Stevie said.

"Good idea," Tess said, unslinging the rifle and holding it out to the career criminal. "Do you remember how to use one of these, Toppley?"

"Oh, I think I can manage," Toppley said.

"Why are you giving it to her?" Stevie demanded.

"Experience counts for everything, Stevie," Tess said.

Chapter 10 - Always Have a Plan-C
Humeburn, Queensland

Outside, the sun had sunk below the horizon, leaving the sky above glowing a fiery red that mirrored the land beneath. Growing up, Tess had considered sunsets like that as depicting a world on fire, and many was the airless summer when she'd had no energy for any thought but one: why had her mother chosen such a forsaken place in which to make her home. But then autumn would arrive. The outback turned from a furnace into a warm land filled with mystery and legend, hope and possibility. But here, now, it had been replaced with the very high probability of death.

The approaching zombie was still a kilometre away, lurching towards her at the very edge of where the road met the wilderness. As it stepped off the road, it stumbled, staggering forward a dozen paces until it tripped on the raised tarmac and fell, face first, onto the blacktop. Hand on her holster, Tess watched as it thrashed, kicked, beat, and slapped its way back to its knees, then to its feet. It was too far away to see the details, but surely it had added new damage to its already substantial wounds. How long before they battered themselves to death on the scorching Australian rocks? How long would it take in the humid jungles closer to the equator, or in the frozen tundra of the far north? Days? Weeks?

She undid the clasp on the gate, pushed it open, and stepped out to meet the zombie. When she reached the stalled bus, she stopped, and there she waited, scanning the horizon, making certain no more approached. No, still only one. And still, she waited. Waited until she could see the zombie wore a camouflage jacket. Waited until she saw those were hiking trousers, not military issue. Waited until she could see the caked blood on its face. Waited until the zombie was clear of the stretch of road the plane would need to land. Waited until the zombie was only twenty metres away. Then she drew her pistol and fired.

Again, she checked the horizon, before walking over to the twice-dead creature. The clothing worried her. It was civilian rather than military.

Camouflage hadn't been in fashion for years, but that was another way of saying coats like that could be found in the front of most op-shops and the back of many wardrobes. Regardless, this woman had probably been a soldier. The deliberate uniformity in the boots, trousers, and jacket indicated someone who'd wanted as close an approximation to military attire as could be found. A tourist, a reservist, or perhaps an active-duty soldier who'd raided a house when she'd needed clean kit.

How were the operations to clear the outback of the undead truly going? The lack of satellites, the broken switchboards, the over-powered and illicit broadcasters clogging the radio spectrum with portentous rumour and light music, a hazy command structure, the ever-changing priorities; it all combined to make for an uncertain picture. She knew the bush security operation was on-going, and her experience on Canberra's walls told her it wasn't going as well as hoped. It was another issue to raise with Anna.

With her boot, she rolled the body off the road. What Harris Global had been doing at this forgotten mine was another. Not that some eight-figure tax avoidance scheme was pertinent to the current crisis, but they were the third largest mining conglomerate in Australia, and a central strut in the creation of a resource stockpile. Harris Global would have to be warned and watched. But after she'd dealt with the Durham refinery. And *that* would have to wait until she'd served the last two warrants. And then, maybe, she'd be able to track down the serial killer.

As she neared the bus, she turned her attention to the tall aerial on the roof. Inside, she confirmed the antenna was for the partially broken CB radio. It wasn't the factory-installed set, but a semi-portable device affixed to the dash with tape. The size of four bricks, and with more, older, tape, holding the casing together, it was a big set and a big aerial. She searched back to when Mick had woken her as they'd approached. They had to have been at least forty kilometres away.

Mulling over the possibilities, and whether their options had increased, she stepped off the bus and walked quickly back to the gate, and to the long row of parked vehicles.

Stevie and Kyle were carrying a single bag each over to the dozer, their free hands clutching long-handled picks. She ignored them since, though they were working slowly, they were actually working, and that would stop if they realised they had an audience. The door to the cabin opened, and PZ209 came out, carrying an armful of rusting shovels. She ignored him, too, and climbed into the first of the grey utility trucks.

Slowly she drove the truck through the gate and down, beyond the bus, parking just beyond the second of the wrecked cars. As she got out, she saw Stevie watching her, though he turned away as she walked back towards the gate.

He *would* be trouble. But if she could keep him active for a few more hours, then let him fill up on beer and food, he might sleep until dawn. Assuming his snoring wasn't louder than the generator, and so a lure for the undead, he'd be no trouble until his hangover wore off, sometime tomorrow around eleven. By which time, one way or another, they'd be far away from here. That was the best-case scenario, but once she had the cars in position, she'd have to prepare for the worst.

If Stevie kicked off tonight, she could cuff him. Kyle, too. But they had to be kept quiet, so they'd have to be gagged. Come morning, they might have to run to the dozer, maybe even run as far as the utility trucks. Leaving the pair of men behind would be as certain a death sentence as the noose, especially if they were cuffed. It was out of her hands, of course. As long as Stevie made the sensible choice, he'd live to swindle, steal, bully, and cheat another day. Experience told her she was expecting a miracle; he'd never made the sensible choice.

By the time she returned to the row of parked vehicles, Kyle was carrying another bag to the dozer while Stevie had vanished.

"Think that's enough blankets and coats, mate," Tess said. "Can you find Toppley? Tell her all the diesel not needed for the generator should go in the back of the utes. And we'll want the paint, and some of the clothes and tools down there, too."

"While you put your feet up?" Kyle asked, his tone resentfully bitter.

"I'm going to disconnect the CB from the bus. An aerial like that will reach much further than the set on the dozer. We'll know when Mick's on his way, and so know when to get moving."

"Oh. Okay," he said, mollified.

There was no sign of Stevie, which, no doubt, was the real reason for the man's ire. Kyle was learning a lesson that was legend in the outback, that Stevie Morsten was the laziest man east of Woomera and west of Dubbo.

She drove the second truck down to the first, climbed onto the roof, and surveyed the horizon, then the mining compound. Had she brought the trucks far enough? Was it too far? The dozer would get them out of the compound, crushing the undead, but it wasn't built for speed or fuel economy. Would it buy them enough time to decamp to the trucks? Probably. Five minutes. Give or take. Leaving the keys in the ignition would buy them a few more seconds, but was it worth the risk? No. She put them into her pocket, and returned to the bus.

With a protest from her increasingly tired limbs, she pulled herself onto the bus's roof. The radio aerial was held in place with tape, with at least one entire roll wrapped along the roof, through the door on one side and out the nearly closed window on the other. The wire itself ran through a hole that had been hacked rather than drilled. Altogether, the ultra-crude installation gave a hint as to why the set had been able to transmit but not receive, and so, perhaps, might be a problem they could fix.

From the compound, a bag in both hands, Kyle was jogging towards her. Predictably, Stevie was nowhere to be seen.

"Good on ya," she called out. "Dump those in the ute, then give me a hand up here."

Removing the aerial wouldn't be difficult, but she'd need to unplug the wires first. She walked over to the edge of the bus, lowered herself down, her muscles pinching with the effort.

"And once I've found the serial killer, then I'll take a day off," she said, stepping back inside. "Wait, no. No, I won't, will I? I forgot about all that digging Toppley said was going on up in Darwin. I'll have to look into that, too." She disconnected the aerial, turned around, and found herself staring at the barrel of a gun.

Her own assault rifle.

Held by Kyle. Outside, on the road, five metres away.

Not just held, he was pulling the trigger.

Couldn't find the safety, she thought, diving backwards even as he finally found the release. The gun roared. The shot went high. The bullet smashed through the glass windscreen.

Tess's dive had taken her backward, into the long aisle which ran the length of the bus. With a kick and a squirm, she got to her knees, and got her sidearm into her hand just as Kyle found the automatic rifle's selector switch. A burst sprayed the cracked window, shattering the glass. Bullets pierced the chassis, ricocheted off the bodywork, punctured the roof and shredded the seats. Tess crouched in the aisle, gun in hand. When the maelstrom ceased, she reared up, ready to take a shot. But she didn't see Kyle. She *did* see the bulldozer as it smashed into the gate, the massive blade crushing the reinforced wire, ripping the pillars from the concrete. Movement, far closer and to her right, caused her to swing and turn. Kyle had run off the road, into the outback, and he still had the rifle.

Tess fired, but was sure she'd missed even before another burst ripped into the bus. Again, the shots went high. Kyle had misremembered or underestimated how high from the ground the bus's floor was. But that didn't stop her hugging it as bullets ripped through metal, raining glass down as the windows shattered.

When the gunfire ceased, she swung up, ready to fire, but again Kyle had vanished. Now it was movement to her left which caught her attention; which made her turn; which made her eyes widen in shocked horror. The dozer was still coming straight towards the bus.

She'd assumed Kyle, and presumably Stevie, wanted to kill her, take the keys, and drive off in one of the utes, but the bulldozer wasn't slowing. If anything, it was accelerating, and it was only metres away.

The window behind her shattered as Kyle fired again. He wasn't trying to kill her, though he'd no doubt rejoice in such a happy accident; he wanted to trap her inside until Stevie did the deed with the dozer's plough.

Shooting at that foot-thick steel was only a waste of bullets and time, and she was low on both.

In a crouch, she sprinted to the rear of the bus, just as the plough carved into the cab. The frame buckled. The bus spun, pivoting and turning even as Tess launched herself through the shattered rear window. She landed hard on the dry, packed soil, and rolled harder, yelling with pain and fury as the dozer continued on, pushing the crushed bus off the road. But still the bulldozer didn't stop. She looked for Kyle, but couldn't see him, and he wasn't shooting. He must have jumped onto the tracked vehicle, which was grinding its way down the runway-road. The monstrous machine slammed into the abandoned car, flipping it onto its back before the plough smashed into the pair of utility trucks.

Tess raised her gun, and fired at the dozer's cab, wasting a bullet on a shot she knew would miss. The dozer rumbled on, down the runway road, turning sharp right, shoving the cars before it as it swung onto the dirt.

Where were Stevie and Kyle going? Did they know? But one by one the cars spun beyond the plough, and the dozer picked up speed, driving west across the outback. Tess lowered her gun, and made her way back to the bus. The aerial was broken, and the radio was ruined. The utes were obviously wrecked. As was the gate, with the left-most support-post completely ripped from the ground and the right-hand gate now hanging by only one hinge.

"General Yoon was right," Tess said to herself. "They're as good as a tank."

Chapter 11 - Inedible Carats
Humeburn, Queensland

Back in the cabin, with PZ209 standing guard by the door, Michaela held a light, while Tess carefully cleaned the blood from Toppley's head wound.

"Your skull's not broken," Tess said. "But your scalp is gashed. You need stitches, but I was never any good at those, so I'll glue it instead."

"I can sew," Michaela said.

"Are you sure?" Tess asked, sorting through the comprehensive, though small, med-kit Mick had left her.

"I make my own dresses," Michaela said. "And I stitched a cut in my leg a year ago when I was out hiking." She rolled up her leg to reveal a nearly straight white scar.

"Then have at it," Toppley said. "After all, the worst that can happen is only death."

"This will hurt, Toppley," Tess said. "Can you stay still, or do you want me to hold you?"

"Teegan, please," Toppley said. "And I have truly been through far, far worse."

"Teegan," Tess said. "What happened?"

"An old woman's forgetfulness," Toppley said. "I forgot men like Kyle can't be trusted. I forgot to keep facing him. I forgot… Ow."

"Sorry," Michaela said.

"No worries," Toppley said with a sigh. "He asked to see the gems. Said he knew they weren't worth anything now, but that he'd never had much and wanted a token. A reminder that life could be different. He spun quite a sad tale about desperate poverty, and how he wanted no more to do with Stevie. I took him to the cabin where I'd found the opal."

"Was it the office with the med bay and the dead body?" Tess asked. "I never searched it properly."

"No, the cabin next door," Toppley said. "It was a one-person dormitory cabin, yet with no nameplate. Everyone else had a printed nametag. Who wouldn't? Someone important enough not to require one."

"And someone who wanted no record of ever being here," Tess said. "It was a bedroom?"

"And living room, much like the others," Toppley said. "Except with a better standard of furniture. Kyle hit me when my back was turned, and took the rifle and ammunition. He must have assumed I was dead or he wouldn't have left me alive."

"That's where I found her," Michaela said.

"Where do we stand now?" PZ209 asked. "It's dark out there. The sun has properly set."

"The utes are completely wrecked," Tess said. "The gate's gone. But so are two of our biggest problems. All I wanted from the bus was the aerial since the bus's CB didn't work properly. If we can speak to Mick before he lands, those extra few minutes will help, but we can cope without them. We'll hear the plane not long after he gets into radio range. Besides, the construction machines will have a decent radio set. Teegan, you inspected those. Which is the safest?"

"For driving?"

"For sleeping in tonight, and maybe driving tomorrow," Tess said.

"We're still sleeping outdoors?" Molly asked.

"Nothing's changed about the undead," Tess said. "Although any zombies that were drifting through the outback will now be heading after the dozer."

"We want the… the dumper truck near the crane," Toppley said, wincing as Michaela sewed. "Other than an excavator at the other end of the lot, it's the only machine with fuel. The dozer had barely a splash. I hadn't topped her up."

"That's a fittingly poetic fate for the pair of them," Tess said. "They'll end up without fuel in the middle of the outback in the middle of the night. What about the generator, did you fill that up?"

"I did. We'll have power until dawn," Toppley said. "Assuming electricity is only being used here, of course, and not somewhere else on the site."

"And where's the rest?" Tess asked.

"Of the fuel?" Toppley asked. "Outside the office. Unless Kyle took it."

"I'll move them now," Tess said.

"I'll move them," PZ209 said, pointing at the gun at her belt. "You can watch my back."

Tess kept emotion from her face. She barely trusted Michaela, and certainly not this mercenary. "Good on ya," she said. "But what's your name, mate? I can't keep calling you PZ209."

He seemed to weigh his options before choosing his answer. "Blaze," he said.

"Good to meet you," she said, inwardly marking him down as one of *those* types of mercenaries, the kind for whom a battlefield call-sign became an identity as much as a name. The kind running so fast from their past, it would take a hail of bullets to stop them, but, inevitably, eventually, that was how they all met their end. She'd met his type before, but thankfully, not often.

Tess peered through the cracked and uncovered window next to the door, checking the shadowy, lamp-lit expanse of the car park. "Looks clear," she said.

Blaze opened the door. Shovel in hand, he went outside first. Tess grabbed a shovel of her own from the dozen leaning next to the window and followed.

"You're not drawing your gun?" Blaze asked.

"Not until I have to," Tess said. "For different reasons now than three weeks ago, of course. Then it was to avoid using it, or escalating a situation to the point where it'd *have* to be used. Now, it's sound and ammo. Best to keep one down, and the other high. How did you end up in that uniform?"

"Wrong place. Wrong time. Wrong person," he said, looking up. "And here I am, Down Under, where even the stars are wrong."

"Most people complain about the heat," Tess said. "Met a bloke a few weeks ago who got heatstroke within seconds of getting off the runway. He was from the U.S., but close to the border."

"I've worked near the equator, I can handle the heat," Blaze said. "But the different constellations, it's like being on an alien planet."

"Most people don't say that until they've met a bit more of our wildlife," Tess said. "Do you see those lights? They've got an asphalt base rather than cement."

To provide the miners with night-time illumination, lamps had been rigged to the tops of wide-based, tapering scaffolding poles. The tallest were at the edge of the wide turning circle where the hanging wires were at most risk of being caught on a digger's bucket or crane's cable.

"Is that important?" Blaze asked.

"The asphalt must have been left over when they laid the runway-road," Tess said. "In itself, there's nothing too odd in that, but where are the road-laying machines? And why didn't they bring any cement up here?"

"Because they had all the asphalt, so why bother with the expense of hauling cement, too."

"If we didn't know something illegal was going on, I'd agree with you," Tess said. "But it's an interesting detail, suggesting someone in their supply chain would notice when cement was missing, but not the machines and tar used for that runway as long as they were returned after use. It's the kind of clue I like, the kind that gives a shape to the thinking that occurred before the crime. The kind of detail that leads to an informant, a witness, a suspect, and a conviction."

"You'd really investigate tax avoidance on a few kilos of black opal?" Blaze asked.

"Nowadays? No, but the best yarns spin on the fine details."

Though the scaffolding was tall and the base was solid, the light shining downward was still weak. To their use of asphalt rather than cement, she added the dangerously criss-crossing net of overhead wires, and the number of broken bulbs in lamps that cast as much shadow as illumination. If she was looking for more evidence, she'd begin by finding out why they didn't bring an electrician with them. More immediately, following Stevie and Kyle's destructive escape, only one working light remained on the broken gate, casting questions on how close in the outback danger might be.

"I might turn on the bus's lights," she said, as they made their way through the construction equipment. "If they still work, they'll illuminate a bit more of the road. But it might lure the undead, leave them between us and the plane."

"How much diesel was in the bulldozer?" Blaze asked, his thoughts clearly on a different topic.

"You mean will Stevie and Kyle walk back here tonight if they break down?" Tess asked.

"We don't want these lights to show them the way," Blaze said.

"Fair dinkum," Tess said. "But it'll show the way for the plane, too."

Small lights had been installed above the doors of the newer cabins, bright enough to read the nameplates, and to see that it was missing on the cabin outside of which a fuel canister had been dropped.

"Only one fuel can," Tess said. "When I saw Kyle heading towards me, he had a couple of heavy bags. Reckon the rifle was in one. Bet there was some fuel as well. That's one question answered. If they don't crash, they have no reason to return."

Another was answered inside the cabin. Curiosity, and a lingering suspicion of Toppley, had her push open the door. On the floor were eleven reinforced metal suitcases. On the desk was a twelfth. She opened it.

"That's a lot of rocks," Blaze said.

"Toppley undersold it," Tess said, picking up an uncut opal the size of her fist. "Once cut, polished, these go for about fifteen thousand dollars a carat."

Blaze, who'd stepped into the partitioned bedroom, stepped back out again. "How many carats in a rock?" he asked.

"It's five per gram, I think," Tess said.

"So how many billions of dollars is there in a ton?" he asked. "Come see."

She walked over to the door. Inside the bedroom, lying next to an unused bed, was an obelisk. From the kaleidoscopic shimmer as it reflected the overhead light, it was black opal, and it was big. Over a metre long and half a metre in width.

"Is that the biggest ever?" Blaze asked.

"It must be," Tess said. "But I think what was going on here was an issue of supply and demand. They'd found a seam so large it required multiple flights from an air freighter, but the value of black opal stays high because of its rarity. Announce the discovery, the value would plummet. But if they— Shh."

Her hand dropped to her holster as she listened. Beyond the bedroom, beyond the main room, from outside the cabin, came a sound.

Footsteps?

Glass shattered as a hand punched through the window, shredding skin as it reached through the broken pane. Tearing flesh as it barged face and shoulder into the splintered window.

"Zombie!" she said, even as a second monster appeared in the doorway. She'd leaned her shovel against the door when she'd entered. Now it was out of reach. The zombie was too close for her to draw and shoot. Instead, she hurled the open metal case from the desk, flinging it towards the doorway. Unlatched, it spilled open as it tumbled through the air. The carrying case, hitting the zombie flat-open, did little damage. The uncut gems did even less, spilling across the floor, but they provided an uneven footing for the zombie's bunny-patterned, soft-felt slip-ons.

The monster toppled forward, sprawling, splayed. Arms and legs thrashed as it rolled into the stack of cases even as she grabbed the shovel from by the door. But Blaze beat her to the kill, stabbing his shovel downward in a two-handed thrust. The blade bit deep into the zombie's neck. The creature bucked, legs jerking upwards as he stamped his boot on the blade, pushing down, decapitating the monster.

Before the second zombie could come in, Tess went outside, shovel raised, and saw a third creature behind it. Two zombies. One in police uniform. One in close-to-camouflage. Both young enough they should have had more of their life ahead than behind.

She swung high, a wild swing that missed everything but the doorframe as the arcing blow slammed into the cabin. She forced herself to calm, bringing to mind Broken Hill and the more useful of the stories from Singapore and Vancouver. She stepped back, swinging low, cleaving the shovel's blade through the zombie's knee. It toppled forward, hands outstretched, even as the other creature advanced, tripping on the thrashing creature. She swung the shovel up, then down, but it took four blows to finish them both.

"Grab the fuel, Blaze," she said, peering into the darkness. The lights around the cabins had been positioned to illuminate nocturnal excursions to the toilet block. They created too many shadows. But were those shadows moving?

"Back to the cabin, eh?" Blaze asked.

"Yep," Tess said, as she finally drew her sidearm.

Chapter 12 - Dancing Penguins
Humeburn, Queensland

"The zombies are out there?" Molly asked.

"Only three," Tess said, standing by the cabin's cracked window, peering outside. "And we only found one fuel can. But one problem at a time. The plan remains the same as before. We'll head over to the dumper-truck and wait there for dawn. But we'll eat first, if it's ready?"

"It is," Molly said. "We can bring it with us."

"I want to wait here a few minutes," Tess said, her eyes roaming across the shadows. "If there are more zombies, I want them out in the light where I'll have a clear shot."

"Can you see any?" Toppley asked, coming over as Molly went back to the kitchen.

"Not yet," Tess said.

"Your logic was flawed," Toppley said. "Earlier, when you said the bulldozer would lure away the undead. It would only lure away those it was travelling towards. Those travelling towards it, towards here, would continue on until they came within sight and sound of us."

"That's just what I was thinking," Tess said. "It isn't war, but it's not a rescue effort, either. But I don't know what it is."

"It reminds me of Selayar Island," Toppley said.

"Where's that?"

"Indonesia," Toppley said. "But the reminiscence stems from the similarity in our situation rather than the geography. I'd arrived by flying boat, just myself and the pilot, meeting a rather skittish group of customers I'd traded with only a handful of times, and usually through an intermediary. We'd unloaded the cargo when an RPG hit the plane. My pilot was dead. My seaplane was sinking. I was stranded. The cargo was ashore, and my customers assumed I was double-crossing them, while I was absolutely certain one of them had to have been involved. Taking fire from all sides, my burning wreck of a plane sent smoke up into the sky, a beacon for their maritime security agency."

"I thought you were a jewel thief," Michaela said, having quietly walked over with two bowls in her hand.

"You move as quiet as a cat," Toppley said.

"It's something every teacher learns," Michaela said. "But why were they shooting at you?"

"She wasn't a jewel thief," Tess said.

"Technically, I was," Toppley said. "When I was twenty I was charged and awaiting sentence for a theft from a jewellers. I was innocent, but a friend had stashed half of what she stole in my room. She denied it. The police believed her, not me. Awaiting trial, I took the other half of my light-fingered former friend's ill-gotten jewels, and fled the country. Afterwards, I worked as a facilitator across the Pacific."

"Facilitating what?" Michaela asked.

"She was an arms dealer," Tess said.

"And medicine, and other essentials," Toppley said. "But yes, I sold guns, usually trading them for raw gems, which I'd resell to a processor, avoiding the hassle of laundering cash. Hence the reputation of being a jewel thief. It suited the journalists covering the story. Far more romantic than bulk-selling AKs and RPGs. Life is never quite as simple as fiction. The good are never quite as kind, the bad are rarely as evil."

"But sometimes they are," Michaela said.

Tess ate her bowl, watching the ruined gate. Previously, she'd identified the fence as the weak point, but now the broken gate offered the undead a far easier entry point. Assuming these new arrivals came from the outback. They could have crossed the creek. The undead who'd fallen to the bottom wouldn't climb out, but how far did the creek extend? Were there other bridges? Had the gates on either side broken?

"We're ready and packed," Michaela said, once more coming over, speaking low, her words a barely audible whisper.

"Get everyone close to the door," Tess said. "But no one's going out there yet. There's movement among the shadows."

"Zombies?" Michaela asked.

"One or two," Tess said. "And I think they're heading to the generator because they're not crossing the open car park to come here. I want to give it another minute before I'm sure."

With a clink and clatter, a rustle and shuffle, bags were gathered and everyone came to stand close to the door.

"Okay, quiet now," Tess whispered. "I'll give a ten-count before we open the door. Teegan, Blaze, tell me what you think? Behind the dumper, are those shadows moving?"

"Probably," Blaze said.

"Definitely," Toppley said.

"We'll give it another minute," Tess said.

Blaze leaned forward again. "Why did the penguin dance in the desert?" he murmured to himself, though just loud enough to be heard.

"Because she was scared," Shannon said instantly.

"You know?" Blaze asked, clearly surprised.

It was such an odd exchange that Tess turned to look at the mercenary, then the teenager. "You lost me," she said. "How would a penguin end up in a desert?"

"It's a song," Blaze said. "About how fear can immobilise you. If we're going out there, let's do it."

"I thought I recognised you," Michaela said, turning to Blaze. "You're —"

But before Michaela could finish, blood arced from her back, spraying over Molly and her daughter.

"Down!" Tess yelled, pushing Shannon and Molly to the hard floor even as Michaela collapsed.

As Tess rolled to her knees, and over to Michaela, her memory replayed the sounds her brain had been slow to process. She'd not heard the shot, but she had heard the sound of a bullet ripping through the wood, smashing into Michaela's chest. Even as Tess reached down in a futile attempt to stem the bleeding, she knew it was too late. Michaela was dead.

Another bullet slammed through the cabin's thin walls. Splinters flew as a third smashed into the frame, causing the door to swing open.

"Shut that!" Tess yelled as a trio of bullets flew through the open door before Blaze kicked it closed, but another trio of bullets caused it to swing open again. Blaze pushed a shovel into the gap between door and floor, wedging it closed. The next shot, a single, came four feet to the right, and one foot above the ground, missing Molly, now clutching Shannon, by less than a hand's width.

"Back behind the counter!" Tess yelled. "Go."

"It's Morsten?" Blaze asked, as they took cover.

"We'd have heard the engine if the bulldozer had returned," Toppley said.

"I saw a shadow by the dumper," Tess said. "But I was expecting a zombie moving towards us or towards the sound of the generator. It must have been Kyle. Either Stevie left him behind, or the dozer broke down a few clicks away."

"So why is he shooting?" Molly asked.

"Because that dumper is the only way out of here other than the plane, and I've got the keys," Tess said.

"How much ammunition does he have?" Toppley asked.

"Hard to be certain, but he's got at least a magazine left."

A bullet slammed into one of the uncovered windows, spraying glass across the floor.

"I'll cut the lights," Blaze said.

"Not yet," Tess said.

"There's only one possible course of action," Toppley said. "Surely you see that?"

"I want to be certain there's no alternative," Tess said.

"An alternative to what?" Molly asked.

"Finishing it," Tess said. "He's got the assault rifle, and I've got a pistol. The dumper is as good as armour, but he can't get a bead on us while we're back here. His only escape is in that dumper, or aboard the plane, but in both cases, he needs us dead. Both for the keys, and to avoid witnesses."

"We can give him the keys," Molly said.

"Yep, and if he asks for them, I probably would," Tess said. "But he must know that if we get out of here, he'll be reported. Within a few weeks, we'll have a description of him in every settlement across the country. If Mick arrives and we're all dead, he can create a new life elsewhere. Once he's sure we're pinned down, he might try to burn us out, or he might wait for the zombies to come in. Either way, he'll have to kill us before dawn so we don't want to give him time to prepare."

"It reminds me of Cambodia," Toppley said. "I'll tell you that story later, but the conclusion to draw is that Kyle killed Morsten. Your pilot would, on finding the bodies, notice that Morsten's was missing. Your former nemesis would get the blame. It will be his description that goes up across the outback."

The door shook as a bullet slammed through it.

"Teegan, will the generator last until dawn?" Tess asked.

"Probably."

"Blaze, get ready to cut the lights. Teegan, you'll need this." She handed the old crook the handgun and the spare magazines.

"What are you going to do?" Molly asked.

"I'm ending this. Teegan, fire a few shots at him. He was by the dumper. Say ten shots, spread over three minutes, then wait a minute. Fire one more every minute. When he stops firing, that's when I've made my move. Everyone else, keep quiet. Kyle!" she yelled. "Kyle. What do you want?"

A bullet came in reply, but only one, into and through the wooden walls.

Tess crawled across the rough boards, over to the selection of tools rejected as weapons earlier in the evening. A short-handled pick designed to be swung one-handed had a point on one tip, a chisel-blade on the other, and rust coating everything between. To that she added a chisel and a hammer.

"Are you sure about this?" Molly whispered.

"No worries," Tess said. "He's a young fool, and I'm an old cop. I'll head out the back, and make my way around to the vehicles. It'll be over in minutes."

Another shot came through the walls.

"When you're ready," Toppley said, crawling away from the bar towards the front door while Tess moved towards the rear wall.

"Blaze, now!" Tess hissed.

Blaze killed the lights. Toppley fired. So did Kyle. A three-shot burst, then another. Wood splintered, metal pinged, glass broke, but in the sudden dark, it was impossible to tell how close the shots had come.

Tess had already opened the door to the corridor and ran along it in a crouch. With the doors on either side closed, there was little light. When the door swung shut behind her, there was none.

The sound of gunfire and splintering wood was muffled, while, in the pitch-darkness, her breathing was amplified. Far sooner than she expected, the pick in her outstretched hand hit the closed door at the hall's far end. She paused, listening until she heard Toppley fire. Was that the third, or fourth shot? She'd already lost count.

Carefully, she pushed open the door, revealing a poorly lit landscape of decaying buildings beyond. Behind the cabin, there were fewer lights, since there were fewer reasons for the miners to come out here after dark. Three scaffolding poles, set in a line eight metres behind the cabin, offered the only illumination. But their bulbs were weak, and the lights were rigged low and directed straight down. It was bright enough to see the figure staggering towards her.

Stevie? Kyle? No. The zombie lurched beneath the nearest of the lights, slamming into the metal pole and with enough force to sever the thin wire. The light went out. Tess blinked, trying to regain the target in the suddenly increased gloom. She swung the handpick upwards in an under-hand blow. The flattened chisel-blade slammed into the zombie's jaw. Flesh tore and gore flew as skin ripped and bone fractured, but the zombie lurched on, oblivious to pain.

Even as the pick arced upwards, Tess turned, ducking under the zombie's swiping hand, reaching up to grip the pick with her left hand, and bringing it down with twice the force. Side-on to the zombie, its arms waving, its knees bucking as it lumbered around, the pick-point sped downwards, clipping the zombie's ear before thudding into its shoulder.

Tess tore the pick free, dragging the zombie towards her as the rusting metal ripped through flesh. In frustration, she let go, pulling the hammer from her belt as she nimbly sidestepped, and again, until she faced the zombie's back.

One arm still swiping, the other now hanging limp, the monster lurched around, and she swung. Once to crack the skull. Again, spraying gore and brain. The zombie crumpled, and she stepped back. Dropping the hammer, she unzipped her jacket, tugging it off, turning it inside out before wiping the gore from her face. An almost futile gesture, she knew, but better than nothing.

Retrieving the pick, her own words of advice about shovels ringing in her ears, she jogged to the edge of the shack.

She heard an unsuppressed gunshot. During the fight, she'd completely lost count of the number of bullets fired. A dull, metallic thud followed. A return shot from Kyle? Yes. And she could see him, or someone, on the roof of the dumper-truck she'd planned to take for her own, and which was almost the furthest vehicle from where she now stood.

Pick in hand, she jogged through the shadows, across ground littered with low piles of broken timbers and long-discarded dirt, staying away from the lights until she heard something ahead, in the dark. Something loud. Feet crunching. Limbs dragging. She knew what caused that sound, but not how many.

Cursing the judge, the engineer who'd modified Mick's plane, Erin Vaughn for deciding warrants should be publicly served, and a dozen others, all the way back to the teacher who'd dissuaded her from pursuing a career as a poet, she sprinted across the wide-open space. Pushing through the tiredness in her legs, the ache in her hip, she ran into the shadows between two excavators, and nearly straight into the arms of the undead.

She slammed the pick in front and pushed the zombie back. Not wasting time in a fight, she dodged around its clawing hands, and ran on, to the rear of the excavators.

There was no time for subtlety. No time for caution. No time to think while hands tugged at her legs. Only time to run and jump and slip over the crawling undead, weaving and dancing through and over the writhing mass of clawing death. Keeping her mouth shut to hold in the scream of horror and pain. Keeping her balance because the alternative was death. Jinking, she dashed along the back of the excavators and towards the steel-shelled truck over which death hovered, awaiting his due.

A metre away, as the ground shifted and shadows rose, she unclipped a tool from her belt, and jumped. The effort sent a jarring needle from her hip down her leg. The impact of her elbow against the side of the dumper-truck made her see stars, but her free hand found the ladder. Even as dead hands curled around her boots, she hauled herself up and beyond their reach, up the outside of the dumper. Inside the deep-sided hopper, she heard footsteps approaching. She jumped up and over and inside. Raising her hand, she switched on the flashlight, shining it directly into Kyle's face.

He was two metres away, the rifle's barrel pointing towards the rear of the hopper, but slowly spinning towards her as she shone the torch in his eyes. Blinded, Kyle released the gun's barrel, his hand automatically raised to his eyes even as his finger curled around the trigger. Tess lunged, jamming the flashlight into his neck, letting go even as her other hand pushed the barrel aside. The weapon jerked as he pulled the trigger. The bullet pinged off one of the hopper's sides, ricocheted off another, and rattled against a third, before vanishing into the night.

Her side flared with pain as Kyle's free hand slammed into her waist. Ignoring the pain, she jabbed her hand at his neck, but hit his jaw. She reached out again, curling her hand around his throat, pushing while she tugged on the rifle, and he pulled the trigger again. The bullet ricocheted once as he lost his grip, but so did she. The rifle clattered to the pitch-dark hopper-bed as his now-free hand clawed at her throat. She slammed her knee up, hard, missing his groin and hitting his thigh, but he slumped an inch. It was all she needed. She twisted his arm up, while grabbing the back of his neck. Pivoting, twisting, adding her weight to his, she threw him sideways.

He landed hard, on his knees, at the edge of the hopper, in the pool of illumination cast by the overhead lights, and next to the tools they'd stashed there a few hours before. Kyle grabbed a shovel, leaning on it as he stood. She dived, slamming her shoulder into his waist. The shovel flew sideways as they both flew towards the edge of the hopper. She landed hard, but he landed harder, on his back, neck, and arms over the edge of the truck.

She flipped to her feet in a move she'd not managed in the gym for a decade. He scrambled for purchase. But his movement caused him to slip, overbalance. Even as he caught hold of the grab-bar at the side of the hopper, his leg slipped over the side. As one leg kicked for purchase on the slick metal, his other slipped on the hopper's edge. He dangled, hands holding the grab-bar, legs kicking against the exterior of the hopper's backwards-sloping lip.

"Help!" he begged.

But she didn't. She stepped back as he slipped. He didn't have far to fall, and it was a soft landing, among the squirming, writhing bodies of the undead. He yelled with fury. Screamed with pain. But even before she'd retrieved the flashlight and shone it over the side, he'd gone silent, torn apart by the undead executioners waiting below.

Chapter 13 - The Questionable Inevitability of Death and Taxes
Humeburn, Queensland

But that was only a job half done.

From the cabin, the handgun roared.

"Clear!" Tess yelled. "Clear, Teegan! Molly! Blaze!"

"We're here!" Toppley called.

"Kyle's dead," Tess called, as she shone the torch across the hopper-floor, looking for the rifle.

"What place did this remind me of, eight years ago?" Toppley said.

"Cambodia," Tess called. "You okay?"

"We're fine. You?"

"No worries," Tess said. "A lot of crawlers out here. Stay put for a few minutes."

Tess relaxed. Properly. And for the first time since they'd arrived. The job was only half done, and their rescue wasn't assured, but at least she knew exactly what dangers she faced. She ejected the assault rifle's magazine, counting ten rounds inside, and only one spare mag in the bag. She walked to the rear of the hopper, shining the light down onto a writhing mass of crawling monsters. There were at least a butcher's dozen, but with potentially more crawlers beneath the truck, and beneath the other vehicles. In the bad light and deep shadows, it would take more bullets than she had to clear them. She clambered back to the front of the hopper. The car park seemed far wider than it had from the cabin where, now, two green-clad zombies beat their bloody fists against the rickety wooden walls. A third, in jeans missing below the knees and with legs missing below the calves, was halfway from the gate, crawling towards the building. Two more zombies crawled towards the dumper, and three, lurching through the gate, had yet to decide in which direction to attack.

"Get back from the door!" she called, unscrewing the suppressor. She took aim. Firing one silence-shattering shot. A second. But it took a third to kill both zombies by the door. A fourth dealt with the feet-less crawler, but not before it had begun dragging itself around to face the truck. The zombies closer to the gate were lurching towards her now, too. So far, so good.

She swung herself down, opened the cab, and jumped quickly inside. Unlike the dozer, the truck's door was far too close to the ground for her liking. Barely two metres of clearance, and that with a lip, a ledge, and a ladder. Maybe zombies couldn't run, but could they climb?

She unzipped her pocket, took out the key, and turned on the engine. It roared. She let it run, long enough to confirm the tank wasn't empty and the battery wasn't flat. Long enough for her to enjoy a moment where hopelessness and despair had been banished, replaced with the very real likelihood of life, rescue, and perhaps, even, sleeping in a proper bed. She put the massive truck into gear and rolled it slowly forward. The monster wheels turned, grinding bone and blood into the already red dirt as the vehicle shuddered forward to the cabin. A metre from the scaffolding, she slammed her foot on the brake.

Before she could shout they should climb up the scaffolding and so, from there, onto the roof of the cab, the door opened. Blaze ran out, shovel raised, Molly and Shannon a step behind.

Tess grabbed the rifle, hauling herself up onto the cab's roof as Blaze stopped by the door, turning outwards to stand guard as Molly pushed Shannon into the cab, throwing in two bags before jumping in herself. Blaze followed, leaving Toppley last, but she climbed in before Tess had to fire.

"That went well," Toppley said, calling up from the cab. "Are you coming in to join us?"

"Best I keep my distance," Tess said. "And wipe down the steering wheel if you can. I was drenched in gore earlier. I'm probably fine, but better to be cautious now than full of regret later."

"Wise words," Toppley called back. "How do you wish us to proceed?"

"Wait until it's time," Tess said, "then reverse out into the middle of the lot. Wait again, then straighten to face the gate. If you use the mirrors, you'll know when it's time to move."

"Understood," Toppley said.

"I don't," Shannon said.

"Shush then," Molly said. "Was it Kyle?"

"It was," Tess said. "Just him. On his own."

She climbed into the hopper, it being a safer perch than the cab. It also possessed the other welcome feature of being out of sight of the undead. On the whole, after the longest day of her life, she decided to call that a positive.

The engine roared. Bone and undead flesh wetly crunched beneath the tyres, and the truck slowly reversed back into the car park.

General Yoon really was correct, Tess thought as the engine ticked over, and the truck idled. These were better than tanks. With a few thousand, they could conquer the undead. And after, they could turn the giant constructors around, and rebuild the world on their way home.

Another minute of bone cracking, flesh grinding, organ pulping, crawler crushing back and forth, and the truck faced the gate.

Tess gathered a couple of the shovels, setting them at a diagonal in the corner, making herself a seat as she turned her eyes star-ward. But before she could enjoy the view, a thunk and clump from the cab was followed by Toppley clambering into the hopper.

"I came to keep you company," Toppley said, holding up the handgun. She picked up a shovel and laid it across the corner opposite Tess.

Tess leaned the rifle against the side, and leaned back against the nearly cool metal. "Six rounds in the mag, thirty in the spare," she said.

"And at dawn?" Toppley asked.

"Listen on the CB for Mick," Tess said. "We'll probably hear the plane before we pick him up on the radio. Maybe not, but it'll be close. We'll have to take a chance on how clear the runway is, how numerous the undead around the gate are. Then we wait to see whether the plane lands or crashes."

"In other words, our future is fluid," Toppley said. "Which is preferable to one which is set in stone. A world of possibilities is open before us."

"Just give me a proper bed, and a half-decent shower," Tess said.

"I've a personal question, if you don't mind," Toppley said.

"Why not?"

"Why did Stevie Morsten keep calling you princess?"

"You want to ask that? I was expecting something... bigger," Tess said.

"It's been bugging me all day. It's petty, but not as insulting as I'd have expected from a man with such an obvious grievance."

"My name," Tess said, "my full, first name, is Countess. My mum was a refugee from Korea. When I was born, she couldn't really speak English. Couldn't read it, either. But she saw a photograph in a glossy magazine all the way from Europe. One of those red-carpet affairs with ball gowns and tiaras. When it came to picking a name, she picked the person she thought the most glamorous, most successful, most happy, and pointed at the legend beneath the picture. Of course, the woman had a title, not a name. So I'm Countess Qwong."

"Ah. One more question. Forgive me, but you don't appear old enough to be the child of a refugee from a war that old."

"My mum was from the other Korea," Tess said.

"Oh. Sorry."

"No worries. She got out," Tess said. She leaned against the cold hard metal of the hopper. "She got out and got to live a life that was more full of joy than sadness, and barely had any pain. Not until the end. My turn for a question. Why did you return to Australia?"

"For cancer treatment."

"Sure, that's what it said in the papers," Tess said. "But you could have bought treatment at any number of private clinics. You can afford it."

"The diagnosis was a reminder of my mortality," she said. "It was time to retire."

"You arranged a plea deal?" Tess asked.

"Essentially. I donated seventy percent of my wealth to charity, and agreed to an eight-year sentence for tax fraud. Two of those years would be served in prison, the rest under house arrest. In return, the remainder of my assets were safe, and I would remain quiet about a number of covert operations in which I assisted. Everyone won."

"The donation was a hundred and fifty million dollars," Tess said. "That's what the papers reported."

"Yes, along with their rather vitriolic editorials on the ethics of the charities being allowed to keep it."

"I'm trying to work out how much the other thirty percent is," Tess said.

"A fortune six months ago, but now worth less than those opals," Toppley said. "Sadly, I wasn't as clever as the court. I had expected my two-year sentence to coincide with the treatment, thus I'd have spent it in a hospital wing, but someone decided to wait until I was cured."

"The kindness of justice," Tess said. "They didn't want you to miss out on the full prison experience. But I'd say you paid your dues in Durham, and here, too."

"So I won't be a prisoner in the refugee camp?" she asked.

"Good question," Tess said. "On the one hand, I could write up a pardon and hand it to you. Forge the prime minister's signature, since I don't think she'd remember not having signed it. On the other, everyone knows you were sentenced to eight years. If I'm trying to keep order in Australia, the *old* order, with the *old* laws, then the *old* sentences have to stand, or be expunged for everyone. You understand?"

"I do. And thank you for being honest. Since I hold the gun, I was expecting you to say something different even if it was a lie."

"But it would have been a lie, and you'd have known it," Tess said. "It makes no real difference in the end. Everyone will be working themselves to sleep for the next decade. How about I get you a job at the airfield in Canberra? That's become Mick's fiefdom. It's the closest I can get to a discharge."

"I was about to suggest a different placement," Toppley said. "You've sent troops to Malaysia?"

"We'll use the border wall with Thailand to create a defensive line," Tess said. "Though this assumes Singapore can be secured. They control the harbour, and most streets, but not all the buildings, and very little of the subway. Last I heard, they're short on supplies. If Singapore can be made safe, it gives us a base to expand operations in Malaysia and

Thailand, while also reinforcing Indonesia. But Singapore is the priority. Don't ask me why, but until then, we're only reinforcing the Thai-Malaysian border. But you want to go there?"

"Cambodia, Vietnam, Thailand, I have contacts there," Toppley said. "Indonesia and the Philippines, too. Those contacts could be of use to you."

"These are people you know from your days as an arms dealer?"

"A facilitator."

"A gun runner to terrorists."

"Freedom fighters."

"How much freedom did they win?" Tess asked.

"Sometimes the battle is more important than the victory."

"Not if you lose the war," Tess said. "Don't you have any qualms about that?"

"Forty years ago, when I was barely twenty, I was framed for a crime I certainly didn't commit. I left the country, but I didn't seek revenge. I made my own way in the world, and I made a sizeable fortune. I didn't have to return. I didn't have to remain silent on the government's clandestine operations. I could have written a book, but I didn't. Ironically, I could have taken a job with Harris Global. They wanted a head of security to manage their mining operations in Nigeria. I turned them down. That is the world in which I operated. The shadow world of spies and mercenaries and off-the-books agents, facilitators as diplomatic proxies. But it is a world of memory, soon to be myth."

"Here's hoping."

12th March

Chapter 14 - An RAAF Upgrade
Humeburn, Queensland

"Commissioner?" Toppley called softly as she kicked Tess's foot. "Are you still human?"

"As much as I ever was," Tess said. Above, the first glimmering threads of a new day were weaving through night's velvet cloak, but sunrise was still hours away. "Is there trouble?"

"The opposite," Toppley said. "We've picked up your pilot on the radio. Our carriage approaches, and will be close enough to hear in a minute."

"If it's too far away to hear the engines, what's that sound?" Tess asked, stretching stiffly as she came fully awake. Her side ached in protest after a few brief hours' exhausted slumber propped against the metal hopper. "Are those zombies?" she asked, even as she leaned over the side to peer down at the writhing pit of crawlers creating a moat around the truck. As she watched, one began to stand, only to be knocked from its feet, toppled back into the seething swarm. "Let's get out of here," Tess said.

"Where are we going?" Molly called up through the open window.

"Out through the gate, beyond the bus," Tess said. "You okay driving?"

"It's not much different to a tractor," Molly called back.

The sound of voices had energised the writhing mass of death. Necrotic flesh knocked and banged against the metallic bodywork and, more flatly, against the tyres. Before Tess could question whether the machine was truly as formidable as the Canadian stories claimed, the engine roared. With a barely perceptible bump, the machine's giant tyres tore over and through the heaving corpses, grinding bones to dust, muscle to pulp, and diseased brain to mulch. Bracing her hands on the hopper's sides, Tess held on as the truck picked up speed.

Enclosed by the vehicle's metal walls, she only had the towering scaffolding-lamps by which to gauge distance until a sharp crack marked them driving into the partially ruined gate. The truck barely slowed. Beyond, and beyond the undead crawling carpet, they sped up, approaching eight miles an hour. Ten.

Sunrise turned the sky ochre mixed with the amber threads of gathering high-level clouds. And up there, still inaudible above the truck's spine-shaking rumble, was a growing speck. Winged salvation, already losing altitude as it sped towards the runway far, far faster than their truck.

With a bump, the truck met the tarred beginning of the runway-road, but the sound of the impact, and even the engine, was drowned by the approaching plane. A plane far louder, and far bigger than Tess remembered. Far, far bigger, with twice the number of engines.

"Your pilot's called in the cavalry!" Toppley yelled.

Tess smiled, and held on.

By the time the truck stopped, the plane, an RAAF C-17 Globemaster, had landed and lowered its rear ramp. From that, a figure in black had jogged out, sweeping his rifle left and right with gloriously comforting professionalism.

"Only one soldier!" Toppley called as she waited at the base of the hopper while Tess climbed down. "Where are the rest?"

Tess turned to look back along the road at the distant mine, and the moving shadows, slowly approaching. "One is more than enough."

Molly, Shannon, and Blaze were already sprinting for the plane. The soldier raised his rifle, aimed into the outback, and fired, the sound of the suppressed shot lost among the engines' idling roar. As the man continued his sweep of the shadowy land, Tess followed Toppley to the plane's ramp. Even before she reached it, she realised she knew the man. Toppley had been correct. It *was* the cavalry.

"Someone ordered a taxi?" Captain Bruce Hawker of the SASR said. "You're missing a few."

"Dead or fled," Tess said, looking back towards the mine. Nearly two kilometres away, it looked far smaller, more desolate, more empty, and it would only get increasingly more so as the thin line of figures lurched erratically after the dumper. "Let's get out of here."

Leaving Hawker to raise the cargo ramp, Tess made her way inside. The windowless interior was configured for the parachute jump over Honolulu. A double row of jump seats along the centre-line had been added to the seats lining the wall, making space for over a hundred parachutists. Toppley, Shannon, Molly, and Blaze were at the far end of the cargo bay, making their way up the steep steps to the control centre above and at the front of the plane. Even as Tess reached the steps, and before the cargo door closed, the plane began its rumbling take-off.

"This is the fun part!" Hawker yelled as she strapped herself in, and he made sure the other passengers were buckled.

Tess closed her eyes as the plane jumped upwards, impersonating a rocket as it soared skywards, tilting, turning, twisting, and, far sooner than she'd expected, levelling off. She opened her eyes, and the first thing she saw was Bruce Hawker, grinning.

"Doctor Dodson wasn't kidding about being a top pilot," he said. "Do you think I can borrow him for Hawaii?"

"Mick's flying?" Tess asked. "I better go have a word."

Leaving the captain to settle the other passengers, she made her way through to the cockpit where Mick sat alone, dwarfed by the jungle of electronics.

"Ah, g'day," he said as blithely as if he'd been driving a car. "Found myself an upgrade."

"You can really fly this alone?" she asked, pulling herself into the co-pilot's seat.

"Most of this gear is for when the enemy starts shooting," Mick said. "And if the zombies begin doing that, we've got bigger problems. Best bit about the plane, though," he added, leaning forward to tap a monitor. "There's CCTV on the cargo hold, so we didn't bring any of the undead with us. You remember that film we watched with the aliens where you said it was over and I said there was another twenty minutes to go?"

She laughed. "It's good to see you, Mick, it really is."

"You, too," he said. "I didn't see Morsten come aboard."

"He ran," Tess said. "Stole a bulldozer, nearly ran me over. Drove off into the outback." She leaned forward to look out the window, but they were already far, far beyond where the bulldozer would have run out of diesel.

"He's a bloke who never listened to the rules," Mick said. "That's the end of him."

"Maybe," she said.

"How'd he end up in Durham?"

"I'm not sure," Tess said. "Didn't get the chance to ask him."

"What about the skinny bloke and the lady with the glasses?"

"He shot her. I killed him."

"Ah. It's been a busy night, then?"

"You could say that. How's Molly's son?" Tess asked.

"Give him a few weeks and he'll be all right," Mick said.

"Good," Tess said. "So how did you get this plane?"

"When I set down in Ballina, Bruce was the bloke who came to welcome us, with his squad, rifles at the ready. He's got a regiment of parachutists ready to jump over Hawaii. After we got the kids to the hospital, and I explained the situation, he said we should use his plane to come get you. Better with rough landings and quick take-offs, you see?"

"Why didn't you bring any of the other soldiers with you?" Tess asked.

"Ah, no, they're not soldiers," Mick said. "The regiment's made up of conscripts who've parachuted before."

"Oh, I see," Tess said. "And no one stopped you?"

"Bruce is the most senior bloke there," Mick said. "Except me, of course."

"I don't know if that's good or bad," she said.

"Don't fret over things you can't control," Mick said. "Rule nine."

"Two days ago you said rule nine was pilots always get the last of the hot water."

"Rule nine-A," Mick said.

"Speaking of water, do you have any?"

"In the locker at the back," Mick said.

Captain Hawker had gathered the others into the ancillary-crew area behind the cockpit. Molly was still buckled in, sipping water. Shannon, next to her, was gulping it. Toppley was in the lavatory, while Blaze seemed to be writing something for Hawker on a small notepad.

"Your son's safe, Molly," Tess said.

"Thank you," Molly said. "Bruce told us, but thank you."

Tess nodded to the captain, but then frowned as he took the piece of paper back from Blaze. Oddly, it appeared to be a caricature of a penguin.

"Good on ya," Hawker said. "And thank *you*, Commissioner. My son will be relieved you kept Mr Blaze alive."

"I'm sorry? Your son will be happy, why?" Tess asked.

"You don't know who this is?" Hawker asked. "It's Dan Blaze. The singer."

"Singer?" Tess asked.

"Entertainer," Blaze said.

"I guess you'd need to have young kids to know," Hawker said. "I took my son to see him in Melbourne the year before last. The Marvel Stadium was completely sold out. Had to be fifty thousand people there. Sure, half were parents, but I think we enjoyed it as much as our kids."

"You're a children's entertainer?" Tess asked, turning to Blaze.

Blaze shrugged.

"Not a mercenary?" she asked.

Blaze gave another wordless shrug.

"He's world-famous," Hawker said. "You've got a TV show, too, don't you mate?"

"I'm only famous among the under-tens," Blaze said.

"Brendon's a fan," Shannon said a little too quickly. "Though I am, too, now."

"I think we all are, now," Molly said.

"You're a kids' entertainer?" Tess asked again. "How did you end up here?"

"During the summer, I tour," Blaze said. "During the spring I record the album. In the autumn, I record the TV show. It's basic numeracy, literacy, and life skills, with a dash of music and a lot of animals. During the winter, I play gigs at children's hospitals. That's what I was doing in Vancouver. I helped as much as I could while the kids were evacuated, and ended up on a plane sent down here. After that, it was a case of being in the wrong place at the wrong time. Ended up on a bus full of convicts on my way to Durham, and to a noose. And now I'm here."

It was, she realised, the most she'd heard him say.

"I've got a few more questions about Durham," Tess said. "But I might ask them when we're back in Canberra. If you're that good, that famous, I think we'll stick you on the radio. It'll be more popular than the prime minister's broadcast. But one question, the penguins, what's that about?"

"It's his best song," Shannon said with an eagerness betraying that, perhaps, she wasn't too old to still enjoy the man's music.

"The song which brought me fame," Blaze said. "The penguin became a recurring theme. It's a lesson about not giving in to fear, no matter how out of your depth you are. When it's lost in the desert, alone and scared, what can a penguin do, except dance?"

"We'll call that rule six," Tess said.

Chapter 15 - Waves of Change
Ballina, New South Wales

"Rice and…" Tess sniffed the plastic tub. "Vegemite?"

"There was no beef at the airport," Mick said. "I couldn't find any bread. But there's a lot of rice. Three C-17s full of it. American food aid, according to the packaging. Not sure how the planes ended up in Australia, because the pilots were gone. Reallocated. You know how it goes?"

"Sure," she said, adjusting her position in the co-pilot's seat before taking a spoonful. The rice was cold, but the flavour was perfect. "Are they using those C-17s for the parachute drop?"

"Yep. And between when they reached Australia and when they got to Ballina, no one thought to empty the cargo," Mick said. "The Vegemite was part of a consignment intended for Brisbane, but redirected just after the outbreak."

"You're saying these planes, full of rice, were already at the airport?" Tess asked, spooning the umami-rich rice into her mouth.

"Parked on an access road, north of the runway. This is what happens when you reallocate people from jobs they know to where someone else thinks they're needed."

"I'll add it to the list," she said.

"What list?" he asked.

"Of things I need to investigate. The Durham Gas Refinery, the airport up at Darwin, Harris Global. Now this."

"Harris Global? What did those crooks do now?"

"They run that place we stayed in last night," Tess said. "Looks like an off-the-books opal mine. Biggest I've ever heard of. Hopefully that's the extent of their deceit because they're running about a third of our national production. Then you've got that bloke back there."

"The convict who looks like a super-villain?" Mick asked.

"You've really got to start watching a different type of movie," Tess said. "But yeah, him. He's a kids' entertainer. World-famous, apparently. Bruce took his boy to see him at the Marvel Stadium. Said it was sold out."

"That bloke's famous?"

"Apparently. He shouldn't have been digging holes in Darwin, but performing on the radio for everyone. Then there's this rice left to rot in the back of planes at the airport."

"You need a team to investigate this," Mick said.

"Like you?"

"Like a dozen flat-foots," Mick said. "Maybe two dozen. Take over the AFP building in Canberra before Anna turns it into another hostel. But if the outback is nearly secure, and if you're now a commissioner—"

"A *deputy* commissioner."

"But if that's who you are, and if that's the job the likes of Erin Vaughn want you to do, you need a team. A pilot and plane, too. If a job's to be done properly, it needs the proper tools."

"You're probably right," she said, finishing the last of the bowl.

"I'm *always* right," Mick said. "Rule twelve, that is. What do you want to do with the passengers when we land?"

"We'll take Blaze and Toppley with us to Canberra," Tess said. "I'll say Toppley is working her sentence, but she can help run the airport. Maybe the entire city. I want to put Blaze on the radio. Hawker said he had a TV show, so we might stick him on the box, too. It'd be good for the kids to hear something other than the prime minister. Something uplifting. Something different. Speaking of which, has there been any news?"

"The opposite," Mick said. "Radio's playing up. Interference has been getting worse all night. All I can offer are some rumours. A few planes were expected before dusk, and never arrived. Soldiers from the Pacific islands, stationed at consulates, marine observatories, that type of place. Oh, but I did hear a story connected to those other warrants."

"Warrants? Oh, of course. I forgot about those. What did you hear?"

"A couple of the helicopter pilots have been running a message-and-medic service between the camps. From what they said, there's no crime been committed, no negligence either, not that's worth us worrying about. Some of the pumps were missing their seals. They were sent to the wrong camps, but they stuck them on a trio of flat-beds, drove like demons, and should have everything working by now."

"The desalination plant, or the power station?"

"They reckon they'll have fresh water by dawn, so I'd say both. Sounds like no crime, just very poor communication."

"Tell me about it," Tess said. "I'll still have to investigate, but maybe we can let it slide. What's wrong with the radio?"

"Solar flare, I reckon," Mick said. "They warned this could be a very active year. Might have been what knocked out the satellites. You know half weren't properly shielded?"

"Says who? And what happened to the other half?"

"It was in a documentary I watched."

"A documentary or a movie?" Tess asked.

"Is there a difference? Speaking of movies, all this talk of mining, when we get back we should watch that film with the miners they send into space."

"When we get back, I'm having a bath, then a sleep. How long until we land?"

"An hour or so," Mick said.

"Then I'll skip the sleep and go interview the witnesses."

"The coast sounds fun," Molly said. "Captain Hawker was telling us what the refugee camp is like, and it doesn't sound bad."

"If you like fish," Shannon said.

"The entire coast is one giant barbie," Hawker said. "They're hauling it out of the sea faster than it can be processed. At the end of their shift, people all head to the beach, have a swim, and have a feed. It's not a bad life."

"What are they cooking on?" Tess asked.

"Coal," Hawker said. "The spare from the power station."

"So it smells of smoke and fish," Shannon said. "I'm not complaining," she added. "Not exactly. I just miss… I miss things being normal."

"You and me both," Tess said. "But the camps are working, then, Bruce?"

"Better than I expected," he said. "Could do with sending some of the tucker to the outback. Before we were recalled for the Hawaiian operation, rations were getting thin. Looked like they had a canning operation up and running at Wooyung."

Tess added that to her mental list, then decided it was getting so long, she was already forgetting things. "Do you have a spare bit of paper, and can I borrow your pen? Cheers. Now, tell me more about the camps."

His description of the coast was a picture of smoke black, with golden yellow sands increasingly stained an industrial grey. The story of the outback, and the operation to hunt down the roaming undead, was told in shades of steel grey and blood red, albeit censored for Shannon's ears.

It confirmed the evidence of her eyes and muscles during the long night, and around Canberra; while focusing on the relief effort overseas, they'd neglected a growing danger in their midst. She was still debating how to approach a solution when Toppley returned from the cockpit.

"Dr Dodson wants you," Toppley said.

"Is there a problem with the intercom?" Tess asked.

"That's only the first, and least, of our problems," Toppley said.

Tess stood, and everyone else followed, crowding into the cockpit.

"Bruce, get on the radio," Mick said. "Decipher the chatter, and tell me what's happening. Sounds like there's been a crash at the airport, but it's being relayed from a plane overhead, not from the tower. I'm picking up dozens of distress calls, none of which make sense. The rest of you lot, find a seat, and buckle in."

"You heard the pilot," Toppley said, ushering Blaze, Shannon, and Molly to the nearest jumpseats.

"What's going on, Mick?" Tess asked.

"The sky is filling up with planes. Air traffic control is down and I'm playing dodgems up here."

"In dodgems, the point is to hit the other car," Tess said. "Where are the planes coming from?"

"The Pacific," Hawker said, tersely, as he continued listening. "All over the Pacific. Approaching from the west. Small islands. Supply flights returning because runways are out of action. Tsunami. They're reporting a tsunami."

Tess looked through the window. They were over the coast, flying south. The sea was to their left, dotted with dozens of small craft, and it appeared as calm as ever. Below, between gargantuan pipes running into the ocean, beachside cooking fires added dark grey wisps to the far thicker industrial smoke. As the sea breeze briefly cleared the air, she saw a small crossroads hamlet was at the centre of an industrial maelstrom. Trucks, campers, and shipping containers provided shelter, ringing skeletal warehouses where the factory machinery had been installed before roof or walls had been finished. But outside, far beyond the edge of the formerly sleepy coastal paradise, a U-shaped ring of cars ran from the water's edge around the new industrial hub. As the wind changed, and the smoke thickened, she spotted a number painted on six of the larger, flatter roofs.

"Twenty-seven," she said. "That's camp twenty-seven. Which place is that?"

"Here," Mick said, briefly taking his hand from the stick just long enough to hold out a notepad.

"That's Wooyung," Tess said, reaching for the map. "We're just north of Ocean Shores." Below, the smoke was thinning as they travelled beyond one of the world's newest cities. Three kilometres inland of the beach, the Pacific Motorway was busier than it had ever been before the outbreak. A long road-convoy of freight-haulers trundled south, another rumbled north, while around and to either side, people and machines tended the patchwork farmland with even greater haste.

It didn't look normal, but nowhere did. It didn't look peaceful, but nowhere was. It looked promising, a framework as skeletal as the new factories, a hint of what could emerge if they learned from their mistakes, and from the past, while focusing on the future.

"Another report of a tsunami," Hawker said. "An oil tanker was overturned and submerged. Another report of another crash at the airport."

Tess turned her eyes back to the sea. There were boats out there, fishing boats and trawlers, though nothing as big as an oil tanker. And then she saw it. Not the tanker. The wave. A towering wall of water stretching to the horizon, reaching up to the sky, sweeping towards the coast. The plane was too high, moving too fast, to see the off-duty workers run, or the surfers drown. But she saw the larger vessels pick up speed, turning in every direction and into each other. And she saw the wave engulf them all.

Part 2
The Bunker

Canberra

11th - 13th March

11th March

Chapter 16 - The Antibody Test
Australian National University, Canberra

As she drove through the unfamiliar campus roads of the Australian National University, Anna Dodson checked the time, then her speed. While she'd allocated time to speak to Tess about serving the warrants, the suicide of Senator Aaron Bryce had been a million-volt bolt from the blue, red, *and* green. In the weeks since the outbreak, she'd known people who'd died, but this was different in ways she had difficulty articulating. As much as that had delayed her, so had speaking to the coroner, then buying the silence of Tess's team of conscripts with an easy duty at the airport. Now, she was late. The Canadian scientists, Dr Avalon and Dr Smilovitz, had requested a meeting with the cabinet. Instead, the prime minister had declared that the six politicians would visit the scientists. No, not six politicians. Five. There were only five now.

Outside the university's School of Medical Sciences, a convoy was parked: one police patrol car, an army four-by-four, a tinted-windowed SUV, and a red convertible at the rear. Three camouflage-clad drivers huddled together on the kerb. They reached for their guns as she parked her battered Subaru behind the convertible. When they recognised her, they jumped to a learned-from-TV approximation of attention. More conscripts, she thought. And there but for a quirk of timing, she might be in uniform, and they might be in the cabinet.

She switched off the wipers, watching the light rain drizzle down the windscreen. Five cars. Five politicians were left in Canberra. Only five, with a few hundred administrators and civil servants to advise and guide. But thousands of conscripts and refugees, and more arrived each day. It was all so chaotic. The new prime minister couldn't take the blame for that, since it was her predecessor's policy. With communications so slow and shaky, those with experience were handed the orders and sent into the field to implement them. After three weeks, the well-oiled ship of government had been hollowed into a leaking barrel. But even as it sailed straight towards a waterfall, a change of direction had come, albeit through the tragic suicide of the previous PM, a thought reminding her of Aaron.

Aaron Bryce was dead. Too many had died for her to mourn them all. When her father, and Tess, had come to Canberra, they'd brought news of the deaths of people from Broken Hill she'd known for much longer. Yet Aaron's death felt closer, more personal. She'd been working with him day and night as their department had grown through the hiring of refugees, then shrunk as their administrative recruits were deployed to implement policy on the ground. Were there signs she should have noticed? If so, it was too late now.

She climbed out of her car and hurried inside. The camouflaged conscript guarding the door told her where to go, but she'd been to the lab twice since the Canadians' arrival. As quietly as she could, she slipped inside the laboratory-classroom, but not quietly enough.

"Got lost?" Oswald Owen, Minister for Production, asked loudly as she entered. Known by everyone as O.O., he'd paid the press to call him the double-O politician, supposedly for his devil-may-care attitude. As he ate his way into middle age, the initials were increasingly a description of his physique.

The lab was small, cluttered, and mostly in boxes as Dr Florence Avalon transferred her experiments to a series of rooms on the other side of the building. Avalon stood in front of a whiteboard winding a neon-green rope around her hand. Leaning against the wall, her colleague and fellow refugee from Canada, Dr Leo Smilovitz, nervously shifted from foot to foot. Behind the whiteboard, trying not to be noticed, were four Australian grad-students, conscripted to be lab assistants to the pair. Facing the scientists, though now looking at Anna, were the other four politicians. Bronwyn Wilson, the new Prime Minister; Oswald Owen, the Minister for Production; Erin Vaughn, the Attorney-General; and Ian Lignatiev, the Minister for Defence.

"Bad news, ma'am," Anna said, addressing Bronwyn Wilson.

"More bad news?" Wilson asked. "Will there ever be any of the other kind?"

A week ago, Wilson had seemed the logical choice during the urgent meeting to appoint a successor to a corpse who was still warm. At sixty-two, she was a veteran backbencher famed for a stare which could neutralise the most acidic of journalists. In the week since, her uncrackable demeanour had fractured under the strain of leadership. Her pallid skin had turned the colour of her iron-grey hair. Her cheeks sagged, and so did her shoulders, stooped under the weight of responsibility.

"It's Aaron Bryce," Anna said. "He's committed suicide. I'm sorry."

"Aaron's dead?" Wilson said. "I... I should write to his parents. To his wife."

"But not now," Oswald Owen said. "Can we get this over with? It's hotter than a kangaroo's pouch in here and smells about the same."

"Does it?" Dr Avalon asked, taking a sniff with apparent curiosity. "I would say the dominant odour is chlorine."

"I was... It was a metaphor," Oswald Owen said.

"Really?" Avalon said. "How curious. But I need thirty-seven seconds." She picked up a pen and pad.

Anna kept her face still. Despite seeing Aaron's body that morning, or perhaps because she was walking such an emotionally taut string, she wanted to smile.

A world-renowned epidemiologist, Dr Avalon, with Dr Smilovitz, had been sent to Australia from Canada by General Yoon. Avalon was only a few years older than Anna, though she'd already accrued a cabinet of awards and produced more than a bookcase of papers and articles, copies of which were stored in the university library. Yes, she was odd. Yes, she was eccentric. But she could certainly identify a metaphor.

"There, done," Avalon said, laying down her pen.

"Is that an important part of the demonstration?" the prime minister asked.

"This?" Avalon replied, glancing at what she'd written. "No, this is just an idea I had to scribe lest I forget. But, as I often say, once written, never forgotten."

"Look, Miss," Oswald Owen growled in his tremble-before-me voice that had been more impressive in the days before his iron-hard jaw had been insulated in jowly fat. "You've got the entire Australian cabinet here. Do you think your work is more important than running the country?"

"Yes, I do," Avalon said. "Isn't that the point? You're trying to save lives. I'm ensuring there is a future for them."

"Perhaps we could return to the demonstration. You had an update on testing?" Erin Vaughn asked, ever the diplomat. A lawyer before she entered politics, prosecuting cases at the intersection of the environment and criminality, she'd been Anna's secret role model since the election. During the governmental merry-go-round of the last decade, with new elections almost every year, and new prime ministers as often, Erin Vaughn held the justice and policing brief under three different administrations. Approaching fifty, she was a woman who prided herself on the sharpness of both mind and appearance. But now she looked unrecognisable, wearing camouflage on which was pinned the crossed-sword-and-baton-badge of a brigadier general. The rank was an unofficial equivalency. Although, in these strange days, nothing was as *official* as it once had been. But the uniform was an alternative to a large entourage, indicating to civilians and conscripts, and to the many overseas military refugees and diplomats, that the wearer had an authority to be reckoned with.

"When will it be ready?" O.O. asked.

"The test is ready now," Avalon said, looking around the half-dismantled lab. "Would you like me to test you?" She walked over to the pair of small sample-fridges, both humming with electricity.

"You've done it?" Ian Lignatiev asked. Square-jawed, with a small forehead and piercing eyes. Even in his late forties he had a face most movie stars would envy, and a physique to go with it. He, too, wore military uniform, though with an easy familiarity, and with a major general's insignia. An active-duty soldier in his youth, and a reservist since he'd entered politics, it had been his idea for the politicians to don uniform. So far, only he and Vaughn had adopted the camouflage. He adjusted his antique and inherited Brown-Bess belt on which was holstered a factory-fresh Mark-3 nine millimetre. "You've actually created a working test?" he asked.

"A third-grader could have done it," Avalon said. "Because I'm drawing on work I first developed while in grade-three. Would you like me to test you now?"

"Hold up," O.O. said. "You've *got* a test? You can test *us*? It *really* works?"

"You asked for a test. I made you a test. I can test you now. What part of that is tripping you up?" Avalon asked in a tone that wouldn't melt butter to which she added a glare that would liquefy basalt.

"When can it be mass-produced?" Lignatiev asked. "To be specific, I want a battlefield test-kit issued to every infantry soldier."

"You mean like a blood test?" Avalon asked. "A pin-prick, touch the blood to the treated paper and watch the colour change, kind of test?"

"Precisely," Lignatiev said.

"Practically impossible," Avalon said. "First, we'd have to repurpose the factories currently manufacturing drinking-water containers into making the casings for the kit. Then—"

"If it's impossible, why did you just say you've done it?" O.O. cut in.

As fun as it was watching the scientist toy with the politicians, Anna had a million items on her job-list before she caught up with yesterday. She turned to the balding man leaning against the wall, and gave him a pleading look. "Dr Smilovitz, please?" she asked.

"We've created a—" Dr Leo Smilovitz began.

"We?" Avalon cut in.

"*Dr Avalon* has created a test, yes," Smilovitz said. "This test reveals whether a subject possesses natural immunity to this virus. Essentially, the test was created by combining a sample of the subject's blood with an extract of infected blood and examining the result. One of these grad students could test ten people an hour." He gestured at the four students, lurking in the corner, taking a grateful break from moving Avalon's equipment from one laboratory to another.

"We're asking whether you can scale it up," O.O. said.

"Down," Avalon said. "You mean scale the physical size of the test *down*, but scale production *up*. You can't scale production up before it's begun. And the answer is never."

"How accurate is it?" Vaughn asked.

"One hundred percent," Smilovitz said.

"Zero," Avalon said.

"Are we supposed to average those?" O.O. asked. "Strewth. Can't either one of you give a straight answer?"

"We ran the test on the grad students, and on the sentry outside," Smilovitz said. "Only one of the students is immune. I then ran it on the entire agriculture department and all the people turning the playing fields into a farm. Out of two hundred and forty-nine samples tested so far, thirty have been found to have immunity. These aren't random samples, but it does suggest between five and twenty percent of the wider population are immune."

"And if you tested more people, you'd get a more accurate estimate?" Vaughn asked.

"There's no point," Avalon said. "There is only one way of proving whether or not the test works. Since we can't do that, why bother?"

Once again, all eyes went to Leo Smilovitz for a translation.

"The test works in theory," he said, "but for definitive proof, we would need to deliberately infect someone who tests immune."

"And then wait," Avalon added. "And if the test doesn't work, congratulations, you've just created another zombie."

"You told us you could create a test," O.O. said.

"And I have," Avalon said. "It's not my fault if *you* don't understand the meaning of the word."

"Careful, Miss," O.O. growled.

"You want to test millions?" Avalon continued, ignoring the increasingly irate, but eternally red-faced, politician. She walked over to the nearest whiteboard, flipped it, and rubbed her sleeve across the equations. In the smudged patch, she began drawing while she spoke. "You want a test? Fine. We've got one. But you want it modified into a self-administered kit and you want it mass-produced? Then we have to produce each of the physical components needed in a testing kit. This then needs to be distributed." She tapped the four indistinguishable and unidentifiable blocky oblongs she'd just drawn. "Factory. Component. Plane. Soldier. See?"

"Leo?" Anna asked.

"We can create an assembly line of civilians and train each to form a specific role," Smilovitz said. "Phlebotomy, preparation, examination. But this will all take time, which is against us. The nature of the virus means —"

Again, Avalon interrupted. "It's not a virus."

The politicians turned to look at her.

"Can you skip the biology lecture and tell us what it is?" O.O. asked.

"For one thing," Smilovitz said quickly, "it appears manufactured rather than something that evolved naturally. And as terrifying an idea as that is, it's of secondary importance at present. I understand why the idea of a test is reassuring. But when you consider the individual steps involved in manufacture, delivery, and use, it would take too long. When you consider the nature of this particular type of infection, it would be ineffective. A graph of when an infected person succumbs, plotted against the time after infection, forms a U-shape. That's based on anecdotal date but there's some biological theory which supports it."

"Meaning?" O.O. cut in.

"Meaning most people turn so quickly they wouldn't have time to test themselves," Smilovitz said. "On the battlefield, a pin-prick test can't be administered while someone is actually fighting. And it is during that fight, within the first ten minutes or so, that about one third become infected. On our graph that is the first leg of the U. The last third seem to succumb around eight hours after, with the remaining third spread out between. Okay?" As he warmed to his subject, his confidence grew. "The test would only be of use to, at most, two-thirds of the soldiers after they've been infected. However, there are bound to be false positives and false negatives. Either would be dangerous on a battlefield, and even more so in an aid-station. Then there's the difficulty of gathering the material needed to make the test."

"You mean zombies?" O.O. said. "You'd want living zombies?"

"Of course," Avalon said.

"By which she means we'd need them, but we don't *want* them," Smilovitz said, pointing at the refrigerator. "It's bad enough having those samples in here. But we'd need more than can be gathered from the zombies shot by the walls. We'd have to capture some, contain them, and harvest the material. This presents obvious risks and ethical questions, but there is also the possibility, out in the wild, or in captivity, that the virus mutates."

"It's not a virus," Avalon muttered.

"Mutates?" O.O. said. "You mean the zombies might learn to run?"

"That's a physiological impossibility," Smilovitz said. "But viruses constantly mutate. If this one did, our test would become useless and we're back to the problem of an infected frontline soldier thinking they're immune, or someone immune thinking they're infected. Either situation would result in a death."

"Then we test the soldiers before we send them to war," the prime minister said.

"And do you only send the immune to fight?" Avalon asked. "Or do you give the non-immune a fast-acting poison to self-administer if they are bitten?"

"Testing is irrelevant," Smilovitz said, "because within eight hours of infection, we'll definitively know whether someone is immune. It's too short a time period to transport samples to a lab. Theoretically, yes, we could create a test a soldier on the battlefield could self-administer. But it would be massively time, labour, and material-intensive compared to issuing everyone with a pair of plastic restraints."

"If testing is irrelevant, why are we here?" Vaughn asked.

"And why don't we send you two back to the Canadian frontline?" O.O. added.

"You don't want a test," Smilovitz said. "You want a weapon. But the first stage was identifying what we are targeting."

"I'm listening," O.O. said.

"Due to the nature of the illness," Smilovitz said, "no one will develop antibodies because no one will recover. This thing effectively kills you before it reanimates the corpse. There won't be any cure. It might, in time, be possible to create a vaccine developed from those who are immune—"

"The British have a vaccine," Lignatiev said.

"Bet they don't," Avalon said.

"It's another secondary issue which we can discuss later," Smilovitz said.

"Tell me about this weapon," O.O. said. "You're talking about something biological?"

"They tried that in Britain," Lignatiev said. "They emptied their labs and threw everything at the enemy. Nothing worked to any great effect."

"We should receive a sample of their vaccine any day now," the prime minister said, turning to Lignatiev. "That's correct, isn't it, Ian?"

"I believe so, ma'am, yes," he said.

"And with that," the PM said, turning back to Avalon, "you could make more? We could vaccinate the world?"

Avalon shook her head. "Seriously? Didn't I just explain myself?"

"A vaccine presents the same issues as an immunity-test," Smilovitz said. "No one will know they've been successfully vaccinated unless they then get infected. There will, inevitably, be side-effects and some for whom it won't work."

"But the Pohms have got one," O.O. said.

"It'll be a placebo," Avalon said.

"They're sending us a sample," Anna said. "And when it arrives you can prove yourself correct. How long until we have a weapon?"

"How short is a goalie's temper?" Avalon said.

"You only really know when the game is over," Smilovitz said quickly. "It's a hockey expression. It'll be months before we have something you can spray from the back of a helicopter over a battlefield. We can provide a rough timeframe after we've begun. For that, we need your approval. We assumed you'd give it, which is why we're relocating to the secure lab, but we'll need more resources. Test subjects."

"What kind?" Anna asked.

"Zombies," Smilovitz said. "Only zombies."

"There's no shortage of them," Lignatiev said. "I think we're done here. Ma'am, my protection detail will escort you back to Parliament House."

"Yes, of course," the prime minister said. "Thank you, doctor."

Erin Vaughn held the door for the prime minister and followed her outside.

"It's not an idle threat, sending you back to the frontline," O.O. said and trailed after Lignatiev, leaving Anna alone with the two scientists.

"Why do people vote for men like that?" Avalon asked as she walked over to a tablet plugged into a pair of portable speakers. "Seven billion possibilities on the planet, and they always pick people like that." She continued muttering, but her words were lost beneath the full-volume blare as she turned the music on. Sitting down, she continued writing on her notepad.

As the lab filled with drums and guitars, and a weirdly atonal screeching, Anna beckoned Smilovitz to step out into the hall.

The four grad students quickly followed. "Should we move the rest of the equipment?" one asked. She had a pixie-cut, elfin eyebrows, and a unicorn t-shirt. No, Anna realised. The text read *Unicode*, though it very definitely depicted a unicorn typing at a laptop. Early twenties, like the other students. One in command yellow, one in a suit and tie, both of which had seen better days, the third in a too-big shirt which was probably recently scavenged salvage. They weren't much younger than her. For that matter, they weren't that much younger than the scientist blaring music inside the partially dismantled lab.

"Actually, Mel, I've a different task for you," Smilovitz said. "There's an ice cream machine in the lobby. Why don't you hunt for the supply room where they stored the ingredients? Come back in an hour."

As the students scurried away, Anna walked over to the bench in the middle of long corridor. She sat, facing the glass-windowed and nearly soundproof lab in which Dr Avalon moved her head in time to the outrageous beat. "How can she work with that noise?"

"She calls it sensory overload," Smilovitz said, coming to sit next to her. "Helps deaden the other inputs, enabling her to focus."

"Really?"

"That's what she says," Smilovitz said. "I think she does it mostly to annoy me."

"Ah. What did she mean that it's not a virus?" Anna asked.

"For one thing, it's artificial."

"You mean it was made in a lab?" Anna asked.

"Almost certainly," he said.

"So it was a weapon?"

"Or an accident," Smilovitz said.

"Where did it come from?" Anna asked.

"There isn't enough data to answer that," he said. "Has there been any news from Canada?"

"General Yoon reached the Saint Lawrence a few days ago," Anna said. "Her army has split. Some went north to secure Quebec. Others went south, towards the United States. More troops are flocking to the flags every day. And more are being sent behind the lines. Within a month, she'll have secured most of the north and centre of the continent."

"From where I sit," he said, pointing at the lab, "*secured* is optimistic."

"They'll have millions of acres of farmland under their control," Anna said. "And we'll need it. Vancouver Island is expecting refugees from Japan. The islands of Hokkaido and Honshu were overrun. They're evacuating to the island of Kyushu, but they're also moving farm equipment to British Columbia. We'll retrain, resupply, and enlist conscripts from across North America, but then Japan will become the next battleground in the northern hemisphere. The American Great Plains have to be secured or there's no way we'll feed everyone."

"I'm glad I don't have your job," he said.

"All I have to do is find shelter, food, and water," Anna said. "You're the bloke responsible for actually saving us all. Yep, if it's a choice between the two, I'm glad I have my job, too. Between five and twenty percent are immune?"

"I'd want to test at least ten thousand before giving you an accurate estimate," he said. "Then I'd like to run another ten thousand tests to adjust for age, ethnicity, and gender. Ten thousand after that to factor in underlying health conditions, and look for a pattern in what causes immunity."

"We have that many people here," she said. "The population dropped since the outbreak, since the fires, and since we sent people to the outback, to the airports, the harbours, and far beyond, but it's rising again swiftly. We could test refugees as they arrive. Or test those working at the new factories."

"Let me refine the test first," he said. "Rather, let *her*. And after we've relocated to the secure lab. Because it will require gathering samples from the… the… infected, I'd prefer we don't begin until we can process the tests in a short period of time. I've seen too many horror movies to want large stores of infected material lying around. Zombies," he added. "They're zombies. I still can't believe I'm having to use that word."

"Tell me about it," she said.

"But if you, personally, want to know, I can test you now."

"Did you test yourself?" she asked.

"I did," he said.

"And you are…?" she asked.

"Immune," he said.

"And Dr Avalon?"

"She refused to be tested. Said if a zombie got close enough for it to matter, we were in far bigger trouble."

"She has a point," Anna said. "Can you really make a weapon?"

"*She* can, yes," Smilovitz said. "But will it kill living people as well? Maybe. It's why we've moved to the new lab. It's a level-three rather than level-four, but I've added a few modifications to improve safety. But as development progresses, we'll need to relocate to somewhere remote. You don't want us wiping out the entire city, eh?"

"Definitely not," she said. "I intended to move some more scientists back in here. It's such a large building, I truly can't afford to let it go to waste. Embassies, offices, obviously hotels, they're all full and we're running out of space. Once the suburbs have been reclaimed, we'll probably need the space here."

"When will that be?"

"Two weeks, maybe three," she said. "I'll find you somewhere more remote before then."

Chapter 17 - A Conscripted City
Canberra

Outside, the drizzle had ceased, leaving nothing but a few puddles, evaporating in the warm midday. This year, their need for rain was greater than usual, but winter wouldn't provide the usual pause for reflection.

Other than the sentry guarding the building's entrance, the camouflaged soldiers were gone, as was Erin Vaughn's police patrol car, Ian Lignatiev's army four-by-four, and the Prime Minister's tinted-windowed SUV. The red convertible remained, as did her own, shabbily honest runabout.

"That Avalon's a strange sheila," an unpleasantly familiar voice said. Oswald 'O.O.' Owen stepped out of the shadow of a pillar where he'd been lurking. In his hand was a paper cup filled with what looked like a nearly frozen ice cream, but he still managed to loom. Six-feet-two, plugged hair, and known for his looks in his youth, he was now better known for his appetites. Food, drink, women, though with a focus on the former as he approached the end of middle age. At fifty-eight, he'd twice missed his chance to be prime minister. Three times, counting the death which had led to the ascension of Bronwyn Wilson. During the midnight debate on a replacement, Wilson's selection had been unanimous. But from O.O.'s demeanour since, he'd not abandoned his ultimate ambition.

"I'd call Avalon someone walking a parallel path to reality," he said. "But with a river of snakes between her and the rest of civilisation."

"Whereas a normal person would say she's on the autistic spectrum," Anna said.

"A psychiatrist, maybe," O.O. said. "And I never met one of them I'd have called normal. Want a slurp? It's not cold enough for a bite."

"Thank you, no."

"Installing the ice cream machine in there was your idea, wasn't it?" he asked. "You wanted to encourage kids to come to some after-school club?"

"A Saturday science club," Anna said. "But their teachers would encourage them to go the first time. The ice cream machine gave them a reason to come back the second week. Were you hanging around looking for food?"

"No, I wanted a convo with those students, and their opinion on our Canadian scientists. Make certain Avalon really is a genius. I'd say the jury's still deliberating."

"The papers of hers stored in the library here weren't enough proof?" Anna asked.

"You can't beat the personal touch," O.O. said, adjusting his coat, and revealing a pair of small pistols in a twin shoulder-holster rig.

"Where did you get those?" she asked.

"Gift from a constituent," O.O. said. "Just the holsters, of course. Anything else would have been illegal last month."

He was, as usual, trying to provoke her. And, as usual, she couldn't understand why. "I'm sure I'll see you later." She took a step towards her car.

"Hang on," he said. "Have you heard any more from those Yanks?"

"Who?"

"The pair of Americans who took that jet up to Canada."

"Not for a while, no," Anna said.

"I'd like to see the footage they recorded," O.O. said.

"Of course," Anna said. "I've not seen it all myself, but it contains nothing we haven't heard reported by others. A large portion were interviews with the people at Nanaimo airfield where Dr Avalon was stranded. You could ask her."

"I'd rather have my eyes licked by a wombat," O.O. said. "But I'd settle for watching a film. I'd like a copy."

"I'll add it to my to-do list," she said, but she'd put it at the bottom of what was growing into a book.

O.O. took another unpleasantly loud slurping sip of the mostly melted ice cream. "Aaron really topped himself?"

"Yes."

"Shame. Bright kid. Didn't seem the sort. Know his father-in-law. Awful man. No redeeming qualities at all. Good for a donation or three, but even *I* didn't feel clean afterwards. Aaron was all right, though. A decent bloke."

Anna said nothing, uncertain as always whether O.O. was trying to ingratiate himself or simply trying to goad her. Before the outbreak, as an independent politician elected as a protest in a truly rural constituency, her vote had been courted by the minority government for which O.O. was Chief Whip. But since *she* had always courted the views of her constituents, and tried to vote in accordance with their long-term best interests, she'd rarely voted with him.

"Yep, shame about Aaron," O.O. added. "So that makes five."

"We have to recall some of the politicians from Hobart," Anna said.

"Nah, they're useless, the lot of them," O.O. said.

"It'll be easier to recall them than to bring back those politicians sent to run projects in the field," Anna said.

"Yes, but I'm saying there's a reason we sent them to Tassy," O.O. said. "Five of us means an odd number, we can make decisions ourselves. Might even be a blessing. Speaking of which, I wanted to trade you a favour."

"I knew you were waiting out here for a reason."

"Always more than one," O.O. said. "I want your vote on the tank design." He took a last slurp of ice cream, then dropped the cup on the footpath, wiped his hands on his coat, and reached into a pocket for a large tablet. "I'll show you," he said, tapping in his code in, and handing the device to her.

Ignoring the sticky case, she swiped through the images. "Three designs?" she asked.

"All based on mining vehicles," he said, unnecessarily captioning what she could see for herself. "Two have tyres, one has caterpillar treads. All have a two-metre-plus clearance, a platform built around the cab, and storage for medical gear, food, and ammo. A wall adds more protection and the top is modular. You can fit and remove a rain canopy or walls depending on whether the machine is deployed to the snow, the desert, or the jungle."

"How would these fare in cities?" she asked. "Singapore, Taiwan, and Japan are the most probable locations for the initial deployment."

"Swipe again. No, again. There. That's the picture. Do you see the ladder? It's essentially a siege tower. We can ride that up to a skyscraper and make entry on the third floor. Fight our way down rather than up."

"Except most tower blocks have more than three storeys," she said. "I was really asking about the turning circle, whether it would get stuck in alleyways."

"Probably not, but there's one way to be certain," he said. "The engine's rated at over twelve-hundred kilowatts. That's more than an M1 Abrams. Slower on-road than an MBT, but faster off it. And we've got ten thousand tyres ready to be installed. Based on the chassis the production line is already set up for, I reckon we can get a thousand machines on the road in two weeks. The next thousand will take two months, but it'll be two thousand a month after that."

"Assuming no bottlenecks," Anna said, swiping back through the pictures. "But a thousand in two weeks?"

"They won't be as pretty as a picture, but these days, who is?"

"And how do we deploy them?"

"From the back of a C-17," he said. "Like I said, the top section can be dismantled, leaving you a platform about the same size as an MBT. Just as sturdy, but with less weight, a less complex engine, and a driving system any miner or bus driver can handle. We can reinstall the top-armour at the frontline. All three meet our requirements," he added, glancing around with a faux-nonchalance bordering on furtive.

"These sound perfect. Too perfect. So why are you asking me out here rather than waiting for the cabinet meeting?"

"Lignatiev still wants his tanks," O.O. said. "The only reason he's not driving around in one is he'd prefer to show off in his helicopter. Good thing all these new vegetable beds and barricades mean he hasn't got anywhere to land it. Instead, he's dug out a design from the 1960s, complete with machine gun mounts for which we don't have the guns, let alone the ammo. It'd take us two months to set up a factory to build a prototype."

"Again, I don't see the problem. Of course we'll use a modern design based on what our factories are already geared up to build and our civilians are able to drive. So why are you asking me now?"

"I just want to get my ducks all lined up before I open fire," he said, taking the tablet back. "After all, we can't waste ammo, can we?"

Anna watched O.O. drive away. He had a secret agenda. He always did. He was playing politics. He always was. But he shouldn't be. Not now. Not when absolutely everything was so critically important.

General Yoon needed ammunition and fuel, and soon she'd need food and medical supplies. And that was just for her army. Singapore needed resupply, as did Taiwan, and Japan needed reinforcement before they lost any more ground. There was Malaysia and Thailand. There was Mexico. India. The entire world needed help and equipment, and they needed it yesterday. But Oswald Owen was working his angles into sharp points to which he could pin his own personal advantage. Some people never changed, she supposed, not even during a crisis.

As she reached for the car door, a gunshot echoed across the rooftops. She listened for a second shot, waiting for the siren. Neither came. Breathing out, she got in, buckled up, switched on the engine, and pulled away from the kerb.

As the greatly expanded agricultural department had begun turning every inch of grass into an experimental crop-bed, and every spare inch of concrete into the foundations for an equally experimental greenhouse, the road signs had come down. Navigating through the university's prettily curving roads, she almost got lost until she saw a Humvee speeding towards her. The vehicle slowed as it neared, but didn't stop. Presumably it was searching for the gunshot, but the direction it came told her the direction to head, and soon she was back into the city proper, and on her short drive back to Parliament House.

She saw no more traffic, at least not moving. Plenty of vehicles partially blocked junctions with more nearby ready to be rolled across to create an unguarded barricade. Most of the guards and sentries had been deployed to clear the outer suburbs. Which wasn't to say that Canberra was deserted. Though conscription into the ever-increasing armed services, or into the even larger engineering and manufacturing corps, had reduced the capital's population, and escape to the bush had reduced it further, refugees had begun to arrive. Some now dug the verge. Others, off-duty after working in prototype factories run in hastily converted office blocks, boarded up the windows of their newly allocated multiple occupancy homes. Many cooked, the plumes of smoke rising from back yards and barricaded kitchen windows. Mostly beef, from the smell. No one would go hungry. Not for a few days. But after then, many would.

Not every old resident of Canberra, or any other city, had been conscripted. A shelter-in-place order had been issued for anyone who could to remain at home for as long as they could. But if they required assistance, they would get conscription along with it. The inequality troubled her, as did the exemptions for the mining barons in their gated mansions, but time would be a great leveller, assuming they overcame the immediate crisis.

Unbidden, she pushed on the accelerator, picking up speed as she crossed the bridge over Lake Burley Griffin, and approached Parliament House.

She parked her car behind Erin Vaughn's police cruiser, and next to the sentries standing guard on the ring road that circled Parliament House. A smile at the sentries received a professional nod in return. Unlike those elsewhere in the city, these were dressed in black utility gear. The kind she thought of as being worn by Special Forces. At least, it was how Special Forces dressed in the movies her dad had taken to viewing every spare minute he had. These soldiers weren't SASR, but their familiarity with their weapons gave her comfort in a way that would have been alien to her only three weeks before. If anything, she now wished there were more of them.

Chapter 18 - Housing and Agriculture
Parliament House, Canberra

In Anna's recently acquired office, the lights were off, but the curtains were open. Originally a large and airy meeting room, its table and chairs had been replaced with a pair of desks. On hers were three large and one small stack of papers. The other desk was Aaron Bryce's, at which a figure sat hunched over a laptop, tapping at the keyboard. For the briefest moment she thought it was Aaron, but of course, no.

"G'day, Hoa," Anna said, as she entered.

The woman at the keyboard nearly jumped. Hoa Nguyen, seventy-three, and six months retired after fifty years in Australia's civil service, had returned to duty after the outbreak. It was she who really ran the department of which Anna was Minister.

"Ma'am," Hoa said, half standing.

"No, don't get up," Anna said, dropping her bag behind her desk, sitting, and kicking off her shoes.

"How were the scientists?" Hoa asked.

"Give them a billy and a match, and you'd get a particle accelerator before you got a cup of tea," Anna said. "Smilovitz is mostly all there, but Avalon is almost entirely somewhere else. But they think they can build us a weapon."

"Think? So they're not certain. And you have reservations?" Hoa asked.

"Is it that obvious?" Anna said. "But yes. Partly, they'll need subjects to test it on. Zombies. Those were people a few days ago. If they could guarantee results, and quickly, it might be different, but they implied it will take months."

"In my experience, with scientists, you can double any time-frame they give," Hoa said. "*And* triple the expense."

"At least we don't have to worry about cost," Anna said. "What are you working on?"

"It's the infrastructure expansion plan from New Zealand," Hoa said. "The documents arrived at the airport yesterday, but only reached my desk this morning. My apologies they didn't reach you sooner."

"It's not your fault," Anna said.

"No, but it *is* my responsibility," Hoa said. "The document contains some useful ideas. I've begun drafting a series of recommendations, and a reply. Speaking of which, albeit obliquely, I heard the first rocket is on the launch pad in the Marshall Islands. As soon as the weather conditions are favourable, they'll launch. We'll have the capability for satellite communications within a few days."

"The capability," Anna said. "Which isn't the same as the reality, but it would be preferable to radio and plane."

Hoa smiled. "We're muddling through, like we used to do not so long ago, but yes, I too will be glad when a semblance of normality returns."

"Is this lot for me to sign?" Anna asked.

"Those three piles require your signature. You should read the paragraph summary, but you don't need to read the details. The ones in the smaller pile need to be read, and a course of action decided upon. Mr Dalgleish's unionisation proposal has arrived. It contains an injury compensation package, life insurance, post-pandemic training, and healthcare. He's also included the wage structure."

"In units of hours worked rather than in currency?"

"Yes, as you requested. And he made the alterations so it can be applied to mine workers as well as soldiers."

"And teachers," Anna said. "And fishers, and who knows who else, but it's probably everyone. Good. So we just need to find an economist to tell us how to convert that into currency, and how to go about paying people."

"I found three economists," Hoa said. "None could agree so I've locked them in a room until they reach a consensus." She raised her watch. "They've had three hours so far. At the bottom, in the red file, are the billeting proposals from Victoria and the Northern Territories. With amendments."

"They made changes? Oh, that is good news," Anna said, picking up the top-most folder, quickly scanning the contents. "They've altered almost every figure."

"And I'm sure the numbers don't add up," Hoa said. "But it means approval of the principle. Senator Bryce was correct. Speaking of whom, I haven't seen him today."

"Oh. Yes, of course. Sorry, you don't know. It's been such a day. Hoa, I'm sorry. I have bad news. Aaron is dead. It was suicide."

"No. No, really?" the old woman asked, suddenly looking her age. She made to sit on Aaron's old chair, but abruptly turned away, pressing a hand against the wall for support.

"His body was found this morning by a team securing the outer suburbs," Anna said. "Tess summoned me to identify him. You were busy at the department, but I should have left you a note."

"Suicide?" Hoa said. "Poor Aaron."

"What was it you said to me last week? There'll be a time for grief, but it isn't now."

"Indeed, yes," Hoa said, straightening. She picked up her laptop. "I'll finish this, have it printed, and I'll pass word about Aaron to everyone in the department. Do you think this will mean some politicians will return from Hobart?"

"Hopefully," Anna said. "But I've been requesting it for a week."

"If only you knew someone who could fly down and bring them back," Hoa said.

"That would be a coup, wouldn't it?" Anna said.

"The most democratic coup in history," Hoa said. "Two reports arrived from Tasmania. One on education, one on domestic economics. I put them in the pile-to-be-read, but only if you want some light relief."

"They're that bad?"

"They are that fantastical," Hoa said. "Perhaps, when we send our reply to Victoria and the Northern Territories, we could request they send a pair of representatives to join the cabinet. I'm sure that the other states and territories will quickly follow suit."

"Perhaps, but let me speak to the prime minister first," Anna said.

"Of course. Ma'am."

Hoa left, leaving Anna alone in the office with Aaron's ghost. Doing her best to ignore him, she picked up a pen and began adding her signature to the piles of papers.

This was her real purpose in Canberra. Hoa ran the department. State and territorial governments administered their regions. But decisions were made by the doctors and mayors, military commanders, cattle-station owners, and mining managers. The strategy could be summed up as stockpile and stay alive, and with priority given in that order. Anna, meanwhile, signed her name with as broad a stroke as the policies she designed, taking responsibility for them all.

No matter how much she relished the rewarding simplicity of muscle-aching labour, she couldn't pick up a shovel and dig foundations. She certainly couldn't return to the complexity of the classroom. There were no taxes to be collected, no manifestos to fulfil, but she had refugees to be housed. But how would they house millions of refugees in a nation of twenty-five million residents? New Zealand and Papua, and the Pacific islands, could take some, but how many?

Aaron had solved the problem by making it someone else's, devolving implementation to regional authorities. The weaknesses of their federal system could, in this disaster, be turned into a strength. No one could foretell how many refugees would arrive, how many would be redeployed overseas, sent to which farm or mine, or returned to a fortified enclave close to their original home. But they *did* know how long it took a ship to sail and a plane to fly. Though boarding could be rushed, the flight and sailing times remained one of the few things unchanged by the outbreak.

Aaron had declared twenty million a month as an arbitrary absolute maximum, and after subtracting the soldiers and conscripts sent overseas, determined an increase of a hundred million over the next nine months. Anna was reasonably sure he'd pulled the numbers out of the air, but it had given them something to work with.

Locally, priority was given to moving refugees away from airports and harbours, and responsibility was given to the individual state, territory, and commonwealth governments. Numbers were allocated proportionally based on the local population at the last census. Internal flights were scheduled to transport refugees from the Asia-facing harbours of Western Australia where most were likely to arrive. The State of Victoria was allocated another seven million refugees this month, with an expected total increase of thirty million by December. A quick scan through the amendments the state government had made, and the total was closer to twenty million.

She smiled. "Thank you, Aaron."

Twenty million might be enough. It might be twice as much as needed. But if it was far less, when boots wearily slogged ashore, what choice would Victoria have but to accept everyone who arrived? In the meantime, locally, they would install water pipes and electricity lines, power stations and treatment plants. The people who knew the land would plan roads and suburbs, and, of course, walls. It would keep people occupied, focused on the future. It would convince them that there would *be* a future. When the refugees came, they would have a roof and drinking water, and somewhere to cook. And if, in a month, the outbreak ended as abruptly as it had begun, she would take the blame. She and the other four politicians.

She was staring at Aaron's desk. It was smaller than hers, and as free of clutter. It had been his idea to commandeer the conference room after she'd accepted the job he'd refused. She'd wanted the promotion no more than he had. In the original post-outbreak cabinet, she had been Minister for Wellbeing and Continuing Education, responsible for morale, and for the national TV and radio broadcasts. When most of the remaining politicians had been sent to safety on Tasmania, she'd expected to be sent with them. Instead, she'd been offered the job Aaron had refused. And now he was gone.

No, now wasn't the time for grief. Not when the pile of papers was still so tall. But she was getting a cramp in her hand. Deciding she'd earned a break, she opened the documents from Hobart.

Some politicians had returned to the hospitals or regiments they'd served with before entering politics. Others had returned to their constituencies. A few had simply disappeared, and too many had committed suicide. The rest had been dispatched to Hobart, partly to keep them safe during the days when it seemed Canberra would succumb like so many other capital cities. But those evacuated politicians had also been tasked with devising a blueprint for the future. The world had changed, so everything about it, from education to healthcare, had to change, too. She picked up their report on economics, scanning the first few pages. They discussed creating a new global reserve currency, seeming to have missed the news that the value of a bank was now measured in how many refugees it could house.

The education report was more promising. An expansion of the School of the Air was included on page one, but most of the document dealt with the re-organisation of universities into life-long learning institutions. She put the document aside, to read more thoroughly later. Perhaps next month. Perhaps next year.

When her hand began cramping again, she checked the time and realised she'd missed the prime ministerial broadcast. It was no great loss since Erin Vaughn wrote it, often with notes and snippets provided by Anna and the other members of the cabinet. The follow-on programme, a dissection by a panel of pundits, comics, and grandees, still had a half hour to run. Rather than a policy discussion, the show was a deliberately irreverent, though broadly patriotic, satire. Bronwyn Wilson had wanted a light-hearted buffer separating her daily speech from the always-grim news bulletin broadcast afterwards. Anna thought it a mistake. They should have stuck to the original schedule where the PM's broadcast was after the news and followed by an informative debate, but her opinion hadn't been asked.

She signed the last document a good five minutes before the messenger arrived to collect them. Still wearing bicycle clips, and carrying a shotgun, he dashed in.

"G'day, ma'am," he said. "Got a delivery for you."

"Please tell me it's pizza," she said.

"What? Oh, sorry, no," he said, looking down at the bag's logo. "The bag's from my previous job. Three weeks ago. They're easier to carry on the bike so I swapped. That's okay, isn't it?"

"No worries," she said. "Whatever works, right? You know, that should be our slogan from now on. I'm sorry, I don't know your name."

"Darryl, ma'am. Darryl Quinn. Mrs Nguyen sent me."

She handed him the signed documents, and he handed her the new ones, and hurried away. But with the documents came a large plastic box. Dinner, sent by Hoa.

Anna smiled.

A pizza delivery boy was now a government messenger, while the teacher she'd once been was a scapegoat-in-waiting. By prime ministerial decree, all cabinet ministers must work from Parliament House, blocks away from their much-diminished departmental staff. The daily broadcast was made from the temporary studio up at the Telstra Tower rather than from the pressroom downstairs or at the ABC studio in Dickson. It was all so chaotic. So accidental. Decisions were made before ramifications could be considered, let alone discussed. But order was slowly emerging. *Very* slowly.

She opened the folder from New Zealand, quickly scanning the contents before reaching for her bag. She wanted her laptop, but her eyes fell first on the much thumbed copy of the British evacuation plan, a thin document which had come from ship to plane to Lignatiev and then photocopied for all the cabinet. The British plan involved redistributing the population along the coast. But her constituency alone was bigger than that Atlantic island, and in Australia, most people already lived within an afternoon's drive of an ocean swim. Had they really developed a vaccine? Surely not.

Smilovitz had said the virus was manufactured. Made. Created. By a human designer. In a lab. Manhattan? She doubted it. A terrorist attack, then? It made little sense, but more so than an attack by a nation state. Who would use this kind of virus as a weapon?

Still searching in the bag, her fingers curled around the small metal tin. Though labelled liquorice pellets, inside was a USB. On it was a copy of the recording taken by the two Americans who'd travelled from Broken Hill to Canberra. The originals were in a bag in her hotel suite, and though no one else in Canberra had seen them, she didn't know who had watched the footage before it had reached her.

Though she'd not had time to review the entire week-long recording, she'd seen enough to make a copy to give to Tess. Rather, she'd *heard* enough to want the police officer's professional opinion. This morning hadn't seemed the appropriate time.

There were two sets of recordings. The first having been made in Nanaimo, the airfield on Vancouver Island where Liu Higson had landed, and at Pine Dock, a remote fishing village on the wrong end of Lake Winnipeg. Those recordings were interviews with Canadians, about where they'd escaped, what they'd seen, how they'd survived the immediate aftermath of the outbreak. Interesting, sure. Except for the climate, it was very similar to the stories from Thailand or Japan.

She'd watched that footage multiple times, particularly the interview with Dr Smilovitz. Not for what he said, but to reassure herself that he had never met the Guinn siblings before. And she'd done that because of what was on the second set of recordings.

In Pine Dock, the siblings had been given military-grade body cameras with a seven-day battery life. Though they had occasionally turned off the cameras, they'd never muted the microphone. The images of their journey through Michigan and Indiana were difficult to decipher, but the sound quality was excellent.

Aside from learning anarchy had gripped South Bend and the surrounding countryside, she'd found two conversations the siblings had not intended to be recorded. Both were discussions of the cartel's attack on Broken Hill, but in both, it was the link to the outbreak that had caught Anna's ears.

Lisa Kempton had been preparing for some kind of apocalypse. To prevent it, years ago, she'd hired Corrie Guinn to develop software with which satellite communications could be subverted. Anna was unclear whether Corrie Guinn had developed the operating system for the satellites or merely a hack. They mentioned air traffic control systems, too, but that conversation was partially muffled by Pete Guinn's methodical chomping of a ration pack.

Nevertheless, Lisa Kempton, the billionaire, had something to do with global satellite communications going down. Kempton had been trying to stop an apocalypse. Smilovitz had said the virus was manufactured. The cartel had attacked Kempton's plane in Broken Hill. It was all linked. But precisely how was as unclear as how she should proceed.

Contact had been lost with the Guinns. While this didn't guarantee they were dead, if President Trowbridge and his CIA escort had disappeared in the Canadian wilderness it was unlikely the Guinns were alive. Certainly, they would be as impossible to locate as Lisa Kempton.

While she certainly wouldn't seek advice from Oswald Owen, nor Bronwyn Wilson, if Anna told Erin Vaughn, she would tell Lignatiev. The military would be deployed in both hemispheres, but was it worth the effort? How many lives would then not be saved?

An old rule of her father's had stayed her hand. A lesson he'd given her when dealing with school-yard bullies who'd continued their torment after the bell: revenge never brings the rain. It had taken her a few bruises, and a few grazes to her knuckles, before she'd truly learned that lesson. Justice, of one sort or the other, required patience. She put the case back in her bag. She'd speak to Tess, and to her father, as soon as they returned to Canberra.

Darkness descended, though she didn't close the curtains. Outside, in the distance, a sudden flurry of noise marked the nightshift heading to work. Thirty minutes later, a louder bustle denoted the dayshift returning to their billets. She returned to her papers and had just finished when a breathless sentry stumbled to a halt outside her door.

"Ma'am! Ma'am!" he gasped. "Ms Dodson."

"Yes, that's me. What is it?"

"You're needed, ma'am. In the Bunker."

"The Bunker? Why?"

"A bomb, ma'am. Someone dropped a nuclear bomb."

12th March

Chapter 19 - The First Wave
The Bunker, Parliament House

The Bunker wasn't supposed to be called that. Technically, it was the Communications and Operations Monitoring Station, so named because they'd chosen the acronym first. With predictable contrariness, the official name had been ditched in favour of the more accurately descriptive nickname. The Bunker was a secure room for the dissemination of reports from spies and foreign agents, from allies and eavesdropped from their enemies. None of which applied in the current crisis. Built as an underground refuge, with an airlock and air filtration system efficient enough to protect from a biological or radiological attack, the designers had been more concerned about a dirty bomb than Armageddon.

In a secure corridor, behind an unguarded sentry post, stairs descended below ground to another long corridor, which led to the Bunker. Beyond a small waiting area, with remotely lockable doors either end, was the first airlock. In normal times, the double-set of transparent, but bullet and bomb-proof, doors were the only ones closed. Now, a second set of far thicker blast doors had been lowered.

Beyond those, a corridor led to the bunkrooms, mess hall, and washrooms for the soldier-operators, as well as to the armoury, storerooms, water reserve, air-filtration, electrical conduit, servers, and generators. In the other direction, the same volume of space was given to the far more spacious private rooms of the politicians. But immediately in front of the blast doors, behind a floor-to-ceiling transparent wall, was the communications centre itself. Rows of monitors and keyboards had been used to access the data processed elsewhere, then displayed on the wall-sized screens dominating the room. In the far corner, a transparent-walled meeting room offered space for politicians and military leaders to debate in semi-privacy. Like the C.O.M.S. wasn't supposed to be called the Bunker, the Secure Executive-Control Restricted Emergency

Transmission Silo wasn't supposed to be called the War Room, but the nickname had, inevitably, stuck.

When the true nature of the outbreak had become apparent, the contents of the armoury had been distributed among the conscripts sent to aid in outback security. The soldiers who operated the communications equipment had gone with them.

With the satellites down, with their allies' data centres offline, little information had been coming into Canberra. As priorities shifted towards production, the Australian data centres had been taken offline in order to preserve electricity and the data stored therein. Fixed-line phones and radio, and a thread-thin web of fibre optics, provided some input, but the most useful information came from hand-delivered eyewitness accounts. In short, the state of the art C.O.M.S. was useless, and so the Bunker had been mothballed. Besides, with only one entrance, if the undead reached Parliament House, who'd want to be trapped in a hole below ground?

That was the situation as Anna had understood it, but when she was confronted by the reality, she came to a shocked halt in the doorway to the communications centre.

Oswald Owen was an island of indifference amid a chaotic maelstrom. The prime minister stared, unblinking, at the wall-sized, but blank, screen. Erin Vaughn tore through maps in the War Room. Lignatiev was tearing strips off a uniformed sergeant, while it appeared the team on duty had been tearing holes in the wall before news of the new disaster came in.

"What happened here?" Anna asked. She'd been in the Bunker once, two weeks ago. Then, it had thrummed with frantic professionals collating what little information had been arriving by radio and hard-line. Now it was more like a building site. Large portions of the floor had been ripped up and the cables ripped out. Monitors had been removed from desks, stacked near the wall, where, again, the panelling had been removed to provide access to the wires behind.

"They've been stripping the command centre for parts to build the new data centre upstairs," O.O. said.

"Who authorised that?" Anna asked.

"You did," O.O. said. "And so did I. We voted on it a week ago."

"We did?"

Along with the politicians, half a dozen camouflaged soldiers, and a couple more wearing black tactical gear of the Special Forces, were trying to not get in the way. Ten dusty civilians, the team dismantling the place before news of the latest calamity arrived, stood at a cowed attention as Lignatiev barked orders. But the Minister of Defence's swearing wasn't restoring calm.

Anna turned back to O.O. "What happened?" she asked. "One of Ian's new recruits dragged me down here. He said someone dropped a nuclear bomb."

"A mushroom cloud was sighted in the Pacific," O.O. said. "Technically, it was three separate sightings, by three different planes, all flying scout ahead of the Hawaiian invasion fleet."

"Was it three mushroom clouds, or one mushroom cloud seen by three different planes?" Anna asked.

"Probably," O.O. said. "Don't ask me which."

"Don't we have any functioning communications systems?" she asked.

"Less than before," he said. "There's a radio link to the airport, and a phone line to the broadcast studio."

"And?"

"No, that's all we've got down here," O.O. said. "We can't even call the barracks. I told you it was a mistake voting for Bronwyn Wilson."

"Have we heard from Guam? Perth? Hobart?" she asked.

"Cup a hand to your ear, and you might hear them yell," O.O. said. "I didn't think they'd do this. And who are *they*, I hear you think. Conscripts. More bloody conscripts because we decided a highly trained specialist was the same as an infantryman, gave them a rifle, and sent them hunting zombies in the bush."

"We should send someone to the university," Anna said. "At least they'd know which wires are liable to electrocute you. They haven't even cut the power."

"There are, quite literally, a million more where those blokes came from," O.O. said.

"Tell me about the cloud," she said.

"I did," O.O. said. "A mushroom cloud was seen at sea. Three reports from three different planes."

"At sea, somewhere near Hawaii, but not over land? Where is the fleet? It can't have reached Samoa yet. Were there casualties?"

"The planes were flying in convoy, ten per wing. One military plane in the lead, the others were civilian. The civilian aircraft were lost. The assumption is the EMP knocked out their avionics."

"There were soldiers aboard?" she asked.

"Conscripts and equipment, yes."

"We lost twenty-seven planes?"

"Twenty-eight," O.O. said. "The pilots in a plane which radioed in were blinded. Both of them. Managed to keep the aircraft airborne long enough to send a radio broadcast. That was their last transmission. No mayday was picked up."

"Twenty-eight planes? That's... thousands of soldiers."

"I hadn't finished," O.O. said. "The plane's broadcasts were picked up by ships. We've lost contact with them, too. But the message was relayed back until it reached a fighter patrol over the coast."

"We lost contact *after* they relayed the message? We need to mount a rescue."

"How? What with?" O.O. said, gesturing at the blank screens. "Those should be displaying all the intelligence we've gathered. I suppose they are, in a way."

"Thousands are dead, perhaps thousands more need rescue," Anna said. "But one or three mushroom clouds spotted in the middle of the Pacific? We don't know where?"

"I'm sure someone does," O.O. said, gesturing at the room. "But they've not told me yet."

Anna looked around the hapless engineers, searching for someone who might be able to give her more information, but her gaze settled on the prime minister. Bronwyn Wilson walked to the War Room. Inside, after the door closed, Anna saw Erin Vaughn turn to her. She saw the younger woman's arms move as she spoke, but the room truly was soundproof. The prime minister sat. Vaughn slapped the wall in frustration and stormed out, heading over to Ian Lignatiev. Anna did the same. Oswald Owen, at a more sedate pace, sauntered after her.

Vaughn reached the uniformed politician first, laying her hand on Lignatiev's arm, whispering something in his ear. Briefly, he took her hand before he saw Anna approaching, and hurriedly let go.

"Owen's briefed you?" Lignatiev asked. A man famous for his self-control, his muscles were tensed with the effort of keeping himself in check.

"There were three sightings of a mushroom cloud," Anna said. "Or maybe three separate mushroom clouds, in the Pacific. The number of casualties, and the number of ships which need rescue, is unknown."

"I don't see how we can mount a rescue operation," Vaughn said.

"I am less concerned with the planes and scout-ships than I am with the troopships heading for Samoa and then Hawaii," Lignatiev said. "There are a million soldiers aboard."

"Conscripts," O.O. said. "Unarmed, too, because you trusted the Yanks to fly weapons there when they can't even fly their new president out of Canada. At least they won't have rifles weighing them down if they have to swim."

"Pull your head in, Oswald," Anna said. "Ian, should we order the ships to return?"

"I can't determine what order to give until we've determined where the ships are," Lignatiev said, "but the cloud was sighted north of Tarawa."

"Tarawa Island, in Kiribati? So it was south of Hawaii?" Anna asked. "But how far south?"

"Tarawa Island is four thousand kilometres northeast of Big Island, Hawaii," Vaughn said.

"All we can conclude is that the bomb detonated somewhere between Australia and Hawaii," Lignatiev said.

"Are we sure it was a bomb?" Anna asked. "Not some kind of accident aboard a sub?"

"Hmm. Maybe," Lignatiev said, automatically looking up at the large, blank screen. "Maybe, but it is more prudent to assume the worst."

A clatter and smash came from her left. One of the conscript-technicians had tripped on an exposed bundle of wires. Trying to carry three screens at once, she'd dropped two.

"This is a nightmare," Anna said. "Who's our expert?"

"No one here," Vaughn said. "The operators and advisors accompanied the Federation Guard to the new military training camps near Wagga Wagga."

"No, they went to bolster the defences at Ermington," Lignatiev said. "I was concerned Sydney would go the way of Melbourne."

"Could have sent them to count polar bears at the South Pole for all the use they are to us now," O.O. said.

"Then I'll..." Anna began. Her first thought was to find Hoa Nguyen. Though the veteran public servant was no expert in disaster management, she would know the names of those who were. "No. I'll get Dr Smilovitz and Dr Avalon. They dealt with biological threats to the species, but I bet they know more about radiation than we do. They could tell us whether this was an accident aboard a sub, or something much worse."

"Are you sure you want to go outside?" Vaughn asked.

"Canberra is as safe as it was an hour ago," Anna said. "The lights are still on, Erin. We're not under attack. Although perhaps we should make contacting Hobart a priority, just in case."

"Agreed," O.O. said. "I've got a famously loud voice. I'll go up to the roof and shout. Or we could send a plane. Ian?"

"There should be a few jets at the airport," Lignatiev said. "I'll send a runner."

"There's engineers at the university," O.O. said. "Professors and academics, but one of those blokes must know more than theory. Let's get some of them here to sort out this chaos."

"I've a team in my department who can handle this," Vaughn said. "Though I suppose I should inform the prime minister first."

They all looked to the War Room where Bronwyn Wilson sat, silent, motionless, staring at the wall.

"Then I'm getting something to eat," O.O. said.

"You're hungry? Now?" Vaughn asked.

"Rome's burning, and I don't have a violin," O.O. said. "So I'll eat, drink, and be as merry as a bloke can be."

He walked away, leaving behind only furious irritation on Lignatiev's face.

"I told you," Vaughn said. "That's why he can't ever be prime minister."

Lignatiev nodded. "Anna, you'll fetch those two scientists? Let me give you an escort."

"No," Anna said. "If they're people you trust, then you can trust them to go to the airport. I've got my car, and it's only a short drive. I'll be back in an hour."

"Then let me get you a sidearm," he said.

"If I had one, I'd shoot at shadows," Anna said. "That would set off an alarm, and even more trouble. No, the last thing we want to do is create a new crisis."

"But do be careful," Vaughn said. "We can't afford to lose anyone else."

Chapter 20 - Off the Scale
Geoscience Australia, Canberra

Outside, the comparative normality of the night-shrouded city was reassuring. Even the lone and distant gunshot offered the reassuring comfort of familiarity. Her car worked, as did the streetlights, and the spotlight on the roof of the sentry's patrol car. The EMP hadn't reached Canberra. But her knowledge of nuclear weapons was limited to the long-term effects of the tests in Emu Fields and Malinga. She knew about the dangers of radioactive seepage into groundwater, about the eternally lingering effects in the soil, and the life-shortening internal destruction wrought on unsuspecting bystanders. How far did the effects of an EMP extend? How far could radiation spread in the ocean? How fast?

At the university, reassuring lights shone from un-curtained windows, behind which workers headed to their improvised office-floor beds, or sleeplessly waited for their first-light shift. The footpaths were deserted, and at the medical science building, the sentry was gone, seemingly replaced by the lab assistant in the unicorn t-shirt.

As Anna parked, the student took a step towards her car, but stopped when Anna got out.

"G'day," Anna said. "Mel, isn't it?"

"Oh, g'day. Hello, ma'am," Mel stammered.

Anna forced a smile. "Guess I'm not who you were waiting for. Life goes on, right? Even now. I need Dr Smilovitz. Is he still here?"

"He's in the new lab," Mel said.

"And where's that?"

Mel turned, and pointed through the doors. "Go inside, go right. Along the corridor, turn left, and listen for the music. She's working late."

"Dr Avalon? Ah."

"If Dr Smilovitz isn't there, he'll have gone to sleep in one of the offices. Go left, not right, and take the big set of stairs up. Offices are to the left at the top of the stairs. No, the right. Yeah, the right at the top."

"Ace, thanks," Anna said, giving the young woman another, less forced, smile. "A friend of mine gave me some advice once. In these dark hours, it seems more relevant than ever. Enjoy the minutes because you don't know how many hours you've got."

Mel gave the politician a puzzled, but polite, nod.

Anna, suddenly feeling twice her age, went inside. As embarrassing in hindsight as the conversation with Mel was, she felt genuinely calmer now. Beset by panic, she'd rushed from the Bunker, intent on doing something, anything, to regain some small measure of control over a situation at the very edge of comprehension. A nuclear detonation was still a tragedy, still a disaster, even now, but though the planes had been lost, many of the power-less ships would still be afloat. A rescue could be mounted. Somehow.

The blaring music provided an audible trail ending at a wide-windowed lab with a row of tables and an array of machines she couldn't identify let alone name. Behind those was a white-walled containment room with an airlock door. In one corner of the wide room, splayed in an armchair far too comfortable to be university-issue, and wearing a pair of ear defenders to block out the din, Leo Smilovitz tapped at a laptop. In the other corner, three tables were arranged in a U, and covered in notebooks, except for the space taken up by the speakers. Avalon, head twisting and rocking in time to the music, held a pen in each hand, both of which darted from one notebook to another, jotting annotations and amendments with an occasional pause to drum a punctuation to the beat.

"You've come to give us a hand with the unpacking?" Smilovitz asked, pulling off his ear defenders.

Anna shook her head. "No. I need your help."

"It's bad news?" Smilovitz asked, closing his laptop and standing up.

"What's bad news?" Avalon asked, glancing up from her notebooks. She looked at the clock, Anna's face, and turned the music off. "How bad?"

"A few hours ago, the pilots of three different planes reported seeing a mushroom cloud in the Pacific, somewhere between here and Hawaii, north of Kiribati. The message was transmitted to ships to planes, to ships to shore."

"You don't know if it was one mushroom cloud or three?" Avalon asked. "And you jumped to the conclusion it was a nuclear detonation, or three, rather than a water spout caused by the eruption of an underwater volcano."

"The pilots in a plane were blinded by the flash," Anna said. "They crashed. We've lost contact with a wing of passenger planes transporting soldiers to Hawaii. Thousands are missing."

"And what do you want me to do?" Avalon asked.

"To help," Anna said. "In our communications rooms, our bunker, they've been pulling the wires from the walls, and sent away anyone who has a clue how to plug them back in. We're relying on eyewitness accounts relayed by radio, and whatever transmissions we can eavesdrop on. It's a mess, and I was hoping you could help fix it, or at least translate the little data we've got."

"But *specifically*," Avalon said. "What do you want to know?"

"Was it one warhead detonating in the ocean," Anna said. "Was it three? More?"

"I can't help with that," Avalon said. "Leo?"

"I think I can," he said.

"Then do that and let me get back to work," Avalon said. She reached across, and turned the music back on.

Smilovitz gestured towards the door.

"You can help?" Anna asked when they were outside.

"Not from here, but yes," he said.

"It doesn't sound like an atmospheric burst, does it?" Anna asked. "That was what we feared. Six high-yield warheads, three in each hemisphere, detonated in the atmosphere to knock out the globe's electronics."

"That wasn't what *I* feared," Smilovitz said. "And the EMP will only knock out the devices without shielding. Each year, that number was decreasing. On the other hand, the absolute number of devices and machines increased exponentially."

"I wondered if it could have been a submarine accident," Anna said. "A reactor meltdown, maybe?"

"Unlikely on all counts," Smilovitz said. "By which I mean it's unlikely for a sub's reactor to melt down, or for that to occur close to the surface. It's more than unlikely for a warhead to detonate while in submarine's silo. If pilots were blinded by a flash, and if others saw a mushroom cloud… Are you sure this was at sea?"

"No," Anna said. "Honestly, I'm not. We think it was northeast of Tarawa Island in Kiribati, and there really isn't much land between there and Hawaii, but the location could have been misreported."

"At what altitude were the planes flying?"

"Again, I don't know," Anna said. "They relayed the message to some ships, who then reported it to some other planes, and ultimately back to a fighter patrol. Contact with the ships has been lost since. What if it was a mutiny aboard a sub? The captain tried to launch a missile without authorisation in order to obliterate a large concentration of the undead. The autodestruct destroyed the warhead while it was still in the tube, or shortly after launch."

"An autodestruct would destroy the missile, not the warhead," Smilovitz said. "Besides, how would anyone in a sub, or on land, know where the undead are most densely gathered without satellite data?"

"Fair dinkum, so no more guessing. I need you to come with me, back to Parliament House, to interpret what data we *do* have."

"Sure," he said. "But you're right, no more guessing. I don't know what's happened to your communications systems, but your bunker isn't the only place data comes into. Can we go to your government's geoscience department?"

"Do you mean Geoscience Australia? Why are we going there? And how do you know about nuclear warheads?"

"Do you have a car? Then I'll tell you as we drive."

Outside, her car had been joined by an army four-by-four in which were two black-uniformed Special Forces. Smilovitz paused when he saw them.

"It's okay," Anna said. "I think they're with me." She raised her voice. "Mr Lignatiev sent you to keep an eye on me? I'm okay, guys, but thanks. I need you to go back to Parliament House. Tell Mr Lignatiev we're gathering some more data from Geoscience Australia. But we'll be back at Parliament House in an hour. He'll understand."

As she got into her car, the four-by-four pulled away.

"Sorry. That brought back bad memories of Kazakhstan," Smilovitz said as he pulled on his seatbelt.

"Kazakhstan? Is that how you know about nuclear warheads?" Anna asked as she pulled away from the kerb.

"Originally, it was my area of expertise," Smilovitz said. "The long-term impact of radioactive decay with a specific interest in the mutations to flora. As a student, I dreamed of working near Chernobyl."

"Really? You *wanted* to go to Chernobyl?"

"Sure. To learn if, by accident from that disaster, we'd accidentally created a solution to one of the planet's many, many, man-made problems. Wildlife thrives there. Thrives and has changed, and is changing still."

"I thought you were an epidemiologist."

"That's Dr Avalon. You're aware we were part of the U.N.'s disaster mitigation team? We were tasked with identifying potential calamities before they became extinction-level events. Antibiotic-resistant bacteria, pressure-cooker volcanoes, ancient anthrax spores revealed in the melting permafrost, each day was a new adventure."

"Sure, yes, I'd read the reports. It was one of those areas of international cooperation I thought our species could be proud of. It's why you were in the far north of Canada, right? But if radiation is your area of expertise, how did you end up hunting for anthrax?"

"Dr Avalon," he said. "I met her in college."

"You were her teacher?"

"Her student," Smilovitz said.

"Really? Sorry, it's just you look older than her."

"I am, but only by a month. According to her, one night, tired of adolescence, my body decided to skip ahead to middle age. I'm not kidding. One morning, she actually said that to me. And I guess she was right. She got her first degree when she was fourteen, and was a professor by the time I enrolled. That's how we met. They had her teach a class to scare off the students not serious about *real* science. I was one of three that survived to the end of the semester."

"And because of her, you switched to biology?"

"Epidemiology. If she hears you call it biology, you'll get a lecture. With homework. Which she will *insist* you complete. No, I didn't switch, not exactly. While I was still working on my thesis, she'd taken the job with the U.N., mostly because it involved less human interaction than teaching. One week after she'd begun, half her colleagues were threatening to quit. She needed a buffer, and asked for me. She calls me her human interface."

"You put your own career on hold just to act as the Avalon-whisperer?" Anna asked.

He shrugged. "I was asked to save the world. How could I say no? It was important work. We stopped four pandemics the like of which the planet hasn't seen in millennia. Wish we could have stopped the fifth."

Anna nodded. From the way the two scientists interacted, it was obvious this man had abandoned his career goals for a romantic dream. But if he didn't mention it, nor would she. "Why are we going to Geoscience Australia?" she asked instead, slowing to detour around the unguarded barricade partially blocking the bridge over Lake Burley Griffin.

"Someone decided you could turn every patch of grass into a truck-garden," he said. "They didn't think to check what cables ran beneath. They severed the data-lines into the university."

"Sorry, that might be my fault. I authorised the agricultural science department to make use of any patch of grass in the city. I expected them to plant crops, but they're creating something far bigger. Every lawn is a different agricultural mini-lab."

"No, it's a good idea," Smilovitz said. "I talked with them, after I finished shouting. Long term, we'll all live in walled-in hamlets. We can have a few big farms in island-nations, and on this island-continent, but most humans, at least for a generation, will live in walled settlements."

"A generation? You think the zombies might live for twenty years?"

"The memory of them will, and so people will demand a basic level of personal security. If you, the government, wish to remain in control, that sense of security must be provided. We have to maximise every inch of soil, and every inch of sunlight. But I would have preferred they did it without cutting the cables. I put in a request to have them repaired, but I guess my turn will come after you guys in parliament. A couple of days ago, I took a tour of your government labs to see what equipment could be repurposed and what should go into storage. Your geoscience building was very interesting."

"Oh, so it was you who Hoa sent?" Anna asked. "I thought the report I received was unusually detailed. I'm reserving government buildings for office and factory space. As the number of refugees increase, the amount of work-space will, too. Time spent constructing walls and laying cables is time better spent producing something we need. But I don't want everything inside chucked onto the scrap heap. So what's there? Some kind of radio to speak to submarines?"

"Sadly, no. Have you heard of E.L.F.? It stands for extremely low frequency, and it is what the name suggests. It's a radio pulse in the three to three hundred Hertz range, which can penetrate seawater to a depth of a hundred metres. You need a truly massive facility. Miles across. China, India, Russia, and the U.S. are the only nations who use it, and all to send one-way signals to their submarines without them having to surface. Because of the physical size of the transmitter, a submarine can't respond in kind, but those nuclear powers all used it as part of their launch system failsafes. Which, by the way, were supremely misnamed. Command and control was a myth, the world over."

"Right. Sure," she said. "Where in the U.S.? Is it anywhere near Canada? Maybe British Columbia, the Saint Lawrence, or anywhere else we might ask General Yoon to investigate?"

"Michigan, I think. But I was expounding on your theory about a sub, and about how we can find out what's happening in the wider world. The internet was always more than social media and movies. You've shut down the data centres, and your power restrictions mean institutions are blacked out, but the cables haven't disappeared. Instruments are still gathering data, and some of them are still transmitting. We need to find somewhere that's still receiving."

"You're talking about weather monitoring? Wasn't that all done with satellites?"

"Not all of it, and I'm talking about earthquakes," he said.

Though the street lights had lit up Jerrabomberra Avenue as bright as day, the lights in the arcing car park were dark. So were the lights on the curved-roof complex, as big as a stadium. But as Anna got out of her car, a startlingly bright light dazzled her. Temporarily blinded, fear returned quicker than the flash. But as she raised her hand to shield her eyes, the light dropped.

"Sorry," a man said. "Just checking you're alive."

"No worries," Anna said, blinking away the white spots, and the man into focus. A neat grey beard edged with white. A face lined with age and worry. Flashlight, slung rifle, a green jacket which wasn't military, but wearing dress trousers with a razor-sharp crease and shoes polished to a mirror.

"Advance and be recognised," he said, before raising the beam again. "Hang on, I know you. You're the politician who said everyone deserved cake."

"Anna Dodson," she said, again blinking away the bright light. "G'day. Are you the guard here?"

"I'm the night-time patrol for everything between here and the caravan park," he said.

"Have you seen any undead?" she asked.

"Tonight? No. But I've heard a few shots from the wall. Other than a few teens, you're the first people I've seen since shift-change. Do you want to go inside? I've got the keys."

"Please," she said, as he went to his truck to collect them. The vehicle wasn't army. It wasn't even police. It was a flatbed road-maintenance vehicle, on the back of which had been rigged four spotlights.

"I'll let you in, ma'am, and I'll wait out here for you."

"There's no need," she said.

"I'm Sergeant Troy Brown," he said. "Retired, re-enlisted. Came to Canberra to help my daughter with her first child, and that's what I did, and it's what I'm doing now. She's a big fan of yours. We both are. She wouldn't approve if anything happened to you. Do you have a torch? Here, take mine. It's as dark as a midwinter coal mine in there."

"Thank you," she said. "We won't be long."

"Why did you want everyone to eat cake?" Smilovitz asked as they stepped inside.

"My opponent, the incumbent, made a quip about me being out of touch with what my constituents wanted," Anna said. "He suggested I should quit the campaign because the only advice I'd ever give someone was to eat cake. He even called me Marie-Antoinette, I assume because he thought I wouldn't know who that was. I explained the causes of the French Revolution, and finished by saying that, a quarter of a millennium later we all deserved three reliable meals a day, and we deserved cake, too. It became a meme, and that helped me win. My constituents still send me cake. Or they did. The sergeant wasn't entirely correct; looks like the back-up lights are on," she added, shining her light around the partially lit vestibule. "Do we need to find the breakers?"

"Nope, the terminals we need are always kept on, so they'll be on the same circuit as the emergency lights. We want the basement." He fished out a penlight. "I always carry a spare dozen of these. Avalon's always losing them."

"Oh, so you're carrying a torch for her?" she asked, as innocently as she could.

Finding the stairs was as easy as following the signs. But once in the basement, in a below-ground corridor with only an occasional illuminated *Exit* sign as a guide, finding the correct set of offices took longer. Only after Smilovitz opened the door did Anna think of the question she should have asked before they'd driven out here.

"How long will this take?" she asked.

"An hour, maybe two," he said.

"I should have asked," she said. "Will you need passwords?"

"I've got those already. Got a copy when I was determining what equipment to mothball," he said, already going inside, taking a cover off a computer that had to be at least as old as her.

"Is there anything else you need?" she asked, as he removed the dustcover from the next machine, a computer so new it still had a transparent sheet covering the flat screen.

"Just a bit of time."

"Then I'll head back to Parliament House, check in there. I'll ask the sergeant outside to wait for you, and drive you there when you're finished."

"Hmm? Oh, sure," he said, his attention already focused on the screen.

Outside, in the dark corridor, she leaned against the wall. Aiming the flashlight down and her eyes up, she marshalled her thoughts. Panic had been replaced by fear, but that had been her unwelcome companion since the outbreak. Nervous exhaustion had popped in for a visit, bringing distraction, confusion, and an unwelcome disorientation. Days were merging into one another, while hours raced like minutes and seconds took as long as years.

This new disaster was in the Pacific, not in Australia. While some kind of rescue operation should be attempted, they must remain focused on the wider goal, on resupplying General Yoon, on evacuating Japan, on reinforcing Singapore, and establishing a defensive line across the Malaysia-Thailand border. As tragic as the loss of the planes was, it truly was only one more small tragedy that shouldn't be allowed to become an ocean of confusion. Yes, when they knew what had happened, they'd have the PM record a public statement for broadcast tomorrow, deploy a rescue operation, but otherwise make sure that the work didn't slow because the zombies wouldn't.

She'd managed two more steps towards the exit when a yell came from behind.

"Ms Dodson!" Smilovitz called, sprinting from the office. "Ms— Oh." He stumbled to a halt.

"What is it?" she asked.

"You need to come and see," he said.

"Seismographs and ocean buoys," he said, pointing at the screen. "That data comes here. You know what a seismograph is?"

"Sure. Measures an earthquake."

"And we use them to monitor nuclear testing," he said. "If we know where the test site is, and can extrapolate dissipation, we can back-work the size of the blast. North Korea, yes? Okay. This is an old system. *Very* old. Designed for monitoring undersea volcanic activity, and now superseded. It's not accurate, but it's still useful. Or it should have been. We know of at least one detonation, and assume it was at sea, but we want the specific location. In the Pacific, a ring of at-sea weather buoys form part of the tsunami detection system. While a satellite uplink is their primary method of data transmission, they also use a simple radio system to transmit data from one to another. That creates a circuit, if you like. If the circuit is broken for a sustained period, the code checks the wave height on the closest active buoys, and if it's raised, an alarm is sounded. A signal is sent by satellite, but also by radio from buoy to buoy and back to shore."

"Okay. So?"

"The weather buoys are gone, and this blast was off the scale. That's not hyperbole, simply a factual statement."

"More slowly. More details. Please," she said.

"This is bad," he said. "A U.S. *Ohio*-class submarine carries twenty-four Trident missiles. The number and force of warheads can vary, but the rule of thumb is that each missile has four one-hundred-kiloton warheads. Four hundred kilotons per missile. Nine thousand six hundred kilotons, or nine-point-six megatons per submarine. By comparison, the 1883 eruption of Krakatoa was two-*hundred*-megatons."

"You lost me at the end there."

"The force of this explosion was more than all the warheads on a single submarine being detonated at once. More than twenty submarines, and the U.S. only has fourteen *Ohio*-class subs."

"This was *all* their submarines? And other submarines? Whose?"

"I'm saying forget submarines," he said. "Three mushroom clouds were witnessed? This data suggests the blast was a lot bigger than that. Hundreds of warheads. A thousand. I can't give you a precise figure with this data here. But even if I could, it would only be an estimate of the yield from which I could back-work the number of warheads. That would give a range, not an absolute figure. Do you understand?"

"Not really. How did this happen?" she asked. "Why? Is there another explanation?"

"Sure, but not a plausible one if our first piece of data is the sighting of three mushroom clouds. The seismological readings from a volcano-triggered earthquake are very different to a nuclear detonation, thus precluding a natural explanation."

"Are you saying that the U.S. government just dumped its entire nuclear arsenal into the Pacific?"

"Detonated, and not necessarily all of it, and not necessarily the U.S. But with that volume of warheads, it's almost certainly either the U.S. or Russia. We know China was increasing the size of its arsenal, but I don't think even they could have secretly amassed so many so quickly."

"There is no Chinese government anymore," she said. "Not in Beijing. Nor is there a Moscow. No Paris. No London, Delhi, Karachi, or Jerusalem. And no Washington. They appointed a man called Trowbridge as president, but I don't think he was given the nuclear football. I've no idea where that is, and doubt the people in Guam would know, either. Guam! Is there anything else you can do here?"

"I need..." He looked around as if seeking answers. "This is the point where I would call our local liaison. If they couldn't help, I'd call the Secretary General and get them to call your prime minister and so on until I had access to the equipment I need. More precise equipment will give us a more precise answer. There should be some, still active, here in the city. I need to know where the missiles came from. Which nation, at least."

"You mean, like me, you want more data," she said. "Do you know where we can find the equipment you want?"

"If I did, we'd be there, not here," he said.

"Fine. Come with me. You can inform the rest of the cabinet. And the prime minister. And you can tell us what we need to do next."

"I've no idea," he said. "I dealt with prevention, and most recently in epidemiology."

"Which is a lot more than me." She took his arm and hurried him into the corridor. "Are you certain this wasn't a naval battle?"

"I can imagine a scenario where a crippled submarine might launch a single warhead to destroy a fleet, but as I said, this was far more than one warhead."

"So it wasn't an act of war," Anna said. "You don't detonate hundreds of warheads in the middle of nowhere to… well, to defeat anyone. Zombies or people."

"No, you're correct," he said. "This wasn't an act of war. It was an act of disarmament. That's all I can think of to explain it, but there has to be a logical reason behind it."

"I haven't been in politics long, but even I know that's not always true."

Her imagination cycling through one scenario after another, each more implausible than the last, she led him upstairs. With each step, she picked up her pace until, when she reached the partially lit entrance lobby, she was running for the door. She skidded to a halt as she reached it. Pushing, then pulling, but neither had any effect.

"It's locked," she said, giving it a shake, then leaned forward, cupping her hands against the glass.

"Did the sergeant lock us in?" Smilovitz asked.

"I can't see him," she said.

"He's having a senior moment," Smilovitz said. "Locked the door when he went to the washroom."

"He's not *that* old," she said. "Never mind, we'll look for another door."

"He said they'd all been locked," Smilovitz said. "I assume there's no hard-line to Parliament House, or to a barracks?"

"Good point," Anna said, shining her light across the vestibule in search of a phone. "There are lines going into Parliament House, but I don't know the number. When they began rebuilding the switchboard, the numbers changed. But I do know the number for my department. Hoa always has someone on duty." Behind the reception desk was an old-fashioned wire-to-wall phone. "But this building isn't connected to the new network," she said, putting the receiver down. "I should have brought a radio. And the escort."

"We'll break the lock," Smilovitz said. "Do you have a gun?"

"Nope, didn't bring one of those either."

Dr Smilovitz shone his torch on a fire extinguisher. "I left mine back in the lab, too. It's hard to get in the habit of always carrying it. That extinguisher will do."

"I'm sure that glass is reinforced," she said, shining her torch onto the doors, then across the reception area and its wide windows, then down a dark corridor to the left. Lining one side of the hallway, between office doors, were display cases, containing examples of every rock in Australia. But above those, a dimly backlit blue arrow pointed towards an exit. "We could try a fire door."

"There's no time," Smilovitz said. "Besides, I wasn't planning to simply smash the lock. A pressurised container makes a decent torpedo, assuming you don't mind the mess? In case it ricochets we'll need some cover," he added. "And I'll need a—"

A loud clatter came from the corridor and the fire escape to the left of the doors. Anna, who'd been shining her light around the lobby in the hunt for a sturdier defensive bunker than the flimsy reception desk, spun around, pointing her light towards the sound. The light glinted off the glass cabinets, and glittered on some of the specimens inside, and illuminated the doors to meeting rooms and offices.

"Maybe we *should* find a different exit," Smilovitz said.

"Or the main breakers, get the lights on," Anna said. "I think they were—"

Even as she began to turn, an even louder clatter came from the corridor, followed by a thump and a crash of breaking glass. A man had lurched out of an open office door, and into an exhibit display-case. He still had the razor-sharp crease in his trousers and the mirror-shine on his shoes, while the green jacket was zipped up tight. But Sergeant Troy Brown's face was twisted, distorted. His eyes were wide, and his grey beard was flecked with blood from where he'd smashed his face into the glass.

"Zombie," Anna said.

"Definitely," Smilovitz said. He flipped the extinguisher, blasting the undead sentry with a jet of pressurised foam, before backing up a step. "Worth a try."

The zombie, now drenched and dripping, lurched towards them, swiping its arms into the display case.

"Got any other ideas?" Anna asked.

The zombie slipped on the now foam-speckled floor, landing hard, on its back, with a thump.

"See, my hypothesis wasn't completely disproved," Smilovitz said.

But even as it landed, the zombie kept moving, rolling, twisting until it was on all fours. Scrabbling on hand and knee and occasionally foot, kicking foam into spray, it lurched forward while they backed up.

Smilovitz blasted it again. And again.

"Get back!" Anna said. "You're not even—"

The zombie got both knees beneath its body, managing to launch itself forward, arms flailing, but legs straight. It lacked the coordination to turn it into a proper leap, landing chin-first with a sickeningly loud crack. Both its outstretched arms were close enough for its hands to curl around Leo's foot. The zombie tugged, pulling itself forward while pulling the scientist off-balance. Leo fell, just as hard as the zombie, landing on his back. The fire extinguisher flew from his hands while the zombie used its own to grab and haul itself up his legs.

Anna grabbed the extinguisher as the scientist kicked, pushed with his hands, trying to get distance between himself and the zombie dripping gore and blood from its broken mouth.

"Don't move!" Anna said.

"Are you kidding?" Smilovitz replied, still kicking.

"No!"

Holding the extinguisher by handle and nozzle, Anna thrust it down on the zombie's head. The extinguisher bounced off, while the undead man's skull slammed, once more, into the hard polished concrete. Despite the thunderclap snap of cracking bone, its hands still clawed, ripping at Smilovitz's trousers.

Anna raised the extinguisher above her head and swung. Skin tore. Bone smashed. Blood arced. The zombie spasmed. Its arms flew out and its head lolled forward as the scientist finally scrabbled out of reach. But the inhuman monster wasn't dead. Its arms flew sideways, almost flapping against the floor while its legs kicked, swimming, dancing, knees and toes smashing into the concrete.

"Fascinating," Smilovitz said.

"Not now, Doc," Anna said, and swung the extinguisher down again. This time it impacted against an already fractured skull. Brain and blood flew across the lobby, across her. But the zombie, finally, was still.

"There's a washroom there," Smilovitz said.

"Hang on," Anna said. "We need the keys. I can't see a wound. Won't find it now. But he got infected, which means more zombies out there, in the streets. Must have come in here, locked the doors, but turned..." She trailed off, walked into the bathroom, still thinking.

"Any keys on him?" Smilovitz asked, following her in.

"No," she said, opening the cleaning closet and pulling out a bottle of bleach. "And no gun. Must have dropped them. You're immune, aren't you?"

"I ran a test, and I'd call this another," he said. "So almost certainly, yes. And I can test you when we get back to the lab."

"We don't have time," she said, drenching her hands with bleach, then rinsing them in the sink. "And we don't have time to find where he dropped the keys. So if you really think you can break down that front door, go find another fire extinguisher."

Chapter 21 - Bad News Loves Company
The Bunker, Parliament House

"Strewth, you look like you've been dragged sideways through a blackthorn jungle," O.O. said, when Anna and Smilovitz entered the Bunker. The description equally matched the communications centre. More panelling had been removed, more wires were exposed, but the screens were still dark. The smell of burning plastic had been added to that of sweat and fear, while a bank of lights above the middle of the room had gone dark.

"It was zombies," Anna said, but before her frustration could boil over, Erin Vaughn and Ian Lignatiev approached.

"Zombies? How many?" Lignatiev asked.

"We only saw one; the sentry guarding Geoscience Australia," Anna said. "He was also guarding a campsite which I know was overfull with refugee-tourists. We should send a patrol to investigate."

"I'll take care of it," Lignatiev said.

"No, send some of these conscripts," Anna said. "Because zombies aren't even close to our biggest problem. Leo needs to update you. And the prime minister. We should tell her as well."

The prime minister was in the War Room, seemingly engrossed in a stack of printed papers.

"Prime Minister, we have news," Anna said. "Leo?"

"Some scientific equipment is still functioning, and sending data back to the city," Smilovitz said. "It's bad news. Very bad." They'd left the door open. Outside, in the main chamber, the dozen uniformed personnel had stopped to listen. "This is only a preliminary interpretation," Smilovitz continued, "but it appears as if multiple warheads detonated in the Pacific within a relatively short time frame, and in close proximity. Maybe a thousand warheads."

"It's over," Vaughn whispered, collapsing into a chair.

Anna turned to the PM who stared ahead, vacant-eyed.

"Do you hear that?" O.O. said. "Dame Nellie's begun to sing, but will she give us an encore?"

"How much immediate danger are we in?" Lignatiev asked.

"None," Smilovitz said. "Which is an under-exaggeration worthy of an Oscar, but it's the end of the scale you need to focus on. At least in the short term. In the medium term, we'll have fallout and radioactive contamination of the oceans to deal with. Right now, it looks, initially, as if the U.S. or Russia detonated their arsenal in the ocean."

"You said this was a preliminary interpretation?" Lignatiev asked. "When can you give us more details?"

Smilovitz shrugged. "In time, and I can't be more precise until I know what equipment I have available."

"I'll spread word to my to men," Lignatiev said, "and have a team search for that zombie." He marched out, Vaughn close behind.

"Ma'am?" Anna asked, turning to the prime minister, but Bronwyn Wilson was, once again, staring into space. Anna turned to Smilovitz. "Leo, can you see if anything can be done with any of that communications gear? If not, we'll have to relocate."

"Somewhere deeper underground would get my vote," O.O. said.

Anna ignored him, and went to find some clean clothes.

She had many spare sets upstairs, mostly provided by Hoa Nguyen who insisted that it was important for leaders to appear professional in manner and dress. But she didn't want to stray too far from the prime minister, not when it would mean leaving O.O. as the sole politician close enough to whisper in Wilson's ear.

Ignoring the corridor leading to the senior politician's private quarters, and where she presumably had an unclaimed room of her own, she ventured down the other hallway.

The armoury door was open, the lock disconnected, the racks of weapons, from nightsticks to shotguns, all long gone, distributed among those sent to the outback or coast. But in the stockroom next door, in a room gloriously well-stocked with disinfectant, were four unopened crates of clothing. The underwear and t-shirts came in many different sizes, though ranging from voluminous to elephantine. The trousers and windbreakers, in one-size-fits-no-one, came with a clasped drawstring at ankle, waist, and sleeves. They'd do for now.

Indulging in the luxury of a wash in the utilitarian bathroom, she stared at herself in the mirror. She certainly didn't look the part of a cabinet minister. Maybe she should have gone upstairs. The clothes in her office were all smart-and-severe outfits in case she had to appear on the national television programme. Which someone should do soon. *Very* soon. Before radio rumours initiated a panic. Not her, but also not the prime minister.

Since her appointment, Bronwyn Wilson had been a broken reed, drowning under the flood of bad news. Gone was the self-assured political veteran, replaced by a walking bundle of uncomprehending indecision. Erin Vaughn would be a competent and reassuring replacement. Or maybe Ian Lignatiev, but only if he could be persuaded to swap his uniform for a suit. Ian *or* Erin, but what should they say? Perhaps the words didn't matter as much as showing that the government, increasingly reduced, was still here.

She grabbed a set of clothes for Leo, and made her way back into the command centre, where, wonderfully and unexpectedly, a map of the world now illuminated the large wall.

"You got the big-screen working!" Anna said.

"Not quite," Smilovitz said, tapping at a tablet. "Think of the map as the screensaver. There's no input yet." He put the laptop down and grabbed a toolbox. "But give me a half hour, and I'll show you the world. Or some of it."

"Where are the other engineers?" Anna asked, realising that most of them had gone and Dr Smilovitz appeared to be working alone. One sentry guarded the door, while four others sat at workstations, headphones on, hand-scribing what they heard. Otherwise, and other than the PM in the War Room, the C.O.M.S. was empty.

"They weren't engineers, and they weren't helping," Smilovitz said. "What's the name of the guy in uniform?"

"Ian. Ian Lignatiev, he's the Minister for Defence."

"Right, he sent some to hunt for that zombie, and took the rest with him. His… I'm guessing it's his wife?"

"Erin Vaughn, the attorney general. They're not married. Well, not to each other, but yes, they're a couple. Worst-kept secret in the A.C.T."

"She said something about going to a radio station. I guess to put out a statement."

"Oh, that's a relief," Anna said. "I was just thinking someone needed to do that."

"Right, but why go to a radio station?" Smilovitz asked. "Don't you guys have a press room upstairs?"

Anna waved her hands to take in the exposed wires. "Fixing that will be your next job, after you've repaired all this. You really don't need any help?"

"No offence, but people mucking about with circuits they don't understand is how you got into this mess in the first place." He pointed to the four people listening to headphones, and writing on notepads. "I've got those four transcribing radio reports. We're noting times and locations, and getting a feel for who is still trying to talk to us. From the places that aren't, we'll learn the boundaries of the EMP. Data should be coming online in about ten minutes. I could use some analysts in the next few hours."

"Like the grad students you had at the university?"

"They'd do, sure. For a start. More would be better. Mel is exactly the woman we need now. She knows the academics, and they'll know whom to enlist. But right now I need to finish this."

"I'll fetch her and the others, and Dr Avalon," she said. Halfway to the door, Oswald Owen sauntered over.

"It's like being a vegan at the corporate barbie," O.O. said. "You've nothing to do, but you can't really leave."

"If you want to go, no one will stop you," Anna said.

"Nah, because everyone arrived together on the company bus," he said, developing his metaphor. "But there'll be clearing up to do soon. I always was a dab hand with a broom."

"That I'd like to see," she said. "But considering the circumstances, a shovel would be more appropriate."

"Ha!" he barked. "I knew you were hiding a sense of humour somewhere."

She'd been serious, not joking, but just nodded, suspecting the man was already drunk. Thinking Oswald, at least, wasn't making the situation worse, she headed through the airlock, and upstairs. While she couldn't protect herself from a nuclear detonation overhead, she didn't want to spend her last few minutes trapped in an elevator disabled by an EMP.

Outside, the sun had risen, and the black-clad Special Forces had gone. But two familiar figures were arguing with the trio of camouflaged conscripts refusing them entry. One was her assistant, Hoa Nguyen. The other, she'd known all her life.

"Dad!" Anna said, hugging her father. "Oh, Dad, I'm so glad to see you but we've had some cataclysmic news."

"I don't like to add to it," Mick said. "But Tess and me were flying over the coast a few hours ago, just after dawn. Yesterday, when we reached the natural gas refinery, we found the lady running the place had built a gallows. We took custody of the prisoners scheduled for their last dance, but as we were flying to the coast, we picked up a distress call. Bunch of kids, mostly, trapped near a new mine. I left Tess and the convicts, took the kids, flew to the refugee camp, switched planes, grabbed Captain Bruce Hawker of the SASR, and returned for Tess. We were above the coast at dawn." He laid his hand on her shoulder, while his lips moved silently as he searched for a way to soften his words. With a shake of his head, he gave up. "A tsunami has swamped the refugee camps."

"A tsunami? I... oh. Where?" Anna asked.

"We reached the coast near Ocean Shores and flew south to Ballina, but the runway had been wrecked before the wave arrived. Told the planes with sufficient fuel to head to the west coast, and led the rest here."

"An hour after dawn?" Anna asked, glancing at the sky. "What time is it?"

"That was two and a half hours ago," Mick said. "Maybe two hours forty minutes. We were travelling at nine-fifty kilometres an hour with a favourable tail wind. I upgraded to a C-17," he added. "Now there's a yarn, longer than we have time for."

"It's later than I realised," Anna said, again glancing at the sky, but then turned her gaze to a lamp above the footpath which, despite the rising sun, hadn't been switched off. "But the lights are still on. Captain Hawker is at the airport? And Tess is there, too?"

"And a few civilians, pilots, and ground-crew," Mick said. "Some refugees from the Pacific who were aboard the planes which followed me back. I've put them in quarantine. They're being watched."

"Quarantine, of course. And how many planes are there, Dad? How much fuel?"

"Depends how far you want us to go. But I can guess," he added. "You want me to return to the coast?"

Anna turned to Hoa who, up until now, had remained silent but listening. "We still don't know precisely what's happened, but it's bad. Very bad. We think thousands of nuclear warheads were detonated together in the remote Pacific. Don't ask me why, or where. Not yet. But that must have caused the wave. We have to mount a rescue operation and there's no point trying to do it from inside the Bunker."

"Ma'am?" Hoa asked. "Are things... okay down there?"

"They're chaotic," Anna said. "The same principle applies as before. People must be transported to somewhere they won't be at risk of infection, dehydration, or starvation. Hoa, you'll have to adapt our plans for overseas refugees. Dad, we need to know how bad the damage is on the coast. And on the west and north coasts, too. Can you send pilots to find out? We'll need runways so we can ferry the people out by air, and then... by then, by tomorrow, we'll have a better idea of what just happened."

"No worries," Mick said. "I can manage that. Can you manage everything here?"

"I'll have to," Anna said.

"Be careful, Anna. Remember rule one," her father said.

"Same to you," she said, and went back inside.

In the command centre, Dr Smilovitz finger-pecked at a tablet until he saw her enter. He hurried to the four transcribing conscripts, taking their notepads, and met her halfway to the War Room.

"I'm ready to give you a preliminary briefing," he said.

"Go on then," O.O. said, slinking out of the shadows. "What's the damage report?"

"It's worse than you think," Anna said. "I've just heard from the airport. Come on, Leo, the prime minister should hear this."

She led him, with O.O. slouching behind, into the War Room. Bronwyn Wilson, eyes on a map of South America, didn't look up. While Erin Vaughn, who'd returned when Anna had been outside, nearly dropped her pad as they entered.

"What now?" Vaughn asked.

"We've more bad news," Anna said. "My father was upstairs. Apparently the sentries wouldn't let him in. A few hours ago, he flew above the eastern coast of New South Wales, near the refugee camps above Ballina. The force of the nuclear detonations created a tsunami."

"A tsunami?" Wilson asked. "We should evacuate. We should leave Canberra before it arrives."

"Ah, no, Prime Minister," Vaughn said with admirable patience. "We're a hundred and fifty kilometres inland, and six hundred metres above sea level."

"Should we go upstairs to the roof, in case?" the PM asked.

"The wave has already hit," Anna said, addressing Erin Vaughn as much as the PM. "I sent my father back to the airport. He's with the flying doctor service. He'll begin organising the evacuation of the coast with help from Captain Hawker of the SAS and Deputy Commissioner Tess Qwong. I can't think of anyone here better qualified."

"No, that was a good idea. Quick thinking," Vaughn said. "They'll send us an eye-witness account?"

"Within a few hours. About five, I think," Anna said. "Once we have it, we can adapt accordingly. But he's already sent word over the radio for planes to redirect here and to other airfields inland."

"More refugees?" the prime minister asked. "Do we have room?"

"Yes, ma'am," Anna said, feeling her patience straining to breaking point. "We were preparing Australia for the arrival of tens of millions of refugees, remember?"

"Good, thank you," Vaughn said. "Keep us updated."

"Sorry, no," Smilovitz said. "That's not even the beginning of the disaster. My initial assessment was incorrect. I can give you an updated, and more accurate, summary."

"Fine. Bring it up on screen," the prime minister said.

"Yeah, no, that'll require an hour inputting data into a graphics programme I've never used before," Smilovitz said, echoes of Dr Avalon clear in his caustic reply. "The main impact site was two hundred kilometres east of Kiribati. That nation is gone."

"Which nation?" the PM asked.

"Kiribati," O.O. said, quietly. "Go on, mate, tell us the rest."

"Tuvalu, Niue, they are also gone," Smilovitz said. "Effectively swept away. Submerged. Samoa has been wiped out."

"Samoa?" Anna asked. "But that's where the fleet was going. Where the Americans had flown troops and equipment."

Dr Smilovitz nodded. "The waters will subside, and there will be some survivors. This is just preliminary data, and it's third or fourth-hand radio reports, so it could be exaggerated. However, the news of Samoa came via a weather station on Mount Fiji, relayed to an overhead aircraft. That plane was out of fuel and had nowhere to land. Before it crashed in the ocean, it radioed what it had heard to any ships still receiving."

"Should we mount a rescue?" Wilson asked. "We should mount a rescue, shouldn't we?"

"He's not finished," O.O. said. "You're not, are you, mate?"

"Other reports from other planes confirm the tsunami," Smilovitz said. "The islands took the worst of it, which means, I think, relatively little damage from the waves to Australia and New Zealand."

"The ocean took a bite out of our coast," O.O. said. "You're saying that counts as relatively little?"

"Yes," Smilovitz said. "It could have been worse, but only numerically speaking, and only for us. This was an omnidirectional event. Like ripples in a pond. Australia was shielded, to an extent, by the island nations east of here. That *were* east of here. Hawaii had no such good fortune. And then there are the Americas."

"What about the Americas?" the prime minister asked. "We need some satellite imagery. Why aren't there satellite pictures?"

"The Americas would have been hit with a wave similar to that which hit our east coast?" Vaughn asked, ignoring the prime minister.

"And right now, we can only estimate the devastation," Smilovitz said.

"What about Guam?" Anna asked. "Is there any word from the American leadership?"

"They took some damage from the tsunami," Smilovitz said. "And this is where I get to the bad news."

"What you just said was bad enough," O.O. said.

"The seismograph was troubling me," Smilovitz said. "I'd like more time with the data. I thought it was one event, the warheads detonating in one place at roughly the same time. I now think it was more than one event."

"There were other bombs?" Anna asked.

"And closer," Smilovitz said. "If this was a targeted, planned strike, it would have been timed for the warheads to detonate at the same time. Instead, the explosions were spread out, both in time and geography. At present, it appears as if the first warhead in the primary impact zone detonated an hour before the last. Most detonations do appear to have clustered together, but again, I'll need more time to assess the data properly."

"You've lost me now, mate," O.O. said. "Try it again in plain English."

"There were other detonations afterwards," Smilovitz said. "Mostly individual events. Single missiles, though perhaps with multiple warheads. But in other locations, far from that first oceanic impact site."

"Are you saying there were detonations here in Australia?" O.O. asked.

"It would explain some of the disruption to communications," Smilovitz said.

"That's neither confirmation nor denial," Vaughn said.

Smilovitz shrugged. "It doesn't help that you recruited a bunch of app-developers who couldn't tell the difference between a fibre-optic cable and a power cord to dismantle a state of the art command and control centre. Actual data, *real* data, is scarce. I'm collating eyewitness accounts and inferring from what damage and disruption there's been, and from the information we're *not* receiving. The EMP, rather the *many* pulses, would have knocked out any unshielded circuits."

"You're saying we don't know if a nuke's been dropped on Australia?" O.O. said. "Tell me that's the last of the bad news?"

"Yes, but no, that's not the bad news, either," Smilovitz said. "The bad news, the worst news, came from Guam. A plane flew overhead, couldn't land because the runway was wrecked, so had to turn around, but they got a report from the ground. The fleet has gone."

"Which fleet?" the PM asked.

"You mean the combined U.S. and allied fleet?" Vaughn asked. "Two aircraft carriers, their combined support vessels, and the civilian transports travelling with them? The tsunami destroyed them?"

"No," Smilovitz said. "The fleet was destroyed by an atomic blast. A single missile, probably launched from a submarine." He glanced at the notepad. "Right now, that's all we know, except that the fleet was deliberately targeted and deliberately sunk. With no satellites to aid in targeting, the submarine would have to, initially, have been within visual range." He held up a hand. "There's one other incident you need to be aware of. A mushroom cloud was seen in the Himalayas."

"In China, India, or Pakistan?" O.O. asked.

"Uncertain," Smilovitz said.

"So the initial, large blast at sea could have been some kind of accident?" O.O. asked. "Nothing else makes sense. But to sink the carrier fleet, that has to be an act of war."

"By who?" Anna asked.

"It truly is the end of everything," the PM whispered.

"It's on-going," Smilovitz said. "That is the most important conclusion to draw. For whatever reason this began, it isn't over yet."

"No, it's not," O.O. said, and made for the door.

"Where are you going?" Anna asked.

"To find jet fuel," O.O. said. "Sounds like we'll need it."

"I guess he means a drink," Smilovitz said as the portly politician stormed across the near empty C.O.M.S.

"The capitals are all gone," Vaughn said. "And the leaderships with them, as far as *we* know, *and* as far as their ambassadors know. We have no idea who is in charge of the nuclear buttons, or even where the new leaders are. But you're implying this will peter out?"

Smilovitz shrugged. "Time will tell."

"Should we relocate to the airport?" Anna asked. "You said you're getting all this information relayed, ultimately, from planes."

"Not all the information," Smilovitz said. "And I can bring more systems back online. But I need more help. Did you speak to Flo?"

"Dr Avalon?" she asked, and realised it was the first time she'd heard him call her anything but her surname. That only doubled her anxiety. "No. I'll go and speak to her now. I'll be back within the hour."

"The worst *has* to be over," Vaughn said, following Anna from the War Room to the airlock-doors.

"We've said that before," Anna said.

"But how many more missiles can there be left?" Vaughn asked.

"Okay, yes," Anna said. "But once the war is over, there's the fallout." She paused to look back at the War Room where the prime minister, once more, stared vacantly at the wall. "We have to do something about Bronwyn. She's in no state to give a broadcast to the nation."

"Certainly not live, but we can record it," Erin said.

"And if not, you should give it," Anna said. "You or Ian."

"I'll take her to her room, let her get some rest," Erin said. "But I went to the tower earlier. I've recorded something we can put out when the time comes."

"I think that time is now," Anna said.

Chapter 22 - The Fragility of Unicorns
Australian National University

It was surreal stepping outside into a magical day where summer's memory met winter's promise. A dense bulwark of clouds held back the sun, while the temperature had fled, leaving in its stead the usually glorious prospect of rain. But it was utterly spoiled by the sight of Oswald Owen. He leaned against the police patrol car, a cigar in one hand, a glass in the other, and an octagonal bottle on the car's roof.

"Fancy a snifter?" he asked. "It's brandy. French, sadly. But beggars can't be picky at the end of the world."

"It's early, but even if it were late, we're working," she said.

"Not yet, we're not," he said. "The real work won't begin for a few hours. When it does, it won't stop for weeks. I told the factories to double production until further notice."

"Production of what?"

"Everything," he said calmly, as if he relished the challenges ahead. "I triaged the list, identified the less critical projects. When we need resources or labour, or cannon fodder, we can draw from them. I've sent word to increase our output of aviation fuel, but word doesn't travel fast these days. The planes will run out before everyone can be rescued, but hopefully not before they land."

"So what do we do about it?" she asked.

"Like you said, make more shovels," he replied, billowing a plume of smoke as dark and portentous as the storm clouds above.

"I'm fetching Dr Avalon and her assistants from the university," she said. "They can help with data analysis. But unless you've a better suggestion, and as long as information is being flown in, we're better running the government from the airport."

"Give me a chair and a glass, and I can work anywhere," he said. "You better take this." He reached into his pocket and pulled out a small pistol, a government-issue 9mm.

"No, I don't need it, and I don't want it," she said. "If zombies breach the walls, the sirens will sound."

"They didn't last night," he said. "Only five of us left, and I don't know if we can count the prime minister. This is the calm at the eye of the storm. The worst is only a breeze away."

To end the conversation, she took the gun, leaving him to wallow. It was only when she reached her car that she remembered there had been an octagonal bottle in the bathroom where Aaron Bryce had committed suicide. Such an oddly shaped bottle couldn't be a coincidence. A bribe from a lobbyist? Probably. But when she climbed into the car, keeping her hands low, she took out the gun and ejected the magazine. It was loaded. Oddly, that only left her feeling even more unsettled.

Replaying her conversation with O.O., and his previous comments during the night, kept her distracted as she drove through the near-empty city. Something he'd said, or done, or not done, had caught at the back of her mind. But what?

As she drove into the university, she was forced to stop by a gang of labourers hauling giant corrugated sheets across the road.

"Let her pass! Clear the road!" a spry man called to the group, stopping those on the footpath while hurrying on those who'd already begun to cross. The man's Scottish accent, redolent of the Isle of Skye on which he'd been born, was as familiar as his face. Liam Dalgleish, a union man from the tips of his arthritic fingers to the top of his egg-smooth head, was an increasingly valuable ally in these strange days. As the workers cleared the road, Dalgleish came over to her window.

"G'day, Liam," she said, bracing herself for the lecture that was his usual way of beginning a conversation.

"Good day to you, Minister," Dalgleish said, both cordially and formally. "A lot of the lads and lasses are talking about a peculiar rumour they heard this morning on the radio. Not on the official channel, but one of those private stations broadcasting from the bush."

"There's been an accident in the Pacific near Hawaii," Anna said quickly. "We'll broadcast an official statement as soon as we have more specific details."

"What kind of accident?" Dalgleish asked.

"A tsunami," Anna said. "There's been some flooding along our eastern coast, and some ships are without power out at sea. A rescue operation is underway, but we may need to redirect resources later. Until then, it's work as usual."

He nodded, satisfied. "Make sure to keep us informed," he said.

She nodded back, and drove on, to the lab.

As she got out of her car, a Humvee full of black uniformed Special Forces drove slowly by. She gave them a semi-formal wave, and received a salute in return. The sentry wasn't outside the lab. The conscripts must have already been redeployed, replaced by this roving patrol.

Inside, as the door swung closed behind her, she paused. The air-conditioning wasn't on, but the power was. Away from chaos of the Bunker, her mind finally cleared. The lights were still on. There'd been no EMP near Canberra. No bomb. But, broadly, it didn't matter if there was. During the last three weeks, the loss of their supposedly ever-reliable communications network had forced them to decentralise command. From the reports she'd seen, mostly it had worked. As long as they kept people informed, they would keep working. Keep producing. Keep fighting. Not forever, but for long enough.

They had planes. They had airports. They had roads. They had a blueprint for housing up to a hundred million refugees. The damage to the coastal harbours would reduce that, while providing them with refugees far closer who now needed a new home. But they still had planes.

Yes, producing jet fuel and getting it to the airports was a problem, but it was one of logistics and production. They'd lost some airfields, and planes, along the eastern coast, but the major population centres were to the north and west. So, assuming three hundred passengers per plane…

She jogged over to the reception desk, grabbing a pen and a pad from next to the defunct phone and scrawled a quick calculation. A hundred million people at three hundred passengers per plane required three hundred and thirty-three thousand flights. But they had thousands of planes. Most of the air fleets of the entire southern Pacific. Some would have a larger capacity, some would have less. Some would have been knocked out of the sky by the EMP. How many? She didn't know.

But with a thousand planes, managing two flights a day, from airports in Australia to airports across Indonesia, the Philippines, Malaysia, Thailand, and even beyond, it would take half a year. The one hundred million target had been plucked from the air by Aaron. At the time, when it had just been the two of them in the office, working away at an hour so late it was early, the number had seemed preposterous. Now it seemed inadequate.

An idea was taking shape. But she needed more information: the number of planes; the number of runways; the amount of fuel which could be processed and delivered; the capacity of the planes. If Captain Hawker had survived, had his parachutists? How many runways could they secure, and how quickly? Where? That last seemed the biggest question, but there were so many others, stacking up faster than she could write, and this was just transport, not food, water, electricity, and basic healthcare.

Their plan, hers and Aaron's, had been centred around the idea that refugees would leave Australia in nearly as great a number as they arrived, returning as soldiers or farmers to land retaken from the undead. There would be no return to areas humming with radioactivity. Nor could they save everyone. In fact, they would only be able to save those close to an airport. A hundred million suddenly seemed wildly optimistic, and with it came a sudden awareness of how many people, globally, would certainly die. She shivered. In turn, that made her realise she was sweating. Signs pointed to a public washroom just off the vestibule. She ducked inside, intending to splash water on her face.

As she entered, the light came on automatically, and she smiled. Yes, the lights were still on. There was still hope. The thought froze when she saw the body.

The grad-student with the unicorn t-shirt, Mel, was hanging from the ceiling, inside an open-doored stall, a length of power cord taut around her neck. Even as Anna took in the scene, she drew the pistol. Holding it by the barrel, she hammered the butt into the glass mirror. Leaving the gun by the sink, she ripped off her thin jacket, wrapped it around the largest shard, and ran to the cubicle. Roughly pushing past the swinging scientist, she braced one foot on the closed toilet seat and her free hand on the stall wall. Leaping up, she sliced the shard of mirror at the taut cord above the hanging woman's head. Two slashes, and the body fell. Anna barely caught the woman, and barely managed to find her footing, as she fell back to the toilet's floor.

With speed rather than care, Anna hauled the scientist out of the cubicle, clawing the severed cord loose. Bending over, she attempted resuscitation. Two breaths. Thirty compressions. Breaths. Compressions. Breaths. Compressions.

She leaned back on her heels. It was too late. The student-scientist was dead. Anna exhaled deep and long, as if she was breathing the last for the dead woman.

Suicide. Another suicide. Why? There were plenty of reasons, of course, but why had no one else realised? Would Leo have if he'd been here? Why hadn't Dr Avalon?

Avalon!

Anna sprang to her feet. She grabbed the gun from by the sink, and dashed outside, sprinting through the lobby, down the corridors, barely slowing when she heard the music, growing ever louder. She only slowed when she reached the lab. Avalon sat at the same U-shaped desk, in exactly the same position as before. The only difference was that two laptops had been added to the rows of notepads. Her head bobbed in time to the music as her hands typed.

Anna opened the door.

Avalon looked up, but didn't stop typing. "You have a gun in your hand."

"Sorry," Anna said, and pocketed the weapon. "Are you okay?"

"Define the parameters of your question," Avalon said, returning her gaze to the screen. "Where's Leo?"

"He's in the Bunker at Parliament House, fixing things."

"He's good at that," Avalon said.

"Dr Avalon," Anna began, and wasn't sure how to continue. "I… can we turn off the music?"

"I don't think that requires collective effort," Avalon said, but switched off the player. "Is that all?"

"No," Anna said. "There's been a series of nuclear blasts."

"You said, earlier. And I told you it's not my area."

"A lot of nuclear blasts. Leo thinks hundreds of warheads were detonated in the Pacific, maybe a thousand. More detonated elsewhere in the hemisphere. We've lost the fleet near Guam, and a mushroom cloud was reported in the Himalayas. A tsunami has struck the east coast."

"I see," Avalon said. Her hands had finally stopped typing, but her gaze remained on the screen. Her brow furrowed. "I still can't help."

"There's more," Anna said, frustrated with the scientist's apparent indifference. "One of your students is dead."

"What?" Avalon asked, and finally looked up.

"It was suicide," Anna said. "I discovered her body in the bathroom near the entrance lobby."

"Which student?" Avalon asked.

"The young woman with the rainbow hair. Mel? She hanged herself with a power cord. I think she's been dead for hours. Where are the other students?"

"Asleep. I sent them to bed at dawn." Avalon stood and walked across the room, pacing back again, stopping in front of the blank wall.

"It was the pressure, the reality of what we're all dealing with," Anna said. "The nuclear blasts must have been the final straw. Every day, we find a few more apartments, a few more houses, with suicides inside."

"Why didn't she talk to me?" Avalon asked.

Anna didn't give the obvious reply that Avalon was about the worst person in the world for anyone in their *best* mind to share their darkest fears. "I need you to come with me. Dr Smilovitz wants your help. You and the other students, and anyone else still here at the university who might know anything about data analysis. We have planes, we have fuel. We'll rescue as many people as we can. Millions."

"Can I see her?" Avalon asked. "Mel. I'd like to see her."

"Of course, yes. And then we should wake your other assistants. Let them know."

"This isn't right," Avalon said, when they were inside the bathroom. She'd taken one look at Mel's corpse and then turned to stare at the stall above which the cut noose hung.

"I know," Anna said. "But grief has to wait."

"No, I mean the body is wrong for a suicide," Avalon said, stepping over the corpse and into the stalls. "Yes. There. Do you see? Rather, do you not see?"

"Do I not see what?" Anna asked, once again confused.

"There are no scuff marks on the walls," Avalon said. "And look at her fingernails, no flecks from the cord. Her hands aren't tied. Her neck isn't broken; she suffocated. So, she looped the cord around the beam in the ceiling, then around her neck, stepped off the toilet seat and didn't kick out? Not once?"

"Not if she truly wanted to die," Anna said.

"That isn't how physiology works," Avalon said. "How would she have reached that beam?"

Anna was a little shorter than the dead scientist, but not by much. Even so, she'd had to jump to cut the cord, one end of which was tightly knotted on the narrow ceiling beam.

"It was staged," Avalon said. "Mel was probably sedated before the noose was placed around her neck. Or she was already dead." She glanced again at the body, but only for the briefest second. "No. Sedated. She was sedated."

Anna looked at scientist and corpse, then back to Avalon. "Where are the other students?"

Uncertain if she was looking for a suspect, or a witness, or more victims, Anna followed Avalon along the corridor, through a set of doors propped open by a cleaning cart, and up a set of stairs to a less frequently visited section of offices. In the corridor, desks and bookshelves had been dragged outside, while a trio of mattresses remained unclaimed. A neat pile of laundered sheets and pillows were stacked next to those. An open door revealed an office turned into a kitchen, complete with camping stove, slow cooker, large fridge, an ice cream machine, and a jungle of extension cables. But the sound coming from further along the corridor cut short her curious inspection. Knocking, as of someone bound and gagged, trying to escape, came from the room ahead and on the right.

Avalon reached for the door as Anna realised an alternative explanation. The scientist pushed the door inward.

"No!" Anna said.

Something pushed the door back, but not completely. A hand was caught in the gap even as its owner pushed and shoved against the door, squeezing the frame on its trapped hand, cutting skin and muscle, oozing red-brown pus.

"Zombies!" Anna said, grabbing Avalon's arm and tugging her back along the corridor.

The door to the office swung open. A student in a star-ship t-shirt staggered out, mouth snapping, arms flailing, gore flying from its self-inflicted, partially severed hand.

Avalon, grabbed a handful of books from the nearest tall stack and hurled them ineffectually at the un-human student. "So they were wrong about the might of the pen," she said as Anna pulled her back again, and then drew the handgun O.O. had given her.

"Get behind me," Anna said.

"Ah, we're experimenting with the sword?" Avalon asked, gamely skipping behind Anna.

A second undead student, in waistcoat, suit trousers, but no tie, staggered through the office door. The undead sci-fi fan was now only ten paces away. Anna raised the gun, pulled the trigger, and nothing happened.

"Safety!" Avalon said.

"It's off," Anna said, flipping it on and off anyway. She pulled the trigger again, and still nothing happened.

"Ammo!" Avalon said.

But Anna turned and pushed the scientist back towards the stairs. "Run!"

Anna followed the scientist down the stairs. At the bottom, Anna grabbed the fire hose from the wall fitment, snaking it back and forth between the bannister and the railings, buying herself time to think.

"Are we fighting or running?" Avalon asked, as she rummaged in her bag.

Above came a thump as the first zombie reached the stairwell.

"If those three get out, they could infect dozens," Anna said. "There are farmers outside, building walls and vegetable plots. But one of them will have a gun, or maybe a radio to call the Special Forces patrolling the campus. Go get them. I'll slow the zombies."

"Not yet," Avalon said. The first of the undead, the student in the waistcoat, had slid down to the landing where the stairs made a one-hundred-and-eighty-degree turn. Thrashing and rolling, knocking hands and feet into the wall, it flopped around the turn, and continued on down the stairs. Except for how its chin slammed into every step, spraying blood, leaving a trail of skin, it almost appeared to be swimming. And it swam right underneath the lower-most coil of fire hose.

Avalon leaned forward, arm extended, spraying something from a canister. "Pepper spray," she said. "I was curious as to whether it might work."

"Run, go!" Anna said, as the zombie squirmed and rolled. Trying to stand.

"Evidently not," Avalon said, reaching again into her bag, this time bringing out a blue-plastic pistol-grip stun-gun. She fired. The zombie jerked as electricity coursed through it. Legs and arms flying left and right, its head and neck bucking.

"Fascinating," Avalon said. "Ah, but no."

As the current ceased, the zombie's movement become more normally erratic. It pushed itself to its feet.

"Here," Avalon said, holding out a short length of metal. "You conduct the next experiment. I'll return shortly."

"Finally," Anna muttered, as the scientist ran.

The undead sci-fi fan had reached the stairs, but had managed to keep its feet as it trip-ran down and into the looped fire hose, against which it pushed and shoved. As its arms reached through the coiled barrier, the hose grew taut, slipping against the hasty knot, but it held. For now. Giving her time to deal with the zombie in the waistcoat.

The object Avalon had given her was a telescopic baton. A sharp flick, and it extended. She swung, a heavy backhand, smashing the metal tube into the undead student's outstretched arms, knocking them aside, but otherwise doing no damage. Anna paced back and swung again, this time a downswing aimed at the zombie's neck, but it lurched to the left, and the blow landed on its shoulder. The creature flinched, and while its hand swiped, Anna had to duck to avoid the ponderous swing of its club-like hand. But her foot slipped, and she sprawled, hitting her head on the floor.

Ignoring the pain, she bounced to her feet, yelling in anger and fury as she hacked the baton two-handed at the zombie's knees and legs, ducking beneath its flailing arms as it fell. As the zombie thrashed on the floor, she aimed another two-handed swing at its bucking head, caused its chin to smash into the floor. A third cracked its skull. A fourth sent brain and gore flying through the air.

The clumsy knot securing the fire hose gave under the weight of the two undead scientists. With a dull clunk, the hose snaked loose. Both zombies slipped, falling to hands and knees at the base of the stairs. As they began to stand, Anna raised the baton, readying to swing when, behind, she heard footsteps. Running.

"Get back!" Avalon yelled, sprinting towards her. In her hands was the gloriously welcome sight of a Colt .45.

Anna pushed herself flat against the wall as Avalon, still running, fired two shots. Both missed. The scientist skipped to a sudden halt, while the zombies staggered upright.

Avalon fired again. Another two shots. This time, she didn't miss.

Chapter 23 - Political Immunity
Australian National University

"I need to change," Anna said looking down at her gore-splattered hands and now-ruined, barely worn, clothes.

"I have clothes in the lab, come," Avalon said.

"I was thinking aloud," Anna said.

"And I have gloves," Avalon said.

"Gloves?"

"For us to wear as we examine the bodies," Avalon said. "We must learn *how* they were infected."

"Bitten, I assume," Anna muttered. Her head was throbbing, but so were her arms. Oddly, her teeth were as well, pulsating in time with her rapid heartbeat.

"Where's the fifth?" Avalon said.

"The fifth?" Anna asked. "There was another student?"

"I sent them to sleep. They were infected, how?" Avalon asked.

Anna, still running on adrenaline, was finding it hard to understand the scientist who was conducting half the conversation in her head. "You mean people don't spontaneously become infected?"

"Indeed. Or I hope they don't. It is possible the virus could mutate, becoming airborne."

"I thought you said it wasn't a virus," Anna said.

"Don't be pedantic," Avalon said. "This way." She began leading Anna back towards her lab. "Three zombies, one staged suicide. So how did those three become infected?"

"Where's the fifth zombie?" Anna said. Reflexively, she drew her handgun. "This didn't work, must be jammed."

"Must it?" Avalon asked, taking it from her, and quickly ejected magazine and spare round.

"You know firearms?" Anna asked.

"I know how they work," Avalon said. "They're remarkably simple. It's baffling their development took so long. Propellant, tube, trigger, bullet. Point, pull trigger, move on. Simple. Boring." As she spoke, she'd dexterously dismantled the pistol. "There's no firing pin. Where did you get it?"

"Oswald Owen gave it to me."

"He's the fat idiot with no indoor-voice?"

"My exercise-deficient colleague, yes," Anna said.

"I don't like him," Avalon said, as they reached the lab.

Anna locked the glass doors after they entered. "Grab your notes, and we'll leave," she said, turning to watch outside.

"In five minutes," Avalon said, taking a syringe from a box. "Give me your arm. I need some blood."

"Why?" Anna asked, turning around.

"To finish an experiment," Avalon said. "Quickly. The work is important. More important than ever before." She pulled up Anna's sleeve and jabbed the needle in before the politician could protest. "The firing pin was removed," Avalon added. "The fat man gave you a broken gun."

"Maybe he didn't know," Anna said. "What are you doing with my blood? Is that the weapon?"

"Not all weapons fire projectiles," Avalon said, bending over her lab table. "Get some plastic gloves. There's a box on the workstation. And you wanted clothes. The suitcases are against the wall. Blue and red. Blue is Leo's. Take anything you want from the red."

Anna tugged off the windbreaker, and ran the tap in one of the deep sinks, enjoying the feel of water on her hands as her brain slowly processed the nightmarish last thirty minutes.

"Despite our most recent experiment, the pen *is* mightier than the sword," Avalon said. "Brute strength and bullets end battles, but information doesn't just end wars, it prevents them. You're immune."

"I'm sorry? That's what you were doing, checking if I was immune?"

"Check the back of your neck," Avalon said, in another of her skip-ahead replies.

Anna raised a hand, and it came away wet.

Avalon took the Colt .45 out of her pocket, slipped on the safety, then walked over to a tower of first-aid kits stacked near the suitcases. She brought them over to a bench. "Sit and don't move."

Anna sat. "I didn't notice," she said. "I didn't feel it. Okay, I *felt* that. I'm immune? How certain are you?"

"Certainty doesn't have gradations," Avalon said. "One is, or one is not. And I am." She affixed a bandage to the back of Anna's neck. "I've cleaned, glued, and bandaged the wound, but you've lost a lot of blood."

When Anna changed her t-shirt, she saw the back drenched red. With that, the last of the adrenaline was banished. "We need to get back to Parliament House," Anna said, sitting down again.

"No, we must discover *how* my students were infected. Drink this." She held out a bottle she'd taken from a fridge.

"What is it?"

"Protein. Sugar. Water. Some fats."

Anna sipped. "Tastes like vanilla. Almost like a milkshake."

"It's the powder from the ice cream machine. They had far more than is healthy in the storeroom. You brought a gun with you, so you're familiar with their operation, yes?"

"I've been with Tess to the firing range."

"Tess?"

"A police officer. A friend."

Avalon held out the Colt .45. "Then take this. But be careful," she added, stuffing her notes into a bag.

"Be careful because it kicks like a jealous kangaroo?" Anna asked.

"Be careful because it's Leo's," Avalon said. "He gets mad when his things get broken."

Five minutes later, they were once more in the stairwell, standing over the corpses of the dead students.

"I'm sorry," Anna said.

"You can't be, because it wasn't your fault," Avalon said. She held out a pair of disposable gloves. "Put those on and remove that fire hose. We need to go upstairs and see where they died. You can be angry," she added as they picked their way over the corpses. "You can be aggrieved. You can be upset. Annoyed. Frustrated. Betrayed. But you can't apologise, because this wasn't your fault. But it *was* someone's."

"Because the virus was made," Anna said as they climbed the stairs and made their way along the corridor.

"And because Mel didn't commit suicide," Avalon said, pausing in the doorway to the office-turned-dorm. "Wait out here."

Anna lingered in the doorway, glancing up and down the corridor, while Avalon went inside, prowling left, then right, occasionally out of sight. The scientist paced, crouched, peered, and Anna simply wanted to sit. She stepped back, intending to lean against the wall, before an ache from her skull reminded her of the bandage, the wound. Instead, she stepped forward, through the doorway, and into the room.

The offices along this corridor had been subdivided by thin walls which the students had removed, extending into the neighbouring four offices. They'd found armchairs and cushions, tables and ornaments, even fabric to hang around their mattresses. More rugs and throws had been hung on the walls, until the zombies had torn them down, leaving only a few scraps of cloth on the bolted ceiling-rail.

A water cooler had provided them with drinking water, while a stainless steel sink had been bolted beneath the window. The zombies had torn that down, too, and knocked free the waste-water pipe the students had drilled through the wall.

Avalon turned around. "Outside," she said.

Anna stepped back into the corridor.

"It was murder," Avalon said, following her outside. "Murder by infection."

"Are you sure?" Anna asked.

"Mel was immune, which is why she was hanged. The other three were deliberately infected. There is a syringe inside. Crushed, unfortunately, but there is no doubt what it contained."

"Under the circumstances, I suppose not," Anna said.

"They would have been sedated first," Avalon said. "I would imagine the compound was in their food. Something given to them. A gift of some sort by the killer. A shame, since their pantry is well stocked with junk food. Your gun has no firing pin."

"You think Oswald Owen killed them? Why?" Anna asked. "But... but... no. Leo and I were locked in the Geoscience building with a sentry who'd been infected."

"He was? Why didn't you say?" Avalon said. "The fat idiot is targeting Leo and me."

"But why?" Anna asked.

"I don't know him," Avalon said. "How could I identify his motivations?"

"I mean, how?" Anna said. "Or, not how, but... I don't know. Who knew Mel was immune?"

"She did. So did I, Leo, and my other assistants. You and your politicians knew. Leo told you yesterday."

"Oswald was hanging around outside here, yesterday after that meeting," Anna said. "And when I came to find Leo, Mel was outside waiting for someone. I thought she was going on a date or something."

"Impossible. She was seeing Lilly."

"One of the other students? Then she certainly wouldn't have conspired in their deaths. So Oswald persuaded Mel to steal a sample of the virus. Gave her some food laced with a sedative by way of payment. He infected the sentry at Geoscience Australia, and then came back here to infect the students."

"Something alcoholic," Avalon said. "Something they would consume here, in their dorm. Meaning they could be infected here. Found here by me when I went to look for them. There's a very old bottle of brandy in there."

"An octagonal bottle?" Anna asked, stepping forward to look. "That's identical to the one Oswald was drinking outside Parliament House, and identical to one found at the suicide of one my colleagues."

"Suicide by zombie?"

"No, Aaron slit his wrist. And that was... no, that had to have been suicide. But it was the same type of bottle. Very old. Hundreds of years old. It's... it's no coincidence. Aaron be connected to this, too, but I still don't know what *this* is." She looked up and down the corridor. "Oh, I wish Tess was here. I'm sure we're missing a lot. This way. We'll find a different way outside."

"All of this began a few hours after he was informed we could make a weapon," Avalon said. "Why doesn't he want a weapon? Why would anyone *not* want to stop the undead?"

"You met the Guinns, didn't you?" Anna asked. "The brother and sister who flew to America?"

"Twice," Avalon said. "Once in Nanaimo, once again in Thunder Bay. Why is that relevant?"

"They know something," Anna said. "They don't realise it, and I don't think they know the extent of it. They suspected a conspiracy behind the outbreak. That's it!" She stopped and turned to the scientist. "That's why you and Leo were targeted. You said to us all that it was manufactured. Created. Artificial. That's why Owen wants you dead, because he worried you'd identify *where* it was created, and ultimately, lead us to him. Do you have paper and pen?"

"Of course. Why?" Avalon asked, opening her bag and withdrawing a notepad.

"I'm sending you to the airport. My father is… well, he's probably in a plane on his way to the coast. Tess and Captain Hawker might have gone with him, but my assistant, Hoa Nguyen, will certainly be there. Give this note to her." She handed Avalon the gun. "And take this."

"Where are you going?"

"To get Leo, and to deal with Oswald."

"Then you'll need the gun."

"No worries," Anna said. "I'm getting an army."

Chapter 24 - The Blood-Red Flag
The Bunker, Parliament House

Having given Avalon her car, Anna jogged back alone, keeping to the footpath and cycle lanes. Utterly anonymous, one more anxious face in what was a growing crowd, though everyone else was staying close to their billets. They looked like the off-duty workers, woken early, or kept awake by the troubling rumours spreading as fast as the unauthorised radio stations could broadcast. She caught a few snippets of those from the open windows and doorways where people gathered, listening, waiting, watching the sky. And behind the radio, on a lower volume, the sound of black-and-white trench-warfare came from the national TV channel, the only station still broadcasting.

Parliament House was busier, too, though here the newcomers were in uniform, a fifty-fifty split between those in camouflage and those in black utility gear. More reassuring still was the welcome sight of the Minister of Defence, Ian Lignatiev.

"Ian, I am so glad to see you," Anna said. "Over here, please, in private. We need to talk."

She led a confused Ian away from his equally confused soldiers. "It's Oswald," she whispered. "He tried to kill the scientists. One of Avalon's lab-assistants stole infected samples for him. He used those to infect the rest of her team, and the sentry at Geoscience Australia."

"Oswald? Are you sure?" Lignatiev asked. "That sounds... no offence, but far more effort than is usual for him."

"I don't think he's working alone," Anna said. "So who, here, do you trust?"

Ian briefly turned to look at the mix of conscripts and Special Forces. "Not everyone," he said turning around again. "Why is he doing this?"

"Because some people knew about the outbreak before it happened," Anna said. "You know how Avalon said the virus was made, manufactured?"

"And you think it was made by Oswald?"

"He's just a small cog in a big international machine," Anna said. "But he's worried the scientists will continue an investigation which will lead them to him."

"There has to be more evidence than that," Lignatiev said.

"Not really, not yet," Anna said. "And it doesn't matter because attempted murder is enough reason to detain him. Once that's done, we need to release an official statement. Rumours are spreading. I'm worried what'll happen at shift-change. Crowds might gather, becoming restless, unruly. Add in zombies, and we'll end up worse than Melbourne. We need to get Dr Smilovitz out of the Bunker, and Oswald in handcuffs."

"The prime minister is in there, too," Ian said.

"Oh. Of course," Anna said.

"Can you go in and get them?" Ian asked. "I'll send a team down with you, but they'll wait outside until the civilians are clear. Although, perhaps that's not wise. Not safe."

"No, it's fine," Anna said. "It'd be quicker if I go in."

"Thank you," Lignatiev said. "Let me redeploy the soldiers I don't trust."

The politician walked over to a trio of black-clad soldiers, and spoke quietly to a woman whose face was mostly scars, and whose web-harness-vest was festooned with as many knives as guns. In any other circumstances, at any other time, had Anna seen her, she wouldn't have just crossed the street, but moved to a different state. The trio broke up, quickly moving among the soldiers, ordering some away, while others fell in, close to the door.

"They've been told there's been an undead incursion and are going to the suburbs as reinforcements," Ian said. "These others, I trust. Major Kelly will enter with you. I'll remain up here with reinforcements."

The scarred woman gave Anna a brief nod. "Are you armed?"

"Ah, no."

"You should be," Major Kelly said. "Sir?"

Lignatiev reached into his bag and withdrew a small nine millimetre in an equally small holster. "Ankle holster is best, yes?" he asked.

"Yes, sir," Kelly said, taking holster and gun from Lignatiev. She ejected the magazine, checked the load, reloaded, and handed it to Anna. "Do you know how to use this?" Kelly asked.

"Point and shoot," Anna said.

"If we hear gunfire, we'll enter," Kelly said. "Otherwise, we'll remain outside until you leave. There are two essential hostages. The prime minister and the scientist. Do not speak to anyone else. We don't know who has been compromised."

"Of course," Anna said. She bent to affix the ankle holster. Leading the way, she headed down to the Bunker.

After Major Kelly had disarmed the solitary sentry outside the airlock, Anna went in, alone. She paused in the corridor outside the sliding doors leading into the communications centre. Dr Smilovitz stood next to one of the headphones-wearing camouflaged conscripts, tapping at a tablet. On the big screen, the map had been replaced with a wall of code, changing as fast as Smilovitz could type one-handed.

O.O. was in the War Room with his back to her. On the table was his bottle. And in front... no, she couldn't see. If she went in to get Smilovitz, Oswald would notice. Anna's hand curled around the gun. She could signal Major Kelly, but was the conscript next to Smilovitz one of Oswald's people? And where were the others? No, it was too great a risk. She'd fetch the prime minister first.

Ducking slightly until she was beyond the transparent walls of the communications centre, she walked quickly along the corridor. Sliding doors led to a semi-public corridor off which were the small chapel, a slightly larger dining room, kitchen, and a medical room. All were empty, as was the security station at the end of the corridor, and another set of doors, which slid open silently as she approached.

The corridor bent ninety degrees as it looped behind the communications room. On the inside was the private accommodation of senior personnel. On the outer side, doors led to washrooms and casual offices which could double as overflow executive dorms. Beyond those, on the other side of their exterior wall, and accessed through the other looping corridor, were the bunk house and mess hall used by the staff, the electrical infrastructure, and pump rooms.

The prime minister's room was at the far end of the corridor. Anna supposed one of the others had been allocated to her, though she'd never bothered to ask. For that matter, she wasn't sure whom she was *supposed* to ask. But since the outbreak, she'd decided if the disaster reached the point where they had to retreat to an underground bunker, there was nothing a politician could do to fix it. Certainly not from below ground. An opinion vindicated by recent events.

She knocked on the prime minister's door, mentally searching for the words to explain the situation to Bronwyn Wilson, and quickly discarding them all in favour of a lie, that she was needed at the temporary broadcast studio at the Telstra Tower.

Inside, something heavy fell over. Anna opened the door, pushing it inwards. The room was pitch-dark, the corridor's second-hand light only adding depth to the weird shadows.

"Ma'am? Prime Minister? Bronwyn?" she asked, and then she saw her. The prime minister lay on the floor. She'd collapsed, her breath a hissing whisper that rose to a rasp as she tried to stand. As Anna stepped inside, the prime minister abruptly bucked backwards, onto her knees, throwing out her arms in a near windmill-wave. From the corridor's dim light, Anna saw the face. Drawn, stretched, contorted by taut muscles drawing eyebrows up in surprise, eyelids wide in blind fury, and mouth open exposing fiercely biting teeth.

"Ma'am?" Anna said, even as Wilson's undead hand swiped out again, this time curling around Anna's ankle, tugging her off balance, and from her feet. She fell, hard. The bandage offered little padding when her head hit the carpet, and for a second, she was stunned. Long enough for the undead prime minister to pull on her leg. Unintentionally grabbing the ankle holster, Wilson pulled herself forward and closer until the clasp on the holster snapped, and Anna, already kicking, was able to roll free.

Anna pushed herself upright, backing away as the zombie-PM thrashed on the floor, now between her and the door. Anna looked for a weapon, and saw the flag behind the desk. The pole was made of ash and brass and had a barely pointed tip. Not a spear, but better than nothing. Wrenching the flag from its stand, she levelled the staff.

Bronwyn was on her knees, mouth open, neck twisting left and right, while her eyes twitched up and down. Anna lunged, spearing the flagstaff forward. The weight of the unfurled banner dragged the blunt tip downward so it impacted against the politician's stomach rather than sternum, but as Anna thrust, the zombie lurched forward. Knees scuffing against the thick carpet, arms batting against the polished ash-wood, Bronwyn Wilson slowly impaled herself on the flagpole. But the banner acted as a bandage, a stopper, preventing the dull spear from penetrating too deeply. The zombie kept pushing. So did Anna, but her hands slipped on the glazed wood, while the monster's fingers clawed ever closer to her face.

With a roar of furious fear, Anna pushed down on the pole with her left hand while lifting with the right, slowly raising the spear tip, and also the zombie, from her knees and to her feet. Wilson's sensible flats scrabbled on the floor, but Anna didn't give her time to find her balance. She charged, pushing and screaming as she shoved the zombie backwards, through the door, and outside. With another furious roar, she tugged the flag free, dropped it inside, and slammed the door closed.

Outside, an undead hand thumped against the reinforced wood. Another clawed. But Anna was safe. Relatively speaking. In the dark. She allowed herself time to exhale, and inhale again, then searched for the light switch. The room lit up, far brighter than she'd been expecting. She picked up the ankle-holster, drawing the weapon even as she looked around the room.

A pair of sliding doors concealed the double-bunk bedroom, while a door on the other side hid the airplane-style toilet. The main room, with its desk, chair, small sofa and table, had no photographs, no mementos. A temporary clothes-rack held a neat row of dress-carriers, above an identical number of shoe-pouches, but those were the only personal touches. Everywhere else, on the desk, on the chair, on the shelves, but mostly on the floor where they'd been knocked after the prime minister had been infected, were books. Strips of paper or cloth marked the pages found to be potentially useful. Histories and agricultural texts, medical books and military memoirs; the prime minister had been seeking answers in books. She clearly hadn't found them.

As Anna took a step towards the bedroom, something cracked beneath her shoe. Glass. A small vial. Of course. How else would the PM have become infected if not deliberately by Oswald Owen?

She checked the pistol's magazine, the safety, and then she walked over to the door. She knew what she had to do. Steeled herself and reached for the door handle.

The lights went out.

But were replaced almost immediately by a soft red flash from the recessed LEDs at the base of the wall. After three one-second flashes, the lights turned a soft amber.

No sirens blared, but the lights were an indication the Bunker had just entered lockdown. Had the Special Forces just made entry? Or had O.O. locked them outside? A thump against the panelled frame reminded her of the pressing danger immediately outside the door. Would it hold? Could she wait? One-handed, Anna raised the gun, reached for the door handle, and paused.

Bronwyn Wilson had been deliberately infected. The previous prime minister had committed suicide. And so had Aaron Bryce. They weren't the only suicides, and other politicians had simply disappeared. When Anna had gone to collect Dr Smilovitz, and then to get Avalon, O.O. had known where she was going. He'd given her a gun which didn't work. He had that bottle, the same type he'd given to Aaron. Whether he wanted the scientists dead or not, *she* had been his target, not them. He had been killing his rivals, the politicians standing in the way of his life-long ambition to rule. Maybe, before this was done, she'd ask him why.

She raised the gun. Again, she hesitated. The zombie did not, slowly battering the wood.

If the Special Forces had made entry, the undead prime minister would have been shot by now. The lockdown had been initiated a few seconds after she'd pushed the PM out into the corridor. There probably weren't any security cameras in the prime minister's private office, but there must be in the hall. O.O. was watching. Remember rule one. It was a saying of her father's to which he'd given many different meanings over the years, but it amounted to not rushing to action before you've had time to think. Check your boots, so she checked hers, reaffixing the ankle holster, and making sure it was concealed.

Quickly, she unclipped the flag from the staff. The top corner was sodden, drenched, glistening in the dim emergency glow. Leaning the flagstaff against the wall, she grabbed the desk. It was far lighter than she'd expected. She laid it on its side, with the legs either side of the door, the table top facing into the room, facing her. The low barrier wasn't much of a barricade, but she didn't want to keep the zombie at bay.

Gripping the flagstaff, she leaned forward, and pulled the door inward, stepping back even as the zombie staggered inside. The zombie prime minister lurched inward, knees slamming into the edge of the upturned table's top. Wilson fell, as Anna had hoped, but landed far further forward than she'd expected, slamming her stomach on the lip of the table. As the undead prime minister thrashed, red-brown gore spilled from the wound in its stomach. Wilson's legs kicked, her head bucked, even as Anna thrust the flagstaff forward, ripping through hair and skin as she tore a ragged gouge through the zombie's scalp. She pulled the flagpole back, and thrust again, putting her entire weight into the blow. Bone cracked, brain oozed, and the prime minister stopped moving.

Chapter 25 - The Treachery of the Opposition
The Bunker, Parliament House

Anna took a second to catch her breath, another to tame her thoughts, and a third to check the gun was concealed. Regardless of risk, it was time the Special Forces came inside and she got out. The corridor was dimly illuminated by the emergency lights. Assuming an undead threat behind each door, she padded quietly down to the junction. And found her way blocked.

The executive rooms were separated from the chapel and other communal spaces by a set of mostly transparent, sliding, airtight doors, which were now closed. To her right was a keypad above which a display read *Code-Three Lockdown*. Unsurprisingly, since the Bunker had been designed for biological hazards, there was no obvious emergency door release. There was an intercom, but she'd be shocked if it worked. When she tried, she wasn't disappointed. Waving her hands at the sensor above the doors did nothing. She appeared to be trapped.

Beyond the sealed doors, down the corridor, a large figure ambled through the door of the small kitchen, a cardboard box of individually wrapped Anzac biscuits under his arm. Oswald Owen.

When he saw her, he grinned, walked over, carefully put the box down, then began miming. He pointed towards the side of the door, while motioning for... for her to do what? Open the doors? Surely not. He saw her puzzled expression, and correctly guessed a quarter of the cause, so took out a notepad on which he wrote, "Open the panel below the keypad."

She let puzzlement deepen her furrowed brow. He *actually* wanted her to open this set of doors? Obviously, he didn't know she suspected him.

The panel was badly concealed, and easily opened. Behind it was a small screen, currently showing a CCTV image of the inside of the main airlock, but she was more interested in the small text command prompt saying *Emergency Override*. Beneath that, two buttons, a *Yes* and a *No*, with the *Yes* glowing a darker shade of blue. She pressed enter on the keypad. The lights switched from emergency-amber back to overhead-white, and the door slid open.

"Not that!" O.O. finished, the first half of his yelled sentence lost behind the soundproof doors.

"Don't take another step!" she said, dragging the pistol from its holster and aiming the barrel at his face.

"What?" O.O. asked, confusion replacing frustrated anger. "Why are you pointing that gun at me?"

"I know you tried to kill me," she said. "Three times now. Congratulations on failing."

"I did what now? And why did you open the doors? Didn't you look at the monitors?" he added, taking another step towards her.

"Seriously, don't," she said, taking another step back. "I mean it. I will shoot you."

"Why? You can't hate me that much. Where's Bronwyn?"

"In her room," she said.

Ignoring her raised gun, he ran down the corridor to the room at the far end, pushing the door open before stepping back. "What happened?"

"What do you think happened?" she said. "Why did you do it? Power, right? Money's not worth anything."

"Why did I do what?"

"Kill Aaron. Kill Bronwyn. That's what this was about, wasn't it?" she said. "You wanted us dead. Your rivals. You weren't trying to kill Leo and Flo, you wanted me dead."

"Why would I want you dead?" he asked, walking towards her, though his eyes were on the long corridor beyond. "But you might just have killed us both. I knew how to initiate the test protocol, not a proper lockdown, and you just overrode it. All the internal doors were locked, the sections sealed. You just opened them."

"Shut up. Stop moving," she said. "We'll wait for the Special Forces, and you're—"

"Too late," he said, pointing behind her. "Take a squiz at that and tell me you still want to hang about here."

She didn't want to look, but she heard something moving in the corridor behind her. A dragging footstep. A thump of a person-sized weight slamming into the wall. She knew what caused the sound, and now understood why Oswald wasn't scared of her gun; it was because he was utterly terrified of the approaching undead. Still, she didn't want to turn, didn't want to shift aim from him.

"Ah, shoot me if you like," he said. "It'd be better than being torn apart." He walked back to the doors. Ignoring the gun aimed at his head, he reached under his coat and drew a handgun from his twin shoulder-holster rig. He raised his gun, aimed, and pulled the trigger. Nothing happened. He drew the other gun. Still, nothing, except the zombie dragged itself closer.

Dressed in camouflage green, but with a red t-shirt beneath and white-soled sneakers on his feet. She knew him. He was one of the conscripts who'd been helping Leo.

"They don't bloody work!" O.O. said, dropping one gun, then ejecting the magazine from the other. "It's got bullets. But it doesn't work." He reinserted the magazine, aimed at the zombie, and pulled the trigger. Nothing happened.

Was he faking? He didn't seem to be, but what O.O. lacked in morality was substituted with an overabundance of animal cunning. She didn't, *couldn't*, trust him. But she *could* shift her aim by an arm's width and fire her own gun at the approaching zombie. So she did.

Nothing happened. She pulled the trigger again. Still nothing. She checked the safety, but it was off.

"It's not you," she whispered. She grabbed his arm, hauled him back, looked again at the control panel. The message had changed to *Secure Door*, with the same *Yes* and *No* options. To her, it was no option at all. She closed the door.

"Not that!" O.O. said, pushing her aside, so he could see the control panel "Why did you do that?"

"Because there's a zombie there," she said, pointing at the walking corpse staggering towards them, "and our guns don't work."

"I know there are zombies. I can *see* there are zombies. But now I can't see what else is going on in this tomb."

"Stop shouting, take a breath, and explain," she said.

"I know the test-code," he said. "Got that a couple of weeks ago, the first time I came down here. The protocol shuts the doors, but sets the camera images to rotate, to cycle from one room to the next. You can view that on the screens behind the emergency panels. That's how I knew you were here."

"And where were you?"

"In the chapel," he said.

"Why?"

In the corridor beyond, the zombie stumbled on.

"Because at this point, I didn't think it could hurt," he said. "What happened to Bronwyn?"

"She was infected," Anna said. "Deliberately. With a syringe of infected blood taken from Dr Avalon's lab. So were Avalon's assistants, and a guard on duty at Geoscience Australia. Who gave you those guns?"

He looked down at the one gun he'd not dropped, still in his hand. "The shoulder rig was a gift from a constituent," he said. "She's a leather worker. Was a jillaroo before a fall from a horse broke her back. Makes holsters, primarily for export to the American market. I asked her to gift me one so I could declare it and get the other mob to ask why a bloke like me would have a shoulder rig if he didn't have a pair of guns to go with it. That set up me up to talk about small-enterprise, and how the little people could take advantage of globalisation if we just gave them a fair go."

"The guns, O.O.," she said.

"Erin Vaughn," he said.

"Vaughn? Mine came from Ian. It's them. They're in it together."

"In what?"

"This. The murders," Anna said. The zombie slammed its fist into the transparent door. "The coup."

"Those two? If it was one, it was both of them. Inseparable they are. Vaughn and Lignatiev. You know they've been dating longer than they've been married to other people? It's why I never trusted them."

"That door's solid. That monster won't smash its way in here," Anna said. "But Leo's still out there."

"If they're infected, so is he," O.O. said. "They've been stabbing people with a syringe full of zombie-blood?"

"I think one of the students stole samples from Avalon's lab. Probably Mel. You were talking with her after Avalon and Leo summoned us all to the lab. Why?"

"That's a crime now, is it?"

"You hung around after the meeting to chat up the students?" Anna asked.

"It's not like that," he said. "She reminded me of my daughter. My son's autistic."

"He is? I didn't know."

"The kid's mother is… out of the picture. My daughter basically raised him. I keep the press sweet, and the deal is they leave my family out of the papers."

"Oh," she said, seeing the man in different light, which added shade to his sinister shadow. "What about the octagonal bottles of Cognac? I found one by Aaron's corpse, and another with the students."

"I gave it to Aaron," O.O. said. "Seemed appropriate since Sir Malcolm gave me the crate as a birthday gift. Said they were worth fifty thousand dollars a bottle. What's a bloke supposed to do with that? Can't drink them. Can't insure them. Certainly can't sell them."

"Sir Malcolm Baker, Aaron's father-in-law?"

"Twisted sense of humour, that bloke, with a soul to match. Since the outbreak, I've been handing the bottles out wherever I go. Why not?"

The zombie slammed its fist into the door.

"Yeah," O.O. said, turning to face the zombie. "Yeah, I gave a bottle to Mel. She'd said she'd always wanted to go to France. Figured a bottle of revolutionary brandy was closer than nothing."

"And you came from the chapel," Anna said. "What happened before that?"

"When I saw you enter the Bunker, I decided that was my moment to take a break," he said. "I went to the chapel. When I came outside, I saw that bloke there, heading towards me. I stuck the place into lockdown. Then came up here and saw you."

"They must have been deliberately infected by Lignatiev's soldiers," Anna said. "The people I *thought* were Special Forces. I hope they aren't. Any ideas how we get out of here?"

"You ask yourself that," he said. "I'm getting a gun."

He walked back along the corridor to the door of the second of the private bedrooms. Before she thought to warn him about potential zombies, he'd entered. She turned back to the undead conscript on the other side of the transparent door. If this man had been deliberately infected, then she must assume Leo had been, too. Except Leo was immune, so perhaps he was still alive. Or was it more likely he'd been shot, or his suicide staged?

O.O. returned, and dropped a long, leather hold-all on the ground.

"You brought a bag down here?" she asked.

"Of course," he said. "Didn't you?" He unzipped it and took out a shotgun. "Not the done thing for a politician to be seen carrying one of these around the streets, even now. Hence the shoulder-holster."

"How many shells do you have?" she asked.

He handed her the gun, then rummaged in the bag until he found the box of shells.

"Any other guns in there?" she asked hopefully.

"Nope, but I've got a boomerang," he said, taking out a long stick, over half a metre in length, kinked two-thirds along with a thirty-degree bend. Though unpainted, it had been polished and stained into a patchwork of russet and honey. "Never could get it to return to me."

"That's not a boomerang," she said as she loaded the shotgun. "It's a throwing stick. For hunting. They don't come back."

"You're kidding? The bloke who gave it to me promised it would. I spent hours chucking it around the garden."

"A gift from another of your constituents, right?"

"Yeah, but a backhanded gift is still a gift. Here," he added, holding it out.

"No worries, I'm happy with the shotgun," she said, loading a last shell. "Besides, didn't you say you'd spent hours practicing? Open the door."

"Then what?" he asked.

"We kill that zombie, head to the airlock, go outside, and to the airport. There's people there I trust. Proper police and proper soldiers."

"Here's hoping I live long enough to regret this," he said. "On three. One. Two—"

He slammed his palm into the door release. As it slowly slid open, the zombie slipped a hand through the door, clawing and grasping, but Anna had raised the shotgun, and even before the door had fully opened, fired.

The slug tore through the zombie-conscript's skull, spraying bone and brain across the opposite wall.

"Poor bloke," O.O. muttered, as the zombie collapsed.

Anna lowered the shotgun, and her gaze, picking a path with care over the fallen zombie.

"There!" O.O. called. "Another one!"

"I heard it," Anna said. "So not so loud."

"There's not much point keeping our voices down now," O.O. said.

Anna raised the shotgun again, and kept walking, slowly heading towards the conscript lurching towards them. Definitely a conscript, going by her neon-pink hair, but not one Anna remembered seeing in the Bunker earlier. She stopped level with the kitchen, waiting for the zombie to stagger closer before raising the shotgun to her shoulder and firing.

"Strewth, sounds louder than a cannon," O.O. said.

"How many conscripts were down here?" Anna asked.

"Four, I think," he said.

The sliding door at the end of the corridor was open. Through the communication centre's transparent walls she saw a third conscript, standing with his back to her, but bent over a console. There was no sign of Leo, and when the conscript swung around, she saw no sign of life in his eyes. The zombie lurched towards the transparent walls, but the door further along was closed. So were the blast doors leading to the airlock.

The door leading to the staff-area along the corridor ahead was open, and through it, an undead conscript lurched.

Anna raised the shotgun, waiting for the zombie to get nearer: a man with nearly a week of stubble, and two days of sweat staining his t-shirt. Another stranger. How many more were down here? To her left, the infected creature inside the command centre had reached the doors. One fist, then the next, languidly slapped against the reinforced material. Anna ignored the trapped monster, focusing on the inhuman beast ahead as it staggered closer. Behind it, the first door along the corridor swung open. Leo Smilovitz stepped outside, a U-shaped contraption of cylinders and wires in his hands.

"Leo, down!" Anna said, even as a small dart flew from the U-shaped device. The zombie's head exploded in a red-brown spray of bone-shrapnel.

"Bonzer," O.O. said. "Is that the weapon you said you'd make for us?"

"That was just a fifteen-centimetre bolt propelled by compressed gas," Smilovitz said, reaching into his pocket and extracting another bolt. "He was the third I've shot, meaning there's one more in the complex."

"I've shot two undead conscripts, and the Prime Minister," Anna said. "So he makes five, and I thought there were only four conscripts down here. What happened?"

"I was going to ask you that," Smilovitz said. "I was following a lead. Literally. Data is coming in, but I couldn't transmit. Since the problem isn't in the command centre, I followed the cables to the conduit beyond the data centre. When the emergency lights kicked in, I hacked into the cameras. From what I saw—"

"Watch out!" O.O. said, raising his arm and flinging the throwing stick down the corridor, and at the zombie which had lurched out of the room opposite that which Leo had been hiding.

With a sickening crack, the heavy stick slammed into the zombie-conscript's head. It collapsed. But it wasn't dead. Its legs kicked. Its arms thrashed, even as a sticky dark fluid pulsed from its cracked skull.

"Mine," O.O. said, walking over to the twitching zombie. "Spent hours throwing that damned thing. Hours!" He picked up the throwing stick, raised it, and smashed it down on the twitching zombie's skull. "Yeah, not bad. I can see the appeal."

"Leo, how many people did you have working down here?" Anna asked.

"Four," he said.

"Because that makes six zombie-conscripts. We have to assume there are more in here. Leo, we need to get outside, but the blast doors are shut. Can you open them?"

"Of course," he said. "Facilities like this aren't a prison, they're built with the assumption that everyone on the other side of the door is dead. There will be a mechanical override built into the frame, but to access it, I'll need my tools."

They turned to look at the command centre and the zombie on the other side, its palms slapping, muffled, against the transparent glass.

"They're in there?" O.O. said, raising the throwing stick. "Then open the door. I'm stepping up to the crease."

"No, you're not," Anna said. "You watch the corridor. Leo, that gun you made, how liable is it to blow up?"

"On a scale of one to ten, I'd say a four."

"Then open the door, and I'll shoot. On three."

When the door opened, the shotgun roared, and the zombie collapsed.

As Leo gathered his tools, Anna walked over to the consoles where she'd last seen four of the conscripts. On the ground were three single-use syringes, and one corpse. Before she'd died, the woman's arms had been pinned to the underside of the desk. Long knives, one per arm, had been inserted between the radius and ulna. Each wound was wrapped with tape, perhaps to stem the bleeding, or perhaps to keep the blades in place. Seated, the victim would have had to keep her neck bent forward, her arms at full extension so as not to further tear the wound. Assuming she wanted to delay death, of course. A strip of tape hung from the remains of the woman's mouth. Otherwise, there were few clues as to what had happened to the poor woman as the other three zombies had torn her apart.

"She was crucified," O.O. said, his voice a hoarse whisper.

"She was bait," Anna said. "She can't have been immune, because they had to have done this before the other three were infected. Maybe this was to bring compliance."

"It was for pleasure," O.O. said. "A gun to the head and the lie that the injection was a sedative would have got them all to stand still for the needle. This is just sadism. I've seen some sick things in my life. Met some bad people. Done business with a few, but this is something else."

"It reminds me of a crime scene Commissioner Qwong described," Anna said. "Except there, the killer took hours."

"Didn't have time here," O.O. said. "Just left her pinned, with the choice of tearing the wounds to bring a quicker death than the zombies would offer. Strewth, I thought the mushroom clouds would be the worst of it."

"We should back away, and not touch anything," Anna said, pulling the older man's arm. "This is a crime scene. Tess will need to investigate."

"We're down to one cop in the entire country," O.O. said. "There won't be an investigation."

"Yes there will," Anna said. "We'll bring back more coppers from the outback. Ah, Vaughn sent Tess to hand-issue warrants on the east coast. I bet she wanted her out of Canberra."

"Do you want the good news or the bad news?" Smilovitz called out. He stood next to a now-removed panel on the metal pillar close to the door. He'd pulled out a trio of wires, and plugged them into his tablet, which he now watched.

"Tell us the bad, mate," O.O. said. "Is it aliens or demons, because the way this day is going, I reckon it's one or the other."

"It's soldiers," he said, pointing at his tablet.

Anna stepped close so she could see. On the screen was a green and white view of the lobby, taken by a camera in the corner next to the blast doors and opposite the stairwell and elevator.

"Is that night vision?" O.O. asked.

"Low-light, yes," Smilovitz said. "They've killed the lights. Sorry, bad choice of words."

The image was far from crisp, but Anna could make out four figures, all with submachine guns. Two were aiming their weapons towards the blast doors. The other two were aiming at the stairs. "Cut the power, kill the elevator, was that their plan?" she asked.

"Part of it, maybe," Smilovitz said.

"And they're on the other side of the blast doors?" Anna asked, peering at the picture. "They must be Ian's people, but I don't think… no, I don't think any are Major Kelly."

"The sheila with the face like a road accident, and voice to match?" O.O. said.

"She escorted me down here," Anna said. "I think she commands Ian's soldiers. Leo, how long will it take them to get in?"

"Ten minutes," Smilovitz said. "But, right now, they're not trying. I can buy us a bit more time. Maybe two hours. But not much longer."

"Where's the back door?" O.O. asked.

"What back door?" Smilovitz asked.

"The escape hatch," O.O. said. "Don't places like this have them?"

"Not in real life, no," Smilovitz said. "This isn't a bunker to keep hundreds alive for a few years. It's not a redoubt in case Canberra is invaded. It's a refuge in case of a biological attack on Parliament. It's got food and water, and enough air to keep a hundred alive for a few weeks. With just the three of us, the air will last a lot longer. But the food is mostly gone. Water, I don't know."

"I know all that," O.O. said. "But I thought there'd be a hatch for the cables or something. This place was a waste of money when it was commissioned. Putting in the bunks and a handful of offices just so the press could report the PM had been taken down to the Bunker. When a politician looks for a rock to hide under, it's time to call an election, that's what I say."

"That's what they were doing," Smilovitz said. "With all of this, dismantling the communications equipment, they were deliberately cutting the Bunker off from the rest of the world."

"It wasn't hard," O.O. said. "There isn't much of the world left."

"Yes, but they could have simply severed the cables entering the Bunker," Smilovitz said. "The wires enter through a conduit just outside. Instead, they left enough incoming data to keep a technician busy while they implemented the rest of their plot."

"By which you mean gathering the unwanted politicians here," O.O. said. "And infecting enough to ensure the rest would get murdered by zombies. Afterwards, those four outside would enter, with cameras to record them stumbling across the undead PM, and us."

"Why?" Anna asked. "If it's a coup, why not just kill us?"

"For legitimacy," O.O. said. "To show the politicians we sent to Hobart that Bronwyn really is dead."

"Fine, we can theorise the rest of it later," Anna asked. "Leo, there really is no other way out of here?"

"If this man here doesn't know of one, I'd be surprised to discover it," Smilovitz said. "But I control the cameras. They can't see inside. Are there more guns down here? What about those two in your holster?"

"They don't work," O.O. said. "Guess who gave them to me. Could you fix them?"

"Maybe," Smilovitz said. "The armoury is empty. I saw that earlier. Is there no other cache of guns?"

"Nope," O.O. said. "We distributed the firearms to the conscripts. I doubt Bronwyn packed a gun. And doubt even more that Lignatiev or Vaughn left some lying around. How quickly can that door slide upward? I'm not dying without a fight, so let's get it over with."

"Can you control the internal locks?" Anna asked. "Could we lure them in here, and seal them in somewhere? Or some of them. If we can get upstairs, we can get outside. Only one of us needs to get to the airport."

"Give me a minute," Smilovitz said, and began tapping at the screen, changing images, occasionally glancing at the ceiling.

"Why, though?" O.O. asked. "Why would Ian or Erin do this?"

"Power," Anna said.

"But they could have had it," O.O. said. "Bronwyn was playing a harp missing half the strings. If we'd had a vote, Ian would have got the job. I would have voted for him. Tell me you wouldn't. So why do all this?"

"Earlier, outside, when you gave me that gun, did you tell anyone where I'd gone?"

"No. Where did you go?" O.O. asked.

"To find Dr Avalon," Anna said.

"Where is she?" Smilovitz asked, looking away from the screen.

"I sent her to the airport," Anna said. "But, Oswald, if you didn't tell them where I was going, how did they know? By then, Mel was already dead."

"Mel's dead?" Smilovitz asked, again looking up.

"Sorry. Yes. And so are your other three assistants. They were infected. Mel was hanged, staged to look like a suicide, but it must have happened hours before I went there. I don't know if Dr Avalon was a target, or if you were, Leo. One of the students was a witness, which, I suppose, is why they were murdered. But were you and Dr Avalon targets, too?"

"Why would we be?" Smilovitz asked. "Ah, hold that thought. We've got movement."

"Are they coming in?" O.O. asked, as he and Anna huddled around the screen.

Two of the soldiers had dashed towards the stairs in the corner opposite the camera.

Before Anna could frame a question, the screen went white. "What just happened?" she asked, even as the door shook, and a loud, though muffled, bang seeped through the thick barrier-door.

"Flash-bang, I think," Smilovitz said.

The image cleared, belatedly showing two people, rifles raised, having descended the stairs. Not just raised, but firing. The two soldiers closest to the stairs were motionless. Even as the other two simultaneously scrabbled for their helmets to raise the night-vision goggles from their flash-blinded eyes, they collapsed. The two loyal soldiers, two women, lowered their guns. One turned back to face the stairs, while the other looked up at the camera. It wasn't a soldier. It was Tess Qwong.

Chapter 26 - Coup Interrupted
Parliament House

"It's a coup, Tess," Anna said as the door finally, slowly, opened.

"But not organised by him?" Tess asked, keeping her gun raised, the barrel a polite few degrees from pointing at Oswald Owen's head.

"Me?" O.O. said. "You think I'm behind this, too? So much suspicion is enough to give a bloke a complex. It was Ian Lignatiev."

"And Erin Vaughn," Anna added.

"Explains the soldiers," Tess said. "Are there any more inside?"

"No," Anna said. "I don't think so. There might be more zombies. There might be more people hiding. But probably not."

Tess lowered her weapon. "Dr Avalon came to the airport, reporting trouble, and told us not to trust Mr Owen."

"He's as innocent as me," Anna said. "At least of this. Is Parliament House safe?"

"No," Tess said. "We've secured the stairwell and the entrance, during which we encountered seven of those soldiers, including the four here."

"They're mercenaries," the woman who accompanied Tess said. Older, and nearing the age where she might even be called old, she held her assault rifle with the confidence of experience, while her face had echoes of familiarity.

"Do I know you?" Anna asked.

"This is Teegan Toppley," Tess said.

"*The* Teegan Toppley?" O.O. asked, stepping out of the airlock and over to the nearest corpse. He unhooked the dead mercenary's suppressed submachine gun. "Talk about the end of the world making strange bedfellows."

"Dream on, mate," Toppley said.

"They infected Bronwyn Wilson," Anna said. "And at least five conscripts."

O.O. fired a burst from the submachine gun into the wall. Bullets ricocheted. Everyone ducked.

"Stop shooting!" Smilovitz called, just before Anna could do the same.

"Sorry, sorry!" O.O. said. "Wanted to make sure the gun worked."

"Not the most sensible idea, considering these," Toppley said, holding up a small bag. "Plastic explosives."

While Dr Smilovitz had worked on opening the door, Anna had watched the screen showing the camera-view of the other side of the airlock. While Tess had guarded the stairwell, Toppley had moved around the room with a bag in hand, even retrieving a small stepladder so she could access the ceiling.

"May I see, please?" Smilovitz asked. He took the bag. "Intriguing. There's a timer rather than a remote detonator. Two timers, in fact. And enough explosives to bring down the building."

"Here you are, Smiley." O.O. held out the submachine gun he'd just fired to Dr Smilovitz. "They wanted to bury us in there?"

"It's a coup, Tess," Anna said. "I think they killed Aaron Bryce, and he wasn't the first."

Another trio of suppressed shots caused them all to spin. O.O. had picked up another submachine gun, but this time, he'd fired into a corpse. "Like I said, I wanted to make sure the guns worked."

"Let's talk as we walk, and do both quickly," Tess said, and took point as they climbed up the stairs.

"You say they're mercenaries?" O.O. asked.

"Low grade amateurs," Toppley said. "Not so much weekend-warriors as vacation-vets. Conscripts, though of a different sort to ourselves. They appear menacing, but have no experience of maintaining a defence or planning a retreat. In short, they are expendable, which suggests their demolition expert wasn't confident the timer would give someone more useful sufficient time to escape up those stairs."

"Did you find a radio?" Smilovitz asked.

"No, but I wasn't looking for one," Toppley said.

"Why do you ask?" Tess asked.

"Slow down a bit," O.O. said breathlessly.

"They had timers rigged to those explosives," Smilovitz said. "Two timers, so one was a back-up, but they must have been waiting for a signal before detonating them."

"Which suggests more people here," Tess said.

"Or more bombs," Anna added.

"Yeah, forget what I just said, and hurry," O.O. said.

Anna was the second to reach the atrium, and the first thing she saw was the gun barrel, though its wielder, having recognised Tess, was already turning to point the weapon back along the corridor. A helmet covered the man's head, a neat goatee covered his chin, while body-armour covered his blue airport overalls. In his hands was a shotgun, while over his shoulder was an MP5 submachine gun with suppressor, presumably taken from the corpse at his feet.

"Any trouble, Clyde?" Tess asked.

"No trouble, Commish," he said. "But some curiosity from the other side of those doors." Even as he spoke, he shifted position, turning ninety degrees, towards the pair of glass doors currently secured by a pair of plastic hand-ties. "Three people in suits. Saw me. Left."

"Probably nothing to do with the coup," Anna said. "But people will have questions."

"They can join the club," O.O. said. "Because I've got no answers for them."

"Clyde, join Teegan at the rear," Tess said. "Shout a warning before you shoot, and don't shoot first."

"Roger, Commish," Clyde said.

"You've found an army," Anna said, as she ran with Tess along the corridor, roughly following the fire-exit signs towards the outside. "And don't I know that bloke?"

"He was with me when I found Aaron Bryce's body," Tess said. "You sent him to work the airport. When Dr Avalon brought her warning, I gathered some people I could trust, and left others guarding the scientist."

"Captain Hawker isn't here?" Anna asked.

But Tess had paused at a corner. "Funnel-web!" she called.

"Stonefish," came the reply. "We're clear, Commissioner."

Tess peered around the corner, then beckoned the others to follow. Just before the doors leading outside were another pair of Tess's team. Two women, both similarly attired to Clyde, wearing blue airport overalls, body armour, and helmets. A woman, with a trio of distinctly un-military nose rings, carried the ADF's standard issue EF88 bullpup-style assault rifle. The other, ramrod straight, wearing enough gems to open a jewellers, carried an MP5 submachine gun, presumably taken from the dead mercenary sprawled near the door.

"Any trouble, Bianca?" Tess asked.

"Not yet," Bianca said. Her accent was as likely to cut glass as the diamonds on the earrings dangling beneath her helmet's strategically repositioned chin strap.

"I thought we came here to arrest him," the woman with the nose rings said, pointing, though not with her gun, to Oswald Owen.

"He's one of the good guys, Elaina," Tess said.

"I'd never describe myself as *good*," O.O. said. "But I'm not evil. Are your soldiers short on weapons?"

"Chronically," Bianca said. "And we're not soldiers. We're Team Stonefish."

"Bianca, Elaina, Clyde," Tess said. "Give your helmets to the politicians and the scientist."

"You mean you're okay with us getting our heads blown off?" Elaina asked. "No offence, but my love for democracy doesn't extend to becoming a decoy."

"A sniper isn't interested in you," Tess said, taking off her body armour. "They'll know you're a soldier by your clothing, and know these three are the targets by theirs."

"You think they have snipers?" O.O. asked.

"If it were me, I would," Toppley said.

"Which is good enough for me," Tess said, handing her bulletproof vest to Anna. "They'll have time for one shot. If it comes, scatter. But we're running outside, and down to the utes parked on the road."

O.O. waved away Clyde's proffered helmet. "No, if there's a sniper, let's give him a truly tempting target. Anna, in those overalls, she looks as anonymous as a recruit. You keep your helmet, and I'll play the sacrificial calf."

Before Anna could object, O.O. had opened the doors and jogged outside.

The road was empty except for a pair of airport emergency vehicles, which O.O. reached without terminal interruption from a sniper. A few seconds later, so did everyone else, taking shelter with three more of Tess's team, one of whom was young enough to be in school.

"*You* can't be SAS," O.O. said.

"We're Team Stonefish," the young man said. "And I thought we were going to shoot him."

"My reputation travels before me," O.O. said. "It's exhausting trying to keep up."

"This is Zach," Tess said, quickly. "And that's Sophia, behind the wheel. They're conscripts I first met at the wall, and whom I trust. The bloke with the shotgun, that's Blaze. He and Teegan Toppley were with me in the outback."

The silver-haired man had his shotgun, and gaze, directed towards the road until Toppley handed him one of the submachine guns taken from the body of a mercenary.

"Who's she?" Anna asked, pointing at the last figure, who clearly wasn't a member of Team Stonefish. The woman sat in the truck-bed of the second airport-response vehicle. In her early twenties, a clotted gash along her forehead had dripped a trail of blood to her chin. With watchful eyes, angrily clenched jaw, and alertly tensed shoulders, she was dressed in the mercenaries' black utility gear Anna had previously associated with the Special Forces. The mercenary's helmet had been removed, revealing close-cropped black hair. Her body armour had gone, too, while her hands and wrists were secured with plastic ties, to which a rope and chain had been added.

"Who added the rope and chain?" Tess asked.

"Didn't want her to escape," the very young man, Zach, said. "I've seen movies. The prisoner always escapes."

"You've got a prisoner?" O.O. asked, pushing his way through the team. "What's your name, Miss?"

The prisoner shook her head.

"She was in charge of the detail here," Tess said. "When I took her prisoner, the others opened fire. That was when Clyde and Blaze began their competition to see who could be shot first." The two older, stern-faced men looked away.

"They attacked first," Zach added in defence of his senior comrades.

"And so we did the same," Tess said. "But now we only have one prisoner."

"Who we'll make sing louder than a lyrebird?" O.O. said. "Smiley, you got any pliers on you, mate? Maybe a drill."

"No, Oswald," Anna said. "We're supposed to be better than that. We have to lead by example, obeying the laws we tell a few to uphold and the many to follow." She turned to the prisoner. "I don't know your name. I should do, since you were guarding this building. I should have asked. But I didn't. I apologise."

The prisoner's eyes narrowed, but more in suspicion than puzzlement.

"You're a mercenary, yes?" Anna asked. "You'll work for whoever pays the most? I can guarantee that we, the Australian government, can pay more than anyone else on the planet. Where did Lignatiev and Vaughn go?"

The mercenary sighed, and gave a wan smile. "I'm not doing this for money. I'm repaying a debt."

"You owe Ian a debt?" Anna asked.

"Not him," the mercenary said. "I don't work for him."

"For Vaughn?" O.O. asked.

The mercenary shook her head. "The worst you can do is kill me," she said. "The people who hired me can make death seem like a gift."

"Oh, I can do worse than kill you," O.O. said. "Someone give me a knife."

"No," Anna said, pointing along the road where a trio of agricultural labourers crouched behind an overloaded pallet of corrugated steel. "There are people watching, Oswald. Constituents. Citizens."

"Show them what we found," the stone-faced man, Blaze, said, not taking his eyes from the road.

"Oh, yeah, this," Zach said, hauling a bag from the front seat and dropping it on the ground.

"Easy on!" Sophia said.

"Sorry," Zach said, bending and unzipping the bag. Inside were small grey bricks.

"Is that a bomb?" O.O. asked.

"Plastic explosive, yes," Smilovitz said, bending down and picking up a brick. "It matches what we found down in the Bunker. No markings, so privately manufactured. Not military issue. Fascinating." He put the brick down and picked up a small box with a pair of wires. "Detonator attached to a timer. No remote. Understandable under the circumstances, but who would have known of the circumstances in advance?"

"Blaze, did you find a radio?" Tess asked.

"No."

"They were expecting the order to come in person," Tess said. She turned to the prisoner. "We found explosives at the entrance to the Bunker, so where were you going to plant these?"

The prisoner shook her head.

"Where were your orders coming from?" O.O. asked. "Answer at least one question or I'll roll up my sleeves, and I don't care if there's a news crew recording it."

"It's okay, Oswald," Anna said, laying a cautioning hand on his arm. "There's no need, because I think I know where Ian and Erin went." She turned back to the prisoner. "Your orders were to make sure no one went down to the Bunker, yes?"

The woman tilted her head in what was neither a shake nor a nod.

"People still work here," Anna said. "Not many. But enough. They would ask why these soldiers were stopping people from going down into the Bunker. The bomb would have sealed the entrance, ensuring that we were trapped down there with the undead who would kill us."

"You were going to trap them with the zombies?" Zach asked.

"But first," Anna continued, "they had to secure their hold on power. They wanted us trapped down there after they'd cut the Bunker's communications with the outside world. Not just to prevent us from getting help, but because they needed all of Canberra, Hobart, Australia, the world, everyone to think we were dead. An explosion at Parliament House would convince everyone in the A.C.T., as fast as the speed of rumour. But they'd need word to get out faster and further than that."

"You mean the broadcast studio they set up at the Telstra Tower?" O.O. said. "That's where they've gone?"

The mercenary stiffened.

"Ha! I saw that," O.O. declared, victorious. "I'd call that a confession."

"Airports and broadcast studios," Toppley said. "They are the essential targets in any revolution."

"Does that ute have a radio?" Anna said. "Switch to the official channel."

Blaze did. Dreary orchestral music, the kind that made a sunny day appear grey, drifted from the speakers.

"That's what they play before the official broadcast," Anna said.

"We've been waiting to hear one all day," Tess said.

"There hasn't been one yet?" Anna asked.

"Nothing. Just that music, and the instruction to stay tuned for something soon."

"Why haven't Lignatiev and Vaughn broadcast something?" O.O. said. He turned to the prisoner. "Are they waiting for you to report the explosion?"

"With this amount of explosive," Smilovitz said, "they'd hear it."

"Then that's their signal, meaning we've still got the element of surprise," Anna said.

"Zach, you drive the politicians to the airport," Tess said. "We'll take the other ute to the Telstra Tower."

"Not a chance," O.O. said. "Me and Ian are overdue for a convo before this is over. The Telstra Tower? Used to love walking around Black Mountain when I was younger, so I'll drive the lead ute."

"No more questions, no more arguments, because we've no more time to waste," Anna said. "Tess, let's move out."

"You've been watching too many movies with your dad," Tess said, but two minutes later, they were driving west.

Chapter 27 - Uphill Battle
Telstra Tower, Black Mountain

"You won't really pay her to join us, will you?" Zach asked while Tess drove, and Anna mentally reframed her understanding of the events of the last few weeks.

Next to Anna was Leo Smilovitz and the notorious crook, Teegan Toppley. The prisoner was still chained up, riding in the back of the other truck, now in front with Oswald Owen behind the wheel. Clyde, Blaze, Bianca, Elaina, and Sophia were crammed inside while the politician wildly steered the speeding truck down the empty roads.

"The mercenary, I mean," Zach said, pointing ahead at the chained woman being thrown from side to side as O.O. veered across the road far more erratically than necessary. "She's the enemy, so will you really let her fight on our side?"

"Put her in the very foremost line," Toppley said. "It was how loyalty used to be proven."

"It depends on what she did," Anna said. "We'll need some jails, but running prisons, with guards and fences, will consume resources we could expend saving others. But her fate will be determined by her guilt. If she was complicit with what happened inside the Bunker, I'll personally dig a big hole to throw her in."

"You mean infecting the prime minister?" Tess asked.

"No," Anna said. "It's worse than that. Do you remember telling me about those two pilots in Broken Hill? This was similar."

"What pilots?" Zach asked. "What was similar?"

"There are some things it's better not to know," Tess said. "How similar?"

"Not identical," Anna said. "But close enough."

Ahead, O.O. clipped the edge of a barricade. There were no guards there, and no people on the footpath, but there were faces in windows, and even in some doorways. From those, the dreary orchestral piece played as citizens waited to hear confirmation of the rumours that must have spread throughout the city. But as long as the music bleakly blared, it wasn't over. Not yet.

"Where are the soldiers?" Toppley asked as they sped through another unguarded barricade.

"There were more a few days ago," Tess said. "Mobile patrols, too."

"He's deployed them elsewhere," Anna said. "He must have. Ian Lignatiev, I mean. This was why he wanted to remain Minister of Defence. During the meeting where we picked Bronwyn Wilson for PM, Aaron Bryce asked Ian if he wanted the top job. Ian said he'd stick with the area he knew best. But this has to be the real reason. If Ian had become PM, Oswald would have taken the defence job. I can guarantee he'd have stuck soldiers on every street corner."

"Conscripts," Toppley said.

"We're still fighters," Zach added.

"But Lignatiev wanted the authority to deploy the soldiers away from here," Anna said. "Julia Dickson committed suicide, Tess."

"Who?" Zach asked.

"The Minister of Defence before the outbreak," Tess said. "She killed herself the day after Manhattan. Rather, it was assumed to be suicide. It was before I reached Canberra."

"It was one of the first suicides," Anna said. "And it was why Ian got the promotion."

"This sounds all rather Roman," Toppley said with a dismissively blithe calm. "Or perhaps the Soviet Union was a stronger influence."

"The mercenaries must have been hired before the outbreak," Anna said. "So did Ian know about the zombies? Did he know about the nuclear war? If he didn't, then what was he planning for?"

"You can ask him in about ten minutes," Tess said.

The thousand-metre-tall Black Mountain swiftly grew ahead of them as Tess struggled to keep up with the demonically speeding Oswald Owen. Accelerating into each bend, and again on each straight, spinning across junctions, and scraping against barriers, O.O. left a trail of rubber, paint, and sparks in his wake. The prisoner chained in the back of his truck received as much attention as the speeding cars from the increasingly large doorstep-crowds. But even the sight of a handcuffed captive, hurled hither and thither, would be forgotten when the broadcast was made.

The orchestral music, playing low through the truck's stereo, abruptly stopped. For a heart-skipping moment, Anna thought they were too late, but instead of Ian or Erin's voice, the music returned.

The two-vehicle convoy sped through the university, down Tourist Drive, and made a sharp turn onto the winding, rising, paved road signposted to the mountain's summit. O.O.'s truck nearly didn't make it, losing a wing mirror as he attempted a handbrake turn between two of the large lumber-harvesters parked at the roadside.

"Are you deforesting the mountain?" Toppley asked, as Tess braked, changed gear, and took the turn more slowly.

"Making a palisade," Anna said. "But only as practice. It's one of many old skills we have to relearn."

Above, the soaring communications tower had disappeared behind the bushy canopies of the closely planted needlewoods. Ahead, O.O.'s truck had disappeared around the winding road's next bend. Tess sped up, and Anna caught sight of O.O's truck just as a burst of gunfire drummed against its side. Glass shattered. The entire truck seemed to shudder. The prisoner went limp. O.O. braked, but Tess sped up.

"Two o'clock, fifty metres back," Toppley said.

"You have to stop!" Anna said.

"Not yet," Tess said, overtaking O.O's truck as another burst of gunfire came from the woodland. Their wing mirror exploded. Bullets slammed into metal, and Tess slammed on the brakes, bringing their truck to a halt just beyond O.O.'s.

"When I say—" Tess began, but Anna had already thrown open the door and jumped out.

She sprinted into the undergrowth, shotgun raised. Leaves and mulch fountained two metres to her left so she zagged to the right, behind a thick trunk, then darted left, diving to the ground even as a shower of bark erupted from the tree behind which she'd sought shelter.

She fired, once, blindly in the direction of the shooter, picked herself up, and sprinted on until a heavy figure knocked her to the ground.

"Stop!" Clyde hissed, pushing her low as a burst came from behind, another machine-bark replied from ahead.

"Get off!" she hissed.

"Stay low," Clyde said, easing to the side, but pushing her gun barrel down. "Wait for the signal."

A stereo trio of metal thumping into wood came from ahead, ending in a softer, wetter, impact, a muted hiss, a truncated scream.

"Clear!" Elaina called from ahead.

"Stonefish!" Zach added.

"Sorry about that, ma'am," Clyde said. Springing to his feet far more lithely than Anna, he reached down to offer her his hand.

"Anna Dodson," Tess said, catching up, and speaking in a tone that had echoes of her father in every syllable. "Don't you *ever* do that again."

"A leader's gotta lead, Tess," Anna said.

Far closer than she realised, barely ten metres away, Elaina and Zach stood over a corpse, with their weapons aimed up the hill. Clyde jogged ahead of them, reaching the corpse before Anna and Tess. He bent down, taking the dead man's submachine gun, then the ammo from the webbing pouches slung across the body armour.

"Heckler and Koch MP5," Clyde said. "But it's not ADF. These mercenaries didn't arm themselves with our weapons. They're well-armed," he added, reaching down to pluck a grenade from the dead mercenary's webbing. "But these are concussion grenades, flash-bangs. Three of them. And this bloke was alone. Do we advance?"

"Does he have a radio?" Tess asked.

"No."

"Then back to the trucks," Tess said. "But bring the grenades."

At the trucks, Leo was bandaging Sophia's arm.

"Are you okay?" Anna asked.

"I got shot," Sophia said, sounding more bewildered than hurt. "I actually got shot. With a bullet."

"It's a through-and-through," Smilovitz said. "But she'll need a hospital."

"The prisoner's dead," O.O. said. "Might even have been the target."

"Not from that range," Clyde said.

"Deploying only one sentry suggests, right here, right now, they're short-handed," Tess said. "That man didn't have a radio, but they'll have heard the shots. We're running out of time."

A sudden blast of trombones and timpani blared from the radio.

"Turn that off!" O.O. snapped, reaching past Zach, into the truck, to switch off the radio.

"But that proves they've not started broadcasting their victory rally," Zach said. "We've still got time."

"What's your name, kid?" O.O. asked. "Zach, right?"

"I'm not a kid."

"No, you're a soldier," O.O. said. "And right now, *soldier*, you're going to drive this woman to the airport. To win a revolution, you've got to control the airport and the transmitter. Smiley, have you got the explosives?"

Dr Smilovitz grabbed the bag from the front of the cab. "You want me to blow up the transmitter?"

"If all else fails," O.O. said.

"Sophia," Anna said, speaking to the injured woman. "Tell Hoa Nguyen what's happened. If Captain Hawker is back, tell him, too. Either way, hold the airport, and prepare an army for an assault."

"An assault where?" Sophia asked.

"Wherever the shooting is," O.O. said. He pointed at Smilovitz, then Clyde. "Smiley, you and the soldier drive the ute to the top. Make some noise. We'll hike the long way, come in from behind. You'll either be the distraction for us to make an assault, or we'll be the distraction while you blow the place down. A pincer movement, that's how we'll win this battle." Everyone except Tess and O.O. turned to Clyde, whose curt nod marked his seal of approval.

"I'll drive them," Anna said. "Oswald and I shouldn't face the same risks. What's that rule of Dad's, if a job's to be done, get it done now. Go on, Tess. I'll see you at the top."

Hunched forward, steering wheel clenched tight, feet tensed, Anna drove the truck up the hill. Clyde was in the passenger seat, with Toppley and Smilovitz in the bench-row behind. Anna's eyes searched the shadows, but her mind already dwelled on revenge. Within minutes, and without another shot being fired, they reached the mountain's crest. Beyond the car park to the lookout point, there was only the barest hint of a view; the trees, in full autumnal majesty, obscured the world beyond their nightmare stretch of tarmac. That was the extent of her universe, the road ahead, and and it was quickly running out.

Ahead, the transmitter rose like a space-age monolith, seeming to grow taller as they approached. But the road curved, dipped, and climbed, as it circled the mountain's peak, and the transmitter was abruptly hidden.

"Get ready to bail," Clyde said. "Out and to the back of the vehicle."

"I've only ever done this the other way," Smilovitz said. "When Flo and I were driving away from the people trying to kill us. But you sound like you've done this before. You're a soldier?"

"A charity worker," Clyde said.

"What kind of charity work involves gunfights?" Smilovitz asked.

"The kind I hoped I'd never have to do again," Clyde said.

Anna hunched behind the wheel, making herself as small as possible. The trees thinned, and through the gaps she saw the entrancing peaks of distant mountains, tempered by the increasingly frequent glimpses of the tower.

They were close. Very close. They *must* have been heard. Lignatiev's people *must* be expecting her. With every metre driven, her foot straining with expectation of stomping on the brake, she expected the trap to be sprung.

And it was.

To their left, a stone retaining wall squatted nearly two metres high, on the other side of which were a row of adolescent trees, stunted by exposure. Beyond those was the levelled ground of the tower's main car park. To her right, a moderately sturdy bar-and-pillar crash barrier prevented rainy-day visitors accidentally ploughing into the wooded slopes below. But ahead, a camouflaged Humvee blocked the road.

The moment Anna saw and recognised it, she braked. But their unseen assailants had seen them, too. Bullets sprayed the road in front, the ricochets bouncing up to thud into the tyres. A second burst went high, as a mercenary with an EF88 assault rifle failed to hit the large target right in front of him.

"Out! Out! Out!" Toppley yelled.

Clyde had already grabbed Anna's collar, pulled her low, and had dragged her halfway outside, through the passenger door, before she'd had time to think.

By accident more than design, the car had stopped at an angle to the road, the front against the stone retaining wall, the rear only a metre from the crash barrier. Clyde pushed Anna down and behind the relatively thicker cover of the wheel-arch as a third short burst from the assault rifle spanged into the truck's engine block. As quickly as it took for the merc to switch the selector to fully automatic, it was followed by a magazine-emptying burst that smashed into engine, door, window, roof, and then the sky.

"Amateurs," Toppley muttered, the word dripping with scorn.

"Cover me," Smilovitz said.

"Why?" Anna asked, but the scientist had already opened the truck's rear door.

Toppley fired a burst from around the rear of the vehicle while Clyde fired from the front, and the scientist grabbed the bag containing the explosives. From ahead, return fire drummed against the road, the car, and a good portion of the trees on the down-slope to their right.

"Two shooters," Clyde said as they all took cover once more. "An assault rifle and a submachine gun, one either end of the Humvee." Another, different, gun barked. "Three shooters," Clyde amended. "Shotgun."

"This takes me back to my youth," Toppley said, ducking down as another erratic burst slammed into the truck.

"Their aim is terrible," Smilovitz said as lead pattered against the retaining wall.

"Killed is killed," Clyde said, ducking low to peer under their vehicle. "Amateur or a sniper, makes no difference if they hit."

"What's the plan now?" Smilovitz asked, crouching low, behind the rear wheel.

"Distract or attack," Anna said. "Any suggestions how?"

"We need the high ground," Toppley said. She pointed back the way they'd driven. "That pillar, supporting the retaining wall, will give us some cover. Go there, climb up to the car park where we'll have the advantage of elevation. Shall we say on three?"

"Make it ten," Smilovitz said, both of his arms inside the bag, his hands moving frantically.

The assault rifle fired another magazine-emptying burst, most of which slammed into the engine. The exposed tyre burst under the impact of a dozen bullets, and the truck sank as it settled onto the rim. From the engine, a wisp of smoke drifted upwards, thin, but already growing thicker.

"Time's up, Leo," Anna said. "What are you planning?"

Smilovitz removed a brick of plastic explosive into which he'd inserted a timer. "Any of you play baseball? No, of course not. What is it down here, cricket, right?"

"Give it to me," Clyde said.

"Timer's thirty seconds," Smilovitz said.

"On ten, we shoot. On twenty, we run," Anna said, edging back along the road. She stood, firing. The shotgun roared, the slugs going wide, but the sound, to which Toppley added her submachine gun, gave Clyde cover to throw. Even as the brick was in the air, all three ducked down.

"Think it was short," Clyde said.

"Doesn't matter, on my mark, fire," Anna said. But their enemy fired first, the bullets slamming into and through the bodywork as the four dived back to the ground.

Clyde aimed his submachine gun beneath the truck, firing a short burst.

"Ten seconds left," Smilovitz said.

"Run!" Anna said, just as the world shook. Her faltering sprint turned into a diving fall as expanding air roared past. Tarmac and fragments of glass and metal tore into her clothes, her skin, as she rolled to a halt, then to her feet, grabbing Toppley, and hauling her over to the wall. Behind, their truck was now on its roof, smoke pouring from the engine. But flames were licking around the Humvee, on its side, and turned parallel to the road.

"Up!" Anna said. "Up!" Still dazed from the pressure of the explosion, from the wall of sound, the rain of debris, she was slow to formulate a longer sentence. Instead, she pushed Toppley up the side of the wall. Clyde, gun raised to his cheek, fired a quick burst towards their enemy, but Anna couldn't see his target.

She hurled her shotgun to the top of the wall, then threw herself up after it, rolling to a crouch next to Toppley, who knelt, looking dishevelled, but amused, aiming her weapon towards the tower.

"That wasn't thirty seconds," Anna said as Smilovitz followed, Clyde hot on his heels.

"Please don't tell Flo," Smilovitz said. "She's always saying I'm terrible at math."

"No movement by the Humvee," Clyde said, crouched by the edge of the wall.

"They're dead?" Smilovitz asked.

"Or they ran," Clyde said.

"Worry about that later," Anna said. "We've given Oswald his distraction, but we can't stay here."

There were no sentries in the car park, and only one vehicle, a camouflaged MRH-90 medium-transport helicopter. A type she knew, and recognised, from Lignatiev's publicity photographs before the last election.

"Ian was retraining as a pilot," Anna said. "I've seen photographs of him in that helicopter."

"Everyone has," Clyde said. "I never trust anyone who uses service as a tool to further their own ends."

"That's his way out, is it?" Smilovitz asked. "Give me a minute. I'll catch up."

Before Anna could ask why, the scientist sprinted towards the helicopter. Clyde ran on ahead, through the car park towards the tower. Toppley ushered Anna after him. She'd managed ten steps when a distant shot made Clyde double over in a crouch, but he also doubled his speed, so she did the same. Eight running strides later, another shot cracked across the mountaintop, and this one was closer.

Clyde took cover at the top of the curving slope that formed an exit to the car park leading back to the road on which the Humvee and their truck now merrily burned.

"They're shooting at Oswald?" Anna asked.

"Defo," Clyde said, twisting his head as he surveyed the windows of the telecoms tower ahead of them. "I see movement. No hostiles."

"There are civilians in there," Anna said. "Broadcast technicians. Some reporters. Even some pundits and musicians. I'm not sure how many, but it must be at least fifty."

A flurry of shots sounded from the far side of the tower.

"Someone should have come to investigate the explosion," Toppley said, as Smilovitz ran to a staggering halt next to them.

Anna glanced back at the helicopter. She'd been expecting an explosion, but the copter was still intact. "You disabled it?" she asked.

"No one will fly away from here in that," Smilovitz said.

"We can't hold this position," Clyde said. "Not with that footbridge there to our left. Looks like it leads straight to the tower's second floor. Advance or retreat?"

Anywhere out in the open would leave them exposed to a sniper up in the tower. Another footbridge led from the tower to the right of the road, while the mountain's slopes were so well managed, a footpath wasn't needed for a descent. If the mercenaries ran, they had an almost certain chance of escape.

"Advance," Anna said.

With Clyde in the lead, they ran down the slope, and back onto the road. Ahead, parked outside the entrance to the tower were two black SUVs, both seemingly empty. Clyde kept his rifle aimed at the tinted windows as he approached, but he should have been looking at the door.

"Down!" Toppley said, firing as Anna half-pushed, half-dragged Clyde behind the vehicle.

Smilovitz, still running, emptied his entire magazine into the doorway. Clyde motioned Anna to advance around the rear of the SUV while he took the front, but when Anna swung around the vehicle, the black-clad figure in the doorway was dead.

"I saw two," Anna called, advancing to the body, sprawled amid shattered glass.

"The other ran," Toppley said, running over to stand between her and the glass doors.

"They're all trying to escape," Clyde said, picking up the dead man's submachine gun. "There's no magazine." He plucked a mag from the mercenary's webbing. "He had ammo, but he forgot to load his gun. Who are these people?"

More shots came from inside: a flurry, a burst, a double-tap.

"If we go inside, we'll be caught in the crossfire," Toppley said.

"The SUVs," Anna said. "We use them as cover, and stop the mercenaries driving away."

"On the politician," Clyde said.

In a close pack, they retreated, guns raised, while inside and beyond the tower, gunfire rose in increasing ferocity.

A pair of figures in camouflage and body armour ran into the lobby beyond the broken doors. Even as Clyde fired, they dived back down the corridor they'd run down.

"I'm going in," Clyde said. "Flush them out. You three stay here."

"No," Anna said. "We—"

"The walkway!" Toppley said, pointing ahead and above, where the walkway formed a bridge over the road. On it, four figures ran. All in camouflage, but one wore a far more professional uniform than the others.

"It's Ian!" Anna said even as Toppley fired.

A mercenary fell, but the other three ran on, and were lost to sight behind the walkway and the trees ringing the car park.

"He can't get away!" Anna yelled, already running back towards the sloped driveway that led into the car park.

"He won't!" Smilovitz yelled, running after her. "He—"

Anna felt something bite into her leg. As she fell, her first thought was *zombie*, but when she saw the blood, she knew it was only a bullet. *Only?* The thought raced across her mind as she tumbled backwards, looking back to the tower, to where a camouflaged soldier stood on the terrace next to the walkway, gun raised. He had a perfect shot. But he made just as perfect a target for Clyde and Toppley as they emptied half a magazine into him.

"Please don't ruin all our efforts by dying," Smilovitz said, crouching next to her.

"Ian's getting away!" Anna said.

"No he's not," Smilovitz said, a thin smile on his face which only grew wider as a second, massive explosion shook the mountaintop.

"You're lucky the bullet didn't break the bone," Toppley said as she bandaged Anna's leg in a corridor inside the Telstra Tower.

Anna, adrenaline spent along with all the energy she'd borrowed to get through the last few hours, simply winced. "Dad always says luck is for those who didn't have timing."

"Then you have perfect timing, because it didn't sever the artery, either," Toppley said. "Dose up on the antibiotics, and you'll be fine."

"But can she stand?" O.O. asked, walking along the corridor.

"Stand? No," Anna said. "I can barely keep my eyes open."

"You'll only have to manage it for ten minutes," O.O. said. "Or you could sit down for the broadcast. Dr Smiley has the cameras ready to roll. There're a few spare outfits in an office down there. Red pantsuits, which don't seem appropriate, but are more prime ministerial than the rags you're wearing."

"I bet they were Vaughn's," Anna said, only half listening to Oswald. "Has Tess found her?"

"There's been no more shooting," O.O. said. "So I'll say no, or not anywhere near here. But if you can't walk, we better carry you."

"No," Anna said.

"The people need to hear from you," O.O. said. "They need to know about the coup. They need to know it's over. A young politician valiantly defeating her foe in defence of her people. It's the perfect story."

"For a month ago," Anna said. "But now they need…" She looked Oswald up and down. "Solidity."

"Charming."

"You know what I mean, and you know it's true," Anna said. "There's been an attempted coup. People will want familiarity. They know you, Oswald."

"They don't like me."

"But they don't distrust you," Anna said. "Not all of them."

"Whoever they see on their screens, whoever they hear on the radio, that's the prime minister," O.O. said.

"I know," Anna said. "And that's why, *this* time, it should be you. I can tie the bandage off, thank you. Take him to the studio. Get him on the air."

"Yes, ma'am," Toppley said with deliberate courtesy that was gone when she addressed Oswald Owen. "You, that way. Go."

Anna watched Toppley take Oswald Owen's arm and lead him back to the studio. Alone in the long corridor, she closed her eyes.

The music playing on the distant speakers cut out, but the silence only lasted a second, replaced by Oswald Owen's strident voice. She couldn't hear the words, but they didn't matter. They never did.

Anna leaned back, feeling sleep approaching, but only until she heard limping footsteps approach. She'd reached for the shotgun even before she opened her eyes, turned her head, and saw Tess Qwong.

"You're limping," Anna said.

"That's something you can look forward to," Tess said, slumping into a chair next to Anna's outstretched leg. "You'll need to get that properly looked at."

"I know," Anna said. "Did you find Vaughn?"

"No. Are you sure that was Lignatiev you saw running to the helicopter?"

"Absolutely," Anna said. "I thought Leo would pull out some wires, disable the helicopter. I didn't know he'd rig a bomb on the door."

"He's a strange bloke," Tess said. "Looks as harmless as a spider, but remember rule one, because he's just as deadly. He said it was revenge for his students."

"How many mercenaries got away, do you think?"

"Can't say right now," Tess said. "But we'll find out. Eight mercenaries are dead and at least two escaped, but we've got three as prisoners, and a barrelful of technicians and producers to interview. Blaze is quizzing them now, making sure they are TV people, not mercs in disguise."

"He's really a children's entertainer?"

"He is."

"You've got to tell me everything that happened to you. When we have time."

"*When* we have time," Tess said. "Something about all of this is wrong, Anna. I don't think Vaughn was even here."

"We've two sides of an equation, but it's not balanced," Anna said, wincing as she straightened her leg. "Lignatiev arranged for all the career soldiers to be deployed from Canberra. The police, too. And I think we know now why Vaughn insisted you and Dad hand-deliver those warrants. They arranged for a lot of politicians to go to Hobart, and killed off those they couldn't otherwise persuade to leave. But… but it doesn't make sense, does it? If I were… I mean, not that I would, but—"

"But this isn't how you'd run a coup," Tess said, articulating Anna's thought. "That's what I was thinking."

"They must have staged the last prime minister's suicide. Having Wilson commit suicide would have been a staggering coincidence, but… no, why didn't Ian take the prime ministerial job himself? He could have kept the Defence Ministry as well. If he was in charge, who could have told him no?"

"Unless he wasn't in charge," Tess said. "I'll find Vaughn. She'll give us the answers. And you need to get medical treatment. Oswald Owen is one steak dinner away from a coronary, and after today, he's our de facto prime minister, so if he asks for steak, who would dare refuse? You know it could have been you?"

"As prime minister? No. As long as the right decisions are made, it doesn't matter who has the title. Oswald Owen is the right person for today. Tomorrow, we'll see. But today the lights are still on, so let's be thankful for that."

Part 3
While the Lights Are On

Canberra

13th March & 14th March

13th March

Chapter 28 - First Class Policing
Canberra Airport

"I made an initial miscalculation," Leo Smilovitz said.

"An *assumption*," Dr Avalon added. "You made an *assumption*."

"Which is a scientific cardinal sin," Smilovitz said. "When the deputy prime minister, Anna Dodson, approached me, she said three mushroom clouds had been sighted. She wanted to know whether it was one bomb or three. When accessing weather and seismographic data, I assumed those reports were correct and there had been a nuclear strike."

"And there *has* been," Avalon cut in. "More than one. More than lots."

"Yes," Smilovitz said. "But by starting with the assumption of one target point, I misread the data. At present, I can confirm over a thousand warheads detonated in the Pacific during a period of one hour, but in between six and twenty different locations, where a location is defined as a rough circle with a diameter of one hundred kilometres. As more data is provided, and with more time to analyse it, I'll be able to form a more specific conclusion."

"A conclusion that will *only* clarify the first strike in the Pacific," Avalon said.

"Yes, indeed," Smilovitz said. "The first wave was clearly fired into the Pacific. The second was manually targeted…"

Tess reached over and turned the radio off.

"I was listening to that," Mick Dodson said, as near-silence returned to their corner of the airport's departure lounge. Beyond the wide windows, Canberra airport was a constellation of lights, shining bright in the dark night as planes were inspected, repaired, refuelled, readied for dawn and a resumption of the evacuation flights from the flooded coast. On the tarmac, the last of the passengers from the last flight to arrive before darkness made their way into the hastily expanded quarantine zone.

"You said you'd stolen the copy of the script from Anna's bedside earlier," Tess said, turning her gaze away from the window.

"I *read* the *report* from Dr Smilovitz," Mick said. "But I was listening to the broadcast to hear if Dr Avalon would let the radio-presenter say another word. Three words into the introduction and she cut him off, and that was five minutes ago. Ace idea sticking the two Canadians on the radio to tell everyone what's happened. And it was an even better idea having them do it as a double-act. She's entertaining, isn't she?"

"In small doses," Tess said. "Which is how we'll get our information for the next few weeks, small doses. Sorry, bad choice of words. But for the immediate future, information will be limited to what news arrives here aboard the planes."

"Until we launch a satellite," Mick said. "Will they mention that tonight?"

"No, that announcement will be kept for tomorrow," Tess said. "Or the day after. I'd prefer they waited until we actually had the rocket in orbit. How long will it take to assemble, do you reckon?"

"Depends on whether the components really are all here in Australia," Mick said. "We sent too much, too hastily, to the Marshall Islands. The islands are gone, the equipment is gone, but it's the loss of the people we'll miss the most. I reckon it'll take another week to find people here who *really* know what they're doing. Finding the components, and transporting them to Woomera, will be more of a trial than constructing the launch site. Compared to that, launch should be as easy as boiling a billy on a stove. Call it a month, factoring in delays. Six weeks at the outside."

"You're guessing, aren't you?" Tess said.

"Ah, but my ignorance comes from a position of experience," Mick said. "We'll get images for a week, that's what Smilovitz thinks. One week and no more. But that'll be enough to find the craters."

"Not at sea," Tess said. "I don't think we'll ever really know how many missiles were fired, and from where. Though I'd settle for learning *why* the missiles were launched."

"Learning something is better than ignorance," Mick said. "Rule eleven."

"Rule twelve. Today's rule eleven was that doctors outrank police," she said, tapping her chopsticks against the side of the bowl. "Why do we only get satellite coverage for a week?"

"Because communication-constellation satellites aren't designed for sustained manoeuvring in orbit," Mick said.

"Did Leo tell you that?" Tess asked.

"No, it was Clyde. He said it would have brought the internet to even the most remote places. He'd been following the technology's development for the charities he worked with."

"He still insists he was an aid-worker?"

"I think he was," Mick said.

"But he was a soldier before," Tess said.

"We're all soldiers now," Mick said with a forlorn sigh. "Soldiers and farmers and everything in between. One week and the satellites will be gone again, but we'll get our pictures of the craters."

"Or clouds," Tess said.

"As long as they're not mushroom-shaped," Mick said. "Speaking of which…"

"There's been another one?" Tess asked.

"Vancouver," Mick said.

"No? Seriously?"

"Plane arrived this afternoon. Landed in Darwin. Ground-chief threw a pilot into an F-35 and sent her straight here. A mushroom cloud was seen to the north of the city."

"What about… I forget the name of the place. On Vancouver Island. The airfield the Canadians were running things from."

"Nanaimo. That's where this plane came from. The EMP knocked out a lot of electronics, but they think they can repair a lot of ships, and some planes. Those that were on the ground."

"There were planes in the air?" Tess asked. "Of course there were."

"The Canadians want assistance with an evacuation," Mick said.

"Of Vancouver Island? But they were sheltering refugees from Vancouver City, from British Columbia, from beyond and across the border."

"Yep."

"We wanted to move refugees there from Japan," Tess said.

"That was before," Mick said.

"*Before?*" She rolled the word around her tongue. "Fair dinkum. We've a new division of the calendar, but I thought it'd have been the outbreak which marked the ushering in of a new era. Old and new. Before and after. Except it doesn't feel like we're in the *after* yet. What did Anna say about Canada?"

"She sent the pilot back to Darwin, with instructions to relay a message north. We'll keep the runway in Darwin clear, and the straighter roads empty. Sent word to Papua, too. Tokua Airport isn't much closer to Canada than Vancouver, but over those distances, every metre matters. The Canadians have no choice but to evacuate, so we better prepare."

"What else can we do?" Tess said, looking down at her half-finished bowl. "But we were preparing for refugees *before*. We'll manage. We'll find a way."

"I hadn't got to the bad part," Mick said.

Tess paused, chopsticks halfway to her mouth. "What? More news on the pilots' grapevine?"

"It's a beer-barrel in this case, and overflowing with a very sour brew," he said. "Jakarta was hit. Twice. The Golden Triangle was hit first, with a second impact site a few kilometres west of the harbour."

"Jakarta? We were going to evacuate half the population. I don't want to even think how many millions must be dead. Dying."

"And that's still not the worst of it," Mick said. "The report came from a boat, upturned, floating a few miles out at sea. The mayday was received by a plane a couple of hours after it happened. Tess, the blast was at ten a.m., our time."

Tess glanced at the clock. Nine p.m. "This morning?" she asked.

"So far, that's the last detonation we've heard of."

"But it might not be the last ever," Tess said. "It really might not be the *after*, not yet." She returned to her bowl, thinking as she ate. "Any word from General Yoon?"

"Not yet. But I do have some good news." He reached into his large green bag, emblazoned with an oil-stained white cross, and pulled out a silver-wrapped package. "I've got some cake."

"When did you find time to bake?"

"Don't worry, I didn't cook it," he said. "It was for Anna. For our new deputy prime minister."

"From whom?" she asked.

"Some blokes down in the fuel store. Two are locals. Local to Broken Hill, I mean. One is from Silverton and his wife's from Mildura. They chose to live there, but I won't hold it against them. They made the cake for Anna."

Tess eyed the package suspiciously. "Considering everything that's happened, do you really trust them?"

"I wouldn't, except Shannon was there when they handed it over. And she ate a slab before I could stop her. If it's poisoned, she'd be dead."

"Is she doing okay?" Tess asked.

"Shannon? Far better now she's half full of cake," Mick said. "Molly's taking it hard. A bit shook up still."

"No sign of her husband?" Tess asked. "I can't remember his name."

"Clarke," Mick said. "No, no sign of him, or the three kids he went looking for. But the other children got onto a plane, and we got Brendon out of the hospital. And into the one here. Molly's spending most of her time with him, but Shannon's been helping me out with my rounds. She'll make a good doctor, in time. I put Sophia and Blaze in to help with the quarantine. You don't need them back, do you?"

"Not tonight," Tess said. "Tomorrow, maybe. Depends what tonight's search uncovers. And that's assuming Anna doesn't want Blaze at the radio station. How is Sophia's arm?"

"It'll be a month before she holds a rifle," Mick said. "And at least two before she could put up with the recoil. But she'll recover full use and movement, and she doesn't need either to be useful to me. That's not the end of the good news, either. At the coast, the waves weren't as high as I thought. The water didn't rise as fast, and didn't come in nearly as far. The sea is receding."

"But leaving salt-water ponds, right?" Tess said. "Nothing will grow there until the rains flush out the salt. By then, any equipment we haven't salvaged will have been rusted or ruined. There," she added, putting her empty bowl on the table. "I've eaten, and it's been an hour. Can I please go?"

"You could sleep, too," Mick said. "She won't escape. Not by air. I've got a guard on the planes."

"But they're not soldiers," Tess said. "Those are pressurised passenger planes. Few of the pilots are Australians, but how many locals could pick Erin Vaughn out of a line-up? With refugees arriving, all those new faces, it will get easier for her to hide in a crowd."

"Then we're agreed that if you don't find her tonight, you'll stop," Mick said.

"Tonight," Tess said. "While the lights are still on."

A new hand-written sign adorned the airport's first-class lounge. *Team Stonefish Strike Squad. Authorised Personnel Only. By Order of the Prime Minister.* The crude fish-and-crossbones motif suggested it was Zach's idea, and it wasn't a bad one. The airlifts would be on-going as long as the lights were on, and so the airport would be given priority with fuel, water, and food supplies. That made it a more sensible base than the fire-ravaged police station on London Circuit, or the mothballed AFP headquarters. At least for now. Longer term, she'd need forensic labs and surveillance equipment, but that could wait until she had the people to operate them. She'd also need cells, but until she had jailers she could trust, the mercenary-prisoners would remain in the airport's detention rooms.

Inside the first-class lounge, the squad had made themselves at home. The soundproof phone and data booths had become their bedchambers; they were too small to be called bed*rooms*. But kitted out with pillows and blankets, they were quieter and more comfortable than elsewhere in the airport. More blankets curtained the broad windows. In daylight, they had a spectacular view of the encircling mountains, which utterly failed to distract from the depressing vista of bedraggled refugees trudging to quarantine.

"Time to move out," Tess called, her gaze going from person to person, judging their reluctance, assessing whether any should be given a night off. "But I bring cake."

"I'm stuffed tighter than a bride in her dress," Elaina said. "That Ms Nguyen is a good cook."

"No she ain't," Zach said. "I couldn't hardly taste the beef."

Bianca laughed so loudly everyone turned to look.

"What?" Zach said. "What's funny?"

"It was a vegetarian dinner," Bianca said, carefully selecting a matching bracelet, necklace, and earrings from a jewellery case that took up a quarter of her pack.

"You mean there was no meat at all?" Zach said, looking in horror at his empty bowl. "None? Gross. I don't think I'll ever eat again."

"The beef's gone," Tess said.

"I heard they're turning it into stock for Vegemite," Bianca said.

"Or meat-emite," Elaina said.

"That stuff smells like koala sick," Zach said. "Tastes like it, too."

"How do you know?" Elaina asked.

"I've been to the zoo," Zach said defensively.

"They're shipping as much beef as they can to the coast, cooked," Tess said. "Until this immediate crisis is over, live herds will be sent directly to the refugee camps. From all I've heard, if you've got beef on your plate, you're in a bad way."

"There, a reason to be grateful it was absent from yours, Zach," Teegan Toppley said. "What entertainment do we have planned for tonight, Commissioner?"

"We're continuing the hunt for Erin Vaughn," Tess said. "It'll be just like this morning when we went to Vaughn's and Lignatiev's houses, but we're looking at a few more places unconnected to them. With most empty properties having been allocated as housing or factory, there aren't many buildings in which someone with a recognisable face can hide. Yes, if she panicked and fled, she could be absolutely anywhere, but if she had time to prepare, I've got three, last, possible locations that she, as a cabinet minister, would know of. Same rules as earlier today. We want a positive I.D., not a fire-fight. Remember, this isn't a movie."

"Because the soundtrack is more... eclectic?" Bianca asked, throwing a glance towards the phone-and-speakers by Zach's bed.

"Because you can really die," Clyde said.

"Something like that," Tess said. "Eyes open for parked military vehicles, or those black four-by-fours, or any other indication someone's recently been there. I'll enter with Teegan and Clyde. Everyone else will secure the perimeter. We don't want a gunfight. We don't need one. Just a positive I.D. Vaughn can't escape the city, and wherever she is, this is her last bolthole. If we can get her on the run, she'll be a lot easier to find tomorrow when Captain Hawker returns with soldiers we know we can trust. If we don't find her, tomorrow, they'll take over the search."

"What happens to us?" Elaina asked. "Do we get a day off?"

"Bad news there, too," Tess said with a smile. "I'm deputising you."

"We're cops?" Zach asked.

"It'll mostly be admin and jailing," Tess said. "Until you finish training."

"Like in martial arts?" Zach asked, his tone rising with sudden enthusiasm.

"Like in psychology, forensics, and data analysis," Tess said. "So I hope you like reading."

While Zach looked disappointed, the other, older, members of the team looked relieved.

"And our kids?" Clyde asked.

"We'll set up a crèche and a school," Tess said. "For your kids, and the rest of the department. Your son is in Hobart, right? The priority is returning the politicians from Tassy, but they should be aboard a plane tomorrow. Once they're here, and once the airlift is over, I promise we'll look into bringing your kids back, or sending you down there, whichever is safer. Grab your gear. And then grab some cake, and we'll see if we can be done by dawn."

"Cake?" Zach asked. "Cool."

"I thought you said you were never going to eat again," Elaina said.

"There's always room for cake," Zach said.

Chapter 29 - Honesty Test
Simpsons Hill, Canberra

Following mathematical rules of her own devising, this week Tess had crossed the line of having spent more of her life as a police officer than not. She counted weekends, but not her initial training; the time in hospital, but not the period of extended leave where she'd searched her soul, and the job ads, for an alternative life. During those years, she'd driven more police cars than civilian models. The Holden Commodores parked outside weren't her first choice in pursuit vehicles. The nearest car's new plain white door interrupted the line of bullet holes which had stitched a fatal tattoo in the vehicle's sides. But the engines were sound, the tanks were full, and the tyres were pumped. More importantly, no other vehicles were available, having been dispatched into the never-never by Ian Lignatiev along with the officers and soldiers who might have stopped the coup.

Lignatiev was dead. The police, and some soldiers and politicians, would soon return. Airlifts were underway. There was pain and suffering, yes, and who knew how many unseen crimes among the crowded refugee camps, but order was returning. Peace would follow. Abnormality was settling in, and she was, once again, doing what she did best: running an investigation.

"We all here?" she asked, inspecting her team. Everyone wore body armour over airport overalls. Helmets, gloves, and knee and elbow pads completed the painting of professionalism, though it was inexpertly shaded by the civilian mix of trainers and hiking boots. And the tools. Everyone was armed with either a shotgun or a submachine gun taken from the dead amateurs at the radio tower. But each also carried a hand-axe, hammer, machete, or, in Elaina's case, a half-metre metal pole with a taped-cloth handle.

"First stop is the leisure centre on the western shore of Lake Tuggeranong," Tess said. "Currently, it's empty, designated as an overflow hospital. We'll drive in convoy straight into the car park. It's too big a site to secure every exit, so we won't even try. We'll drive up, lights on. When we get there, use the spotlights to blind any watchers, and let them run. Clyde, Teegan, and I will take the lead car. Bianca, Elaina, Zach, you're in the second."

Keeping her reservations to herself, she climbed in. They *were* civilians, with the possible exception of Clyde and Toppley. But along with the first planes to arrive from the coast had come news of localised outbreaks. With the chaos, the panic, the loss of shelter, order, and weapons, little would prevent the number of infected from rising. Canberra's quarantine was being applied rigidly, to civilian and soldier alike. Watching them were the aircrews. With no one else to call on for that essential duty, there certainly were no others for Tess to recruit for what she increasingly believed was a fool's errand.

Half an hour later, that feeling seemed to be confirmed. The leisure centre was empty. There had been people there, and recently, though the collection of empty stubbies and roach-singed roll-ups in the bottom of the now-drained pool suggested people far younger than Vaughn.

The second property, an office block, was full of workers operating lathes, presses, and drills with enough proficiency to prove they'd been there for days.

The third place on the list was Bronwyn Wilson's old home. An unassuming house on Enid Lorimer Court, at the base of Simpsons Hill, it had been removed from Anna's re-housing list out of respect for its owner.

"The prime minister lived around here?" Clyde asked. "I thought we paid for the PM to live in a mansion."

"I don't think she had time to move into The Lodge," Tess said. "Remember, she wasn't prime minister for very long."

"But will the next one beat her record?" Toppley asked.

"Oswald Owen?" Tess asked. "Depends what happens when the politicians from Hobart return. But I can't see many people wanting to take the top job when the last two were murdered and the current incumbent is likely to shoulder the blame for every mistake made in the next few months. If someone does fancy a try, they'd have to contend with Anna, and since she blew up the last pretender to the throne, they'll think twice."

"As I recall, it was the scientist set the bomb," Toppley said.

"But it'll make for a more rousing yarn if we say it was Anna," Tess said. "I think this is the road." She parked in front of the barricade.

The road was blocked with a simple pillar-and-bar barrier, and a note warning that the entire street was closed, and the properties were reserved for official use. Tess paused at that sign, shining her torch on it to read it again. According to Anna, only Wilson's house had been reserved. The sentry post was currently unguarded, but someone had occupied it long enough to add a chair, a small fan, a larger fridge, and an insulated cable running to the nearest of the supposedly secured houses.

Above, a quarter of the streetlights still cast their dim glow on the dry roadway. Another twenty temporary lights were dotted across the grassy slope of Simpsons Hill immediately opposite the row of homes. Distantly spaced, the lights cast a shadowy glow over stacks of timber, and sealed shipping containers.

"Are they building dormitories there?" Toppley asked.

"I'm not sure," Tess said. "But this road isn't as secluded as I thought. Not if people are working here during daylight." As if to emphasise that, a porch-light came on behind them, a door opened, and a face appeared long enough to see the guns in the hands of the civilian-clad deputies. The door was hurriedly shut.

"Maybe that was her," Zach said.

"She's grown a beard since yesterday?" Elaina asked.

"You know what I mean," Zach said.

"There's a pillowcase pinned to the door," Tess said. "Whoever lives there claims to have done so since before the outbreak, and has been sheltering inside ever since."

"Or they only go out at night," Toppley said. "That's what I would do. Wait until dark, and raid nearby houses until I had enough to stay even longer."

"Perhaps, but he'll be getting houseguests next week anyway," Tess said. "Anyway, Vaughn *could* be anywhere, but we came to check Wilson's house."

She walked along the footpath at the base of the hill, scanning the properties, unsure which they were looking for until she saw a light flashing around the interior of a house. Too powerful to be a match, too steady to be a fire, gone too quickly for it to belong to a legal resident hurrying to their bathroom.

Tess raised a hand, and the squad came to a loud halt.

"Trouble?" Toppley whispered.

"People," Tess said. "A light inside. No car outside. No streetlights working on that side of the street. No sentries on guard. This is starting to look viable."

"They'll have heard our engines," Clyde said.

"So we'll move quickly. Clyde, Toppley, make your way around to the back. I'll go in the front. Elaina, Zach, watch the road here. Remember, if you see someone running, it might be me. Bianca, you're with me. I'll go to the front door. You'll go to the bay window. When I signal, shine your torch inside. I'll enter through the front. Don't follow. Keep low. Remember it might be me who comes running outside."

It was her own fault, she thought as she unslung the shotgun. After the first two properties had been so empty, she'd concluded Vaughn had run, and so had been going through the motions with this last property. Driving too close. Talking too loud. Walking too near.

Inside, from a window to the right of the door, another light briefly shone. The same torch? Or a different flashlight held by a different hand? Were the missing mercenaries still protecting Vaughn?

Wishing Hawker had returned with his soldiers, she jogged across the road, straight to the front door. According to the number, this *was* Wilson's home. Inside, she heard a cupboard open, a drawer close, shoes squeak, metal clink on metal. Opting for sound and fury, she levelled the shotgun at the upper hinge, stepped back, and fired. The shotgun's roar shattered the silence of the suburb. The slug smashed through the hinge. The door spun inwards, pivoting then thudding to the floor as the one remaining hinge failed under the weight.

"Police!" she yelled as Bianca shone her light through the nearest window.

A stronger glow came from inside, beyond an alcove-doorway.

Aiming low, Tess fired a slug into the floor, quickly switching her aim ahead as she yelled, "Police. Surrender! You're surrounded."

"We do!" came a yell in return. "We surrender."

Tess stopped, puzzled. The voice was male and unfamiliar, and the words were unexpected.

"Throw out your guns," Tess said. "Then kneel on the floor, hands behind your heads."

"We're unarmed!" the man called.

"Teegan!" Tess called.

"We're here," Clyde replied, far closer, and already inside.

"By the kitchen door," Toppley added. "We have them covered."

Tess stepped forward, and through the alcove, into the kitchen where three people now knelt on the floor: a man nearing thirty, a woman about the same age, and a younger man. Early twenties, he was shorter, though more muscled, than the older man, but had the same elongated chin, razor-sharp cheeks, and terrified brown eyes. All wore dark clothing, their heads covered in dark ski-hats, though the woman's was maroon rather than black, and the younger man's shoes had white soles unevenly shaded with a marker-pen. In the middle of the kitchen were four large black holdalls. Three were stuffed and zipped, but the partially full bag was open, and full of packets.

Tess lowered her shotgun, and tapped the badge around her neck. "I'm Commissioner Tess Qwong. Explain yourselves. Quickly."

"We were just looking for food," the woman said. "That's all. We weren't going to take anything else."

"You're wearing ski hats," Tess said. "And you coloured the white part of your shoes. Try again."

"It was my idea," the older man said. "We live down the street, and we knew who lived here. And we knew Ms Wilson. Used to do her gardening. We knew she was dead. She didn't need the food here, so we came to take it."

"Just the three of you?" Tess asked, placing the shotgun on the kitchen counter. She plucked three pens from the jar by the cordless phone.

"Just the three of us, yes ma'am," the oldest said.

"Are you armed?" Tess asked, taking three pieces of paper from the pad by the phone.

"No, ma'am," the older man said.

"You should be," Tess said. "Nowhere is safe from the undead these days, not even inside the city wall." She dropped the pens and pieces of paper in front of the prisoners. "This is a field honesty-test. You said you'd heard the prime minister was dead. I assume on the radio. We came here looking for her killer. Staying on your knees, shuffle around so your backs are to one another. Good. I'll ask you some questions. If your answers match, I'll believe you're just looters. If not..." She picked up the shotgun. "First, write down your name. Surname, too." She waited as they scrawled. "Now write the names of the other two." She waited. "Where are you living now?" She waited. "Where did you last eat a meal together that wasn't where you now live?" She had to wait a little longer as the younger man, brow furrowed, lips moving, decoded the question. "Teegan?"

Toppley collected the pieces of paper. "Close enough a match for government work," she said. "Though this gentleman needs a lesson in how many u's are in *restaurant*."

"Take them outside, Teegan. Have them sit on the kerb. Clyde, wait here while I search the rest of the property."

Wilson's was a small house belonging to an ageing woman with fading dreams. The living room could have been a set for a furniture catalogue, right down to the picture frames. The photographs inside, though, were Wilson's. One showed her standing next to the prince on a royal visit ten years ago. In another, she was sandwiched between two of the more recent prime ministers at the launch of a Hobart-class destroyer. In a frame larger than the others, she wore a headscarf while standing outside a mosque with a robed sheikh. Pride of place seemed to go to an older picture, slightly faded, where she stood on a red carpet with a film star whom Tess almost recognised. No friends. No family. Just an implied political importance belied by the mundane suburban setting.

There was no television or sofa, just six armchairs arranged symmetrically around a coffee table, overlooked by the photographs. In the corner, a drinks cabinet contained one bottle of nearly everything, and each, except for the scotch, was nearly full.

Technically it might be a living room, but Wilson hadn't lived in it. She'd arranged the furniture for meetings, but the hint of dust on chairs and bottles suggested she'd not had many of those recently, either. The spare bedroom was set up as an office, and did contain a small TV set pushed into the corner, almost forgotten. The microphone plugged into the desk phone was far more expensive. On the walls, instead of pictures, she'd hung install-yourself soundproof panels. Bronwyn Wilson had a reputation as always being good for a sound bite, and it was in here that she'd crumbled her punditry-morsels onto the airwaves. From the extra cushions in the chair, the jars of mints, and the book of crossword puzzles, Tess got the impression the politician spent most of her life waiting in this room for the press to call.

The master bedroom *did* contain a bed, and the wardrobe contained clothes, though most of the dress-carriers also carried the label of the hire company to which they could be returned.

"Strange place," Clyde said, from the doorway. "No personal touches at all."

"There are a few," Tess said. "But there's something staged about them. Something staged about the whole place. It feels as deliberately fake as if she'd filled the place with soft toys and the walls with children's drawings. She was trying to project an image out there, but in here, in her bedroom, I'd expect to find something that gave an insight into her real self."

"She wasn't married, right?" Clyde asked.

"No," Tess said. "No kids. No spouse."

"No sign of an extended family," Clyde said.

"Let's be gracious and assume that she kept all that back in her constituency," Tess said. "Or maybe at her office in parliament. The alternative, considering how she died, is just too bleak."

"What do you want done with the looters?" Clyde asked.

"It's their lucky day," Tess said. "Finish emptying those cupboards in the kitchen and bring the bags to the car. I'll send Zach in to help you."

Tess returned outside. "Zach, go help Clyde." She turned to the three looters. "Listen up. Our strike force is hunting the mercenaries who were working with Erin Vaughn, so you're doubly lucky. Firstly, that it was us who found you and not them. Secondly, because I don't have time to take you in for processing. Canberra is in lockdown. If you've been listening to the radio, you know. The walls are guarded. No one leaves. No one enters unless they go through quarantine. There's no escape, but if you *have* been paying attention to the radio, you'll know there's nowhere on Earth to escape to. The shelter-in-place order will expire tomorrow, and everyone will be conscripted. But since you're out here looting, you must have run out of food of your own. Go to the airport. Report for duty. I'll check around dawn. If you're not there, your names will be broadcast on the morning news as wanted for questioning in connection with the coup. Got it? Go."

"That's it?" Elaina asked, as the three cautiously got to their feet, then more quickly, hurried away. "Aren't we arresting them?"

"We'd have to feed them, watch them, arrange a trial, a punishment," Tess said. "For petty looting, it's not worth our time."

Zach staggered outside, struggling under the weight of an overly full bag. "This one's mine," he declared.

"It's not," Tess said. "Because we're not keeping it. We'll drop the bag off at the emergency depot on our way back."

"We can't keep any of it?" Zach asked. "Not even the biscuits?"

"One pack of biscuits," Tess said. "But only one, and you're sharing with everyone. Anything else would be stealing, and if we don't keep the law, we can't expect anyone else to."

"Have we anywhere else to search?" Toppley asked.

Tess walked across to the dark lamppost, leaned against it, and looked up at the sky. "I don't think so," she said. "I can think of a dozen places I'd hide, and I barely know this city. Vaughn could be anywhere. Lignatiev had a helicopter up at the transmitter. He guessed things might go north. Vaughn might have assumed the same and made a plan of her own. She had the time, and authority, to arrange a road-route through the walls and beyond. Wilson's house seemed a logical place for her to hide, but perhaps it was too obvious. It's hard trying to think like a criminal."

"We think just like everyone else," Toppley said. "Because we are just like everyone else. Criminality, for most people, is a matter of timing, marking the difference between borrowing an item and keeping it."

"I won't say you're completely wrong," Tess said. "But—" She stopped, turned, and looked back at Wilson's house. "*Timing.* The mercenaries were hired before the outbreak. They had to have hidden somewhere."

"A rental property, one assumes," Toppley said.

"But afterward, they had to hide somewhere no one would be billeted," Tess said. "A building not in danger of re-allocation, and Anna was in charge of the list. Anna and *Aaron Bryce*. We searched most of the reserved properties this morning, and these were the last three. Senator Aaron Bryce owned a mansion in Redhill, but he committed suicide in suburbia, and he lived in the smallest room in a hotel. And it *was* suicide, I'm sure of it. Not murder. Anna said he was struggling, out of his depth, refusing promotions and responsibility, but is that enough to warrant suicide? I assumed it, partly because there'd been so many other political suicides before my arrival here. Suicides I now suspect were murders."

"You think he had some involvement in the conspiracy?" Toppley asked.

"I hope not," Tess said. "Because it would mean the trail doesn't stop with him. His father-in-law, Malcolm Baker, is in contention for most corrupt man in the country. However, Vaughn and Lignatiev didn't pay for the mercenaries themselves. But that's an issue for tomorrow. Tonight, I want to pay Aaron's house a visit. Get everyone back in the cars, and tell them we're driving to Redhill. We won't find Vaughn there, but we might find where they were plotting. Maybe we'll find out what they were plotting to do next."

In most respects, Vaughn no longer mattered. She'd lost all authority and all chance of acquiring power. But Sir Malcolm Baker was a very different matter. His mining interests made him an even more influential figure than he'd been a month ago. His old contacts gave him influence among the politicians returning from Hobart. Worse still, Sir Malcolm had a connection to Oswald Owen. In which case, the coup might barely have begun.

Consulting her notebook, then the map, she drove the lead car through a suburb of million-dollar homes. The properties reallocated to refugees were noticeable by the caravans in the driveways, the DIY-store huts and cabins on the front lawns, the new fences and occasional sentry posts.

Two streets away, according to her map, Tess pulled the car in. Elaina parked the follow-car behind. Tess switched off the engine, grabbed her shotgun, and climbed out. The silent street nearly hummed with the hushed watchfulness of sleeping citizens woken by the unfamiliar sound of an engine. She could sense them, in their beds, some at their windows, breath held, hoping the vehicles' arrival didn't also mark the arrival of the same dangers from which they'd fled.

"Lights off," she whispered as Zach and Toppley turned theirs on. "I want you to wait here. Quietly." She took off her helmet, and then her body armour, and put them into the car. "Clyde, lose the helmet and the submachine gun, then lend me your arm. We're taking a night-time stroll."

"You want us to play the old couple getting a few minutes away from the kids?" he asked, handing his helmet to Zach.

"Less of the old, thanks," Tess said. "But yeah. You have a sidearm? Keep it ready."

Arm in arm, keeping to the occasionally illuminated footpath, they made their way to Endeavour Street.

Even with the hastily built fences, the houses were pleasant. Roomy. Spacious drives were bordered by neat flowerbeds. Those on the uphill side of the sloping road even had a view, though darkness hid it from her. They were more expensive properties than she could afford, but they weren't truly high-end. They were the homes of upper management, not the board. She got the impression Sir Malcolm had bought his daughter and son-in-law the smallest property he could get away with.

Senator Bryce's home was a corner-plot ringed by a pale blue painted wall and a privacy hedge to which an unseasoned wooden fence had been added. Part of the hedge had been crudely hacked down, making way for support posts to be planted in its stead, while more support props jutted out onto the footpath. A sturdy metal gate secured the drive, though with wooden panelling behind. But it was what was on the gate that caught her eye. The painted *Hospital No Entry* was clearly legible even under the faint glow of the streetlamp opposite. The note pinned to the gate was less so. She stepped closer, squinting. It said something about being a temporary measles and chicken-pox ward for the nearby hospital.

Above the fence, she could see a two-wing house, with the upper-floor rooms on either wing having matching balconies. There were no lights, however, nor any sounds. Deciding they'd lingered long enough, she tugged on Clyde's arm, continuing on around the corner.

"No lights," Clyde said when they were out of earshot.

"No sentries," Tess said. "But that note on the gate said it was an overflow ward. And it's not. We're using the leisure centre for that."

"Good ruse, though," Clyde said. "Have we found it?"

"I think so," Tess said. "Let's get the others."

"The house appears empty," Tess said when she and Clyde had returned to the cars. "Someone's pretended it was an overflow ward for the hospital. We're going to take a look. The windows are dark, but we'll assume Vaughn is inside. Remember, the goal is to make her run, not get into a firefight. Dawn's only a few hours away, and if we can confirm she's here, we can put out a bulletin on the radio. But in case the hospital did claim the house, and word never made it up to us, fingers off triggers. Teegan, Clyde, and I'll make our entrance through the front. Clyde, grab that crowbar. We'll smash the fence. No point being subtle. Zach, Bianca, Elaina, in five minutes, drive both cars up to the front, sirens on. Shine the spotlights in the windows, and tear down the main gate. It's metal, so use a chain. Any shots, we'll fall back. Let her escape around the back. At this point, the evidence she's left behind is more useful than her. Questions? Let's go."

Taking the lead, Tess ran back to Aaron's house, this time with the shotgun in her hands. With the streetlights still on, she kept her torch off. She pointed at the nearest section of fence. Clyde stepped forward, running his gloved hand over the fence in search of a helpful gap. Toppley stepped back, submachine gun raised, while Tess looked up, watching for movement or lights in the windows visible above the fence.

With an achingly loud crack, Clyde wrenched a fence-panel loose. Another crack, and he'd torn it free. A third, and he'd pulled off a second panel, creating a gap just wide enough for Tess to enter.

"Make for the front door," Tess said, bending and squeezing her way through. As she ran up the drive, she noted the complete absence of any cars, but she did see the hint of a light in a downstairs window. A reflection, a genuinely sick child, or a sleepless Vaughn waiting for dawn?

On either side of a dwarf-tree shrubbery, where the evergreens were carved into meaningless peaks, marble slabs, covered in scuffed dirt, led to the double front doors. Square white pillars supported an equally white porch-roof hiding a bank of lights shining on the red-stained front door.

Tess levelled her shotgun. "Go in fast," she whispered as Clyde and Toppley caught up. "Go in low. Clyde to the left. Teegan the right."

She levelled the shotgun at the bottom hinge.

The roar shattered the suburb's unnatural stillness. The door shook until the second slug ripped away the upper hinge. Even as Tess shifted aim to the lock, the door slid sideways, twisting as it clattered to the tiled floor. Forgetting her instructions, or simply ignoring them, Clyde sprang inside ahead of her. The light slung beneath his submachine gun's barrel tracked the weapon's path as he swept up and left, stepping quickly into the hall.

Tess followed, adding her own beam to his, picking out details, looking for threats. A large hallway lay in front, with open double-doors to left and right, and a closed single door immediately ahead. A wraparound staircase began to her right, just beyond the open door. It rose to a balcony landing from which three corridors led left, right, and towards the back of the property, and down which a figure appeared. Bearded, in body-armour but no helmet, carrying a stocky long arm.

"Police!" Tess yelled, even as a gun roared. Automatically, unsure who was the shooter and who was the target, she fired back. The shotgun's slug tore through the balcony-landing's opaque-glass safety barrier, and into the mercenary's leg. As he screamed, Tess realised the shot she'd heard hadn't come from that man. Clyde had spun to the right, and fired through the open doors, before ducking down into a crouch and firing another burst. Tess looked from him to his target, and saw a second mercenary, bleeding, prone, probably dead.

From behind came a low groan.

Tess spun. "Toppley's down!" she said.

But Toppley wasn't dead. "Behind you!" the old crook yelled.

Tess ducked, pivoting around as bullets sprayed above her head. To the left, beyond the open doorway, stood another mercenary. Dressed only in t-shirt and shorts, she was working the mechanism of a machine pistol. Tess fired. Blood arced as the slug ripping through the woman's stomach and spine. Her shrill scream rang louder than a siren, but only briefly, becoming a gargling whimper as the mercenary died.

As Tess stepped into the room, another automatic burst came from behind as Toppley, still prone, fired up the stairs. They were on a knife's edge, the battle able to spin either way.

The closed door at the end of the hall opened just far enough for someone throw something through.

"Grenade!" she yelled, diving backwards, into the room while Clyde dived to the right.

The hall filled with white light and noise as the concussion grenade exploded.

Disorientated, head ringing, temporarily blinded, Tess barely registered the damp pool of blood through which she rolled as she tried to get back to her feet. The walls, and the angle of the staircase beyond, had partially shielded her. Vision slowly returning, she crawled, to the doorway.

In the hallway, Toppley sat against the wall, rifle in her lap, head in her hands. Clyde was in the doorway of the room opposite, on his knees, trying to push himself upright. But beyond him, a shadow straightened, silhouetted by the weakly reflected lights outside: the mercenary Clyde had shot. The man's body armour had taken the impact.

"Clyde!" she called, even as she drew her handgun, but her arms were too slow and the words came out weak.

Clyde didn't see the merc's boot as it slammed upwards into his face. He sprawled sideways, but turned it into a roll. As the mercenary reached for his sidearm, and before Tess could find a clear shot, Clyde had drawn a knife from his boot. He dived, not forwards, but to the side of the man, stabbing the blade, underarm, deep into the mercenary's thigh.

As the merc screamed, Clyde twisted the blade, pushing the man's leg down while pushing himself up. Dragging the blade free, his left arm hooked around the man's gun hand, clamping it as his right hand, gripping the knife under-hand, plunging the blade into the mercenary's neck.

Now holding the dying man, Clyde released the knife. As he grabbed the gun from the dying mercenary, he spun himself and the nearly-dead merc, putting the almost-corpse between himself and the shadows. A bullet thudded into the merc's chest. Clyde fired back, two shots, into the corner of the room. Releasing the now very dead mercenary, he darted into the shadows, disappearing from Tess's view.

Wondering, once again, what the man had done before he'd become an aid-worker, Tess staggered down the hall, towards the door through which the flash-bang had been thrown.

Outside, sirens blared. Flashing lights reflected around the ceiling. That dispelled her hesitancy. The people with Lignatiev in the Bunker and at the Telstra Tower might have been amateurs and hobbyists, but the mercenaries in this house were professionals. She couldn't let them engage the rest of her own amateur squad.

Torch in one hand, pistol in the other, she pushed the door open with her foot, moving in quickly, sweeping gun and light leftward and—

The door swung closed behind her. Her feet flew from underneath, kicked away before she realised. Gun and torch went flying. But as the beam turned and twisted, she saw a figure in black, a face covered in a roadmap of scars, above which was a helmet with a set of night-vision goggles, currently up.

"Kelly," Tess hissed.

The mercenary didn't reply, but moved quickly. Not towards Tess, but to the fallen flashlight which she grabbed and turned off. The room went completely dark. A soft click marked Kelly dropping the night-vision rig over her eyes. Tess pushed herself to her knees, and dived, but not forward, to the side, turning the dive into a roll, ignoring the agonised yell from her hip as she straightened and ran into the wall, hands slapping and searching until they found the light switch.

Artificial day returned. Kelly screamed, snatching the night-vision rig from her eyes even as Tess grabbed her fallen handgun, aimed, and fired. Two shots, which hit the mercenary's body armour, making her stagger backwards. But Tess's third slammed into Kelly's face.

Pushing down pain and emotion, Tess ran back out into the hall.

Clyde was back at the front door, standing above Toppley, a pistol in each hand. One was aimed up the stairs, the other aimed directly at Tess until he recognised her, and shifted the barrel upwards. Toppley was gone, but Elaina was now crouched in the doorway, submachine gun uncertainly raised.

"Where's Teegan?"

"Took two to the vest," Clyde said. "Bruised but fine."

"Major Kelly's dead," Tess said. "Hold the door. I'm going upstairs."

Limping, she holstered her handgun, picked up her shotgun, and pushed herself up the stairs. After three steps, she grabbed hold of the bannister as old wounds gave newer injuries a tour of her exhausted body.

Adrenaline didn't last as long as when she was younger. Pain made itself known far more quickly. But experience had come with age, too. Experience taught her people like Kelly fought or fled, and the shooting had now stopped. If there were others, they'd have run when the sirens sounded outside. Probably. But as she reached the landing, she levelled the shotgun, and kept her finger on the trigger as she went room to room, kicking open one door and the next until she found the bodies.

14ᵗʰ March

Chapter 30 - A Dinosaur of a Caravan
The Australian National Museum

Tess forced herself to finish checking the rooms on that hallway. She returned to the landing-balcony. "No one else comes up here, Clyde. No one else comes in. Especially not Zach."

"Roger," he said. "Ma'am, what did you find?"

"A crime scene," she said, and forced herself to check the other two upstairs corridors, and the rooms beyond. Both were shorter, but led to his-and-her master rooms, both identical in design, both barely lived in. Both, thankfully, were empty. Though the rooms had been searched, looted, the beds hadn't been recently used.

Even more slowly than before, she returned to the landing, and then downstairs. Bianca had joined Elaina in the door, and both women held their weapons uncertainly.

"They're all dead or gone," Tess said. "Bianca, take Zach and drive Teegan to the airport. Zach stays with Teegan. Find Mick Dodson. I want twenty people. Armed. People he trusts. Aircrew who've seen action. And I want the coroner. And I want them here in ten minutes."

"I can use the radio," Bianca said.

"No, I want this message delivered in person," Tess said. And she wanted Zach away from here. "Clyde, Elaina. Hold this position. I'll finish the sweep."

More slowly, putting off the moment she'd have to return upstairs, she went through the downstairs rooms, turning on lights as she went.

Aside from the recent battle, the house was barely changed from when Aaron and his wife had lived there. The floor was scuffed, but the ornaments remained untouched and on display. The mercenaries had even added a few out-of-place rugs to the silk-threaded sofas, and sheets to cover the coffee tables. They hadn't looted. They hadn't wantonly destroyed. They'd known they might have to leave hurriedly, and the discovery of the bodies would lead to an investigation, and so had minimised the evidence they'd left behind.

Dirty plates had gone into the dishwasher. The boxes of disposable gloves next to it suggested they'd even made the effort not to leave fingerprints when they'd unloaded the machine, replacing plates and glasses in their proper cupboards. The fridge remained stocked with the food bought before the outbreak, but the mercenaries had been here since then, give or take. And they had been eating rations packed in one of the four black, reinforced, coffin-shaped boxes stacked in the room in which she'd killed Kelly.

The topmost box contained weapons and ammo. Each gun had its own slot in the custom made box, but the long sniper rifle caught her eye. She'd seen Kelly with it on the city's walls, but clearly it was intended for something other than shooting the undead. What was their original plan, before the outbreak, if it involved assassinating people at long range? Did it matter now?

Another coffin-shaped crate was empty except for a single compressed bag containing the mercenaries' waste, and most of that was empty vacuum-packed rations. It couldn't have been their only waste, not for the at least three weeks they'd been here. The rest must have been taken somewhere, dumped or buried. The other two coffin-sized containers held food, some medical kit, a sat-phone, radios, and empty space.

"Interesting," she murmured. The radios were interesting in that they were inside the crates. The sat-phone confirmed the boxes were packed before the satellites went down, but did it mean they weren't expecting the failure of global communications? There were no spare sets of body armour, nor of night-vision goggles. They had enough weapons to equip a small army, but that was never their intent. No, their original plot involved a handful of killers, a sniper rifle, sat-phones, suppressed submachine guns, and encrypted short-range radios.

Tess turned around, to look at the corpse of Major Kelly. "Were you really ever a soldier?"

She walked over to the body of the dead assassin, and undid the button at the corpse's collar. Around the woman's neck hung a silver chain with a pair of identification discs on which was the name *B Kelly*, but those could be easily forged. Or stolen, because there was another chain, made of gold, and around that, with holes drilled in each, were three gold coins. It was what she'd been expecting after the corpse in the Bunker, after the victims upstairs.

Behind the kitchen, and through a utility room larger than her bedroom in Broken Hill, a door led into the garage. Inside was only one vehicle, a New South Wales park ranger utility truck. Stacked neatly by the rear wheels were four petrol cans. Each full. Inside, on the back seat, were five sets of park ranger uniforms.

The truck was a diesel, so the petrol was for the house. They'd have torched it as they left, but they'd planned for that not being possible, so had maintained a light-touch protocol, leaving few clues behind. But, due to the bodies, if they suddenly fled, the hunt wouldn't be for mercenaries, but for a serial killer.

Reluctantly, Tess returned upstairs. From the landing, the left-and-right corridor led to the two wings, and the two master bedrooms. The other corridor led to the guest rooms, one of which was larger than the two master rooms. Possibly used by Sir Malcolm when he visited his daughter and tormented his son-in-law. In that room lay the body of a tortured man. Not Sir Malcolm. Not anyone Tess had ever seen before. But she thought she could put a name to him.

He had bruises on his chest, a broken arm strapped and held in a sling. They'd caused pain, yes, but nothing which would leave a permanent mark except the bullet hole in his skull. Rigor mortis had yet to set in, so he had been killed recently. Probably within the last few hours.

In the room opposite, perhaps originally intended as a nursery though it only contained a pair of dusty chairs, was the body of a woman. Around fifty, she hadn't been tortured, but shot once in the head, then wrapped in a thin sheet, probably to make it easier to carry her up there. A trio of industrious early-morning ants had found their way to the body. More would come soon, but taken with the beginning of decomposition, it suggested the woman had died recently.

Next door were the children. Two of them. Twins. Fourteen years old. A boy and a girl who'd had their throats cut. It didn't appear as if they'd been tortured, but the autopsy would determine that. In the room at the back, overlooking the swimming pool, was the last corpse. A woman. Early forties. The mother of the twins. Her arms and legs were a map of scars. None deep. Each around ten centimetres long, collectively forming an overlapping diamond pattern that ran up her arms, up her legs, across her chest, but stopped at her neck. Tess stepped back, making sure she'd remember the woman's face, and returned to the stairs, then to the front door.

"What did you find, ma'am?" Clyde asked.

"I wish I didn't have to tell you," Tess said. "There are five bodies upstairs. A woman in her late fifties, a man in his late forties, a woman who's a few years younger, and two twin boys, fourteen years old."

"You know their ages?" Elaina asked. "You know who they are?"

"Not the older woman," Tess said. "She's probably a neighbour, a witness. Maybe hired help. But the others, yes, I know them from information Anna gave me earlier. The man is Erin Vaughn's husband. The woman was married to Ian Lignatiev. The boys are his sons. They were murdered. The older woman and the Lignatievs were killed yesterday. Mr Vaughn was shot a few hours ago. I think they were hostages. In that room at the end of the hall, there are four black storage containers. Gather the weapons and ammo from the bodies. Make sure the guns are unloaded. Put them in the container with the plastic waste, then bring all four outside, load them on our ute. We'll log them in as evidence. Don't go upstairs."

Tess went outside, enjoying the cool night air. Above, clouds had blanketed the sky, hinting at rain to come. Serial killers, nuclear war, zombies. What would come next? But at least the lights were still on, here in Canberra.

The sound of engines had her walking back down the drive, through the broken-open gates, and to the road. Flashing amber lights marked the arrival of reinforcements from the airport, five service-trucks. Mick was behind the wheel of the lead vehicle, Blaze in the passenger seat. Bianca following in a truck so close she'd clearly been trying to take the lead.

"This is a crime scene," Tess called out, even as the trucks stopped. "Blaze, take ten people around the back. I want these vehicles parked on the roadside not blocking the entrance. Bianca, on the gate. No one comes in until the coroner arrives. Mick, these are your people, get them deployed."

"Kasey," Mick said, turning to the stocky woman who'd been driving the third truck. "You heard the commissioner. Clear the road, then form a perimeter. Tess?"

She led Mick up towards the house, though not indoors. "It's torture and murder, Mick, like in Broken Hill. Major Kelly was here. It was a real fight we only survived thanks to luck and Clyde."

"Who was murdered?" Mick asked.

"Lignatiev's wife and children, Vaughn's husband, and a woman who was probably just in the wrong place at the wrong time."

"How old were the kids?"

"Fourteen. Twins. Boys," Tess said. "I don't think they were tortured, but their mother was."

"Like in Broken Hill with that pilot who was skinned alive?"

"Similar, but different. Lots of shallow cuts forming a diamond pattern. Would have taken time, though, so that's the same as Broken Hill."

"So it's a different serial killer?" Mick asked. "Or is the killer's M.O. evolving?"

"Neither," Tess said. "The killer, or killers, enjoy causing pain, or at least have no qualms about it, but it's a means to an end. In the garage, there's an NSW park ranger truck with four ranger uniforms. That was how they intended to escape. In uniform, aboard an official truck. It's not far to the state border, and what conscript would stop them if they said they'd been ordered to eliminate a cluster of zombies nearby? But it's a diesel truck, and next to it are four petrol cans."

"To burn the house down?"

"Defo," Tess said. "Douse the bodies, and the cuts wouldn't be found in an autopsy. But if we found the bodies before they had a chance to torch the place, we'd be looking for a torturer, a serial killer, not a cartel gangster."

"Cartel? That's who they were?"

"Kelly had three gold coins hanging around her neck like they were a necklace," Tess said. "And I think she was the torturer here. I could be wrong, but I think we got them all. Kelly and her people were hired to kidnap Vaughn's and Lignatiev's family. She used them to make sure those two politicians did what they were supposed to."

"Like kill those students, and try to kill Anna," Mick said.

"I think Kelly or one of her people did the actual deed," Tess said. "But Lignatiev and Vaughn provided access. Who would notice Kelly when she was playing bodyguard, tagging along when Vaughn went to speak to Bronwyn Wilson, or when bringing a message to the last prime minister, or to the students, or whomever else?"

"And how many others did she kill?" Mick asked. "Kelly was on the wall with us."

"Yep. With a sniper rifle," Tess said. "But me and my team got lost on our way to the suburb we were meant to be clearing, otherwise I'd be dead and listed as a casualty of friendly fire."

"You found Aaron's body, though," Mick said. "I'd call that a coincidence."

"I'd call it guilt," Tess said. "He had to have known some of what was going on. But I'm sure he committed suicide."

"If he did, how voluntary was it?" Mick said. "But that's not the question I really want answered. Did any of them get away?"

Tess stepped aside as Elaina and Clyde carried one of the black boxes out through the front door. "I don't think these are the same gangsters who were in Broken Hill," Tess said. "The timing's wrong. I want to know how many more of them were here before the outbreak. Was it two teams? Did they arrive together? Lignatiev managed to recruit his own private army of sorts to protect him at the Telstra Tower, and who he left to be murdered in the Bunker."

"I thought they were reservists," Mick said. "Isn't that how he met them?"

"So far only one has been confirmed as a reserve soldier. I'm still waiting on the identification of the others, but there was one bloke at the tower who had a corporate I.D. on him. Belonged to the newspaper Malcolm Baker bought last year."

"And this is Aaron Bryce's house, right?" Mick asked.

"Paid for by Baker," Tess said. "Is he the source of the money which paid for these mercenaries? Or did he pay for Lignatiev's amateur bodyguard? When were they recruited?"

"You want to find Sir Malcolm?" Mick asked.

"He had a place in Brisbane, I think," Tess said.

"Ah, so he might have drowned."

"We should be so lucky. I'll have to speak to O.O., inform him of what's happened. But when you get back to the airport, leave word for Captain Hawker. If I'm going to Brisbane, I want professional backup."

Elaina approached, pausing a polite distance away. "That's the last of the boxes," she said. "Do you want us to gather anything else?"

"No, you and Clyde are done for the night," Tess said. "We'll drop these off at the evidence lock-up and you can get some sleep. Mick, can you keep a lid on this place?"

"What do I tell the neighbours?" he asked, pointing across the road to a house where a few lights had come on.

"The truth, more or less," Tess said. "We were mopping up from the coup. We got the last of them. Now we're waiting on the coroner. I'll speak to Mr Owen, and to Anna."

Mick nodded.

Tess took one last look at the house. She hoped it marked the end of something, not the beginning. Elaina at her side, she walked over to their ute, where Clyde had finished securing the crates.

"You're bleeding, mate," Tess said, pointing at the gash on the man's forehead, and the growing bruise, an angry yellow under the streetlights' amber glare.

"Could have been worse," he said. "Are we still hunting Vaughn?"

"Nope," Tess said. "She's hiding from a murderer as well as us. She'll turn up in time, but we could waste weeks looking for her. Assuming she's even still alive. We'll log this, then I'll brief the prime minister."

"We're taking this to the airport?" Elaina asked, climbing into the driver's seat.

"The museum," Tess said, pushing the bag of food taken from the looters at Wilson's house across the backseat, and climbing in. "It's supposed to be a food store and evidence lock-up."

"There's food at the museum?" Elaina asked.

"Not just food," Tess said, as she drove the quiet streets. "Not much food, really. Any artefacts, paintings, and antiques we want to keep for future generations are being stored there. But originally, when the shops, businesses, and factories were requisitioned, the assumption was all the excess food could be collected and stored, and then redistributed. But, predictably, people took what they found, leaving very little to go to the central reserve."

The museum occupied a waterside promontory bulging into Lake Burley Griffin, south of the university and across the tranquil lake to the northwest of parliament. Their journey was slow, finding barricades increasingly occupied, especially around the university. At the museum, they found a guard.

The lights in the car park shone down on rows of juggernaut rigs, though none had a trailer. Around the entrance to the museum, a space had been left empty. There, behind a desk-and-partition barricade, stood a trio of teenagers who, like Zach, should have been in school, and an older woman in an odd uniform.

They parked their truck, climbed out, and Tess saw the woman was wearing a police uniform, not from Australia, but Indonesia.

"*Apa kabar*," Tess said, with a smile and a nod, nearly exhausting her Indonesian vocabulary. "G'day. I'm Tess Qwong. Deputy Commissioner with the AFP and senior officer here in Canberra."

"*Brigadir Polisi* Sri Susanti," the officer said, snapping to attention and giving a crisp salute the three teenagers attempted to copy.

Tess smiled. "Welcome to Australia."

"Thank you," Susanti said. "But when is my return flight to Jakarta? I was told I could return."

"Jakarta? I've got to drop this evidence off. I'll come and speak with you afterwards."

The police officer's eyes narrowed. "Attacked? Bombed?"

Tess nodded. "I'm sorry."

Susanti handed Tess a large set of keys. "One city, a different city. One life, a different life. Does it matter where and which?"

"A question I ask myself every day," Tess said, as she took the keys. "Leave those for now," she said as Clyde went to untie the crates. "Bring those bags of food we took from the looters, but we'll grab a trolley from inside for the evidence."

Inside the museum, half the lights were on, while, except for a half-metre-wide aisle, the corridors were completely full. High-sided trolleys and shopping carts loaded with paintings lined both walls. Between, against, and even on top, ceiling-high stacks of wooden crates, plastic storage boxes, and cardboard containers teetered and bulged.

"It's much fuller than last time I was here," Tess said, as she picked her way over a fallen suitcase, leading the other two down the artificial alley and into the marginally emptier space of the atrium. "And with less order. They've been dumping it wherever there's a gap."

The last time she'd been to the museum, a dragon of a woman had been yelling at everyone for the damage they were causing. But she'd been maintaining some semblance of order among the chaos. Either she'd given up, or she'd gone, because this place was less like a treasure hoard guarded by a dragon, and was now just a dump watched over by the skeleton of a dinosaur.

"We should bring Zach here," Elaina said, looking up at the two permanent exhibits dominating the high-ceilinged hall. "He'd love having a ride on that."

"Who wouldn't?" Clyde said with wistful longing, taking a step towards the old car and pink caravan, though his way was blocked by a large trolley, stacked with paintings, and jammed between four large wooden crates. "A 1955 FJ Holden. Two-point-two litre engine, three-speed transmission, whitewall tyres, red upholstery, and weighs a whisper over a ton. But the caravan's the real beaut. A home away from home. The epitome of the post-war Australian dream."

"I was talking about the dinosaur skeleton," Elaina said with a snort of laughter.

"Oh, the muttaburrasaurus?" Clyde said, with clear disinterest. "About twice the length of the Holden, and eight times the weight. But those are just bones, while the car is a gem."

"Tell you what, mate," Tess said, "when we've a bit of time, we'll clear some floor space and see if she can drive. We're so short of living space, you can sleep in the caravan." She pointed at the corridor unnaturally narrowed by long rows of transparent boxes whose interiors glittered. "Stack those paintings next to the dino, and use that cart to bring in the evidence. The meeting rooms down that corridor are where we're storing evidence. Food gets stored in the cafe, so give me those bags, and I'll drop them off there."

"Looks like jewels in those crates," Elaina said, pointing to an open box half-buried beneath an upturned bronze elephant.

"Don't tell Toppley," Clyde said as he dragged a three-metre-long seascape from the two-metre-long cart.

"Do you really believe that story she told about the diamond mine, the casino, and the jet-ski?" Elaina asked.

Clyde's reply was lost beneath the squeak of the wheels.

Tess picked up a bag, and picked a path between the dumped loot and to the cafe.

The salvaged artefacts had spread through the wall-less entrance of the open-plan cafe, with more crates and boxes stacked on the chairs and tables, and even against the ceiling-height windows. Through the occasional gaps, she could see the dark expanse of the lake. Beyond were lights, though. Parliament House? Possibly. It would have been a fantastic view once.

"And it will be again," she said, with a determination she couldn't quite believe.

Making her way between the serving counters, she entered the well-lit kitchen. Cluttered and musty, it still had the faint hint of cooking. Was that cumin and garam masala?

She lowered the bag to the floor as she sniffed again, then angled towards the bin on which a pair of early-working flies were sleepily perched. The bin was half full of wrappers and a few empty cans. The microwave timer was blinking on one. Inside was a bowl, covered in cling-wrap, the contents still hot.

Her hand on her holster, she slowly turned around, seeing the kitchen with different eyes. The bowl didn't belong to the guards outside, not if it was still hot. The cooking-programme had been paused before it had chimed. If the guards knew someone else was inside, they would have said. Almost certainly. A thief would have taken the food away, leaving only a lurker, a fugitive, someone hiding.

Looking for clues as to the diner's identity, looking for places they might hide, she made her way back to the kitchen door. Drawing her gun, but keeping it low, she pushed the door open, letting instinct take over, her eyes roaming the junk-room cafe. A fire door was only partially concealed by a stack of plastic boxes. It offered an obvious way outside, but would the lurker have fled? Or would they have hidden, assuming that these newcomers would dump their treasure and leave? Her eyes fell on the exhibits in the main atrium beyond. There was *one* obvious place to hide.

Slowly, gun low, she made her way out of the cafe, but paused behind a trolley full of century-old portraits, covered in nearly as much dust. Shoulder height, they offered concealment, if not cover, and a clear view of the caravan.

"Come out!" she called. "You're caught."

Silence stretched, but it was less complete than before. A squeak from a leather seat, a gentle spang from the suspension as weight inside moved, a clunk from the hinges as someone tested the door. It opened, though only an inch.

"Hands up, come out slow," Tess called, taking a step away from the paintings. Even as she saw the gun barrel emerge, Tess dived.

Bullets shredded the portraits, slammed into the floor, ricocheted off the trolley's frame. The gun firing at her was a fully automatic, and with a silencer.

Tess ducked behind a stack of plastic boxes full of small objects wrapped in tissue paper. Spotting better cover, she chose her words with care.

"It's over!" she called, diving forward in a roll which caused her spine to protest, her hip to scream as she landed on every bruise she'd acquired during the last few days. But as the next burst slammed into the plastic boxes, turning porcelain ornaments into shrapnel, Tess curled behind the giant bronze Buddha, relatively confident she was safe.

"Good place to hide," she called out. "Few people come to the museum, and none of them linger long." Another burst from the submachine gun sprayed the statue, the bullets then dancing off in every direction. "Yep, you've got water, light. Food, of course. Privacy, of a sort. And most deliveries are dropped off in daylight. That was your mistake, of course." Another stream of lead slammed into the bronze, but this time, at least two punctured the outer shell, pinwheeling around inside what Tess suddenly realised was a *hollow* statue. "Your mistake," she continued, now scanning for deeper cover, "was forgetting the one person who might deposit evidence at night is a cop."

There were other pockets of shelter, but none looked sturdier than where she now sat. Slipping into a half crouch, gun raised, she got ready to fire and run, ducking when she heard a shot. One. Loud. From her right, and followed immediately by the sound of breaking glass as the caravan's front window shattered.

"Got you covered, Commish," Clyde called.

"You're surrounded," Tess said. "Surrender or die, and pick quick."

Silence.

It stretched.

Finally, a voice replied. A familiar voice. A woman's voice. "I can't leave," Erin Vaughn said.

Tess nodded to herself in satisfaction at a hunch confirmed. "Major Kelly is dead, Erin. So are her team. We killed them about an hour ago."

"She's dead?" Vaughn asked, a faint hint of hope in her voice.

Tess was tempted to lie, but there was too great a chance it would backfire, that Vaughn would ask to speak to her husband. "The hostages are dead," she called.

"Dead?" Vaughn asked.

"Yes. Shot. All of them. This morning."

"Even the twins?" Vaughn asked.

"Yes," Tess said. "They died after Owen's broadcast yesterday, after he reported news of the attempted coup. Your husband died some time tonight."

"I'd have died if I went back to Aaron's house," Vaughn said. "I knew that. And I knew they'd kill him soon after. So I couldn't go back. I thought... I don't know. I loved Johno. I did. But I loved Ian, too."

"You were coerced," Tess replied. "You had no choice. You couldn't have saved them. But you can save others. We need information. Who was Kelly? Who was she working for?"

"Kelly wanted you dead," Vaughn said. "It's why I had you sent to the coast."

"So you didn't know about the bombs, the tidal wave?" Tess asked.

"Know? I didn't know about any of it," Vaughn said. "They got Ian first. Months ago. First I knew was when I woke up, naked, in a shack in the middle of the bush. I was leverage. And then... But then..." She trailed off into a sob.

"You can help us, and help Australia, Erin," Tess said. "You'll be locked up in a cell from which there'll be no escape, no rescue, but no assassination. You'll be a prisoner, but you'll be safe."

"Ian said that. Ian said I'd be safe," she said, and Tess could sense she was losing Vaughn.

"Was it Malcolm Baker?" Tess asked. "How much did he know?"

"I... I don't know," Vaughn said. "You can't help me, and I can't help you."

"You can save your people," Tess said.

"*My* people are dead!" Vaughn cried in a primal wail as the caravan's door swung open. Submachine gun raised, she ran out.

Before Tess could speak, a burst came from her left, and Erin Vaughn crumpled, sprawling on the priceless, worthless artefacts surrounding the caravan.

"Cease fire!" Tess said, jogging forward, but Vaughn was dead.

"Sorry, Commish," Elaina said as she and Clyde came out of cover.

"Yeah, sorry," Clyde said. "I acted on instinct there. Saw the gun and fired."

"No worries," Tess said, guessing it had been Elaina, not Clyde, who'd fired. "Caravan's empty. She wasn't sleeping there. Just hid there when she heard us enter."

"Was she alone?" Elaina asked.

"In every possible meaning of the word," Tess said, holding up the object she'd picked up from the floor of the caravan. "She ejected the magazine before she ran outside. Just one last suicide for the books."

"Was she telling the truth?" Elaina asked. "She was really just another victim?"

"No, she wasn't a victim," Tess said. "She shot at me first. Despite her words, her grief, her instinct was to shoot, not talk. She could have come to me, or to Anna. She could have gone to the AFP months ago, if that's when this began. But she didn't. She went along with it. There was no helping her. No saving her. No, despite the questions I want answered, better it ended this way. It's better than a noose."

Epilogue - While the Lights Are On
Australian National University, Canberra

"No offence, Tess, but you look worse than me," Anna Dodson said as Tess collapsed into an armchair opposite the sofa on which Anna reclined, her bandaged leg extended. "You should get some sleep," she said. "At least one of us should be on their feet."

"After this, yes," Tess said. "I appointed Zach as my official driver. And after this, he's driving me home." She gestured through the glass walls at where Zach stood, braced in a rigid at-ease position, shotgun slung, and unloaded.

"He should be returned to school," Anna said. "And if I had a say in the matter, I'd be there, too."

Parliament House was still off-limits until it had been confirmed no more explosives were hidden within. In the meantime, Oswald Owen had taken up semi-permanent residence at the Telstra Tower. Anna had moved to the university, and a glass-walled teaching room just inside the entrance to the School of Medical Sciences.

"You wouldn't prefer somewhere more private?" Tess asked, straightening a little as, outside, a trio of shovel-carrying workers stopped to gawk.

"It's important to be seen," Anna said. "More so now than ever. Oswald wanted to be out and about, talking and meeting people, reassuring them. But he'd get too many awkward questions, which I can always answer by saying I'll take them to the prime minister. Tomorrow, I'm leaving for a tour of the airfields. Dad's doing his best, but the need for quarantine zones is creating a bottleneck. There must be a mathematical solution so I asked Flo to find me the answer."

"Does that mean her research for a weapon is on hold?"

"I think," Anna said slowly, with a glance through the glass walls. "I think we need to re-evaluate what is possible, and within what timeframe, when considering our much depleted resources."

"You're hoping the zombies will be dead by the time we can manufacture one," Tess said.

"I'm hoping they'll all die tomorrow," Anna said. "But, for now, all our efforts must go into saving as many people as possible. Or almost all our efforts."

"Do you want me to come with you to the airfields?"

"I do. You'd make me feel less outnumbered by my bodyguards." Anna pointed to the pair of SASR privates standing to attention on the other side of the glass doors. Another pair, also recently returned from the outback, were at the front of the building. "But your investigation is more important than my grip-and-grimace tour. Oh, but I would like you in proper police uniform for the televised session of parliament."

"If I can find one," Tess said.

"Sorry, Tess, Leo already has. He's remarkably good at finding things. I think he threatens to send them to Dr Avalon if he doesn't get his way."

"When do the politicians arrive?" Tess asked.

"New South Wales arrived this morning. We're expecting the others this afternoon. The politicians we sent to Hobart should be in the air now."

"And the parliamentary session is scheduled for this evening?"

"It'll start at six, so an hour after shift-change. Oswald wants as many people as possible to watch it."

"And that's at the Telstra Tower?"

"No, it'll be up at Parliament House, assuming Captain Hawker is satisfied it's safe, but we won't announce the location in advance."

"It's a gamble," Tess said. "There could be a challenger."

"Not on live TV. Not after a coup," Anna said. "Who'd want to be prime minister now? In two years, it'll be a different story. But right now, no one wants the responsibility. They'll reaffirm their oaths, and the nation, or some of it, will watch and listen as O.O. gives a detailed report on everything that's happened. Or nearly everything." Anna turned to look out the window, wincing as she stretched the stitches on her injured leg.

"There's more bad news?" Tess asked.

"More of the same bad news," Anna said. "There seems to be a naval war on the open seas. Russia, China, and the U.S. are attacking each other and themselves. Other ships often seem to get in the way. It seems that a first-strike order was issued before the outbreak, but to every side. As to which nation *did* strike first, I'm not clear. Some ships obeyed the orders. Some didn't. Now they're all trying to sink one another."

"An order from before the outbreak?" Tess asked. "That tallies with what I've learned from investigating the murders."

"We received a report from New Zealand," Anna said. "I recognise the names of the people who signed it. They're the same as last week. If they had a coup, it was much more efficient than ours. But they reported learning of a mushroom cloud over Sao Paulo yesterday."

"It happened yesterday, or that's when they heard about it?" Tess asked.

"It happened yesterday morning. It's possible another was seen yesterday evening in Kochi, that's on the western coast of India. It seems, whatever the cause of this war, not everyone has yet realised we've all lost."

"If you're the commander of a nuclear sub, and you've fired one missile, why not fire the rest?" Tess said. "Is there anything we can do?"

"We lost our navy at Guam," Anna said. "There are a few vessels at sea, but we don't know who our enemy is. So, no, Tess, we can do nothing but wait, and hope. There is better news, of a sort, in that there've been no more detonations close to Australia."

"Just that one blast a hundred kilometres out to sea?" Tess asked.

"For which we're still waiting on confirmation," Anna said.

"The lights are still on and we're calling that good news," Tess said, glancing up at the dim glow from the overhead bulbs, unnecessary on such a bright day, but a welcome comfort.

"We heard from Vancouver," Anna said. "Contact has been lost with General Yoon. Mushroom clouds were seen along the Saint Lawrence. The reports are confused, but it sounds as if Montreal, Quebec City, Ottawa, and Toronto were all hit."

"They were deliberately targeting General Yoon?"

"Leo says no one can deliberately target anyone," Anna said. "I think that's wishful thinking. But we have to assume the general and her army are gone. Vancouver Island is being evacuated. We are withdrawing from the Northern Hemisphere."

"And Japan? They were expecting an evacuation."

"Everyone wanted help, but we can't provide it," she said, briefly closing her eyes. "Our resources are limited. We have a bottleneck in transporting aviation fuel from the refinery to the airports. Within a week, we'll have to drastically reduce the number of planes we can operate, and so the number of people we can rescue. But within a week, we'll have a better idea of what medium-term damage the bombs have caused."

"Like a nuclear winter?"

"Leo says no. Flo says maybe," Anna said. "If most of the detonations took place at sea, there won't be much dust catapulted up into the atmosphere. And it is that radiation, and the effect on the fish, on the rainfall, on our crops, which is my greater concern. And then there are zombies. But the lights are still on, and we're still alive, so tell me what you've learned."

"I skimmed the recordings the Guinns made," Tess said. "All I can say, so far, is Lisa Kempton knew something was going to happen, and that the cartel were involved."

"Why would a drug cartel want to destroy the planet?" Anna asked. "They would be destroying their customers, too."

"Power," Tess said. "Real power. The power of an empire. This wipes the slate clean, allowing them to establish themselves as a new authority. A new nation. But what I haven't determined is whether they were behind the outbreak or the nuclear war, or whether they were planning something else which was derailed by these catastrophes. It matters because it'll indicate what kind of resources they have. What size of an army. They didn't send many people here, but that doesn't mean they haven't got far more elsewhere. However, our key focus has to be locating them while we're able to put a bomber in the air."

"Eliminate them now, yes," Anna said. "I agree. Do you know where to look?"

"No. Vaughn had nothing on her in the museum. There were no clues left in Aaron Bryce's house. I've got Elaina and Bianca going through Vaughn's office. Sophia and Toppley are searching Lignatiev's. I'd prefer proper investigators, but until we know who to trust, I'll stick with my team."

"But the coup is over? There are no more conspirators?" Anna asked.

"There are no other hostages, so I think it's over. For now. The prisoners we took at the Telstra Tower all used to work for a hedge fund. They're not reservists, just members of a corporate hunting club. They didn't know of any deeper plot, and while I doubt they knew very much of the plans at all, they did give me the name of the person who owned the shell company that paid their wages."

"Sir Malcolm Baker?" Anna asked.

"Him, yes," Tess said.

"And you want to question him?"

"Assuming he's still alive, yes. We think he was in his house near Brisbane. If he was the money, he'll confirm there are no further threats to the government. Not of that kind, anyway. He'll tell us where to find the cartel, and then we can bomb them into dust."

"And if he's dead, would Lisa Kempton know where to find the cartel?"

"Probably," Tess said. "But if she knew something was coming, she'll have disappeared into a bunker somewhere."

"But she had an office in New York," Anna said.

"Probably. I've no idea. Why?"

"Dr Avalon wants to go to Manhattan to collect samples from patient zero, or as close to patient zero as she can find."

"How?" Tess asked. "We don't know precisely where it began."

"She thinks she can work that out," Anna said. "And if we can find it, we might find out who began all this, and why. It might help with the weapon, if we ever have the time and resources to develop one."

"So you're sending a team to Manhattan?"

"I'm sending her. And Leo, of course," Anna said. "By ship. Leo also wants to go to Britain to find a sample of this vaccine they claimed to have. We were supposed to receive a sample, and the formula, but it never arrived. Ian said he'd organised that, but I think he was lying."

"A ship. From here to Britain, then to New York? The voyage would take weeks."

"A month, at least," Anna said. She smiled.

"Oh, no," Tess said. "You're not serious?"

"You always said you wanted to travel, Tess."

"I should find Baker first," Tess said.

"You have a week," Anna said. "If you've not found him, someone else will take over. We must stop the cartel, Tess. I hate to think what kind of new world people like that would create."

"Then I'm grabbing some sleep before the broadcast," Tess said. She stood, stiffly, just as the room dimmed. The lights had gone out. The fan had stopped humming. Outside, the soldiers had both half-raised their weapons, while in the corridor, people had stopped, turning to one another in baffled confusion.

Her weary limbs, bruised muscles, and cut skin forgotten, Tess quick-stepped to the light switch on the wall. She flicked it once, twice, and a third time in desperate hope, but the lights wouldn't turn on.

To be continued…

Printed in Great Britain
by Amazon